The Best AMERICAN SHORT STORIES 1987

The Best
AMERICAN SHORT STORIES 1987

Selected from
U.S. and Canadian Magazines
by ANN BEATTIE
with SHANNON RAVENEL

With an Introduction by Ann Beattie

HOUGHTON MIFFLIN COMPANY BOSTON 1987

ISSN 0067-6233
ISBN 0-395-41341-9
ISBN 0-395-41342-7 (pbk.)

Printed in the United States of America

Q 10 9 8 7 6 5 4 3 2 1

Contents

Publisher's Note

The *Best American Short Stories* series was started in 1915 under the editorship of Edward J. O'Brien. Its title reflects the optimism of a time when people assumed that an objective "best" could be identified, even in fields not measured in physical terms.

Martha Foley took over as editor of the series in 1942. With her husband, Whit Burnett, she had edited *Story* magazine since 1931, and in later years she taught creative writing at Columbia School of Journalism. When Miss Foley died in 1977, at the age of eighty, she was at work on what would have been her thirty-seventh volume of *The Best American Short Stories*.

Beginning with the 1978 edition, Houghton Mifflin introduced a new editorial arrangement for the anthology. Inviting a different writer or critic to edit each new annual volume would provide a variety of viewpoints to enliven the series and broaden its scope. *Best American Short Stories* has thus become a series of informed but differing opinions that gains credibility from its very diversity.

Also beginning with the 1978 volume, the guest editors have worked with the series editor, Shannon Ravenel, who during each calendar year reads as many qualifying short stories as she can get hold of, makes a preliminary selection of 120 stories for the guest editor's consideration, and selects the "100 Other Distinguished Short Stories of the Year," a listing that has always been an important feature of these volumes.

In the ten years that have passed since then, there has been growing interest in the short story, and the form itself has grown. The range of approaches and techniques and stances it attracts is ever broader. And so is its audience. In response to this anthology's increasingly enthusiastic readership, this year's volume introduces a new feature. Each of the authors of the twenty stories selected by the guest editor has been invited to describe briefly how his or her story came to be written. Most have accepted what is clearly a challenging assignment, and their short essays appear at the back of the volume in the "Contributors' Notes" section.

The stories chosen for this year's anthology were originally published in magazines issued between January 1986 and January 1987. The qualifications for selection are: (1) original publication in nationally distributed American or Canadian periodicals; (2) publication in English by writers who are American or Canadian; and (3) publication *as* short stories (novel excerpts are not knowingly considered by the editors). A list of the magazines consulted by Ms. Ravenel appears at the back of this volume. Other publications wishing to make sure that their contributors are considered for the series should include Ms. Ravenel on their subscription list (P.O. Box 3176, University City, Missouri 63130).

Introduction

IT'S OFTEN BEEN SAID that short stories are so popular now because they are an ideal form for our time. This is said in the same spirit, it seems to me, as announcing that finger food that can be eaten in one bite is preferable at cocktail parties. Similarly, a large group of people seem to believe Andy Warhol's proclamation that "in the future, everyone will be world-famous for fifteen minutes." My own feeling is that in the future, still only a chosen few will be noticed, and then — if they're lucky — for fifteen minutes. I do believe that television has altered our ideas about concentration, yet at the same time we must have wanted that: the beast in the jungle has been replaced by the Betamax in the bedroom.

But if everyone, everywhere, can concentrate so briefly, those are not the people I've met as I've taught and given readings and been interviewed. I don't meet people who, if they read one story and are impressed by it, don't read another by the same author. It would be ridiculous to assume that they are resistant to reading many stories sequentially. I don't find that they think that stories, being shorter, are more accessible than novels. While academics may debate What's-a-poem/What's-a-story/What's-a-novel, very few readers are confused by this. I think that they have a gut reaction to the different forms, and that they know what they're reaching for just as well as the writer knows, right away, whether something he or she wants to express is best cast as poetry or prose. All are distillations, but chronological time is very important. There is the time of the story (Lee K. Abbott's "Dreams of Distant Lives" exists in the present moment, in the time that it takes to tell the story), but as time unfolds, and as the character remembers, the story expands. Connoted time, the implications of any situation, may take us far and wide. But first we have to be willing to take a journey. We have to make an imaginative leap in the first place, taking time out to risk that words may, at least to some extent, change our world.

In his introduction to last year's *Best American Short Stories*, Raymond Carver wrote that stories have more in common with poetry than with the novel. I agree with that, and often wonder why so many people who have presented themselves as commentators on the so-called resurgence of the story have concerned themselves so much with the external, literal world in which the story transpires and have ignored the writers' use of language. In an essay in the January–February 1987 issue of *American Poetry Review*, C. K. Williams writes, "We are taught that it is associative necessity which determines metaphor, but this is not the case. It is actually the ability of the poet to *dissociate*, to reach into the realm of chance, to fuse the unlikely with the undeniable, which determines the intensity of metaphor." I think that sensitive readers know that, and don't assume that analogies were plucked like glistening plums and added to, or superimposed on, the narrative.

Writers are held in high esteem (leaving aside the pop-press presentation of writers: all those articles that condescend to writer and audience alike, in which the writer's advance is stated and there is an accompanying picture of the writer in the kitchen, holding a whisk, as proof that he or she can whip up a nifty dessert) because they are thought of as adventurers, of sorts: divers into metaphors and parachutists over distant lands of discontinuity. And the reader, one hopes, comes to be convinced not that it is an uncomplicated world, but that there is something important in the disparities and complexities. Indeed, the writer may be disassembling and finding oddities beneath what might have passed for coherence. In the best writing, though, what emerges becomes too convincing to appear concocted.

For the writer, finding a theme is one thing (it requires patience, originality, and faith) and presenting it compellingly and convincingly is another. Beyond our vision, what we have is language — the written word. The right word can provide enormous resonance or succinctly suggest any number of complexities (for example, Tim O'Brien's use of the word "encyst"). Yet the writer has to be extremely precise as well as innovative: it is necessary to be careful because people are resistant; they encounter a barrage of language every day. Some of it is self-inflicted. (We *can* turn some of it off; apparently the average American is as dedicated to his remote control switch as cavemen were to their clubs.) Much of the rest of the noise has to do with the current belief that everything and everyone needs discussion. Poets and fiction writers, as far as I know, don't feel this way. They realize that what they are providing is extraneous to matters of absolute survival; they know that they have to deliver things sneakily or they will not arrive at all; they have no grand point to make, or they would have written an essay in the first place. They want to persuade. They want to get their way. They are grown-up children, with greater skills.

But the times are difficult. No doubt some of the current overtalking is revisionist: a reaction against the touchy-feelie philosophy that predominated a couple of decades ago, and at the same time a return to a stratified, hierarchical society in which self-appointed authorities deliver the word (and usually a product) to the masses. Almost everything takes the form of an exposé, but while facts may be exposed, little is revealed about the beauty and wonder of our existence. Those who are not actively involved in announcing and proclaiming seem to be getting increased respect. (Consider the boom in the art market, where words are not the medium at all and, as well, where there is a reappearance of narrative painting.) While it is not yet the day of the poet, there are still a considerable number of people who are turning away from instant analysis and toward the implications of art. The analyzers are not in the business of being surprised (*Saturday Night Live*'s parody of news reporting is a good example of alleged objectivity), but surprise is what good writing is all about, and readers are attuned to it. Something ineffable about the quality and texture of what they read lets them know when the writer has been surprised, and the sheer energy of that surprise conveys itself in the writing. I do not forget my shock — and how entirely impressed I was — when, for example, I first read Mary Robison's story "Yours," and learned what the doctor wanted to tell his wife about people who had not quite enough talent. Or the sock-to-my-stomach word, that absolutely perfect one word, with which Raymond Carver concluded his story "What Is It?" — doubly brilliant, because while the reader finds himself or herself sad, pronouncing the word "gleaming" makes the muscles move so that the mouth is smiling. This year, I read Madison Smartt Bell's story with fascination and dread, simultaneously tantalized by the events and as done-in as the character by their implications. It was like being on a roller coaster. I had to enjoy the ride I was being taken on, but at the same time it shook me up a little too much. Other times, the writer's timing was perfect. I had forgotten that things were not in sharp focus, so convincing was the guiding narrative that was moving me through Kent Haruf's story "Private Debts/Public Holdings," that when the sentence — surely banal out of context — appeared that read, "She was wearing slacks and a loose green blouse," my eyes widened with surprise. It might as well have been neon-green, or the wildest thing imaginable. She was *real.* Of course!

Stories are fabrications, mimetic enough to convince, off-kilter enough to carry weight. It's often the spark that convinces us and not the fire, in this world where facts are too often manipulated into meaninglessness. As I see it, writers are willing to take a chance; they like to tempt fate a little. Few writers — even those with outlines and copious notes — sit down to doggedly prove anything. Rather, they like to see if they can shake themselves up, if there are questions that can be raised, narrow roads that may widen. Flannery O'Connor's remarks about things needing to exist literally in a story before they can exist figuratively are quite telling about the process: what exists must exist persuasively, in its own right (hard enough to do), and only then can it enlarge into a metaphorical existence. And then it is not that something *is* a metaphor, but that a melding has occurred, a true transformation has resulted, and things are now joined, not to be separated. Of course the intelligent reader, however impressed, does not care to believe that there is one truth. That is why the perceiver turned to art to begin with. Like the whispered secret that becomes, in repetition, something entirely different, the remembered story, through time, becomes a worry bead transformed into a boulder. It is the writer's task to suggest that something is inevitable — which is of course a difficult thing to do in a world in which not much is inevitable. The starting points, the basic *givens,* are often so strange that it is difficult to imagine what the correct theorum should be that might apply, say, to Joy Williams's characters' predicaments in "The Blue Men." Abstracted, her world looks to me like the peninsula of Florida that becomes neither rectangular nor triangular, so that it seems entirely appropriate that the car ride at the end takes the course it does. In some of these stories, such as John Updike's exhilaratingly sad "The After-life," what is strange is in the process of being discovered, for character and reader alike, as both move through time. Craig Nova's story begins, in effect, at the end. Lee K. Abbott's story implodes.

The visual — paintings, photographs — come at us, at least on the surface, all at once. There is, on some level, simultaneity. Time is frozen. But in a story, we may hear a voice before we associate it with a character, have no idea of the character's world even if we can assess him or her, and the ending is not foretold as we begin the story. To some extent, when we read fiction, we're sleuthing to get the facts, and we have to have good instincts so that we don't get thrown off. I think that with most stories — this group, at least — we're not meant to antici-pate what we're moving toward. The stories are mysteries to which we will be exposed. The sureness is in the writing. Look at the first paragraph of Mavis Gallant's story "Kingdom Come." Someone is clearly in charge of telling us a story; the suspense is in the substance of the things observed, not in our inability to become attuned to the method of delivery. Looking at Mavis Gallant's story, and at Kent Haruf's, and at Craig Nova's, I suddenly realized that when the tone established the narrator as competent and in charge — when there was clearly an au-thority — the tone of a fairy tale never seemed far away. In retrospect, I'm sure that Craig Nova realized that "The Prince" might well have begun: "Imagine this: in a land far away . . ."

But in some ways, it seems even more compelling, and more shocking, to realize that we are reading a fairy tale that refuses to be a fairy tale. Nova's story becomes a kind of comment on the genre. And it is surprising to realize how powerfully that genre reflects our times.

I spent years being puzzled by people — people who were well acquainted with my work — who would come up to me at readings or receptions and say, with a gleam in their eye, "Wait till you hear *this*," and then proceed to tell me some shocking story. Usually their delivery was very good: the punch line came unexpectedly, and hit hard. These people wanted me, at the very least, to see the world as absurd, wicked, grotesque, and chaotic, often with some depravity thrown in. Then they had a back-up story that substantiated even grimmer truths than their first story. Considering that early on I was writing (with few exceptions) about what seemed to me in many ways to be sadly *un*-provocative people, people who were meant to provoke the reader because they were themselves having trouble understanding or articulating their despair, I wasn't quite sure why tales of horror were seen by my informants as a necessary sort of secret salute. Then I realized that I was thinking about it too hard, personalizing it; it wasn't really the subject matter of my stories, but an assured delivery that made people think that I needed shaking up. That I needed it for their satisfaction at seeing me squirm and, paradoxically I suppose, as reinforcement for me. It was a while before I realized that *any* storyteller will be seen as a person playing a game: we're holding out — we know what happens, right? (Wrong, most often. I'll hazard a guess that Ralph Lombreglia forgot the swimming pool himself until it had to appear again, and even that Kent Haruf didn't know which dance would be Jessie's last.) People who meant to entertain me by shocking me thought I was taking something literal — actually, this was a compliment, because they took an improvisation for the real world — and making it hypothetical. Since this has largely been true of what's been going on in the society at large (with the proliferation of explicators), I was just a convenient and temporary public figure to get even with or to try to outguess.

One of the conclusions I have reached is that people want order, but some part of them craves anarchy, and writers are seen to embody both elements: in a sane, reasonable way, writers will present a situation, but the components of that situation, and the implications, can be dynamite. How exactly should Joy Williams's characters act in response to their largely inherited world? In Craig Nova's story, how alienated is the prince, and how might he become better adjusted? In Tim O'Brien's story, how should Lavender's death have been dealt with? These stories pose questions — they mean to pose questions — but it is not just a sly fade that the writers do after implying that there are problems. They try to have their vision radiate metaphorically. They put in the mouths of characters unlikely solutions so that we may think about more likely ones. Because the world assumes a status quo, and because writers don't believe this, my questions above end up sounding silly. Yet a lot of critics still condescend to writers and their readers by assuming (although they will do almost anything to avoid saying this in its primitive form) that answers should be apparent after an experience. Perhaps there should be balance, texture, and the right sound of language to go along with the material — perhaps these things, and others, might make a story transcendent — but finding the exceptional way to articulate the ordinary is a significant task. Even ordinary things confuse us.

Poets and painters and fiction writers may offer a channel for rediscovery. The ongoing state of things is such that as soon as we arrive in one place, something necessitates our moving on to another. Parking meters are profitable for this reason. There isn't a story in this collection that doesn't contain or express anxiety. Reading them, you'll go to funerals, fight a war, come close to drowning, slip on the stairs in the dark, career around in a car out of control, lose your kingdom, wonder whether your children are safe, and consider electrocution. In terms of shock value, of course, none of these stories outdoes the daily newspaper. Neither do they seem to be exciting adventure stories, except perhaps in paraphrase. Instead, they present strong revelations about ordinary, private matters. There are things that get whispered about that writers are there to overhear. Shadows behind the curtains that can be brought into focus. It's a serious business, writing and reading stories; we sense, as we do in times of need, who our friends are. There is a poem that I'm very fond of by Gregory Orr. At its conclusion there is a trapped fly (no apologies to Flannery O'Connor needed; no one will doubt its simple existence) that functions, as well, as the perceiver's projection and also as a metaphor. It reminds me how much art matters — how much trust we put in it, how vulnerable we can become.

READING LATE IN THE COTTAGE

There aren't that many pages left.
I'm getting nervous; what if
the author means to surprise me
by leaving the last twenty blank?
Now all sounds disturb me:
embers letting fall on the hearth
their heavy grey petals;
cattle outside, tearing the grass
with their teeth; and close by,
the screech of the luminous
insect trapped in the lightbulb.

In the stories I selected, I found questions that disturbed me, implications I had not thought of, and observed living humans illuminated by art. I picked the stories, I suppose, for the same reason I have picked people and places (when I have been the one to choose). I picked them because they surprised me.

ANN BEATTIE

SUSAN SONTAG

The Way We Live Now

FROM THE NEW YORKER

AT FIRST HE WAS just losing weight, he felt only a little ill, Max said to Ellen, and he didn't call for an appointment with his doctor, according to Greg, because he was managing to keep on working at more or less the same rhythm, but he did stop smoking, Tanya pointed out, which suggests he was frightened, but also that he wanted, even more than he knew, to be healthy, or healthier, or maybe just to gain back a few pounds, said Orson, for he told her, Tanya went on, that he expected to be climbing the walls (isn't that what people say?) and found, to his surprise, that he didn't miss cigarettes at all and reveled in the sensation of his lungs' being ache-free for the first time in years. But did he have a good doctor, Stephen wanted to know, since it would have been crazy not to go for a checkup after the pressure was off and he was back from the conference in Helsinki, even if by then he was feeling better. And he said, to Frank, that he would go, even though he was indeed frightened, as he admitted to Jan, but who wouldn't be frightened now, though, odd as that might seem, he hadn't been worrying until recently, he avowed to Quentin, it was only in the last six months that he had the metallic taste of panic in his mouth, because becoming seriously ill was something that happened to other people, a normal delusion, he observed to Paolo, if one was thirty-eight and had never had a serious illness; he wasn't, as Jan confirmed, a hypochondriac. Of course, it was hard not to worry, everyone was worried, but it wouldn't do to panic, because, as Max pointed out to Quentin, there wasn't anything one could do except wait and hope, wait and start being careful, be careful, and hope. And even if one did prove to be ill, one shouldn't give up, they had new treatments that promised an arrest of the disease's inexorable course, research was progressing. It seemed that everyone was in touch with everyone else several times a week, checking in, I've never spent so many hours at a time on the phone, Stephen said to Kate, and when I'm exhausted after the two or three calls made to me, giving me the latest, instead of switching off the phone to give myself a respite I tap out the number of another friend or acquaintance, to pass on the news. I'm not sure I can afford to think so much about it, Ellen said, and I suspect my own motives, there's something morbid I'm getting used to, getting excited by, this must be like what people felt in London during the Blitz. As far as I know, I'm not at risk, but you never know, said Aileen. This thing is totally unprecedented, said Frank. But don't you think he ought to see a doctor, Stephen insisted. Listen, said Orson, you can't force people to take care of themselves, and what makes you think the worst, he could be just run down, people still do get ordinary illnesses, awful ones, why are you assuming it has to be *that*. But all I want to be sure, said Stephen, is that he understands the options, because most people don't, that's why they won't see a doctor or have the test, they think there's nothing one can do. But is there anything one can do, he said to Tanya (according to Greg), I mean what do I gain if I go to the doctor; if I'm really ill, he's reported to have said, I'll find out soon enough.

And when he was in the hospital, his spirits seemed to lighten, according to Donny. He seemed more cheerful than he had been in the last months, Ursula said, and the bad news seemed to come almost as a relief, according to Ira, as a truly unexpected blow, according to Quentin, but you'd hardly expect him to have said the same thing to all his friends, because his relation to Ira was so different from his relation to Quentin (this according to Quentin, who was proud of their friendship), and perhaps he thought Quentin wouldn't be undone by seeing him weep, but Ira insisted that couldn't be the reason he behaved so differently with each, and that maybe he was feeling less shocked, mobilizing his strength to fight for his life, at the moment he saw Ira but overcome by feelings of hopelessness when Quentin arrived with flowers, because anyway the flowers threw him into a bad mood, as Quentin told Kate, since the hospital room was choked with flowers, you couldn't have crammed another flower into that room, but surely you're exaggerating, Kate said, smiling, everybody likes flowers. Well, who wouldn't exaggerate at a time like this, Quentin said sharply. Don't you think *this* is an exaggeration. Of course I do, said Kate gently, I was only teasing, I mean I didn't mean to tease. I know that, Quentin said, with tears in his eyes, and Kate hugged him and said well, when I go this evening I guess I won't bring flowers, what does he want, and Quentin said, according to Max, what he likes best is chocolate. Is there anything else, asked Kate, I mean like chocolate but not chocolate. Licorice, said Quentin, blowing his nose. And besides that. Aren't *you* exaggerating now, Quentin said, smiling. Right, said Kate, so if I want to bring him a whole raft of stuff, besides chocolate and licorice, what else. Jelly beans, Quentin said.

He didn't want to be alone, according to Paolo, and lots of people came in the first week, and the Jamaican nurse said there were other patients on the floor who would be glad to have the surplus flowers, and people weren't afraid to visit, it wasn't like the old days, as Kate pointed out to Aileen, they're not even segregated in the hospital anymore, as Hilda observed, there's nothing on the door of his room warning visitors of the possibility of contagion, as there was a few years ago; in fact, he's in a double room and, as he told Orson, the old guy on the far side of the curtain (who's clearly on the way out, said Stephen) doesn't even have the disease, so, as Kate went on, you really should go and see him, he'd be happy to see you, he likes having people visit, you aren't not going because you're afraid, are you. Of course not, Aileen said, but I don't know what to say, I think I'll feel awkward, which he's bound to notice, and that will make him feel worse, so I won't be doing him any good, will I. But he won't notice anything, Kate said, patting Aileen's hand, it's not like that, it's not the way you imagine, he's not judging people or wondering about their motives, he's just happy to see his friends. But I never was really a friend of his, Aileen said, you're a friend, he's always liked you, you told me he talks about Nora with you, I know he likes me, he's even attracted to me, but he respects you. But, according to Wesley, the reason Aileen was so stingy with her visits was that she could never have him to herself, there were always others there already and by the time they left still others had arrived, she'd been in love with him for years, and I can understand, said Donny, that Aileen should feel bitter that if there could have been a woman friend he did more than occasionally bed, a woman he really loved, and my God, Victor said, who had known him in those years, he was crazy about Nora, what a heart-rending couple they were, two surly angels, then it couldn't have been she.

And when some of the friends, the ones who came every day, waylaid the doctor in the corridor, Stephen was the one who asked the most informed questions, who'd been keeping up not just with the stories that appeared several times a week in the *Times* (which Greg confessed to have stopped reading, unable to stand it anymore) but with articles in the medical journals published here and in England and France, and who knew socially one of the principal doctors in Paris who was doing some much-publicized research on the disease, but his doctor said little more than that the pneumonia was not life-threatening, the fever was subsiding, of course he was still weak but he was responding well to the antibiotics, that he'd have to complete his stay in the hospital, which entailed a minimum of twenty-one days on the IV, before she could start him on the new drug, for she was optimistic about the possibility of getting him into the protocol; and when Victor said that if he had so much trouble eating (he'd say to everyone when they coaxed him to eat some of the hospital meals, that food didn't taste right, that he had a funny metallic taste in his mouth) it couldn't be good that friends were bringing him all that chocolate, the doctor just smiled and said that in these cases the patient's morale was also an important factor, and if chocolate made him feel better she saw no harm in it, which worried Stephen, as Stephen said later to Donny, because they wanted to believe in the promises and taboos of today's high-tech medicine but here this reassuringly curt and silver-haired specialist in the disease, someone quoted fre-

quently in the papers, was talking like some oldfangled country
GP who tells the family that tea with honey or chicken soup may
do as much for the patient as penicillin, which might mean, as
Max said, that they were just going through the motions of
treating him, that they were not sure about what to do, or
rather, as Xavier interjected, that they didn't know what the hell
they were doing, that the truth, the real truth, as Hilda said,
upping the ante, was that they didn't, the doctors, really have
any hope.

Oh, no, said Lewis, I can't stand it, wait a minute, I can't believe
it, are you sure, I mean are they sure, have they done all the
tests, it's getting so when the phone rings I'm scared to answer
because I think it will be someone telling me someone else is ill;
but did Lewis really not know until yesterday, Robert said tes-
tily, I find that hard to believe, everybody is talking about it, it
seems impossible that someone wouldn't have called Lewis; and
perhaps Lewis did know, was for some reason pretending not
to know already, because, Jan recalled, didn't Lewis say something months ago to Greg, and not only to Greg, about his not
looking well, losing weight, and being worried about him and
wishing he'd see a doctor, so it couldn't come as a total surprise.
Well, everybody is worried about everybody now, said Betsy,
that seems to be the way we live, the way we live now. And, after
all, they were once very close, doesn't Lewis still have the keys
to his apartment, you know the way you let someone keep the
keys after you've broken up, only a little because you hope the
person might just saunter in, drunk or high, late some evening,
but mainly because it's wise to have a few sets of keys strewn
around town, if you live alone, at the top of a former commercial building that, pretentious as it is, will never acquire a door-
man or even a resident superintendent, someone whom you can
call on for the keys late one night if you find you've lost yours
or have locked yourself out. Who else has keys, Tanya inquired,
I was thinking somebody might drop by tomorrow before coming to the hospital and bring some treasures, because the other
day, Ira said, he was complaining about how dreary the hospital
room was, and how it was like being locked up in a motel room,
which got everybody started telling funny stories about motel

rooms they'd known, and at Ursula's story, about the Luxury Budget Inn in Schenectady, there was an uproar of laughter around his bed, while he watched them in silence, eyes bright with fever, all the while, as Victor recalled, gobbling that damned chocolate. But, according to Jan, whom Lewis's keys enabled to tour the swank of his bachelor lair with an eye to bringing over some art consolation to brighten up the hospital room, the Byzantine icon wasn't on the wall over his bed, and that was a puzzle until Orson remembered that he'd recounted without seeming upset (this disputed by Greg) that the boy he'd recently gotten rid of had stolen it, along with four of the *maki-e* lacquer boxes, as if these were objects as easy to sell on the street as a TV or a stereo. But he's always been very generous, Kate said quietly, and though he loves beautiful things isn't really attached to them, to things, as Orson said, which is unusual in a collector, as Frank commented, and when Kate shuddered and tears sprang to her eyes and Orson inquired anxiously if he, Orson, had said something wrong, she pointed out that they'd begun talking about him in a retrospective mode, summing up what he was like, what made them fond of him, as if he were finished, completed, already a part of the past.

Perhaps he was getting tired of having so many visitors, said Robert, who was, as Ellen couldn't help mentioning, someone who had come only twice and was probably looking for a reason not to be in regular attendance, but there could be no doubt, according to Ursula, that his spirits had dipped, not that there was any discouraging news from the doctors, and he seemed now to prefer being alone a few hours of the day; and he told Donny that he'd begun keeping a diary for the first time in his life, because he wanted to record the course of his mental reactions to this astonishing turn of events, to do something parallel to what the doctors were doing, who came every morning and conferred at his bedside about his body, and that perhaps it wasn't so important what he wrote in it, which amounted, as he said wryly to Quentin, to little more than the usual banalities about terror and amazement that this was happening to him, to him also, plus the usual remorseful assessments of his past life, his pardonable superficialities, capped by resolves to live better, more deeply, more in touch with his work and his friends, and not to care so passionately about what people thought of him, interspersed with admonitions to himself that in this situation his will to live counted more than anything else and that if he really wanted to live, and trusted life, and liked himself well enough (down, ol' debbil Thanatos!), he *would* live, he would be an exception; but perhaps all this, as Quentin ruminated, talking on the phone to Kate, wasn't the point, the point was that by the very keeping of the diary he was accumulating something to reread one day, slyly staking out his claim to a future time, in which the diary would be an object, a relic, in which he might not actually reread it, because he would want to have put this ordeal behind him, but the diary would be there in the drawer of his stupendous Majorelle desk, and he could already, he did actually say to Quentin one late sunny afternoon, propped up in the hospital bed, with the stain of chocolate framing one corner of a heartbreaking smile, see himself in the penthouse, the October sun streaming through those clear windows instead of this streaked one, and the diary, the pathetic diary, safe inside the drawer.

It doesn't matter about the treatment's side effects, Stephen said (when talking to Max), I don't know why you're so worried about that, every strong treatment has some dangerous side effects, it's inevitable, you mean otherwise the treatment wouldn't be effective, Hilda interjected, and anyway, Stephen went on doggedly, just because there *are* side effects it doesn't mean he has to get them, or all of them, each one, or even some of them. That's just a list of all the possible things that could go wrong, because the doctors have to cover themselves, so they make up a worst-case scenario, but isn't what's happening to him, and to so many other people, Tanya interrupted, a worst-case scenario, a catastrophe no one could have imagined, it's too cruel, and isn't everything a side effect, quipped Ira, even *we* are all side effects, but we're not bad side effects, Frank said, he likes having his friends around, and we're helping each other, too; because his illness sticks us all in the same glue, mused Xavier, and, whatever the jealousies and grievances from the past that have made us wary and cranky with each other, when

something like this happens (the sky is falling, the sky is falling!)
you understand what's really important. I agree, Chicken Little,
he is reported to have said. But don't you think, Quentin observed to Max, that being as close to him as we are, making time
to drop by the hospital every day, is a way of our trying to define
ourselves more firmly and irrevocably as the well, those who
aren't ill, who aren't going to fall ill, as if what's happened to
him couldn't happen to us, when in fact the chances are that
before long one of us will end up where he is, which is probably
what he felt when he was one of the cohort visiting Zack in the
spring (you never knew Zack, did you?), and, according to Clar-
ice, Zack's widow, he didn't come very often, he said he hated
hospitals, and didn't feel he was doing Zack any good, that Zack
would see on his face how uncomfortable he was. Oh, he was
one of those, Aileen said. A coward. Like me.

And after he was sent home from the hospital, and Quentin had
volunteered to move in and was cooking meals and taking telephone messages and keeping the mother in Mississippi informed, well, mainly keeping her from flying to New York and
heaping her grief on her son and confusing the household routine with her oppressive ministrations, he was able to work an
hour or two in his study, on days he didn't insist on going out,
for a meal or a movie, which tired him. He seemed optimistic,
Kate thought, his appetite was good, and what he said, Orson
reported, was that he agreed when Stephen advised him that
the main thing was to keep in shape, he was a fighter, right, he
wouldn't be who he was if he weren't, and was he ready for the
big fight, Stephen asked rhetorically (as Max told it to Donny),
and he said you bet, and Stephen added it could be a lot worse,
you could have gotten the disease two years ago, but now so
many scientists are working on it, the American team and the
French team, everyone bucking for that Nobel Prize a few years
down the road, that all you have to do is stay healthy for another
year or two and then there will be good treatment, real treatment. Yes, he said, Stephen said, my timing is good. And Betsy,
who had been climbing on and rolling off macrobiotic diets for
a decade, came up with a Japanese specialist she wanted him to
see but thank God, Donny reported, he'd had the sense to re-

fuse, but he did agree to see Victor's visualization therapist, although what could one possibly visualize, said Hilda, when the point of visualizing disease was to see it as an entity with contours, borders, here rather than there, something limited, something you were the host of, in the sense that you could disinvite the disease, while this was so total; or would be, Max said. But the main thing, said Greg, was to see that he didn't go the macrobiotic route, which might be harmless for plump Betsy but could only be devastating for him, lean as he'd always been, with all the cigarettes and other appetite-suppressing chemicals he'd been welcoming into his body for years; and now was hardly the time, as Stephen pointed out, to be worried about cleaning up his act, and eliminating the chemical additives and other pollutants that we're all blithely or not so blithely feasting on, blithely since we're healthy, healthy as we can be; so far, Ira said. Meat and potatoes is what I'd be happy to see him eating, Ursula said wistfully. And spaghetti and clam sauce, Greg added. And thick cholesterol-rich omelets with smoked mozzarella, suggested Yvonne, who had flown from London for the weekend to see him. Chocolate cake, said Frank. Maybe not chocolate cake, Ursula said, he's already eating so much chocolate.

And when, not right away but still only three weeks later, he was accepted into the protocol for the new drug, which took considerable behind-the-scenes lobbying with the doctors, he talked less about being ill, according to Donny, which seemed like a good sign, Kate felt, a sign that he was not feeling like a victim, feeling not that he *had* a disease but, rather, was living *with* a disease (that was the right cliché, wasn't it?), a more hospitable arrangement, said Jan, a kind of cohabitation which implied that it was something temporary, that it could be terminated, but terminated how, said Hilda, and when you say hospitable, Jan, I hear hospital. And it was encouraging, Stephen insisted, that from the start, at least from the time he was finally persuaded to make the telephone call to his doctor, he was willing to say the name of the disease, pronounce it often and easily, as if it were just another word, like boy or gallery or cigarette or money or deal, as in no big deal, Paolo interjected, because, as Stephen continued, to utter the name is a sign of health, a sign that one has accepted being who one is, mortal, vulnerable, not exempt, not an exception after all, it's a sign that one is willing, truly willing, to fight for one's life. And we must say the name, too, and often, Tanya added, we mustn't lag behind him in honesty, or let him feel that, the effort of honesty having been made, it's something done with and he can go on to other things. One is so much better prepared to help him, Wesley replied. In a way he's fortunate, said Yvonne, who had taken care of a problem at the New York store and was flying back to London this evening, sure, fortunate, said Wesley, no one is shunning him, Yvonne went on, no one's afraid to hug him or kiss him lightly on the mouth, in London we are, as usual, a few years behind you, people I know, people who would seem to be not even remotely at risk, are just terrified, but I'm impressed by how cool and rational you all are; you find us cool, asked Quentin. But I have to say, he's reported to have said, I'm terrified, I find it very hard to read (and you know how he loves to read, said Greg; yes, reading is his television, said Paolo) or to think, but I don't feel hysterical. I feel quite hysterical, Lewis said to Yvonne. But you're able to *do* something for him, that's wonderful, how I wish I could stay longer, Yvonne answered, it's rather beautiful, I can't help thinking, this utopia of friendship you've assembled around him (this pathetic utopia, said Kate), so that the disease, Yvonne concluded, is not, anymore, out there. Yes, don't you think we're more at home here, with him, with the disease, said Tanya, because the imagined disease is so much worse than the reality of him, whom we all love, each in our fashion, having it. I know for me his getting it has quite demystified the disease, said Jan, I don't feel afraid, spooked, as I did before he became ill, when it was only news about remote acquaintances, whom I never saw again after they became ill. But you know you're not going to come down with the disease, Quentin said, to which Ellen replied, on her behalf, that's not the point, and possibly untrue, my gynecologist says that everyone is at risk, everyone who has a sexual life, because sexuality is a chain that links each of us to many others, unknown others, and now the great chain of being has become a chain of death as well. It's not the same for you, Quentin in-

sisted, it's not the same for you as it is for me or Lewis or Frank
or Paolo or Max, I'm more and more frightened, and I have
every reason to be. I don't think about whether I'm at risk or
not, said Hilda, I know that I was afraid to know someone with
the disease, afraid of what I'd see, what I'd feel, and after the
first day I came to the hospital I felt so relieved. I'll never feel
that way, that fear, again; he doesn't seem different from me.
He's not, Quentin said.

According to Lewis, he talked more often about those who visited more often, which is natural, said Betsy, I think he's even
keeping a tally. And among those who came or checked in by
phone every day, the inner circle as it were, those who were
getting more points, there was still a further competition, which
was what was getting on Betsy's nerves, she confessed to Jan;
there's always that vulgar jockeying for position around the bedside of the gravely ill, and though we all feel suffused with
virtue at our loyalty to him (speak for yourself, said Jan), to the
extent that we're carving time out of every day, or almost every
day, though some of us are dropping out, as Xavier pointed
out, aren't we getting at least as much out of this as he is. Are
we, said Jan. We're rivals for a sign from him of special pleasure
over a visit, each stretching for the brass ring of his favor, wanting to feel the most wanted, the true nearest and dearest, which
is inevitable with someone who doesn't have a spouse and children or an official in-house lover, hierarchies that no one would
dare contest, Betsy went on, so we are the family he's founded,
without meaning to, without official titles and ranks (we, we,
snarled Quentin); and is it so clear, though some of us, Lewis
and Quentin and Tanya and Paolo, among others, are ex-lovers
and all of us more or less than friends, which one of us he
prefers, Victor said (now it's us, raged Quentin), because sometimes I think he looks forward more to seeing Aileen, who has
visited only three times, twice at the hospital and once since he's
been home, than he does you or me; but, according to Tanya,
after being very disappointed that Aileen hadn't come, now he
was angry, while, according to Xavier, he was not really hurt but
touchingly passive, accepting Aileen's absence as something he
somehow deserved. But he's happy to have people around, said

Lewis; he says when he doesn't have company he gets very sleepy, he sleeps (according to Quentin), and then perks up when someone arrives, it's important that he not feel ever alone. But, said Victor, there's one person he hasn't heard from, whom he'd probably like to hear from more than most of us; but she didn't just vanish, even right after she broke away from him, and he knows exactly where she lives now, said Kate, he told me he put in a call to her last Christmas Eve, and she said it's nice to hear from you and Merry Christmas, and he was shattered, according to Orson, and furious and disdainful, according to Ellen (what do you expect of her, said Wesley, she was burned out), but Kate wondered if maybe he hadn't phoned Nora in the middle of a sleepless night, what's the time difference, and Quentin said no, I don't think so, I think he wouldn't want her to know.

And when he was feeling even better and had regained the pounds he'd shed right away in the hospital, though the refrigerator started to fill up with organic wheat germ and grapefruit and skimmed milk (he's worried about his cholesterol count, Stephen lamented), and told Quentin he could manage by himself now, and did, he started asking everyone who visited how he looked, and everyone said he looked great, so much better than a few weeks ago, which didn't jibe with what anyone had told him at that time; but then it was getting harder and harder to know how he looked, to answer such a question honestly when among themselves they wanted to be honest, both for honesty's sake and (as Donny thought) to prepare for the worst, because he'd been looking like *this* for so long, at least it seemed so long, that it was as if he'd always been like this, how did he look before, but it was only a few months, and those words, pale and wan looking and fragile, hadn't they always applied? And one Thursday Ellen, meeting Lewis at the door of the building, said, as they rode up together in the elevator, how is he *really*? But you see how he is, Lewis said tartly, he's fine, he's perfectly healthy, and Ellen understood that of course Lewis didn't think he was perfectly healthy but that he wasn't worse, and that was true, but wasn't it, well, almost heartless to talk like that. Seems inoffensive to me, Quentin said, but I know what you mean, I remember once talking to Frank, somebody, after all, who has volunteered to do five hours a week of office work at the Crisis Center (I know, said Ellen), and Frank was going on about this guy, diagnosed almost a year ago, and so much further along, who'd been complaining to Frank on the phone about the indifference of some doctor, and had gotten quite abusive about the doctor, and Frank was saying there was no reason to be so upset, the implication being that *he,* Frank, wouldn't behave so irrationally, and I said, barely able to control my scorn, but Frank, Frank, he has every reason to be upset, he's dying, and Frank said, said according to Quentin, oh, I don't like to think about it that way.

And it was while he was still home, recuperating, getting his weekly treatment, still not able to do much work, he complained, but, according to Quentin, up and about most of the time and turning up at the office several days a week, that bad news came about two remote acquaintances, one in Houston and one in Paris, news that was intercepted by Quentin on the ground that it could only depress him, but Stephen contended that it was wrong to lie to him, it was so important for him to live in the truth; that had been one of his first victories, that he was candid, that he was even willing to crack jokes about the disease, but Ellen said it wasn't good to give him this end-of-the-world feeling, too many people were getting ill, it was becoming such a common destiny that maybe some of the will to fight for his life would be drained out of him if it seemed to be as natural as, well, death. Oh, Hilda said, who didn't know personally either the one in Houston or the one in Paris, but knew *of* the one in Paris, a pianist who specialized in twentieth-century Czech and Polish music, I have his records, he's such a valuable person, and, when Kate glared at her, continued defensively, I know every life is equally sacred, but that *is* a thought, another thought, I mean, all these valuable people who aren't going to have their normal four score as it is now, these people aren't going to be replaced, and it's such a loss to the culture. But this isn't going to go on forever, Wesley said, it can't, they're bound to come up with something (they, they, muttered Stephen), but did you ever think, Greg said, that if some people don't die, I

mean even if they can keep them alive (they, they, muttered
Kate), they continue to be carriers, and that means, if you have
a conscience, that you can never make love, make love fully, as
you'd been wont — wantonly, Ira said — to do. But it's better
than dying, said Frank. And in all his talk about the future,
when he allowed himself to be hopeful, according to Quentin,
he never mentioned the prospect that even if he didn't die,
if he were so fortunate as to be among the first generation of
the disease's survivors, never mentioned, Kate confirmed, that
whatever happened it was over, the way he had lived until now,
but, according to Ira, he did think about it, the end of bravado,
the end of folly, the end of trusting life, the end of taking life
for granted, and of treating life as something that, samurai-like,
he thought himself ready to throw away lightly, impudently;
and Kate recalled, sighing, a brief exchange she'd insisted on
having as long as two years ago, huddling on a banquette covered with steel-gray industrial carpet on an upper level of The
Prophet and toking up for their next foray onto the dance floor:
she'd said hesitantly, for it felt foolish asking a prince of debauchery to, well, take it easy, and she wasn't keen on playing
big sister, a role, as Hilda confirmed, he inspired in many
women, are you being careful, honey, you know what I mean.
And he replied, Kate went on, no, I'm not, listen, I can't, I just
can't, sex is too important to me, always has been (he started
talking like that, according to Victor, after Nora left him), and
if I get it, well, I get it. But he wouldn't talk like that now, would
he, said Greg; he must feel awfully foolish now, said Betsy, like
someone who went on smoking, saying I can't give up cigarettes,
but when the bad X-ray is taken even the most besotted nicotine
addict can stop on a dime. But sex isn't like cigarettes, is it, said
Frank, and, besides, what good does it do to remember that he
was reckless, said Lewis angrily, the appalling thing is that you
just have to be unlucky once, and wouldn't he feel even worse
if he'd stopped three years ago and had come down with it
anyway, since one of the most terrifying features of the disease
is that you don't know when you contracted it, it could have
been ten years ago, because surely this disease has existed for
years and years, long before it was recognized; that is, named.
Who knows how long (I think a lot about that, said Max) and

who knows (I know what you're going to say, Stephen interrupted) how many are going to get it.

I'm feeling fine, he's reported to have said whenever someone asked him how he was, which was almost always the first question anyone asked. Or: I'm feeling better, how are you? But he said other things, too. I'm playing leapfrog with myself, he is reported to have said, according to Victor. And: There must be a way to get something positive out of this situation, he's reported to have said to Kate. How American of him, said Paolo. Well, said Betsy, you know the old American adage: When you've got a lemon, make lemonade. The one thing I'm sure I couldn't take, Jan said he said to her, is becoming disfigured, but Stephen hastened to point out the disease doesn't take that form very often anymore, its profile is mutating, and, in conversation with Ellen, wheeled up words like blood-brain barrier; I never thought there was a barrier *there*, said Jan. But he mustn't know about Max, Ellen said, that would really depress him, please don't tell him, he'll have to know, Quentin said grimly, and he'll be furious not to have been told. But there's time for that, when they take Max off the respirator, said Ellen; but isn't it incredible, Frank said, Max was fine, not feeling ill at all, and then to wake up with a fever of a hundred and five, unable to breathe, but that's the way it often starts, with absolutely no warning, Stephen said, the disease has so many forms. And when, after another week had gone by, he asked Quentin where Max was, he didn't question Quentin's account of a spree in the Bahamas, but then the number of people who visited regularly was thinning out, partly because the old feuds that had been put aside through the first hospitalization and the return home had resurfaced, and the flickering enmity between Lewis and Frank exploded, even though Kate did her best to mediate between them, and also because he himself had done something to loosen the bonds of love that united the friends around him, by seeming to take them all for granted, as if it were perfectly normal for so many people to carve out so much time and attention for him, visit him every few days, talk about him incessantly on the phone with each other; but, according to Paolo, it wasn't that he was less grateful, it was just something he was getting used to, the visits. It had become, with time, a more ordinary kind of situation, a kind of ongoing party, first at the hospital and now since he was home, barely on his feet again, it being clear, said Robert, that I'm on the B list; but Kate said, that's absurd, there's no list; and Victor said, but there is, only it's not he, it's Quentin who's drawing it up. He wants to see us, we're helping him, we have to do it the way he wants, he fell down yesterday on the way to the bathroom, he mustn't be told about Max (but he already knew, according to Donny), it's getting worse.

When I was home, he is reported to have said, I was afraid to sleep, as I was dropping off each night it felt like just that, as if I were falling down a black hole, to sleep felt like giving in to death, I slept every night with the light on; but here, in the hospital, I'm less afraid. And to Quentin he said, one morning, the fear rips through me, it tears me open; and, to Ira, it presses me together, squeezes me toward myself. Fear gives everything its hue, its high. I feel so, I don't know how to say it, exalted, he said to Quentin. Calamity is an amazing high, too. Sometimes I feel *so* well, so powerful, it's as if I could jump out of my skin. Am I going crazy, or what? Is it all this attention and coddling I'm getting from everybody, like a child's dream of being loved? Is it the drugs? I know it sounds crazy but sometimes I think this is a *fantastic* experience, he said shyly; but there was also the bad taste in the mouth, the pressure in the head and at the back of the neck, the red, bleeding gums, the painful, if pink-lobed, breathing, and his ivory pallor, color of white chocolate. Among those who wept when told over the phone that he was back in the hospital were Kate and Stephen (who'd been called by Quentin), and Ellen, Victor, Aileen, and Lewis (who were called by Kate), and Xavier and Ursula (who were called by Stephen). Among those who didn't weep were Hilda, who said that she'd just learned that her seventy-five-year-old aunt was dying of the disease, which she'd contracted from a transfusion given during her successful double bypass of five years ago, and Frank and Donny and Betsy, but this didn't mean, according to Tanya, that they weren't moved and appalled, and Quentin thought they might not be coming soon to the hospital but would send presents; the room, he was in a private room this time, was filling up with flowers, and plants, and books, and tapes. The high tide of barely suppressed acrimony of the last weeks at home subsided into the routines of hospital visiting, though more than a few resented Quentin's having charge of the visiting book (but it was Quentin who had the idea, Lewis pointed out); now, to insure a steady stream of visitors, preferably no more than two at a time (this, the rule in all hospitals, wasn't enforced here, at least on this floor; whether out of kindness or inefficiency, no one could decide), Quentin had to be called first, to get one's time slot, there was no more casual dropping by. And his mother could no longer be prevented from taking a plane and installing herself in a hotel near the hospital; but he seemed to mind her daily presence less than expected, Quentin said; said Ellen it's we who mind, do you suppose she'll stay long. It was easier to be generous with each other visiting him here in the hospital, as Donny pointed out, than at home, where one minded never being alone with him; coming here, in our twos and twos, there's no doubt about what our role is, how we should be, collective, funny, distracting, undemanding, light, it's important to be light, for in all this dread there is gaiety, too, as the poet said, said Kate. (His eyes, his glittering eyes, said Lewis.) His eyes looked dull, extinguished, Wesley said to Xavier, but Betsy said his face, not just his eyes, looked soulful, warm; whatever is there, said Kate, I've never been so aware of his eyes; and Stephen said, I'm afraid of what my eyes show, the way I watch him, with too much intensity, or a phony kind of casualness, said Victor. And, unlike at home, he was clean-shaven each morning, at whatever hour they visited him; his curly hair was always combed; but he complained that the nurses had changed since he was here the last time, and that he didn't like the change, he wanted everyone to be the same. The room was furnished now with some of his personal effects (odd word for one's things, said Ellen), and Tanya brought drawings and a letter from her nine-year-old dyslexic son, who was writing now, since she'd purchased a computer; and Donny brought champagne and some helium balloons, which were anchored to the foot of his bed; tell me about something that's going on, he said, waking up from a nap to find Donny and Kate at the side

of his bed, beaming at him; tell me a story, he said wistfully, said
Donny, who couldn't think of anything to say; *you're* the story,
Kate said. And Xavier brought an eighteenth-century Guate-
malan wooden statue of Saint Sebastian with upcast eyes and
open mouth, and when Tanya said what's that, a tribute to eros
past, Xavier said where I come from Sebastian is venerated as a
protector against pestilence. Pestilence symbolized by arrows?
Symbolized by arrows. All people remember is the body of a
beautiful youth bound to a tree, pierced by arrows (of which he
always seems oblivious, Tanya interjected), people forget that
the story continues, Xavier continued, that when the Christian
women came to bury the martyr they found him still alive and
nursed him back to health. And he said, according to Stephen,
I didn't know Saint Sebastian didn't die. It's undeniable, isn't it,
said Kate on the phone to Stephen, the fascination of the dying.
It makes me ashamed. We're learning how to die, said Hilda,
I'm not ready to learn, said Aileen; and Lewis, who was coming
straight from the other hospital, the hospital where Max was
still being kept in ICU, met Tanya getting out of the elevator
on the tenth floor, and as they walked together down the shiny
corridor past the open doors, averting their eyes from the other
patients sunk in their beds, with tubes in their noses, irradiated
by the bluish light from the television sets, the thing I can't bear
to think about, Tanya said to Lewis, is someone dying with the
TV on.

He has that strange, unnerving detachment now, said Ellen,
that's what upsets me, even though it makes it easier to be with
him. Sometimes he was querulous. I can't stand them coming in
here taking my blood every morning, what are they doing with
all that blood, he is reported to have said; but where was his
anger, Jan wondered. Mostly he was lovely to be with, always
saying how are *you*, how are you feeling. He's so sweet now, said
Aileen. He's so nice, said Tanya. (Nice, nice, groaned Paolo.) At
first he was very ill, but he was rallying, according to Stephen's
best information, there was no fear of his not recovering this
time, and the doctor spoke of his being discharged from the
hospital in another ten days if all went well, and the mother was
persuaded to fly back to Mississippi, and Quentin was readying

the penthouse for his return. And he was still writing his diary, not showing it to anyone, though Tanya, first to arrive one late-winter morning, and finding him dozing, peeked, and was horrified, according to Greg, not by anything she read but by a progressive change in his handwriting: in the recent pages, it was becoming spidery, less legible, and some lines of script wandered and tilted about the page. I was thinking, Ursula said to Quentin, that the difference between a story and a painting or photograph is that in a story you can write, He's still alive. But in a painting or a photo you can't show "still." You can just show him being alive. He's still alive, Stephen said.

The Afterlife

THE BILLINGSES, so settled in their ways, found in their fifties that their friends were doing sudden, surprising things. Mitch Lothrop, whom Carter and Jane had always rather poked fun at as stuffy, ran off with a young Jamaican physical therapist, and Augustina, who had seemed such a mouse all those years — obsessed with her garden and her children's educations — took it rather raucously in stride, buying herself a new wardrobe of broad-shouldered dresses, putting a prodigiously expensive new slate roof on the Weston house, and having in as a new companion another woman, a frilly little blue-eyed person who worked in Boston as a psychologist for the Department of Social Services. Ken McEvoy, on the other hand, was one day revealed in the newspapers as an embezzler who over the course of twenty years had stolen between two and five million from his brokerage firm; nobody, including the IRS, knew exactly how much. The investigation had evidently been going on for ages, during which time Ken and Molly had been showing up at cocktail parties and dinner parties and zoning hearings and church suppers with not a hair out of place, smiling and looking as handsome a couple as ever. Even now, with the indictment in the paper and the plea-bargaining stage under way, they continued to appear at gatherings, Ken quite hilarious and open about it all and basking at the center of attention; he had always seemed rather stiff and shy before. What had he done with all the money? It was true they had two foreign cars, and a place on the Cape, and trips to Europe in the years they didn't go to Florida, but then so did everybody, more or less.

And then the Billingses' very dearest friends, Frank and Lucy Eggleston, upped and moved to England. It was something, Frank confided, they had thought about for years; they detested America, the way it was going — the vulgarity, the crowdedness, the violence. They both, Frank and Lucy, were exceptionally soft-spoken and virtual teetotalers, with health diets and peaceable hobbies; Frank did watercolors, Lucy bird-watched. A juncture came in his career when the corporation asked him to move to Texas; he opted to take early retirement instead, and with his savings and a little inheritance of hers, plus the ridiculous price their house brought — ten times what they had paid for it in the early sixties — they moved to England, at a time when the pound was low against the dollar. Why defer a dream, they asked the Billingses, until you're too old to enjoy it? They found a suitable house not in one of the pretty counties south of London but up in Norfolk, where, as one of Lucy's early letters put it, "the sky is as big as they say the sky of Texas is."

The letters were less frequent than the Billingses had expected, and on their side they proved slower than they had promised to arrange a visit to their transplanted friends. Three years had gone by before they at last, after some days in London to adjust to the time change and the currency and the left-right confusion, took a train north, got off at a station beyond Cambridge, and were greeted in the damp and windy spring twilight by a bouncy, bog-hatted shadow they recognized as Frank Eggleston. He had put on weight, and had acquired that rosy English complexion and an un-American way of clearing his throat several times in rapid succession. As they drove along the A-11, and then navigated twisting country roads, Carter seemed to hear Frank's accent melt, becoming less clipped and twitchy as his passengers and he talked and warmed the car's interior with their growly, drawling Americanness.

After many a turning in the dark, they arrived at Flinty Dell — a name no natives, surely, would have given the slightly gaunt mustard brick house, with its many gables and odd-sized, scattered windows, behind its high wall and bristlings of privet. Lucy seemed much as ever; a broad-faced strawberry blonde, she had always worn sweaters and plaid pleated skirts and low-heeled shoes for her birding walks, and here this same outfit seemed a shade more chic and less aggressively "sensible" than it had at home. Her pleasant plain looks, rather lost in the old crowd of heavily groomed suburban wives, had bloomed in this climate; her manner, as she showed them the house and their room upstairs, seemed to Carter somehow blushing, bridal. She escorted them through a maze of brightly papered rooms and awkward little hallways, up one set of stairs and down another, and on through the kitchen to a mud room, where she and Frank outfitted themselves with scarves and Wellingtons and fat leather gloves and canes and riding crops and rakes and shovels for their dealings with the constantly invigorating out-of-doors. A barn went with the place, where they boarded horses. The village church was just across the pasture and through the wood on a path. Some obscure duke's vast estate stretched all about, with miles and miles of wonderful riding. And then there were fens, and a priory ruin, and towns where antiques could be had for almost nothing. It was all too much to take in, or to talk about so late at night, Lucy said, especially when you must be exhausted and still on funny time.

"Oh, no," Jane said. "Carter was de*ter*mined to get on your time and he wouldn't let me take even a nap that first awful day. We walked all the way from the National Gallery to the Tate in the rain, which had this huge retrospective of this horrid Kitchen Sink school."

"Such fun you make it sound," Lucy said, tucking her plump freckled calves under her on the tired-looking sofa. The living room was rather small, though high-ceilinged. The furniture, which they must have bought here, clustered like a threadbare, expectant audience about the tiny grated fireplace, as it vivaciously consumed chunks of wood too short to be called logs. "We thought we'd be going down to London every other day but there seems so much to do *here*."

The birding was incredible, and Lucy had become, to her own surprise, quite involved with the local church and with village good works. Frank was painting very seriously, and had joined an artists' association in Norwich, and had displayed a number of watercolors in their biannual shows. Some of his new works were hung in the living room: wet gray skies and tiny dark houses in the lee of gloomy groves scrubbed in with purple and green. Having poked the fire, and added more chunks (whose smoke smelled narcotically sweet), Frank pressed drinks upon the Billingses, though, as all agreed, it was already late and tomorrow was a big day. Lucy was going to drive them to the sea while Frank rode in the local hunt. Scotch, brandy, port, Madeira, and several tints of sherry were produced; Carter remembered the Egglestons as abstemious, but English coziness seemed to have teased that out of them. Carter drank port and Jane cream sherry as they gave the American news: Mitch Lothrop and the Jamaican bodybuilder live in Bay Village and have a baby, while Augustina has turned the Weston place into some sort of commune, with a total of five women living in it now. Ken McEvoy is out, having served less than two years, and has been given a job by one of the big Boston banks as an accountant, because he's supposedly an expert on fraudulent bookkeeping. Though he and Molly still drive their old Jaguar and a Volvo station wagon, it's obvious he must have stashed millions away, because they're always flying off now, even just for weekends, to this place they seem to own in the Bahamas. And so on.

Frank and Lucy had grown smilingly silent under this barrage of imported gossip, and when Carter stood and announced, "We're boring you," neither of them contradicted him. He had lost count of the times Frank had refreshed his port, or poured himself another brandy, and the freckles on Lucy's shins were beginning to swarm; yet he felt he was cutting something short, standing at last. All seemed to feel this — this failure, for all their good will, to remake the old connection — and it was in an atmosphere of reluctance that the guests were, sensibly, led up to bed, Lucy showing them the bathroom again and making sure they had towels.

In the night, Carter awoke and needed to go to the bathroom. All that port. A wind was blowing outside. Vague black-on-blue tree shapes were thrashing. Turning on no light, so as not to wake Jane, he found the bedroom door, opened it softly in the dark, and took two firm steps down the hall toward where he remembered the bathroom was. On his second step, there was nothing but air beneath his foot. His sleepy brain was jolted into action; he realized he was falling down the stairs. As he soared through black space, he had time to think what a terrible noise his crashing body would make, and how the Egglestons would be awakened, and how embarrassing and troublesome it would be for them to deal with his broken body. He even had time to reflect how oddly selfless this last thought was. Then something — some*one*, he felt — hit him a solid blow in the exact center of his chest, right on the sternum, and Carter was standing upright on a landing partway down the stairs. He listened a moment, heard only the wind as it moaned around the strange brick house, and climbed the six or so steps back to the second floor.

He remembered now that the bathroom was reached by turning immediately left out of the bedroom and then right at the bannister that protected the stairwell, and then left again, at the second door. He crept along and pressed this door open. The white toilet and porcelain basin had a glow of their own in the moonless night, so again he did without a light. His legs were trembling and his chest ached slightly, but he felt better for having emptied his bladder. However, emerging again into the dark hall, he couldn't find the way back to his bedroom. Walls as in a funhouse surrounded him. A large smooth plane held a shadowy man who actually touched him, with an abrupt oily touch, and he realized it was himself, reflected in a mirror. On the three other sides of him there were opaque surfaces paneled like doors. Then one of the doors developed a crack of dim blue light and seemed to slide diagonally away; Carter's eyes were adjusted to the dark enough to register wallpaper — faintly abrasive and warm to his touch — and the shiny straight gleam, as of a railroad track, of the bannister. He reversed his direction. There seemed many doors along the hall, but the one he pushed open did indeed reveal his bedroom. The wind was muttering, fidgeting at the stout English window sash, and as Carter drew closer to the bed he could hear Jane breathe. He crept in beside her and fell swiftly asleep.

Next morning, as he examined the site of his adventure, he marveled that he had not been killed. The oval knob of a newel post at the turn in the stairs must have been what struck him on the chest; had he fallen a slightly different way, it would have hit him in the face — smashed in his front teeth, or ripped out an eye — or he could have missed it entirely and broken his neck against the landing wall. He had no memory of grabbing anything, or of righting himself. But how had he regained his feet? Either his memory had a gap or he had been knocked bolt upright. If the latter, it seemed a miracle, but Jane, when he confided the event to her, took the occasion not for marveling but for showing him, as one would show a stupid child, how to turn on the hall light, with one of those British toggle switches that look like a stumpy rapier with a button in its tip.

Carter felt rebuffed; he had told her of his nocturnal adventure, while they were still in bed, in hushed tones much like hers when, thirty years ago, she would confide a suspicion that she was pregnant. The Egglestons, downstairs at breakfast, responded more appropriately; they expressed amazement and relief that he hadn't been hurt. "You might have been *killed!*" Lucy said, with a rising inflection that in America had never been quite so pert, so boldly birdlike.

"Exactly," Carter said. "And at the time, even as I was in midair, I thought, What a nuisance for the poor Egglestons!"

"Damn white of you," Frank said, lifting his teacup to his face. He was in a hurry to be off to his hunt; he had been up for several hours, doing a painting that needed dawn light, and there were blue and yellow under his fingernails. "Not to pop off on us," he finished.

"It happens," Carter told him. "More and more, you see your contemporaries in the *Globe* obituaries. The Big Guy is getting our range." This outburst of theology was so unexpected that the three others stared at him with a silence in which the chimneys could be heard to moan and the breakfast china to click. Carter felt, however, unembarrassed, and supernaturally serene. The world to which he had awoken, from the English details of the orange-juiceless, marmalade-laden breakfast set before him to the muddy green windswept landscape framed in the thick-sashed and playfully various windows, reminded him of children's books he had read over fifty years ago, and had the charm of the timeless.

He squeezed his feet into Lucy's Wellingtons and walked out with Frank to admire the horses. This Norfolk earth was littered with flint — chalky, sharp-edged pebbles. He picked one up and held it in his hand. A limestone layer, porous like bone, had wrapped itself around a shiny bluish core. He tried to imagine the geological event — some immense vanished ocean — that had precipitated this hail of bonelike fragments. The abundant flint, the tufty grass so bursting with green, the radiant gray sky, the strong smells of horse and leather and feed and hay all bore in upon Carter's revitalized senses with novel force; there seemed a cosmic joke under mundane appearances, and in the air a release of pressure which enabled the trees, the beeches and oaks, to attain the size of thunderheads. The air was raw — rawer than he had expected England in April to be. "Is the wind always like this?" he asked the other man.

"Pretty much. It's been a tardy spring." Frank, in hunting coat and jodhpurs, had saddled a horse in its stall and was fiddling with the bridle, making the long chestnut head of the animal, with its rubbery gray muzzle and rolling gelatinous eyeball, jerk resentfully. The physical fact of a horse — the pungent, assaultive hugeness of the animal and the sense of a tiny spark, a gleam of skittish and limited intelligence, within its monstrous long skull — was not a fact that Carter often confronted in his other life.

"Doesn't it get on your nerves?"

"Does 'em good," Frank said with his acquired brisk bluffness. "Scours you out."

"Yes," Carter said, "I can feel that." He felt delicate, alert, excited. The center of his chest was slightly sore. His toes were numb and scrunched inside Lucy's boots. With a terrible shuffling of hooves and heaving of glossy mass, the horse was led from the barn and suddenly Frank was up on it, transformed, majestic, his pink face crowned by his round black hat, he and the horse a single new creature. The two women came out of the mustard brick house to watch its master ride off, at a stately pace, down the flinty driveway to the path through the wood. The trees not yet in full leaf were stippled all over with leaflets and catkins, like a swathe of dotted swiss. Frank, thus veiled, slowly vanished. "A grand sight," Carter said, feeling that some such entertainment, astonishing yet harmless and intangible, would be his steady diet here. He felt weightless, as if, in that moment of flight headlong down the stairs, he had put on wings.

Lucy asked them which they would like first, the walk to the river or the drive to the sea. Then she decided the two should be combined, and a supply of boots and overshoes was tossed into the car. Carter got in the back of the little Austin — red, though it had looked black at the station last night — and let the two women sit up front together. Jane occupied what in America would have been the driver's seat, so that Carter felt startled and imperiled when she turned her head aside or gestured with both hands. Lucy seemed quite accustomed to the wrong side of the road, and drove with a heedless dash. "Here is the village, these few houses," she said. "And the church just beyond — you can't see it very well because of that huge old chestnut. Incredibly old they say the tree is. The church isn't so old."

On the other side of the road, there were sheep, dusted all over with spots of color and mingled with gamboling lambs. The river was not far off, and they parked by an iron bridge where water poured in steady cold pleats down the slant face of a concrete weir. Embankments had been built by stacking bags of cement and letting natural processes dampen and harden them. Lucy led the way along a muddy path between the riverbank and a field that had been recently plowed; the pale soil, littered to the horizon with bonelike bits of flint, was visibly lifting into the silvery, tumbling sky. The wind was scouring dark trails of soil upward, across the plowed miles.

"It's been almost a drought," Lucy said, her voice buffeted, her kerchief flattened against her freckled cheek. Her squinting eyes were a pale color between blue and green, and this beryl, beneath this sky, had an uncanny brilliance. "Oh, look!" she cried, pointing. "A little marsh tit, doing his acrobatics! Last week, closer to the woods, I saw a pair of waxwings. They generally go back to the Continent by this time of year. Am I boring you both? Really, the wind is frightful, but I want you to see my gray heron. His nest *must* be in the woods somewhere, but Frank and I have never been able to spot it. We asked Sedgewick — that's the duke's gamekeeper — where to look for it, and he said if we got downwind we would *smell* it. They eat meat, you know — rodents and snakes."

"Oh dear," Jane said, for something to say. Carter couldn't take his eyes from the distant dark lines of lifting earth, the Texaslike dust storm. As the three made their way along the river, the little black-capped tit capered in the air above them, and as they approached the woods, out flocked starlings, speckled and black and raucous.

"Look — the kingfisher!" Lucy cried. This bird was brilliant, ruddy-breasted and green-headed, with a steel-blue tail. It flicked the tail back and forth, then whirred along the river's glittering surface. But the gray heron was not showing himself, though they trod the margin of the woods for what seemed half a mile. They could hear tree trunks groaning as the wind twisted their layered crowns; the tallest and leafiest trees seemed not merely to heave but to harbor several small explosions at once, which whitened their tossing branches in patches. Carter's eyes watered, and Jane held her hands in their fat, borrowed gloves in front of her face. At last, their hostess halted. She announced, "We better get on with it — what a disappointment," and led them back to the car.

As they drew close to the glittering, pleated, roaring weir, Carter had the sudden distinct feeling that he should look behind him. And there was the heron, sailing out of the woods toward them, against the wind, held, indeed, motionless within the wind, standing in midair with his six-foot wingspread — an angel.

The wind got worse as they drove toward the sea. On the map, it looked a long way off, but Lucy assured them she had often done it and back by teatime. As she whipped along the narrow roads, Carter in the back seat could not distinguish between her tugs on the steering wheel and the tugs of the wind as it buffeted the Austin. A measured, prissy voice on the radio spoke of a gale from the Irish Sea and of conditions that were "near cyclonic," and Jane and Carter laughed, though Lucy merely smiled and said that they often used that expression. In a village especially dear to her, especially historical and picturesque, a group of people were standing on the sidewalk at the crest of a hill, near the wall of a churchyard. The church was Norman, with ornamental arcs and borders of red pebbles worked into the masonry. Lucy drove the car rather slowly past, to see if there had been an accident.

"I think," Carter offered, "they're watching the tree." A tall tree leaning from within the churchyard was swaying in the wind.

"Bother," Lucy said. "I've driven too far — what I wanted to show you was back in the middle of the village." She turned around, and as they drove by again several of the little crowd, recognizing the car, seemed amused. A policeman, wearing a rain cape, was pedaling his bicycle up the hill, very energetically, head down.

What Lucy wanted the Billingses to see in the village was a side street of sixteenth-century houses, all of them half-timbered and no two leaning at the same angle.

"Who lives in them?" Carter wanted to know.

"Oh, people — though I daresay more and more it's trendy younger people who open up shops on the ground floor." Lucy backed around again and this time, coming up the hill, they met a police barricade, and the tree fallen flat across the road. Just half of the tree, actually; its crotch had been low to the earth, and the other half, with a splintery white wound in its side, still stood.

The three Americans, sealed into their car, shrieked in excitement, understanding now why the villagers had been amused to see them drive past under the tree again. "You'd think *some-body*," Jane said, "might have said something to warn us."

"Well, I suppose they thought we had eyes to see as well as they," said Lucy. "That's how they are. They don't give anything away; you have to go to them." And she described, as they bounced between thorny hedgerows and dry-stone walls, her church work, her charity work in the area. It was astonishing, how much incest there was, and drunkenness, and hopelessness. "These people just can't envision any better future for themselves. They would never *dream*, for example, of going to London, even for a day. They're just totally locked into their little world."

Jane asked, "What about television?"

"Oh, they watch it, but don't see that it has anything to do with them. They're taken care of, you see, and compared with their fathers and grandfathers aren't so badly off. The *cruelty* of the old system of hired agricultural labor is almost beyond imagining; they worked people absolutely to death. Picking flint, for instance. Every spring they'd all get out there and pick the flint off the fields."

That didn't seem, to Carter, so very cruel. He had picked up bits of flint on his own, spontaneously. They were porous, pale, intricate, everlasting. His mind wandered as Lucy went on about the Norfolk villagers and Jane chimed in with her own concerns — her wish, now that the children were out of the house, to get out herself and be of some service, not exactly jump into the ghetto with wild-eyed good intentions but do something *use*ful, something with *peo*ple . . .

Carter had been nodding off, and the emphasized words pierced his doze. He felt he had been useful enough, in his life, and had seen enough people. At work now — he was a lawyer — he was conscious of a curious lag, like the lag built into radio talk shows so that obscenities wouldn't get on the air. Just two or three seconds, between challenge and response, between achievement and gratification, but enough to tell him that something was out of sync. He was going through the motions, and all the younger people around him knew it. When he spoke, his voice sounded dubbed, not quite his own. There were, it had recently come to him, vast areas of the world he no longer cared about — Henry James, for example, and professional ice hockey, and nuclear disarmament. He did not doubt that within these areas much excitement could be generated, but not for him, nevermore. The two women in front of him — Lucy's strawberry-blond braids twitching as she emphasized a point and Jane's gray-peppered brunette curls softly bouncing as she nodded in eager empathy — seemed alien creatures, like the horse, or the marsh tit with his little black-capped head. The two wives seemed as stirred up and twittery as if their lives had just begun, and courtship and husbands and childbearing were a preamble to some triumphant menopausal ministry among the disenfranchised and incestuous. They loved each other, Carter reflected wearily. Women had the passion of conspirators, the energy of any underground, supplied by hope of seizing power. Lucy seemed hardly to notice, while talking and counseling Jane, that she had more than once steered around the wreckage of limbs that littered the road. Through the speeding car windows Carter watched trees thrash in odd slow motion and overhead wires sway as if the earth itself had lost its moorings.

Then, out of the bruised and scrambled sky, a rain pelted down with such fury that the wipers couldn't keep the windshield clear; it became like frosted glass, and the car roof thrummed. Lucy lifted her voice: "There's a lovely old inn right in the next village. Would this be a good time to have a bite?"

Just in dashing the few yards from the parking lot to the shelter of the inn, the three of them got soaked. Inside, all was idyllic: big old blackened fireplace crackling and hissing and exuding that sweet scent of local woodsmoke, carved beams bowed down almost to Carter's head, buffet of salmon mousse and Scotch eggs and shepherd's pie served by a willing lad and blushing lass, at whose backs the rain beat like a stage effect on the thick bottle panes. They ate, and drank beer and tea, and over Lucy's protests Carter paid.

Next door, an antique shop tempted tourists through a communicating archway, and while the storm continued, Lucy and her visitors browsed among the polished surfaces, the silver and mirrors, the framed prints and marquetry tables. Carter was struck by a lustrous large bureau, veneered in a wood that looked like many blurred paw prints left by a party of golden cats. "Elm burl, early eighteenth century," the ticket said, along with a price in the thousands of pounds. He asked Jane if she would like it — as if one more piece of furniture might keep her at home.

"Darling, it's lovely," she said, "but so expensive, and so big."

"They ship," he responded, after a few seconds' lag. "And if it doesn't fit anywhere we can sell it in town for a profit." His voice didn't sound quite like his own, but only he seemed to notice. The women's conversation in the car had obligated him to show that power, male power, did more than induce weariness in the holder. Elm burl: perhaps that was the charm, the touch of attractive fantasy. In America, the elms were dead, as dead as the anonymous workman who had laid on this still glamorous veneer.

Lucy, deepening her hint of a British accent, courteously haggled with the manager — a straggly fat woman with a runny red nose and a Gypsyish shawl she held tight around her throat —

and got four hundred pounds knocked off the price. Carter's plunge into this purchase frightened him, momentarily, as he realized how big the markup must be to absorb such a discount so casually.

There were forms to sign, and credit cards to authenticate over the telephone. As these transactions were pursued, the storm on the roof abated. The tree buyers stepped out into a stunning sunlit lapse in the weather. Raindrops glistened everywhere like a coating of ice, and the sidewalk slates echoed the violet of the near-cyclonic sky.

"Darling, that was so debonair and dashing and untypical of you," Jane said.

"Ever so larky," Lucy agreed.

"Kind of a game," he admitted. "What are the odds we'll ever see that chest again?"

Lucy took mild offense, as if her adopted fellow countrymen were being impugned. "Oh, they're very honest and reputable. We've dealt with these people a few times ourselves."

A miraculous lacquer lay upon everything, beading each roadside twig, each reed of thatch in the cottage roofs, each tiny daisy trembling in the grass by the lichen-stained rough field walls. Then clouds swept in again, and the landscape was dipped in shadow. Many trees were fallen or split. Little clusters of workmen, in raincoats that were pumpkin-colored instead of, as they would have been in America, yellow or Day-Glo orange, buzzed with saws and pulled with ropes at limbs that intruded into the road. Waiting to be signaled past such work parties took time, while the little Austin gently rocked in the wind as if being nudged by a hand. Carter caressed the sensitive center of his chest, under his necktie: his secret, the seal of his nocturnal pact, his passport to this day like no other. It had felt, in the dark, like a father's rough impatient saving blow. "How much farther to the sea?" he asked.

"Well might you ask," Lucy said. "On a day of smooth sailing, we'd be there by now." The cars ahead of them slowed and then stopped entirely. A policeman with a young round face explained that lines were down across the road.

"That does rather tear it," Lucy said. The detour would add

fifteen miles at least to their journey. The landscape looked dyed, now, in an ink that rolled across the pale speckled fields in waves of varying intensity. Along a far ridge, skeletal power-line towers marched in a procession, their latticework etched with a ghostly delicacy against the black sky. A band of angels.

Jane consoled Lucy. "Really, dear, if I saw too many more charming villages I might burst."

"And we see the sea all the time when we're on the Cape," Carter added.

"But not *our* sea," Lucy said. "The *North* Sea."

"Isn't it just ugly and cold and full of oil?" asked Jane.

"Not for much longer, they tell us. Full of oil, I mean. Well, if you two don't really mind, I suppose there's nothing to do but go back. Frank *does* like an early supper after he's been on a hunt."

It was growing dark by the time they reached Flinty Dell. Exposing to view a small, drab Victorian church, the ancient chestnut had blown down — a giant shaggy corpse with a tall stump torn like a shriek, pointing at the heavens. The tree had fallen across the churchyard wall and crushed it, the outer courses of sturdy-seeming brick spilling a formless interior of rubble and sand.

Frank came out into the driveway to meet them; in the dusk his face looked white, and his voice was not amused. "My, God, where have you people been? I couldn't believe you'd be out driving around in this! The hunt was called off, the radio's been canceling everything and telling people for Christ's sake to stay off the roads!" He rested a trembling hand on the sill of the rolled-down car window; his little fingernail still bore a yellow fleck.

"In this bit of a breeze?" Lucy asked him, birdlike.

Jane said, "Why, Frank darling, how nice of you to be worried."

And Carter, too, was surprised and amused that Frank didn't know they were beyond all that now.

The Prince

FROM ESQUIRE

AMONG THOSE WHO had come to see the sale of the prince's last piece of property were André, a farmer, and his wife, Marie. They brought their child, too, and stood at the front of the crowd and stared at the prince, who acknowledged them once; then Marie and André were forced to go home, since they weren't able to act freely in public, and all they felt was turmoil, although André felt violent, too, and remorseful, and was set on getting drunk.

On the day the last piece of his property was to be sold, the prince shaved with the same care he had taken on the morning of his wedding. His cheeks and chin were so smooth as to seem powdered. The prince was a man of forty, close to six feet tall, heavy but not fat, since he still ran the same miles and did the same sit-ups that had been required of him when he had been in his teens. Until a few years before, the prince had hunted deer on a piece of land his uncle owned in the north, and he hunted them without a blind. He sat absolutely still in the cold until he had his chance. He had been invited, when he had been in his early twenties, to be a member of an Olympic bobsled team, but he had turned it down. In private he spoke to his father, who agreed that any public display was vain and childish. They had been in the father's study, and the prince had said, "All competitions are odious. Invariably they imply contempt for someone." The prince felt that he had said enough, but his father was staring at him, so the prince said, "I'm not speaking of having to kill someone. That's an act of infinite cruelty in which considerations like contempt are made laughable." The prince had a mustache to cover his slight harelip, which actually made him handsome, or striking, the more so when he smiled enough to show the thin, slick scar.

The property was about two hours from Paris by car. There was a house of medium size, twenty rooms not counting servants' quarters, and it was surrounded by two hundred acres. There were gardens, an arbor covered with vines (beneath which a party of thirty could easily be seated), an orchard, a vineyard, fields, and seventy-five acres in timber.

Occasionally the deer got into the orchard, and the prince had told the gardener to go to the barber in the closest town (about twenty minutes away by car) and to buy all the clippings from a week's worth of haircuts; the hair was brought home in a gunny sack, divided into small bunches, and hung from the trees. The deer didn't like the smell of human hair, and the orchard was left alone after the bunches had been hung from the trees.

In addition to the land, house, furniture, and wine cellar, there was also a '29 Rolls (with a crushed fender), a green '59 Aston (with a creased side), and a blue '63 Chevrolet pickup in good running condition. The prince drove the pickup rather than the cars. There was farm machinery, too: a tractor, a rake, disc, harrow, a baler, and a new John Deere manure spreader. There had been the usual hand tools as well, but when the prince saw the men putting away the tools, which had, in some cases, been handed from father to son for generations, he suggested to the manager that the tools be taken home by the men who had used them, even though allowing these things off the property was a violation of the court order that had been granted to cover the prince's debts. There was a library, too, and it had, in addition to perfectly bound books from the sixteenth century, some of the more elaborate erotica known in Europe.

The prince finished shaving, dressed, and packed his bag, a good leather one. The court allowed him two trunks, but he took only the leather bag, and one mutton-leg gun case in which there was a Holland & Holland shotgun.

There was a small platform set up in front of the house. It

had a fresh, green canopy, and the prince sat under it on a lawn chair next to the auctioneer's podium. He wore a dark suit and a white shirt and a dark-red tie and perfectly shined shoes. From his chair he saw the orchard. Now almost everyone who had an orchard hung bundles of hair from the apple trees, and the deer stayed out of all of them. The prince stared at the trees now, thinking of the time when, after the idea had caught on, there hadn't been enough hair to go around. One of the orchard owners came to the prince and asked if there was anything else that worked as well. The prince told him to sprinkle human urine around the edges of the orchard. "Ah," said the apple grower, nodding his head. "You've got to do it after every rain," said the prince, and the grower nodded again and left. When the rains began, the prince drove along the road that went next to the grower's small orchard, usually passing it after dark, so that the lights of the car went over the grower and his family, two tall, ugly sons and two heavyish daughters and a wife, as they all stood or squatted at the edge of the orchard, drinking wine and pissing for all they were worth. In those days the prince's wife and son had been alive.

On the day of the sale, people came to see the contents of the house: the furniture that had been polished with beeswax for hundreds of years, the tapestries, paintings, rugs, china and crystal, linen, the Gambia side-by-side shotguns, the safe filled with worthless bonds, a flag bloodied in the First World War, and champagne glasses for five hundred guests. There was even a new Wang word processor, which an American friend had sent to the prince when it was clear the prince no longer had a secretary. The American friend had hoped the machine would be used to keep up with the ever-mounting and more strident letters from creditors and then from their lawyers. But the prince had left the machine in its white foam packing and cardboard boxes, preferring to go broke in the old style. And although it was true that the people from the region were interested in the things to be sold, some of which they had polished and maintained from earliest memory, they had come to see the prince, too.

The prince stared at the empty orchards, and then turned and watched how each piece of furniture was being tagged with a small sticker on which there were lines of various thicknesses.

On a table next to the prince there was an electric typewriter and another small machine with a window on it. From these two there were cables running to a van that had been parked on the lawn. There was a computer inside the van. The tags, before being applied to a piece of furniture, were passed in front of the machine with the window, and soon the typewriter began to type (with unseen fingers) as it made a catalogue. It reminded the prince of a player piano he had seen when he was a young boy in Paris.

A young lawyer, a man who represented creditors, had come to the prince a month before the sale, offering to arrange with Christie's or Parke-Bernet and some private collectors a sale of some of the more interesting things. The prince thanked him for his consideration, and told him that all would be welcome at the sale. The young lawyer blushed when he left, not entirely certain himself whether because he saw that his suit was a cheaper imitation of the prince's or because he'd been shown what vile stuff money was. As far as the prince was concerned, that vileness would be shared by all, or at least witnessed by all. Until this point the young lawyer had thought the finest thing was to be rich, and as he walked from the room (the furnishings of which were now being carried onto the lawn) he knew that he would not forget the gentle and much too understanding look in the prince's eyes.

The men from the auctioneer continued with their tags, and the prince listened to the typewriter as it went along. There must have been five hundred people standing in front of the house, on the lawn and walk, and the prince noticed that in the front row, not twenty feet away, there were André, Marie, and their child. He gazed at André and Marie, and they kept their eyes on his face, and all of them stayed that way for some time, enough even to be indecent without some words to break the lingering moment, and it seemed that all of them, at one point or another, were about to say something, but all found it impossible, including the prince, who went back to staring at the orchards in which there had been hung bundles of human hair. After a while, André and Marie left, Marie pulling the little boy by the hand, and he was crying because he had never seen so much furniture being moved onto a lawn and was angry because he was not allowed to see the end of it all.

In the time before the sale, André rented a few acres from the prince and raised cows and made cheese that was dried in straw baskets and dusted with pepper. It was sharp and delicious. During the harvests, the time of haymaking or apple picking, he hired himself out to the prince's estate manager. Marie was young and tall, had reddish hair, a slight stoop, and was oddly pretty, in spite of the fact that one of her eyes was almost, but not quite, crossed.

It had been André who had ridden his bicycle to the police station to report the accident in which the prince's wife and son had been killed, since the accident had taken place not far from where André lived. It had been an oddly gentle automobile accident: the car hadn't been hit very hard and wasn't even badly dented, but the impact had been at the wrong angle. No one who had seen the car would have believed it had been involved in an accident where people had been killed. The prince in no way blamed his wife's and his son's deaths for his financial failures. The boy had been ten and had enjoyed the early-morning exercises with his father and those cold hours on the stand in the fall, waiting for deer.

André and Marie were married about two years after the prince's family had been killed, and once, a few weeks after the wedding, the prince went to town to pick up the groceries he bought on credit. After the truck had been loaded with a side of beef, crates of melons and wine, the prince went to a café that had a few tables outside, an awning that flapped pleasantly in the breeze, and a view of the fields and orchards beyond the town's stone walls. The prince stayed there for a couple of hours, drinking brandy and paying for it out of pocket, since he was at the stage where he felt comfortable only with really large debts, which by themselves, given their size, almost inspired confidence in his lesser creditors. The prince left when he saw it was getting late and that the owner of the café wanted to go home. He got into the pickup and began the drive back to his large and empty house.

André and Marie lived on the road the prince took home. The house had two whitewashed rooms, a concrete floor, and it was close to André's barn, which was on the other side of the road. The barn was white, too, and kept as clean as the house.

The prince drove well, considering the number of brandies he'd had. As he came close to André's house, he slowed down (as he always did when there was any chance of coming across people or livestock), and as he did so (feeling the crates of wine and melons and the side of beef shift against the cab of the truck, almost, as the prince imagined, against his shoulders), he saw that the door of André's whitewashed house was open.

The house was very close to the road. It was now after dark. There was no electricity in the house, and the newly married couple lived in the mornings and evenings by a kerosene lamp: it threw a yellowish, sickly light onto the road. The prince went more slowly, thinking that since the door was open André was on the road between the house and the barn. The prince was puzzled by the open door, since it was fall and the evenings were cool after the sun went down. As the truck came very close to the house, the prince heard a shout and the sound of a table being turned over and the voice of a woman as she said that all she wanted was to be left alone.

The truck came to a stop, and although the prince had no desire to intrude or to embarrass by being a witness to the argument, he found it impossible to put the truck into gear and drive away: more than anything else there was a familiar tone in Marie's voice. It was the same one that the prince had in his own voice when he came up against the limits of things, whether events or character, limits that always left him with a feeling of utter helplessness. The prince heard, as he sat in the truck, a dish being broken and the sound of a heavy table being pushed along the stone floor. The woman spoke again, more quietly, and the prince got out of the truck and walked the few steps to the door of the house.

Marie was sitting against the white wall of what was both the living room and kitchen, and both hands were pressed against her temples. She sat with her legs apart, crossed Indian style, and her skirts were hiked up to her waist. As the prince stepped into the room he saw that she was crying and that her nose was bleeding. The quick, steady drops fell onto her underclothes and onto the clean, whitish floor. The table and chairs had been overturned, and the large earthen bowl out of which soup was served was broken. André stood over his wife, one arm half cocked, the hand of it made into a fist. When the prince came into the room, both Marie and André looked at him, and for one moment all of them did nothing but stare at one another. Then Marie started crying harder, and she did so not for her hurts (which weren't that small, either) but for the shame of being so exposed, sitting on the floor with her husband about to hit her while she bled on the underwear she had asked a cousin in Paris to buy and send to her. So in Marie's expression when she looked at the prince there was only hatred. The prince turned away. After a few moments she moved her eyes away from him to her husband, who dropped his fist and made it into an open, flat hand.

"Cover yourself up," said André, and Marie gave the prince another look of hatred and then smoothed her skirts over her legs and leaned against the wall. One hand held under her nose to catch the blood, and the prince picked up a napkin from the floor and handed it to her, but she said, "No, that's a good one. For company," and then stood and went to the corner of the room where there was a basin and a pitcher of water. She bathed her face, and the prince heard the splashing of water as he said to André, "I'm sorry to have intruded."

"It won't happen again," said André, who now looked at the darkish spots on the floor.

Marie lifted her skirts and tucked them into her waistband and removed her underwear and tried to get the blood out of it before taking a damp rag to her long legs. André watched the prince's face, and then stared at the floor again.

"It won't happen again," he repeated.

The prince's nod was half agreement and half threat. He lingered a moment or two more, though, for a particular reason, which was that he wanted André to know that even though he was appalled at his own bad manners and intrusion, he also wanted André to know that the difference between this one lapse and the next was not large for the prince, or, to put it differently, the prince lingered a moment or two more to let André know how lucky he was to still be alive.

Then he apologized again for the intrusion and went out to the road. He got into the truck and drove the rest of the way to his house in the scented early-fall air, and after he parked the truck at a side door and as the last of the servants unloaded it, he went to his wife's dressing room and looked through her bureaus until he found some of her underthings (which had come specially from Paris and had never been worn), and these, along with a silk skirt he found in a closet, he wrapped up in brown paper and then tied with a piece of string. The next day he sent the package to Marie, who, without opening it, returned it. She brought it back herself and knocked on the front door of the prince's house.

"Here," she said. "It was bad enough that you saw what happened. I would have thought you'd have known better than to do anything about it."

"Of course," said the prince, "with my apologies," and took the package back.

Marie pulled her hand away when it touched the prince's.

"I am a married, respectable woman," said Marie, "no matter what you saw the other night."

"I didn't, in any way," said the prince, "intend anything indecent."

Marie watched him as he stood on the steps of his house, holding the package of brown paper and string, and then turned and began to walk down a path that went between the lawns. When the prince was putting the package away he remembered her as she walked along the path and found that she was close to being right: he had intended something. He suddenly felt the weight of the house and the completeness of his personality descend upon him: sometime soon in the not too distant future, although the prince didn't know exactly when, his checks would begin to bounce, too.

The prince continued to drive by André and Marie's house. He looked at her face, smiled to her, or to her and André if they were together — not spying, but seeing them as often as any other tenant or villager, not more, not less. And as the months and years passed by, the prince was certain that there were no new marks on Marie's face, and he knew that she had become pregnant and had given birth. After a while, the prince saw her walking with a young child.

At first, at these chance meetings, Marie gave the prince the same hard stare as the night the prince had come into her house and the same scowl as when she had returned the package, but as the months and years passed she stopped scowling, although she still stared straight before her, and after a while she dipped her head, and then smiled. And a few months before the sale, when the prince had been driving the pickup from the village (being then unable to get anything more on credit, no matter what the terms), Marie had stopped him, or had let him know by a shake of her reddish hair and a look in those eyes that were almost crossed, that she wanted to speak to him. The prince slowed down, putting on the brakes that now squeaked, and stopped a few feet from her house. He parked so that the bed of the truck was in front of the door, and when he stepped out and faced her, the bed was between them. The prince was wearing the same leather jacket and scarf he had worn the night André had been caught with his raised, clenched fist. It was now an early-fall afternoon and through its light haze there was a chill, a faint reminder of the days and evenings of December and January.

Marie stood in the doorway.

"I thought you might want some cheese. The last we made was good," she said.

"It's always been good," said the prince.

"Sometimes it's better than others," said Marie. "Here."

"I've eaten this cheese since I was a child," said the prince.

"Here," said Marie again, as though she touched the word with the tip of her tongue, and although she held nothing in her hands, the prince knew she meant for him to come around to her side of the bed of the truck and into the house. But the prince stood just outside the doorway. It was a small town and the prince didn't want any gossiping (especially since his checks had started to bounce). Marie stood back from the threshold, and from the road it looked as though the prince were standing before an empty door. Marie handed the prince a slice of bread with a piece of cheese. The prince ate it and found the cheese sharp and tasty, rich with mold. Marie gave him another piece on a slice of pear. The prince tasted the fruit, saw Marie's odd eyes, the way she held her head, her lips as she bit into her piece of pear. Then, after the prince finished, Marie gave him a large wedge of cheese wrapped in brown paper and tied with a piece of string.

"Thank you," said the prince, "give my regards to André," and was careful not to touch Marie's hands as he took the package. He got back into the truck and drove to the house, which was now filled only with furniture, and as he drove, he thought of Marie's eyes on the night she had been outraged. The prince took a good bottle of wine from the cellar and made his dinner out of the cheese. Afterward, when it was dark, he walked into the orchard and cut down all the bundles of human hair, since there would be no cider made that fall and the prince didn't like the idea of apples rotting on the ground. It took a long time for the deer to return. The prince brought the bundles of hair into the house and burned them in the fireplace and then went to bed with the sharp, oddly intimate odor in his nose.

Now, as the furniture was being brought into the sunlight and tagged and as the electric typewriter worked at a terrific speed cataloguing the things from the house, the prince looked up and saw André, Marie, and the child.

Marie had bruises along the left side of her face, along her jaw and forehead. The last of the fall sunlight had a dusty, hazy quality, and it softened the contours of the gardens, lawns, the leafless orchard, and the hills beyond. André, Marie, and the prince looked at one another. The prince saw that the bruises were the color of a ripe pear. André flinched, and looked away, and Marie, while still looking at the prince, pulled a sweater over her shoulders and then took the hand of the little boy and began to walk away, although she looked over her shoulder as she went, keeping her eyes on the prince, who now found it impossible to look at André or Marie or the marks on her and kept his eyes steady or at least open and his head up, although he had to tremble to do so.

As Marie began to walk through the crowd, one of the auctioneer's assistants brought a book from the library to be catalogued, and since there was no title on the leather-bound book, the assistant began to flip the pages back and forth as he approached the table where the typewriter was, and as he did so, some of the book's plates could be seen, one in particular, which the assistant held up for the auctioneer to see, and in the hazy fall light there was exposed the sheen of a photograph of silk, and a curved hand, a breast, a buttock, a nipple, the limp sagging of a black stocking at a young woman's ankle. There was a man there, too, and there seemed to be an animal, a tiger or a leopard, watching the figures.

The auctioneer, who had been looking for coins beneath the cushion of a wing chair, said, "My God! My God! Don't you have any sense? This is not to be brought out here . . . There are children and women! What do you mean? . . . " But the assistant seemed not to hear, and for a moment anyway he continued to flip the pages so that the slick images could almost, but not quite, be seen by the people who stood on the lawn, and even the auctioneer had trouble making out those graceful and thin young women with their skin stretched tight over their ribs. There was the imprint of a breast in new snow and a woman next to it, sitting with a fur coat slipping from her shoulder . . .

The people who stood on the lawn saw the prince as he watched Marie finally turn her back to him and continue walking with the little boy, and as they saw his face, they said, *"Le livre,"* over and over until the air had the quality of being filled with buzzing insects. The prince stood, and everyone saw the trembling in his neck and face. It appeared that some of the secrets of the prince's family were coming out, or at least there had been revealed the private interest of one of those who had filled the safe with worthless bonds and who had brought home a flag bloodied in the First World War. The people nodded and murmured. In fact, the prince was remembering the shameless intimacy in Marie's eyes, and in the obvious way she showed the bruises the prince realized he had not only dissolved his land and house into bankruptcy, but some private, precious thing as well.

"That was one of my uncle's books," said the prince in a voice that was loud enough for all to hear. "Do you suppose I could keep it? As something to remember him by?"

The assistant glanced at the auctioneer, who knew there were plenty more of them in the house, and who said with a voice almost liquid with generosity, "Of course, of course." The assistant closed the leather-bound book, gave it to the prince, and then typed something into the computer. André, Marie, and the child had disappeared into the hazy, soft light. The prince stood with the book under his arm and said to the auctioneer, while facing people he had known from his childhood, "I'm sure there will be no difficulty with the sale. Everything seems correct."

At the end of the path on the driveway there was parked a new and very expensive sports car. The prince's bag and the mutton-leg gun case had been put into it earlier, and now he walked through the people who had come to see him.

The car was driven by a woman whose nationality could have been one of many: she was dark, had fine, high cheekbones, full lips, and she wore tailored pinstripe trousers and a white blouse, very little makeup, had long fingers and legs, and she drove the car very well. The prince and the woman had been spending a little of the last year together, and the prince was pleased that she had been there at the end, or almost at the end, and that she hadn't begun to ignore him as the others had begun to do, although the prince knew she had a new man, a young Arab with money. The woman's name was Bristol.

The prince still held the book under his arm when he climbed into the passenger's side of the car.

"Do you still want to go to Paris?" said Bristol.

"Yes," said the prince, "please, to De Gaulle airport."

They drove quietly for a while. The prince smelled the leathery odor of the car as they drove and saw the dry, brownish hillsides. The prince's shoulders were still trembling, and then he found, as though a hood had been dropped over him, that his eyes were closed and that he was bent forward and that before he could stop he had allowed the sounds of two sharp sobs, or snorts, to get free.

Bristol drove without saying anything.

"I'm sorry," said the prince.

After a few miles more, Bristol said, "What are you going to do?"

"Immediately?" said the prince.

"No," said Bristol, "about living."

The prince stared at her for a moment without answering.

"About money," said Bristol.

"Oh," said the prince, "yes, I see. I'll have a little something left. I speak languages, went to Oxford, and can be trusted in small things. I'll be all right."

Bristol made no gesture, no attempt to soothe, aside from pointing out things that had changed along the road. They came to the airport, and Bristol parked and walked with the prince to the lobby.

"All right then?" said Bristol. "What about immediately?"

"I have an invitation," said the prince. "I'm going to New York."

Bristol raised an eyebrow.

"The invitation is to shoot deer," said the prince.

"But they're selling your rifles," said Bristol.

"I have a shotgun," said the prince. "In America they have something called a slug."

"Like gangsters?" said Bristol, with a smile.

"Yes," said the prince, "like gangsters."

They paused for a minute. The prince looked at Bristol, and she knew he was thinking of the Arab, but he said nothing. He took the book from under his arm and threw it into a trash bin that was close by.

"My uncle's," said the prince. "He had lovely manners but he was such a scoundrel."

The prince stood before her, oddly mute, wanting to explain about the book, but not being able to say a word, and as he stood before the tall and beautiful woman, he seemed bewildered by the attempt to speak.

"Why don't you come along?" said the prince, finally.

Bristol shook her head.

"The Arab isn't that bad," she said.

"Of course," said the prince. "Thank you for the lift."

Bristol gave him a kiss on the cheek, and the prince checked in at the counter and then went down the tunnel to the airplane. He took the Concorde, and when it was halfway to New York, the stewardess gave him a glass of wine and a pear. The prince held the wine and watched the cloudy wastes below. He felt again the sensation of having a black hood dropped over his head, and again leaned forward and made the same sound as in the car, not knowing whether it was for the way Marie's bruises looked in the pale sunlight, the shameful knowledge in her eyes, the wedge of cheese she had given him, the smell of burning hair, the sight of the grower's family lined up and pissing in their orchard, or the moment at the auction when the package of his wife's things would be brought out and sold.

Favor

FROM THE NEW YORKER

FROM AROUND THE corners of the house, from as far away as the orchard, hens shied into the yard, scurrying as they felt other hens behind them, then lagging back to feed. Two chesty matrons tumbled into a smaller black hen. She darted under a strand of wire, and when the old man turned, he could detect only her back in a fine mesh of grass shadow. She was getting wild, and Sandoval's mouth set in a hard line. He didn't want her to hide out all morning, but there was little he could do that wouldn't scare her more. He chided, "Damn cheeks, do I got all day? Leave that Lola alone. Doan go after her, now, you, or —"

He left the threat hanging over them as the hens, in a sudden gang, crowded forward. Sam looked up, startled; Lola had been the old man's wife's name. "That little one's Lola?"

Sandoval shrugged without troubling to glance Sam's way; a precise economy, long ago decided on, ruled even his movements. "Cheek, cheek-cheek, pretty cheek," he called to the black hen, his Adam's apple working as he clucked. The yard was bare except for some briarlike roses under the eaves, where the rain spilled in torrents after storms: his wife's roses, which he had clipped down cruelly after she was dead, as he pruned down almost everything too` far, until there was little left to bloom. She had been seventy, and not five feet tall, and she used to come and put her body between those roses and him with his shears. Old Man Sandoval was a miser; he wanted nothing to yield too generously, too unthinkingly — worst of all, to give in such a way that he could not get his hands on what had been given and cunningly husband it. He dreaded the leaf-dappled, camouflaged clutch, the apple dropping into the irrigation ditch. He had never had any children.

On the woodpile, Sam cradled the old man's shotgun, broke it, and peered down the barrel. Snugged to his shoulder, the walnut of the long, trim stock had a bracing heaviness. The gun was a beauty, in mint condition, and it would be impossible to find another like it. Sandoval had lost a hen and a rooster, and he'd been telling Sam how it happened: From below the bedroom window had risen the reek of skunk, but when the old man tried to climb from bed his knee stabbed him with pain, and he had to lie there, staring at the ceiling, through the hens' ruckus. Sam missed the noisy banty rooster, Chico, with his rakish tail feathers, but when he tried to figure which of the hens was gone he couldn't; they were too alike to him, with their peckish feuding, and the only hen he recognized was Lola. Sandoval had brought the gun outside for Sam to examine, because tonight, Sandoval said, there would be a moon, and he was going to wait for the skunk in the rocks behind his henhouse, wait all night if he had to — an oath sworn as the old man bent and gingerly felt his knee.

Sam meant to try the gun in the arroyo behind his own house, but he was waiting until his wife, Jenny, a painter, would be in her studio, and no longer nursing a cup of her inevitable pitch-black coffee in front of their kitchen window. She was sure he did too many favors for the old man as it was, and she refused to admit any trace of Sandoval's charm. Last evening, Sam had come home, kissed her, and said, "Jen, I finally figured out why he props cardboard around his truck."

She wiped away the kiss, studying him with some dislike. "You figured out what?"

He steered her to a window. Below, in the far corner of Sandoval's yard, was the rust-spotted Chevrolet, with scraps of salvaged cardboard tipped to rest against it. "Did you ever notice that?"

"No, I never noticed that."

"Well, listen." He was still excited. "He props that cardboard up to protect his tires from the sun. He thinks it's going to make the rubber last longer."

"Oh, Sam, nobody could think that."

"He does."

"How do you know?"

"I just know. It was bothering me, and I figured it out. I'm getting to understand how he thinks."

He wanted to kiss her again, but she said, "I think that's so sad," and didn't say what was sad — the old man or Sam's wondering about him. Sam heard the rebuke: no insight into Sandoval's cunning would ever impress Jenny, she was so sure that time spent with the old man was another way Sam avoided repairs on their own house.

Their house: he hadn't predicted it would work as a wedge between them. At first, Jenny had handled the confusions of renovation fairly well, but before long the recriminations began. There were too many problems he hadn't foreseen, and she acted as if she should have been warned exactly how hard it was going to be. Sam could have prodded more skeptically through the house as a buyer, remarking its shortcomings and pretending to the real estate agent that the sale could fall through, but he had been helpless — for Sam the house was love at first sight. The roof had proved to be dirt covering old, warped planks, glossed over by tar, whose bright black glister had falsely reassured him, when he climbed the ladder and leaned over the parapet, that the roof was sound. The tar had been new, but the dirt below it dampened with rain, and by November a strand or water, tinted red by the dirt, leaked across kitchen quarry tiles Sam had painstakingly laid. "The kitchen was the only room finished," Jenny said, "and now it's ruined" — though it wasn't, though a little water couldn't hurt quarry tile and butcher block, but Jenny, shaking the dirty pages of a sodden cookbook, refused to be comforted by the truth. A house in the country — there were always things wrong, he told her, especially with an old house, an unimproved house, a house they could afford: hadn't she known it would need patience? Lately she rarely bothered to argue, and he found her silences more disconcerting than quarrels — they never made love after a silence. He was a carpenter, a mender, a rescuer, and he hated knowing there was something wrong between them that he couldn't get at, and Jenny had let him live with that fact for the last edgy year. He wondered what he could try that he hadn't already; he could stay home more often, but the house oppressed him with the sense of things left undone. Originally, the house's imperfections had seemed an aliveness, even a richness — part of its character, he would have said, and did say, in selling the house to Jenny. Those flaws turned against him, settling into grim, long-standing grudges, when he had meant to shoulder all burdens so handsomely, to tend to all the details before they could occur to Jenny as nuisances. Now, no matter how hard he worked, Sam seemed errant, and for Jenny his sunny afternoons spent in the old man's company were wasted, symptomatic of Sam's failure to be absolutely (inhumanly) responsible. *Responsibility* is a favorite word of Jenny's lately, and *separation* is another. *You have no sense of,* and *Maybe we ought to think about.*

Sam lit a match and held it to a cigarette, though cigarettes were something he'd almost given up. Sandoval was hobbling across the yard, his fedora tilted to the back of his head, his unshaven jaw exposed to the sun. The edges of his eyes were red and inflamed, the lids sly and deeply arched. His hat and his breath both smelled old. He fished a cigarette from the bib of his overalls. Sam stood up for him, and they shared the match, and calmly smoked.

"I'll do it," Sam promised. "I'll get him for you."

When the school bus stopped, Naranjos's blind mare hooked her big dusty head over the fence so the passing children could stroke her nose. Late last year Jenny and Sam's mailbox had been shot by someone driving by, and now that it was fall the wasps that were everywhere searching out niches had climbed in through the bullet holes. Sam sprayed the inside of the mailbox, slammed its door, and then he and Jenny ran. Wasps threaded out through the bullet holes and waited — a dozen wasps, two dozen, their abdomens jerking in rage.

"Is the wind this way?" Jenny asked. She didn't want to breathe it; she thought she was pregnant. She hadn't told Sam, though if he'd been anything except entirely self-absorbed he would have guessed it by now — she had even stopped drinking coffee. Last week, she'd taken the little jar into town, to her gynecologist's office, and he was supposed to call tomorrow morning early, but Jenny already knew what he would tell her. The wasps drifted from the mailbox; it was hard to tell if they were flying or had been blown away.

Sam said, "It can't hurt you. It hasn't hurt them."

To Jenny he sounded disappointed. "Maybe they'll come back and you can kill them over again."

This was cheering, and he agreed, "Maybe," swinging the spray can as they walked back up the road, pausing for the old man, who was leaning against a tree; by the innocence in his face, Jenny knew they'd been ambushed. The tree was another thing that the old man had mutilated in pruning, but it appeared to have forgiven him, and bore apples in hard, small hundreds. There were none left now, and Jenny wondered where they'd gone; certainly he'd given few enough to them. She had a reason to like Sandoval, because he had signed the grant of easement that had finally cleared the title of their house to the bank's satisfaction, but her gratitude had been whittled away each time her husband disappeared to run the old man's errands.

Sam clapped Sandoval between the shoulder blades as he hunched over, coughing into a rag of handkerchief; he cleared his throat and croaked, "Good, good, *gracias, hijo,*" as if his life had been saved.

You old actor, Jenny thought; you old cheat. *Hijo* was a word that couldn't fail to move Sam, but all the affection went one way — it went from Sam to the old man. She leaned her cheek against Sam's back, so that he was between her and Sandoval, because sometimes she had the uncanny sensation that Sandoval knew exactly what she was thinking. His voice reverberating through his own shoulder, Sam told the old man what time to expect him tonight (What time to expect him tonight?), and Sandoval limped away through his dwarfed trees. Jenny knew he was old, he was alone, and it was wrong to resent whatever use he made of Sam, but Jenny knew a number of troublesome truths that seemed to have only negligible influence on her emotions. She knew it should be simple to make up with Sam, and she knew she had a very good reason to try, and she would — she would try, if only things between them hadn't locked into a pattern so stubbornly wrong, which had not, any of it, been her fault.

The mattress rocked as Sam got out of bed, and, asleep, Jenny said, "What?"

"Me," he whispered into her hair. It took him annoyingly long to dress, because he needed warm work clothes and couldn't remember where they were. On the bureau he found a billed cap and tugged it on, and then he lifted long johns from the floor and, from a corner, Levi's that were both grass-stained and oily. There was something evil about pulling on cold, dirty blue jeans in the dark, he felt, but he needed clothes that wouldn't show against the night. He emptied his pockets of change — dime against dime could betray him to a wild thing.

From the bed, while he searched for his jacket, she asked, "Do you really have to kill something?"

"The old man's losing chickens, Jen."

"You don't want to."

"I'm not in love with the idea, no."

She got up, went down on her knees, and drew his jacket out from under a chair; he wondered what impulse of helpfulness this was. "Stingy old bastard," she said.

"Well, maybe." He shrugged into the cold denim, and found a glove.

"He is. Why do you have to go? Can't he find some nephew of his or something?"

"You know he can't."

She found his other glove, balled it up, and rubbed her upper lip with it. "What's this smell?"

She was naked; he liked her small, suspicious face. "Cloves. That's a hunting glove, it can't smell too human. Give it."

"He can't find anyone else because they all hate him. I hate him. You're never here."

"Back to bed." She obliged. It was like telling a fairy tale: Sam said, "You're going to sleep again, nice and warm, and before you're up I'll be home. You'll think this was a dream."

The chill in the grass wet his sneakers as he trotted down the slope, across the road, into the weedy margin of the old man's orchard, through the still, small trees. A briar caught in his sneaker laces. Bending to pick it out, he found himself looking into the eye of a goose — whose? — worrying her own breast in deft, diving nips. Finished, she sleeked her cheek against brown feathers. They regarded each other so intently that when, nearby, an apple fell, Sam jumped. Coming out from the trees, he found the old man's kitchen lit.

Sandoval had laid the shotgun across the kitchen table. Sam liked the lamplight guttering across the rough adobe walls to the shadowed ceiling, and the warmth from the wood stove was nice, but he had to leave now if he wanted to do any good. He shook his head, from superstition, when the old man said, "You're gonna get him, I know." When the kitchen door latched behind Sam, the dark was darker; he'd lost his night vision.

At the henhouse he squinted through a chink, and though he could distinguish nothing inside, the hens continued their dovish burbling undisturbed. He clambered up the sandstone reef; his foot slipped, a pebble skipped away and struck, and down the valley a dog began to bark, waking another dog farther away. Sam climbed until he found the right shelf, wide enough to lie on, not too high for a good view. There was, for some reason, a rusty car fender lying on this shelf, and when he pushed it away its racket silenced the hens. He lay down flat, and as the stone chilled his stomach he concentrated on the smell of Jenny's hair, at that moment the most pleasant warmth he could come up with. He tried to work this warmth down to his fingers and freezing toes, but it remained in a ball in his chest. Below, nothing stirred, and the hens started in again. Sandoval's kitchen light blinked out, and Sam was glad, because it meant the old man trusted him enough to go back to bed. Or, he worried, it meant the old man was saving electricity, sitting waiting in the dark for Sam to succeed.

For an hour, then another, Sam lay counting alternately stars and the barks of distant dogs, guessing he would be able to spot in the grass the white chevron between snub ears, and wishing he felt better about killing the skunk. Lying there, he had begun to sympathize with it — the poor plank henhouse invited plunder, and the hens sounded idiotically cozy. Jaw to the shotgun's stock, Sam ran through his reasons. What he hated was the old man's sadness about his hens, and killing the skunk would put a stop to that. Fair enough — Sam was willing to take on this responsibility for that motive, and in his mind he had already neatly finished off the skunk's existence, leaving only the cold wait until he pulled the trigger. But the shape he finally observed, at the bottom of the reef, circling another rusty fender that lay there, moved nimbly, without a skunk's toed-in, tail-up shambling, and with many fractional hesitations and scent checks that were, to a skunk, quite unnecessary; what was coming through the cold green grass put its feet down briskly, kept its ears pricked and its tread light, and was, Sam saw, a fox.

Where the brush was deepest, the fox feinted in and out, keeping low, reluctant to show itself fully, but it was exposed as it skinnied under the fence and jumped to the henhouse ramp, where it paused. Its ears pointed forward, then back, and if Sam had whispered, the fox would have caught it. It sat, fitted its tail around its feet, and squared its shoulders silkily, as a hunting cat does for a bit of last-minute concentration — Jenny would have loved seeing that. The fox crouched, its ears angled now at the doorway, within which the hens were still foolishly burbling. Fox or skunk, Sam thought, the old man's loss was the same, and this death the end of his trouble. Sam made up his mind, a stone by his elbow chinked against another stone, the shotgun kicked into his shoulder, and the fox tucked into the doorway. The report echoed down the valley; Sandoval's kitchen went bright. Sam patted his jacket down for another shell, and cursed his confidence when he knew there wasn't one; he made the climb down sandstone, its cold grain scraping his hand. The hens sounded as if they were all dying bloody deaths, but by the time Sam had run to the henhouse door and knelt there, not even sure what he could do if he cornered the fox inside, he found only the fluttering hens, and feathers rocking down through shadow, and nothing else.

In the warm kitchen, Jenny said, "You missed because you didn't really want to kill it." She was in her nightgown, making coffee, and she seemed very pleased with herself, with her own version of what had happened. "Was it beautiful?"

"Very. All sleek and fat from chickens. You should have seen the old man, Jen. He was so disappointed in me."

"Well, I'm not."

For once, he thought, but said, "He couldn't believe I'd missed."

She surprised him: "That was hard for you, letting him down."

"He trusts me, Jen. I'm going to have to spend the afternoon wiring the henhouse up, so he can lock it right. It needs a new door."

"Not this afternoon, you can't."

"I have to fix the way the fox got under the fence as well. Why not this afternoon?" In spite of himself, he was irritated. Well, he'd been up half the night.

"We have to go into town," Jenny said.

"Why both?"

"Because I'd like it." Behind him, she scrubbed her chin along his denim jacket, with its night smell of faint cold grassy dustiness; he always seemed a little strange to her when he came back from hunting. She rubbed the hair at his neck, which needed a trim. She said, "My doctor called, and he says that I'm pregnant, but I've known that. I've just known."

His reaction to her words was physical — a startling in his chest, like alarm. He could understand the million metaphors and references to hearts, because that was where this happened. But he was quiet; misinterpreting that, she rushed on. "If only it wasn't such a rotten time for it, I know. If only we hadn't been having problems. I can't tell how I feel about a baby, Sam, can you?"

He meant to be cautious with her. He didn't want the answer he made now to be counted against him at any future time, to be entered into the list of his failures of intuition, and a part of himself was rapidly calculating and rejecting responses. She pushed his back. "Come on, Mr. Fox." She pushed harder. "Say something."

The part of him that answered her hadn't considered strategy at all; it was only guesswork, but Sam said, "I love you."

Wasn't there sometimes a period of grace, after you happened to do something right, when you could do no wrong? When the old man had counted up his chickens and found them all there, when the fox didn't return, when Jenny brushed her hair sing-ing, Sam guessed he had entered such a time, though a stray question from his former, troubled existence haunted him: If he had killed the fox that night, what would Jenny be like now? He knew what she would be like, and it wouldn't be good. He had come so close to killing the fox for the old man, and it would have proved to be, for Jenny, a kind of last straw. God, it was scary what he went through life not knowing.

But for now Sam believed he had pulled off an astonishing feat: he had got three — ah, four — lives into a kind of har-mony.

It began to smell like snow, though there was no snow. It oc-curred to Jenny that there were things that had stayed undone since they had moved in which would still be undone when nine months were up — her baby would be born into an imperfect house, and this cost her some peace of mind. She stood before the house in the evening, filled with impatience. Outside, it was exactly as it had been for the last fifty years. The front of the house was eroding adobe, of a soft, quilted fawn, the same shade as the bluff that backed and appeared to shelter it. This bluff was the only thing Jenny unequivocally loved about the house. The separate bricks had weathered to a compact round-edness, all corners gone, and where the mortar had fallen out the façade buckled into a series of chinks, hollows, and inlets deeper than her fingers. In short, repairs were urgently needed, and Sam was gone again, down to Sandoval's yard, splitting kindling for the storm. The old man, Jenny knew, saved his gnarliest, hardest cedar for Sam.

She shrugged to herself, pulled her sweater higher around her throat, and cut down the slope to Sandoval's yard, where she sat on a bucket. The old man was sitting, too, not far from her bucket, but not near, either, and they nodded formally. Sam drove the wedge into a stump, extremely hard; the maul de-scended in heavy clops, again and again, and sometimes he let it fall and knelt to wrestle with the roots, trying to work them farther apart with his hands. The heartwood creaked like a saddle as the wedge inched deeper in.

"It's going to snow soon," Jenny said. "Can't you feel it?" She wrapped her arms around herself. Neither of them appeared

to hear, but they were far beyond small talk. Sam had told her
he thought the henhouse was safe enough now, and that the
shot had surely terrified the fox. He'd told her, too, that the
apples were in the old man's attic; sitting on her bucket, Jenny
considered all that the old man would never, ever dream of
giving away, and found she didn't care. She supposed that the
way she thought of him now was the way Sam had thought
about him all along — Sandoval was the way he was, and you
had to accept him as that. Jenny was much more interested,
now, in what was happening in herself.

It was colder, it seemed almost too cold to snow, and finally it
snowed. Naranjos's blind mare slept under snow, and her
furred nostrils left white vapor in the air. Jenny and Sam, returning home from a late movie in Santa Fe, saw the mare as
they turned into their lane, and Jenny said, "Poor horse."
  "Snow can't hurt a horse," Sam said. "It's probably warmer on
her back than nothing." Brilliant light, low to the ground, prodded around the blind curve before them, and because it was
hardly wide enough there for two vehicles to pass, Sam pulled
onto the road's side, which was frozen hard. Jenny nestled
against him, holding a handful of her hair across her face and
breathing through it. The pickup's heater wasn't working properly, and her nose was cold. "Sam," she said, lifting her chin
sharply. He looked where she was looking. By light flashing in
circles from the snowplow's cab, Sam saw the fox crossing the
lane, running just in front of the ice jetting from the slanted
blade, and though the snowplow was coming slowly, the fox
almost didn't make it — his head was cocked so that the black
hen could rest, a dead weight, on his narrow shoulder, and he
could not see where he was going, and he could not let go.

MAVIS GALLANT

Kingdom Come

FROM THE NEW YORKER

AFTER HAVING SPENT twenty-four years in the Republic of Saltnatek, where he established the first modern university, recorded the vocabulary and structure of the Saltnatek tongue, and discovered in a remote village an allophylian language unknown except to its speakers, Dr. Dominic Missierna returned to Europe to find that nobody cared. Saltnatek was neither lush nor rich nor seductive, nor poor enough to arouse international pity. The university survived on grants left over from the defense budget, and even Missierna had to admit he had not attracted teachers of the first order. He had wasted his vitality chasing money for salaries and equipment, up to the day when an ungrateful administration dismissed him and the latest revolutionary council, thanking him for nothing, put him on a plane.

He was still in mourning for his Saltnatek years. It grieved him to hear, at a linguistic congress in Helsinki, younger colleagues in the most offhand way confusing Saltnatek with Malta and Madagascar. Saltnatek consisted of an archipelago of naked islands, one of which had been a port of call for cruise ships early in the century. Most tourists had not even bothered to go ashore: there was nothing to admire except straight rows of undecorated houses, and nothing to buy except shells of giant sea snails, on which the nation's artists had carved in a spiral pattern "WHEN THIS YOU SEE, REMEMBER ME." The motto was thought to have been copied from the lid of a snuffbox found in the pocket of a drowned naval officer during the Napoleonic wars. (Missierna supposed the box was probably a lucky piece, even though it had not turned out to be providential. He kept this to himself; he was not in the business of offering speculations.) Even that trifling commerce had come to a stop when, just after the First World War, a society for the protection of sea snails urged a boycott of mutilated shells — a prohibition that caused Saltnatek great bewilderment and economic distress.

In Helsinki, his heart galloping, his voice trembling sometimes, Missierna disclosed the existence of a complex and living language, spoken by an inbred population that produced children of much thievishness, cunning, and blank beauty. He stood on a stage too large for him, fuzzily lighted, in an auditorium the size of a concert hall. Nine men and three women sat, singly, in the first fifteen rows. They were still and unresponsive, and as soon as he had finished reading they got up in the same quiet way and filed out. There were no questions: he had brought back to Europe one more system, and no one knew how to make the old ones work.

If he was disappointed, it was in part because he was no longer young, and it was almost too late for his competence, perhaps his genius, to receive the awards it deserved. Although he was far less vain than any of the substandard teachers he had interviewed and hired for Saltnatek, he still hoped that at least one conclusion might be named for him, so that his grandchildren, coming across his name in a textbook, could say, "So this is what he was like — modest, creative." But all that anyone said at the Helsinki congress was "You have demonstrated nothing that cannot be shown through Hungarian."

During the years when he was so obsessively occupied, Europe had grown small, become depleted, as bald in spirit as Saltnatek's sandy and stony islands. The doubting voices were thin and metallic. No one was listening. His colleagues said, "One step after the other," and "One at a time." They trod upon discarded rules of address, raked the ground to find shreds of sense and reason. Salvation was in the dust or it was nowhere. Even if he were to reveal twenty new and orderly and poetic methods of creating order by means of words, he would be told, "We had better deal with matters underfoot, closer to home."

He was a divorced parent, which meant he had children and grandchildren but no place in particular to go. Saltnatek had been like a child, and he had stayed with it longer than with any other, had seen it into maturity, and it had used and rejected him, as children do, as it is their right. It was not in his nature to put out emotional ultimatums. In the past, it could have been his business — he should have made it his business — to observe the patterns of exchange among his real children, even if the information, tabulated, had left him depressed and frightened. He could have taken them as an independent republic and applied for entry. Even now, he considered inviting himself for next Christmas. He would surely obtain the limited visa no one dares refuse a homeless old man, a distinguished relative, not poor, needing only consideration — notice taken of his deafness, his stiff shoulder, his need to get up and eat breakfast at five o'clock, his allergies to butter and white wine.

What to take on the Christmas exploration? The first rule of excursions into uncankered societies is: Don't bring presents. Not unless one wants to face charges of corruption. But then, like any scholar fending off a critic, he could justify the gifts, telling himself that another visitor might taint the society in a manner deadlier still, whereas he, Missierna, sat lightly. He had been a featherweight on his children; he had scarcely gone near them. A present from parent to child surely reinforces a natural tie. When they were young, he used to bring home one wristwatch and make them draw lots. For professional trips he had packed radio batteries; his travels had taught him that new republics run out of them soon. He had taken ski boots wherever there were snowy mountains, except in places where snow was sacred. He had always shown a sense of patience, a good-tempered approach to time, as he cut through the thorn patch of transit visas, six-month-residence permits, five-year research grants. To enter one's own family, he supposed, one needed to fill out forms. All he would have to understand was the slant of the questions.

From his hotel room in Helsinki, Missierna saw the Baltic and gulls skimming over the whitecaps. At night ghosts floated along the horizon. He took it for granted they were ghosts — having lived among people who saw a great many — and not simply the white shadows of summer.

An insurance actuarial study gave him six more years to live if he went on as he was, eight if he gave up smoking, nine and a half if he adopted an optimistic outlook. What about white magic? What about trying to add a few more summer nights by means of poems and incantations? Why not appeal to a saint — a saint so obscure that the direct line from Missierna's mind to the saint's memory of a mind would be clean, without the clutter of other, alien voices? He could begin by repeating his own name, before deciding what conjury should come next.

His grandchildren surely lived on magic. There was fresh daylight every morning. Clothes dropped on the floor were found clean and folded. A gray-haired man at the congress, who said he had once been Missierna's student, had told him that very soon, by law, children were going to be asked to acknowledge their parents, instead of the other way. There would be some cold refusals, Missierna supposed, and some selfish ones, and some inspired by embarrassment. There might be cases of simple antipathy, too. Most children would probably accept their parents, out of pity, or to keep a strong thread of filiation, or to claim an inheritance, or to comform to an astral pattern. Some, to avoid the sight of adult tears. A few might show the blind trust that parents pray for. The new insecurity, the terror of being cast off, was already causing adults to adopt the extreme conservatism that is usually characteristic of the very young. A mistrust of novelty and change surely accounted for Missierna's sparse audience, the silence in the auditorium, the unwillingness to know something more.

In Saltnatek, toward the end, he had heard some of the cool remarks that said, plainly, he was not a father; heard them from students he had taught, reared, nurtured, and who were now ready to send him packing: "You can't say we didn't warn you." "I tried to tell you that someday you'd be sorry." "I'm sorry if you're sorry. But that's all I have to be sorry about." From his own children there had been monitory signals, too, which he had mistaken for pertness: "Can't you ask a waitress for a cup of coffee without telling your life story?" "Other parents don't take the wrong bus." "Please don't get up and dance. It makes you look silly." Their eyes were clean, pure, but bedeviled by unease and mortification. The eyes of children are the eyes of petit bourgeois, he decided. They can't help it; they are born wondering if their parents are worth what the bus driver thinks.

For twenty-four years the eyes of Saltnatek had appraised him, and had then turned away. He had become to himself large and awkward — a parent without authority, dispossessed, left to stumble around in an airport, as if he were sick or drunk.

He could still recite by rote the first test sentences he had used for his research:

"Now that you mention it, I see what you mean."

"There is no law against it, is there?"

"I am not comfortable, but I hope to be comfortable soon."

"Anyone may write to him. He answers all letters."

"Look it up. You will see that I was right all along."

At the outset, in Saltnatek, he had asked for a governmental ruling to put a clamp on the language: the vocabulary must not grow during the period of his field work. Expansion would confuse the word count. They had not been sure what to call him. Some had said, "Father," which was close in sound to his name, as they pronounced it. His own children had for a while avoided saying even "you," dropping from their greetings such sentences as "What did you bring us?" and "Are you staying long?" They were like long-term patients in a hospital, or rebels interned. Their expression, at once careful and distant, seemed to be telling him, "If you intend to keep coming and going, then at least bring us something we need."

His children were not proud of him. It was his own fault; he had not told them enough. Perhaps he seemed old, but he appeared young to himself. In the shaving mirror he saw the young man he had been at university. In his dreams, even his bad ones, he was never more than twenty-one.

Saltnatek was his last adventure. He would turn to his true children, whether they welcomed the old explorer or not. Or he could find something else to do — something tranquil; he could watch Europe as it declined and sank, with its pettiness and faded cruelty, its crabbed richness and sentimentality. Something might be discovered out of shabbiness — some measure taken of the past and the present, now that they were ground and trampled to the same shape and size. But what if he had lost his mixture of duty and curiosity, his professional humility, his ruthlessness? In that case, he could start but he would never finish.

At Helsinki he heard young colleagues describing republics they had barely seen. They seemed to have been drawn here and there for casual, private reasons. He did not like the reasons, and he regretted having mentioned, in his lecture, sibling incest in that village in Saltnatek. He had been careful to admit he had relied on folklore and legends, and would never know what went on when the children tore all their clothes off. Repeated actions are religious, but with children one can never decide if they are heathen, atheistic, agnostic, pantheistic, animist; if there remains a vestige of a ritual, a rattled-off prayer.

Say that he used his grandchildren as a little-known country: he would need to scour their language for information. What did they say when they thought "infinity"? In Saltnatek, in the village, they had offered him simple images — a light flickering, a fire that could not be doused, a sun that rose and set in long cycles, a bright night. Everything and nothing.

Perhaps they were right, and only the present moment exists, he thought. How they view endlessness is their own business. But if I start minding my own business, he said to himself, I have no more reason to be.

Was there any cause to feel uneasy about the present moment in Europe? What was wrong with it? There was no quarrel between Wales and Turkey. Italy and Schleswig-Holstein were not at war. It was years since some part of the population, running away, had dug up and carried off its dead. It seemed to him now that his life's labor — the digging out, the coaxing and bribing to arrive at secret meanings — amounted to exhumation and flight.

The village children had wanted white crash helmets and motorcycles. He had given them helmets but said he could not bring in the bikes, which were dangerous, which would make the ancient windows rattle and the babies cry. Besides, there were no roads. Some of the village women turned the helmets into flowerpots, but the helmets were airtight, there was no drainage, the plants died. The helmets would never rot. Only the maimed giant snails, thrown back into the ocean, could decay. Missierna, the day he resolved that helmets do not die, and so have no hope of resurrection, wondered whether the time had come to stop thinking.

He should have mentioned in his lecture that the village children were of blank but unusual beauty, that they wanted steep new roads and motorcycles. It might induce plodding, leaden, salacious scholars to travel there and seduce them, and to start one more dull and clumsy race.

All this he thought late at night in his hotel room and in the daytime as he walked the streets of Helsinki. He visited the Saltnatek consulate, because he was curiously forlorn, like a parent prevented by court order from having any more say in his children's fate and education. He entered a bookstore said to be the largest in Europe, and a department store that seemed to be its most expensive. On a street corner he bought chocolate ice cream in a plastic cone. He did not return the cone, as he was supposed to do. He believed he had paid for it. He crossed a busy road, saying to himself, "The cone is mine. I'm not giving it up."

So — he had become grasping. This slight, new, interesting evaluation occupied his mind for some minutes. Why keep the cone? It would be thrown away even in Saltnatek, even in the poorest, meanest dwelling. Children in their collective vision now wanted buses without drivers, planes without pilots, lessons without teachers. Wanted to come into the world knowing how to write and count, or never to know — it was all the same conundrum. Or to know only a little about everything. He saw helmets on a window ledge, ferns growing out of them. By now, the women had been taught to use pebbles for drainage. Saw children tearing uphill on the motorcycles other visitors had brought. Imagining this, or believing he could see it — the two were identical — he understood that he would never go back, even if they would have him. He would live out his six actuarial years on his own half-continent. He would imagine, or think he could see, its pillars rotting, seaweed swirling round the foundations. He would breathe the used-up air that stank of dead sea life. He might have existed a few days past his six more years in the clearer air of Saltnatek. Then? Have fallen dead at the feet of the vacant, thievish children, heard for a second longer than life allows the cadence of their laughter when they mocked him — the decaying, inquisitive old stranger, still trying to trick them into giving away their word for Kingdom Come.

SUE MILLER

The Lover of Women

FROM MADEMOISELLE

Lloyd Abbott wasn't the richest man in our town, but he had, in his daughters, a vehicle for displaying his wealth that some of the richer men didn't have. And, more unusual in our midwestern community, he had the inclination to do so. And so, at least twice a year, passing by the Abbotts' house on the way to school, we boys would see the striped fabric of a tent stretched out over their grand backyard, and we'd know there was going to be another occasion for social anxiety. One of the Abbott girls was having a birthday, or graduating, or coming out, or going away to college. "Or getting her period," I said once to my brother, but he didn't like that. He didn't much like *me* at that time either.

By the time we'd return home at the end of the day, the tent would be up and workmen would be moving under the cheerful colors, setting up tables and chairs, arranging big pots of seasonal flowers. The Abbotts' house was on the main street in town, down four or five blocks from where the commercial section began, in an area of wide lawns and overarching elms. Now all those trees have been cut down because of Dutch elm disease and the area has an exposed, befuddled air. But then it was a grand promenade, nothing like our part of town where the houses huddled close as if for company; and there probably weren't many people in town who didn't pass by the Abbotts' house once a day or so, on their way to the library for a book, or to Woolworth's for a ball of twine, or to the grocery store or the hardware store. And so everyone knew and would openly discuss the parties, having to confess whether they'd been invited or not.

My brother Jacey usually had been, and for that reason was made particularly miserable on those rare occasions when he wasn't. I was the age of the youngest daughter, Pamela, and so I was later to be added to the list. By the time I began to be invited to the events under the big top, I had witnessed enough of the agony, which the whimsicality of the list cost my brother, to resolve never to let it be that important to me. Often I just didn't go to something I'd been invited to, more than once without bothering to RSVP. And when I did go, I refused to take it seriously. Sometimes I didn't dress as the occasion required, for instance. At one of the earliest parties I attended, when I was about thirteen, I inked sideburns on my cheeks, imagining I looked like my hero of the moment, Elvis Presley. When Jacey saw me, he tried to get my mother not to let me go unless I washed my face.

"It'll look worse if I wash it," I said maliciously. "It's india ink. It'll turn gray. It'll look like dirt."

My mother had been reading when we came in to ask her to adjudicate. She kept her finger in the book to mark her place the whole time we talked, and so I knew Jacey didn't have much of a chance. She was really just waiting for us to leave.

"What I don't understand, John," my mother said to Jacey — she was the only one who called him by his real name — "is why it should bother you if Doug wants to wear sideburns."

"*Mother*," Jacey said. He was forever explaining life to her, and as far as he was concerned, she never got it.

"This isn't a costume party. No one else is going to be *pretending* to be someone else. He's supposed to just come in a jacket and tie and dance. And he isn't even wearing a tie."

"And that bothers you?" she asked in her gentle, high-pitched voice.

"Of course," he said.

She thought for a moment. "Is it that you're ashamed of him?"

This was hard for Jacey to answer. He knew by my mother's tone that he ought to be above such pettiness. Finally, he said, "It's *not* that I'm ashamed. I'm just trying to protect him. He's going to be sorry. He looks like such a *jerk* and he doesn't even know it. He doesn't understand the *implications.*"

There was a moment of silence while we all took this in. Then my mother turned to me. She said, "Do you understand, Doug, that you may be the only person at this party in artificial sideburns?"

"Yeah," I answered. Jacey stirred restlessly, desperately. He could see where this was heading.

"Do you understand, honey, that your sideburns don't look real?" her voice was unwaveringly gentle, kind.

Well, I had thought they might almost look real, and this news from someone as impartial as my mother was hard to take. But the stakes were high. I nodded. "Yeah," I said.

She pressed it. "That they look, really, as thought you'd drawn them on?"

I swallowed and shrugged. "Yeah," I said again.

She looked hard at me a moment. Then she turned to Jacey. "Well, darling," she said. "It appears he does understand. So you've really done all you can, and you'd better just go along and try to ignore him." She smiled, as though to try to get him to share a joke. "Just pretend you never saw him before in your life."

Jacey was enraged. I could see he was trembling, but he had boxed himself in with his putative concern for my social welfare. I felt the thrill of knowing I was causing him deep pain.

"Mother," he said, as though the word were a threat. "You don't understand *anything.*" He left the room, slamming the door behind him.

My mother, who never discussed the behavior of one of us with the other, didn't even look at me. She bowed her head in the circle of lamplight and continued to read her book. I left her, too, after a moment, and was in my room when I heard Jacey hurtling past my door and down the stairs again. His rage had been feeding on itself and he was yelling even before he got anywhere near her. "Let me tell you something, Mom. If you let him go to the party like that, I'm not going. Do you hear me? I'm not going." His breathing was audible to me from the top of the stairs — he was near tears — but my mother's answer, which was long, was just a murmur, a gentle flow of her voice for a while. And though he ran out of the house afterward, slamming the front door this time, he was at the party when I got there later. He was dancing and following my mother's advice to pretend he didn't know me.

The reason my entry into his social world, particularly the Abbott part of it, was so painful, so important to my brother, was that he had already fallen in love with their family, with everything they stood for. In an immediate sense, he was in love with the middle Abbott girl, Eleanor. She wasn't the prettiest of the three, but she seemed it. She was outgoing and sarcastic and very popular; and Jacey wasn't the only boy at Bret Harte High trying to close in on her. He spent a long time on the phone each evening talking either *to* her or *about* her to girlfriends of hers who seemed to manage her social life through messages they would or wouldn't take for her. He was with her whenever he could be after school and on weekends. But here he was at a disadvantage because he, like me, had a part-time job all through high school, which the other boys in our circle of friends didn't. In this difference between us and the others we knew socially lay, I think, a tremendous portion of the appeal Eleanor Abbott had for my brother.

My father was one of the few in Haley who had died in the Second World War, killed by American bombs, actually, while being held prisoner by the Germans. Most of the fathers of our friends had had large enough families by the time America got involved that they didn't go. But my father enlisted when Jacey was two and I was on the way. He died only a few months before my birth, and my mother brought us back to live with her parents here in Haley, the small town in Illinois where she'd grown up.

I can't remember my Grandfather Vetter well — he had a heart attack when I was still quite small — but Grandma Vetter was as important as a second parent throughout my childhood. She died when I was ten. We had just sat down to dinner one night when she said, "I think I'll just lie down for a little while," as though that were what everyone did at the beginning of a meal. My mother watched her walk down the hallway to her room on the first floor, and then went directly to the telephone and called the doctor. Grandma Vetter was dead by the time he arrived, stretched out on the bed with her dress neatly covering her bony knees. I remember thinking that there was some link between the way she looked, as though she *were* just resting and would get up any minute, and the way the table looked, every place neatly set, every plate heaped with food, as though we would sit down any minute. I was very hungry, and looking at the table made me want to have my dinner, but I knew I shouldn't care about the food at a time like this — my mother and brother were crying — and I was ashamed of myself.

Throughout my childhood my grandmother preferred Jacey to me — he was a more polite, conscientious boy — and this left my mother and me with a special bond. She was, as I've indicated, incapable of overt favoritism, but she told me later that my infancy provided her with a special physical comfort after my father's death, and I often felt a charge of warmth and protectiveness from her when my grandmother was critical of me in one way or another, as she often was.

My mother was the only woman in our circle who worked. She taught second grade at the Haley Elementary School, moving to third grade the years Jacey and I would have been her pupils. And, as I've said, we boys worked, too, starting in seventh and eighth grade mowing lawns and delivering papers. By our senior years of high school, each of us had a salaried part-time job, Jacey at the county hospital, I at a restaurant in town. It wasn't that others in our world led lives of great luxury — few besides the Abbott girls did. Our home, the things we did, the kinds of summer trips we took were much like those of our friends. But my brother and I provided ourselves with many of the things our friends' parents provided them with, eventually even paying most of our own way through college. We were "nice" boys, ambitious boys, but there was a price for our ambition.

Somehow we must have understood, too, and yet didn't question, that although our lives were relatively open — we could number among our friends the richest kids, the most popular kids — our mother's mobility in Haley was over. She was single, she needed to work. These facts constituted an insurmountable social barrier for her. Yet it seems to me I barely noticed her solitude, her isolation from the sociable couples who were the parents of my friends. And even if I had noticed it, I wouldn't have believed it could have a connection to the glorious possibilities I assumed for my own life.

Because of our relative poverty, our lives were full of events that were beyond contemplation for our friends, but which then seemed only adventurous and exciting to me. I remember one summer coming back from a trip to California by car, we ran out of money. My mother stopped in Las Vegas with a nearly empty gas tank and about three dollars' worth of change in her purse, and won over two hundred dollars — more than enough to get home on — with her second quarter in the slot machine. That kind of thing didn't happen to friends of ours, and somehow, as a result, their mothers seemed more childlike to me, less grown-up, less strong. I thought there was no one else like my mother.

But Jacey yearned for everything she, he, we, were not; and in his senior year of high school, he particularly yearned for Eleanor Abbott.

Now I'm finally able to see that at least a part of my passionate embrace of the role of rebel in high school had to do with a need to deny the embarrassment I could not, out of loyalty to my mother, let myself feel about all those aspects of our lives that I was slowly beginning to perceive as difficult or marginal. I *did* think the Abbott girls and their endless parties ostentatious, ridiculous; but in addition, some private part of me angrily yearned for the ease and gracefulness of their kind of life, their sure sense of who they were and how they fit in, as much as Jacey yearned overtly for it.

At the time, though, I thought his yearning, particularly his yearning for Eleanor, was shallow and contemptible. She was a year ahead of me in high school, but even I knew she wasn't smart. In fact, she was in biology with me because she'd flunked it the first time around. I couldn't understand what attracted him to her, especially since I knew she hung around at least as much with three or four other senior boys.

One summer afternoon, though, the last summer before Jacey went off to college, the drive-in where I worked closed early because the air-conditioning was out of order. I came straight home, hot but elated to have an unexpected day off.

My mother had gone up to Chicago to visit a college friend, and I expected Jacey might still be sleeping, since he was working the night shift as an orderly at the county hospital. I was hot, as I've said, and I felt like celebrating my release from routine, so I charged down the basement stairs two at a time to raid the big freezer. My mother kept it stocked with four or five half gallons of various flavors of ice cream. As I opened the case and leaned into the cool sweet darkness, the freezer seemed to exhale up at me. I heard a rustling noise from the front part of the basement, a whisper. I shut the freezer slowly, my heart thudding, and moved silently toward the doorway. I don't know what I expected — thieves perhaps — but it wasn't what I saw in the few seconds before my brother shouted "No!" and I turned away. He and Eleanor Abbott were naked on the daybed set up near the wall of the coal bin, and Eleanor Abbott was sitting on him. He was in the process of reaching up with his body to cover hers from view when I looked at them. The light in the basement was dim, and they were in the far corner — it was like looking at silvery fish in an unlighted aquarium — but the vision lingered with me a long time, clear and indelible.

I left the house immediately — got my bike out of the garage and rode around aimlessly in the heat all afternoon. By the time I came home, it was twilight and my brother was gone. I went down to the basement again. I went into the front room and I lay down on the daybed. I turned my face into its mildew-smelling cover, and imagined that I was breathing in also the rich, mysterious odor of sex.

I remember being less surprised at my brother than I was at Eleanor Abbott. I thought about the three or four other boys she went out with — some of them more seriously than my brother, I knew from gossip at school. The possibility arose that Eleanor Abbott was having sex, not just having normal sex as I'd been able to imagine it with girls I knew, but actually *sitting* on all of the boys she went out with. The possibility arose that Eleanor Abbott, whom I'd seen as utterly vacuous, utterly the conventional rich girl, was a bigger rebel even than I, in my blue jeans and secret cigarettes, in the haircut I now modeled on James Dean's.

My brother never mentioned what I'd seen, and the silence

seemed to increase the distance between us, although I felt a respect for him I'd never entertained before. I saw that even his life could contain mysteries unguessed at by me.

He went away to college that fall on a partial scholarship. I saw Eleanor Abbott around school. Sometimes she'd smile at me in the halls or say hello, especially when she was with friends. I felt that I was somehow comical or amusing to her, and I felt, at those moments, genuinely exposed, as though what she seemed to think of me was all I really was — a joker, a poser. I discovered, too, that she dominated my fantasy life completely, as she perhaps knew when she'd laugh and throw her head back and say "Hello, Doug" when we met. Once I actually walked into a door as she passed.

She went to college the next year, to a women's college in the East. My brother mentioned her several times in letters to my mother, letters she read aloud to me. He said that he'd gone to visit her, or had her to Amherst for the weekend. I don't know what visions this conjured up for my mother — she never offered her opinion of any of the Abbotts except to say once that Lloyd Abbott had been "kind of a dud" as a young man — but for me, images of absolute debauchery opened up. I could hardly wait to be alone in my room. I found these images nearly impossible, though, to connect with my actual living brother when he came home at Christmas or Easter, ever more trig, ever more polished.

Eleanor didn't come home at Easter break, I remember, and Jacey seemed to have no trouble finding other women to hang around with. This shocked me, his betrayal of her, in a way that her early possible wildness did not. It seemed cynical. Her wildness I had romanticized as hunger, pure appetite.

Sometime in early May, I was sitting at the dining room table doing some homework when the phone rang. My mother was in the kitchen, and she called out, "I'll get it." She came out to the telephone stand in the hall. Her voice, after the initial hello, was cool and polite, so I assumed it was some social acquaintance of hers and went back to my chemistry. She was silent on the phone a long time, and then she said, sharply and angrily, "No, that's impossible." Her tone made me look up. She had turned her back to me, as though to shield me from whatever was going on. After another, shorter silence, she said, "No, I'm sorry. I can't do that. If you have something to say to my son, you'd better talk to him yourself." I started to stand, my heart thudding, thinking of the various misdeeds of the last weeks, the last months. I ran around at the time with a small gang of misfits, and we specialized in anonymous and, we thought, harmless acts of vandalism — setting a car upside down on its owner's front lawn, breaking into the school cafeteria and urinating into the little cartons of orange juice.

"That's right," my mother said stiffly. "I'm very sorry." And she hung up.

After a moment, she turned and saw me standing there, looking, I'm sure, terrified and puzzled. Her worried face relaxed. She laughed. "Sit down, darling," she said. "You look as though you're about to meet your maker."

She came into the dining room and put her hands along the back of the chair opposite me. "That wasn't even about you. It was Joan Abbott, about John." The vertical line between her eyebrows returned. "I'm going to ask you one question, Doug, and if you have no idea, or don't want to answer, just tell me."

I nodded.

She looked down at her hands, as though she was ashamed to be doing what she was about to do. "Is there any sense, you think, in which John has . . . oh, I don't know, it sounds ridiculous . . . *corrupted* Eleanor Abbott? Led her astray?"

My mind was working in several directions at once, trying to reconstruct the phone call, trying to figure out what the answer to her question might really be, trying to figure out how much I wanted to tell her and if I told her anything, how to put it.

"Well, I know he's made love to her," I blurted finally. She looked startled only for a second. I could feel a deep flush rise to my face. "But not because he's *talked* about it." She nodded, I think, approvingly. "But I would have said that Eleanor was pretty much in charge of her own life. I mean, she had lots of boyfriends. That she slept with, I think. Even in high school." By now I was talking down to my chemistry book. "I mean, I think he liked her more than she liked him. Not that she didn't like him. I mean, I don't know."

"I see," my mother said. I looked up at her. Suddenly she

grinned at me and I felt the pinch of love for her that came only occasionally at this stage of my life. "Well, that was clear as a bell, Doug."

That June, Pamela Abbott, who was in my class, had a tent party to celebrate our graduation. I had been eagerly anticipating seeing Eleanor there, telling her I was going to Harvard in the fall, trying, as I see now, the appeal of my conventional success where the romance of my rebel stance had failed. My brother had been home for a week but he hadn't mentioned her, and some secret, competitive part of me hoped she was done with him and would find in my embrace the intensity she had sought in vain in his.

There was no sign of Eleanor. I danced with her sister and asked about her; she simply said that Eleanor couldn't make it. But what I heard from the others in the course of the evening, in little knotted whispers, was that Eleanor had, in some sense, broken with her family. Run away somehow. She'd flunked or dropped out of school (something no boy in our world, much less a girl, would ever do), and had taken a job as a waitress or a dancer or an airline stewardess, depending on who told the story.

When I got home that night, I saw the light on in my brother's room. I went and stood awkwardly in his doorway. He was reading in bed, the lower part of his body covered with a sheet, the upper part naked. I remember looking at the filled-in, grown-up shape of his upper body and momentarily hating him.

"Thought I'd report on the Abbott party," I said.

He set his book down. "I've been to the Abbott party," he said, and smiled.

"Well, everyone was there, except *you*."

"I'm surprised you still go," he said.

"I'm surprised you don't," I said.

"I'm *persona non grata* there," he said flatly.

After a pause, I said, "Eleanor wasn't there either."

"M-mm," he said. "Well, I'm not surprised."

"I heard she'd left school," I said.

"I heard that, too," he answered.

"What's she doing now?" I asked.

"She hasn't told me," he said.

"So you're not in touch with her?" I asked.

"No, I've outlived my usefulness to Eleanor." I was surprised to hear the bitterness in his voice.

"How were you *useful* to her?"

"I should think that would be easy enough to imagine."

I didn't know what to say.

"I mean," he said, "even aside from the little scene in the basement."

I shook my head, confused and embarrassed at the reference.

"Look," he said. "Eleanor was looking for a way not to be an Abbott, to get away from that whole world. And it turns out that it takes a lot to get away. It's not enough that you sleep around with boys from your world. But when you start fucking boys from across the *tracks*," he said. He was agitated. He sat up, throwing back the covers, and got out of bed. He walked to the dresser, lighted a cigarette and turned to face me.

"You mean she was sleeping with guys we didn't know — from Fountain Park or something?" I was nervous as I tried not to look at his nakedness.

He stood leaning on the dresser. He inhaled sharply on the cigarette and then smiled at me. "No, I mean she was sleeping with *me*. And she made sure her parents found out about it."

I was silent for a moment, unable to understand. "But *we're* not from across the tracks," I said.

He cocked his head. "No?" he asked. "Well, maybe I'm not talking about literal tracks."

"I don't believe that," I said after a pause. "I don't believe in what you're talking about."

He shrugged. "So don't believe in it," he said. He carried the cigarette and ashtray back to bed with him, covered himself again.

I persisted. "I mean, we're just the same as them. We're just as good as they are."

He smiled. "Ask the Abbotts about that."

"The *Abbotts*," I said, with what I hoped was grand contempt in my voice, forgetting for the moment my eagerness to attend Pamela's party.

"Okay, ask Mom. Ask her about how well *she's* lived in Haley all these years. Ask her whether she's as good as anyone else around here." Then, as though something in my face stopped him, his expression changed. He shrugged. "Maybe I'm all wet," he said. "Maybe you're right." He tapped an ash into the ashtray. "I mean, this is America after all, right?"

I stood in the doorway a minute more. "So what do you think Eleanor is doing?" I finally asked.

"Look, I don't care what she's doing," he said. He picked up his book, and after a few minutes, I left.

I went to Harvard in the fall, as did Pamela Abbott — though in those days we still called her part of it Radcliffe. The year after that my brother moved to Cambridge to study architecture at Harvard. Gingerly, we began to draw closer together. We still occupied entirely different worlds, mine sloppy and disorganized, his orderly and productive. I thought it emblematic of this that I was so utterly unattracted to the women he preferred. They were neat, wealthy, Waspy, and to me they seemed asexual. I was drawn to ethnic types, women with dark skin, liquid black eyes, wild hair. But I had none. My wild women were abstracts, whereas Jacey had a regular string of real women in and out of his apartment; and I could never look at them, with their tiny pained smiles, without thinking of Eleanor perched on top of my brother in the basement the day I wanted ice cream.

We both continued to go home each summer to be with my mother, and it was the summer following his first year in Cambridge, the summer before my junior year, that Jacey fell in love with the oldest Abbott sister, Alice.

Alice had been a year ahead of him in high school, had gone to a two-year college somewhere and then married. She was arguably the prettiest of the sisters, the most conventional, and, if she hadn't been older than he was at a time when that constituted a major barrier, she was probably the one my brother would have been attracted to in the first place. If he had fallen in love with her back in high school, I think their courtship might have proceeded at a pace slow enough, tender enough, that her parents might ultimately have been reconciled to it; the issue of our marginal social status might have been overcome if it hadn't been combined with Eleanor's sexual precocity, if Alice had come first.

But Alice had married someone else, someone acceptable,

and had had two children. And now she was back home, something unmentioned having happened to her marriage. The children were preschoolers, and I was startled once that summer to walk past the Abbotts' house and see a tent set up in the backyard with balloons and streamers floating in the protected air beneath it. I heard children's shouts, someone crying loudly, and I realized that the cycle had begun again for the Abbotts.

I don't know where Jacey met Alice — there certainly were enough people in whose homes they might have bumped into each other — and I can't imagine how he explained himself to her in the context of what her family thought had gone on between him and Eleanor, but he began to see her secretly that summer, arranging to go to the same parties, to meet accidentally. I went out with Pamela every now and then without having any romantic interest in her; we mostly commiserated on how dull Haley was, talked about places in Boston we missed, and she told me about Jacey and Alice.

I said I didn't believe her.

"Alice told me," she said.

"But *secretly?*" I asked.

"She's afraid of my parents," Pamela said.

"But she's a grown woman, with children. I mean, she's been married, for God's sake."

"Oh, that," Pamela said, waving her hand contemptuously.

"What do you mean, 'Oh, that'?" I asked.

"That was practically an arranged marriage," she said. "They think that Alice has peanut shells for brains or something, so they sort of suggested after she graduated that maybe it was time to tie the old knot, and they sort of suggested that Peter was the one to do it with."

"I don't believe it," I said. "No one could be that malleable."

She shrugged. "Look, Alice is the good one, and Eleanor was the bad one, and I'm the one who sort of gets off the hook. That's just the way it works."

We sat in silence for a minute. "What do you hear from Eleanor?" I asked.

She looked at me sternly. "I don't," she said.

I'm not sure that Jacey even slept with Alice that first summer, and from what I knew via Pamela, Alice was feeling fragile about the end of the marriage, and tentative about getting involved with someone seemingly as dangerous as Jacey. To me, who saw myself as the truly dangerous potential in our family, this was amusing. But it was striking to me back in Cambridge that year that he stopped seeing other women. The seemingly endless parade in and out of his apartment stopped; and I was the one, finally, who had women.

I only had two, but it was enough to perplex me thoroughly. I was very involved with theater groups at Harvard; I'd been in one production or another practically nonstop since midway through my freshman year. Now, as a junior, I was getting lead roles; and the exotic women I'd dreamed of having, theatrical women who ringed their eyes with black pencil, were interested in me. But somehow, both my romances fell flat; they didn't seem as gripping as the roles I played, or even as exciting as the tense, delicate relationship Jacey was now maintaining by mail with Alice. Though he wouldn't really talk about Alice with me, about what she was like or what they did together, I knew he was determined to have her, to rescue her the following summer, and I watched it all with intense interest.

The summer started and then progressed somewhat as the first one had. There were frequent phone calls, the arranged meetings. But then Jacey brought Alice to our house.

I suppose they had problems finding places to go together privately, and they finally decided they had no alternative. At first it was when my mother was away, off on her annual trip to a college classmate's in Chicago. I was sitting in the living room, watching television, and I heard them come in. I looked up to see Alice, then Jacey, going upstairs. I could hear the murmur of their voices off and on through the night after I went to bed, and the sounds of their lovemaking, but it didn't bother me as it might have if it had been Eleanor. They left sometime in the dead of the night.

He brought her to the house every night my mother was gone, and we never spoke of it. I don't know what they did in the weeks after my mother's return, but in mid-August, he brought Alice to the house when my mother was home. She didn't hear them come in. She was in the backyard watering the plants. And then for a while I could hear her moving around the kitchen. At about ten o'clock, though, she crossed to the bottom of the stairs and stopped, hearing their voices. Then she came into the dining room where I was.

"Who's upstairs with John?" she asked.

"I think it's Alice Abbott," I said.

"Oh," she said. "How long is she likely to stay?"

"I don't know," I said. "But I wouldn't stay up and wait for her to leave."

The next morning when I woke, I could hear Jacey and my mother talking in the kitchen, their voices floating out the open windows in the still summer air, hers steady and his impassioned, occasionally quite clearly audible. From what he said, I could tell she felt he needed to make his courtship of Alice open. It even seemed she was trying to get him to move out if he wanted to sleep with Alice, perhaps rent a room somewhere. "But it's because I *do* love her, Mother. It couldn't be more different from Eleanor. Eleanor was just an *idea* I had."

I don't know what my brother and mother agreed on, but he didn't move out and he didn't, to my knowledge, ever bring Alice to the house again. And then, just before he was to go back to Cambridge and reclaim his apartment from a subletter who was leaving early, it was over. Her parents had found out and simply said no, and apparently Alice didn't have the strength or the financial independence to defy them.

There were several days of phone calls, when my mother and I sat shut into the kitchen or our respective rooms trying not to listen to Jacey's desperate voice rising and falling, attempting to persuade Alice that it could work if she would just make the break.

And then even the calls stopped, and he just stayed in his room until his job ended and he could leave. And that's literally how he did it. He came home from his last day of work, took a shower, and started loading up his car. My mother tried to persuade him to stay overnight and start the trip the following morning, but he argued that he'd have to drive through at least part of one night anyway, and it might as well be at the beginning of the trip. "Besides," he said, "the sooner I get out of this fucking town the better." That he would use such language in front of my mother made it clear to me, finally, how deeply lost in misery my brother was.

When he left, my mother stood looking after his car for a long time. I went up onto the front porch, but she didn't follow. Finally I called to her, "Are you coming in, Mom?" And she turned and began to climb the stairs. I had a sudden revelation then of my mother's age. She had always looked the same age to me, but at that moment she looked as tired as Grandma Vetter had when she told us that she was just going to lie down for a bit.

We had a fairly silent dinner, and afterward, over coffee, she said to me, "Do you think your brother will be all right?"

"Well, he's not going to do anything stupid to himself, if that's what you mean."

"That's not what I mean," she said, her quickly raised hand dismissing even that possibility.

"I know," I said. I felt ashamed. Then, impulsively, I said, "I just wish he'd never met the Abbott family."

She sighed. "If John hadn't met the Abbotts, he'd have had to invent them, one way or another. There are no ends of Abbotts in the world, if that's what you need. And he just needs that somehow." She picked up the chipped yellow cup and sipped her coffee. "Well, really, I know how."

I was startled. "What do you mean, you know how?"

She sat back in her chair wearily and looked at me. She shook her head slowly. "I think John had a hard time, a terrible time, with the way you both grew up, and it made him want — oh, I don't know. Not money, exactly, but kind of the sense of place, of knowing where you belong, that money can give you. At least in a town like Haley." She shrugged. "And the way he grew up — that was my fault."

I answered quickly. "No it wasn't, Mom. If he feels that way, it's his responsibility. I mean, I grew up however he did, and that's not the way I feel."

"Yes, but you're different from John."

I started to protest again, but she lifted her hand to silence me. "No, listen. I can explain it." Then she sighed again, as if coming around to some central, hard truth. "You know that after Charlie — your father's — death, I was just . . . I was just a *mess*. I hurt so badly that some mornings, I'd be crying before I even woke up. And then I had you." She looked up at me. "And poor old John, well, he just got lost in there. I just didn't have anything for him."

She shook her head. "He was such a sad-sack kind of kid anyway. He'd always been jumpy and intense, even as a baby. I just couldn't settle in and be loving to him. He was too nervous. Whereas *you*," she smiled at me, "you just slept and smiled and nursed. Even when you were a toddler I had to pin a sign on the back of your shirt saying 'Don't feed this child' because you'd go around the neighborhood and everyone would just *give* you things.

"And I swear, as I remember it, I spent weeks just sleeping with you in bed after you were born. I got dressed for meals, but that was about it. Otherwise I'd just sleep and sleep and sort of come alive just to nurse you or change you. I just couldn't believe Charlie wasn't coming back. I was twenty-four years old." Her face was blank, remembering things I couldn't possibly understand.

She cleared her throat. "And John just floated away from me. My mother was right there, you know, and terribly concerned about me, and she sort of took him over. That was what she felt she could do for me. I can remember early on, sometimes I'd hear him crying or calling for me, and then I'd hear her, and after a while he'd stop, and I'd be *glad*. I'd just hold you and go back to sleep. Or more like a trance, it really was. I'll never forgive myself."

I wanted to comfort her. "But he loved Grandma Vetter," I said. "I mean, he ended up getting a lot *out* of that."

"Well, yes, I think he did, but in the meantime, making that shift from me to her was terrible for him. And also, I'm not so sure having my mother as a substitute was so good for him. I mean, she was born in another century. All her values and rules, while they're perfectly good ones, were ones that sort of . . . stiffened John, fed *that* side of who he was. And I, I knew that he, much more than you, needed to learn to relax, to be playful. But I just didn't, couldn't, help him." She twirled her cup slowly in its saucer. "And then I was working and he was so good and reliable, and *you* were the one always in scrapes."

I felt a pang of something like guilt. "But he turned out fine, Mom. He turned out great."

"Oh, I know he did, darling, but I'm talking about something else. I'm talking about why John struggles so hard to have certain things in his life. Or even certain people."

I frowned at her, not sure I understood.

"I let him go, Doug, don't you see?"

I shook my head, resolute on her behalf.

She looked at me for a moment, then suddenly she said, "All right, I know. I'll tell you. It's like one time I remember, I was driving you boys back from some trip somewhere, and we were coming home through Sandusky. We were going to stop at my great-aunt's for the night. Viola. She's dead a long time now. And I just couldn't find it. I tried for about an hour and a half, but nothing was where it was supposed to be by my directions. And so I finally just pulled over — I was so aggravated — and I said out loud, 'Well, that's it. We're lost.' And I was so busy looking at these directions and maps and things that I didn't notice John for a few minutes. But when I finally looked at him . . . well, I've never seen a child so terrified. I asked him what the matter was and he said, 'You said we were *lost!*' And suddenly, by the way he said it, I knew he thought I'd meant *lost,* in a sort of fairy-tale sense — like Hansel and Gretel, or someone being lost in a forest. *Never* getting home. Starving to death."

She shook her head. "You know, most kids his age — he was five or six, I think — don't think they're *lost* as long as they've got their mother with them. But he had so little faith in me, in my ability to protect him. I knew right then that I'd lost John. Just lost him." She shook her head again, sadly.

After a moment I said softly, "I think he'll be all right, Mom."

"Oh, I know he'll be all right, honey," she said. "I know it! That's what breaks my heart." And for the first time in my memory since Grandma's death, I saw my mother cry.

I went over to Jacey's apartment more frequently that fall than I had in the past. I had a sense of him as a trust that my mother had placed in me. I'm not sure what made for my conviction that she had never spoken about him to me, but I felt secure in it. And I felt she'd somehow asked me to help her pay a debt to Jacey that she, and therefore perhaps I, too, owed him.

It didn't make much difference to our relationship, because Jacey simply wouldn't speak to me about anything intimate; but in fact, I liked the order and the quiet in his carefully furnished apartment. On Sundays, I almost always bought English muffins and the *Times* and walked over there. We'd sit quietly all morning, eating and going through the paper, occasionally reading aloud or commenting on some story.

But as the fall wore on, I found more and more, when I dropped over unexpectedly, that he'd come to the door in a bathrobe or towel and tell me that it wasn't a good time. He never smiled or suggested in any of the ways some of my friends might have that it was because there was a woman inside. But I knew that's what it was, and I was happy for him, though a little surprised after the intensity of his feeling for Alice. But it was clear to me, by now, that Jacey was a lover of women, that he needed and enjoyed their company in a way that some men don't — perhaps, I remember speculating then, because of my mother's painful turning away from him as a young child. That he was again able to be interested in them seemed to me a sign of health, and I wrote my mother that Jacey was, as I put it, "beginning to go out a bit," though he hadn't actually spoken to me about it.

He invited me to early dinner one Friday in late October. He said it had to be early because he was doing something later on. It was a cold, rainy night, and I remember a sense of nostalgia swept over me as I walked the short distance to his apartment, stumbling occasionally over the bumps in the rain-slicked brick sidewalks. I was in the throes of another dying romance, powerfully disappointed because the woman I thought I had loved was so much more mundane than I had originally conceived of her as being. Jacey had made a fine meal — scallops and salad and a very good wine. We had several cups of coffee afterward, and I remember thinking how thoroughly in charge he was of his own life. He went into his study to get some slides to show me, and the doorbell rang.

"Shall I get it?" I asked.

"Sure," he called back.

A woman stood under the porch light, wearing a poncho, her head bent down, her face lost in the shadow of her hood. As I opened the glass door, she raised her head. It was Pamela Abbott. She looked startled, but her voice was smooth. "Hello, Doug," she said.

I said hello. For a few confused moments, I thought that she'd somehow come to my brother's apartment to see me, but as I followed her in, I realized this couldn't be, that it was, of course, John she had come for. Even then I couldn't make my mind work to understand it.

Jacey greeted her coolly and took her wet poncho, shaking it away from him several times before he hung it up. She sat down at the table and I joined her. He was standing. He asked her if she wanted some coffee. She shrugged. "Sure, if you're having some."

While he was in the kitchen, I felt compelled to make small talk. "So, Pamela," I said. "What's up?"

She shrugged again.

"I mean, God," I said, feeling more and more like an idiot, "I'm really sweating out this *facing life* business. Trying to decide what in hell I'm going to do next year, you know?" She looked steadily at me and didn't respond. "Do you have any idea what you're going to do?" I asked.

"I don't know," she said. "I'll probably go to New York and get a job in publishing, I think."

"God, that sounds exciting. But it's rough, isn't it? I mean, to get a job?"

"I don't know. My father has a couple of connections. I don't think it'll be too hard to get some shit lower-level thing."

Jacey was standing in the doorway now, a cup of coffee in his hand. "And then climb the ladder, using his connections all the way," he said sharply. I looked at him, but his face was blank. He walked over to her and set the coffee in front of her. She shrugged again. She looked at him as he went back to his seat. I watched her watching my brother, and saw that she was frightened of him. I realized that I should have left as soon as she arrived, that she was what he was "doing" later. We sat in silence for a minute. Jacey lighted a cigarette and the smell of sulphur and burning tobacco hung in the little room.

"Well," he said suddenly to Pamela. His voice was still sharp. "Do you want to go to bed?"

She looked quickly at me and then away. After a moment she raised her shoulders. "Sure," she said without emotion, as though accepting some punishment. He stood up. She stood up. I stood up. I was trying to meet my brother's eye, and it seemed to me for a second I did, but his gaze slid quickly sideways. He walked out of the room first, and she followed him, without looking at me again.

I left the apartment immediately. My heart was pounding in my ears. I walked along the black river in the rain, across the Western Avenue Bridge and all the way up to the boathouse on the other side, trying to understand what my brother was doing to himself, to Pamela, to me. He who was so private, who kept his life and emotions so masked, had exposed himself and Pamela to me, had shown me how contemptuously he could treat her, how despicable he could be. He who had felt used, I know, by Eleanor, and who, I could guess, had felt abused by Alice, was now doing both to Pamela. It seemed to me like a violation of everything I would have said he believed in. And I felt slapped that he had asked me to witness it all, as though he were exposing also my pretensions to understand anything about life.

I was cold and drenched by the time I got home. I took a long shower, grateful that both of my roommates were out, and went to bed early. I lay awake for a long time, thinking about Jacey, about myself, about how we grew up.

I didn't get in touch with my brother or go to his apartment again for several weeks. Finally he called. It was a Sunday. He said he'd gotten the *Times* and made breakfast and he wondered if I wanted to come over. I said okay, not enthusiastically, and then I said, "Will there be just the two of us?"

"Yes," he said. "That won't happen again."

It was cold outside, gray. The trees were nearly stripped of leaves and I had the sense of winter coming on. John had a fire going in the fireplace and had set breakfast out on the coffee table. I was, for once, repelled by the orderliness. I wondered if I'd ever again see my brother in a spontaneous moment. I swallowed some of his good coffee.

"I wanted to apologize," he said.

"Oh," I said.

"What I did was wrong."

"Did you tell that to Pamela?" I asked.

"What business is that of yours?" he said, flaring suddenly.

Then he looked away, into the fire for a moment. We were sitting side by side on the couch. "Yes," he said tiredly. "You're right. And I did say it to her. I'm not seeing her anymore. I wanted you to know that." Then he slouched lower in the couch and started to talk. He told me that Pamela had come over unexpectedly almost as soon as school started. It upset him to see her, and he had a lot to drink while she was there, as she did. He said she did most of the talking, about her family, about Alice, about Eleanor. She seemed eager to align herself with him against her parents. She told him that they were stupid, rigid. Worse, they were cruel. She said that they had destroyed Eleanor and were destroying Alice, that she was the only daughter smart enough to see the process, the pitfalls on the one hand of resisting too hard or, on the other hand, of caving in. She called her father a tyrant, a bastard. She said that Jacey couldn't imagine the kinds of things said about him, about our family, in their house.

And then, drunk, she said how wonderful she'd always thought he was, how much she admired him, how much she wanted him. She thought they ought to sleep together.

Drunk, too, and angry, he had done it. Then he had passed out, and in the morning she was gone. He said he had thought that that was probably it, that she'd seen herself as fulfilling some part of what he called her "Abbott destiny" by having him as a lover.

But she kept coming over, and he kept sleeping with her. He said he knew it was wrong, that he didn't even like her really. But that in some ways it was like having Alice again, and it was like getting back at her too. And so he just kept doing it.

He got up and poked the fire. He sat down again, this time on the floor. "And then I began to feel *used* again," he said. "It was crazy; I was using her, too. But I began to feel that somehow I was just . . . some bit *actor* in some part of their family drama. She kept telling me she *loved* me; and I just kept getting more and more cruel to her. More angry." He looked at me suddenly.

"I guess inviting you over was a way of seeing how much she'd take, how low she'd go." He turned away again. "I was pretty far gone, too, in some kind of rage I'd lost control over. But finally I just said I wouldn't see her anymore. I was trying to be kind, but it ended up being a pretty ugly scene. Lots of tears and yelling."

I thought of Pamela, so flip, so sure of herself. "Did she not want to stop?"

He shrugged. "She claims she's in love with me. She threatened to tell Alice we were lovers if I wouldn't see her anymore."

"God!" I said. "Think she will?"

He shook his head. "I don't know. She may. I'm hoping that it'll seem so uselessly cruel that she'll decide not to. But it's her family. And I took that risk when I slept with her. And there won't be anything more between me and Alice anyway, so maybe it'd be for the best. Maybe it'd confirm all the terrible things her father has to say about me and make things easier for Alice."

"That's pretty magnanimous of you," I said.

He looked at me and smiled. "Not entirely. I'd like to be able to let go of Alice. It's been hard. I mean, I've been in love with her for a year and a half and I've slept with her maybe ten times. And I never will again. She still writes to me all the time, even though I can't answer. That kind of stuff. I mean, maybe it's part of the whole thing. Why I slept with Pamela in the first place. To push that possibility away forever."

That was the end of my brother's involvement with the Abbott girls. He told me a few Sundays later that he thought Pamela must have said something to Alice or to her family, because the letters abruptly stopped, but otherwise we didn't speak of them again. I went home the following summer and he stayed in Cambridge. He had a drafting job with a little design company. Alice was still living at home and I saw her a few times during the summer. At first I didn't recognize her. She'd put on at least twenty-five pounds. She didn't say hello to me, but I didn't really expect her to. In fact, as by some unspoken agreement, we each pretended not to know the other when our paths crossed.

In the fall I moved to New York. I saw Pamela there, occasionally, for a few years. We still had friends from college in common. She was an assistant editor at a good publishing house, and I was trying to get any kind of acting job. We'd talk when we met, a little edgily. She'd ask about Jacey, and I'd ask about Alice and Eleanor, as if they were vague acquaintances and not a part of who we both were. She was in touch with Eleanor again, but Eleanor refused to see the family at all. She was a stewardess, and she loved it, loved to travel, Pamela said. Alice lived at home and let her parents run her children, her life. Pamela went home every now and then for a few days, which was about as long as she could stand it, she said.

Our only really difficult conversation was our last one, when I had to tell her that Jacey had gotten married. She looked pained for the smallest fraction of a second, and then the tough smile reemerged. "Well, I assume that whoever it is is rich."

"Why do you assume that?" I asked. In fact, Jacey's wife, an architect too, did have some money, perhaps even as much as the Abbotts had. But I knew enough now to know that that really wasn't rich. And Jacey seemed happy no matter what.

"Isn't that the only kind of girl he's ever been interested in?" she asked jauntily. "Hasn't he been trying to marry *up* since about the day he had his first erection?"

There were so many levels on which her remark offended me — the insult about Jacey's intentions, the implied insult about his, and therefore my, social class — that I wasn't able to choose at which level I wanted to respond. I answered quickly, almost without thinking, "Why do you assume that for him to have married one of you would be to marry up?"

She looked at me for a moment with her mouth open, and then she turned away.

I didn't see her again before I moved to Chicago. I wanted to be nearer my mother, who wasn't well, and I'd gotten a good job with a repertory company there.

My mother got worse over the next three years — she had cancer — and I often went down and spent two or three weeks in the old house with her when there were breaks in my work. One summer night we were driving past the Abbotts' and the tent was up again. Dance music swelled out on the summer air.

The band was playing "Blowin' in the Wind" to a bouncy fox-trot rhythm. My mother looked over at the soft yellow lights, the moving figures. "Imagine a child of Alice's being old enough to dance," she said. And I recalled abruptly that she had known all the Abbotts, all the children in town, as second graders. That in some sense we remained always young, always vulnerable in her vision. She didn't think of the pain we'd all caused each other.

She died in the early winter of that year. I went down frequently in the fall. We sat around at home in the evenings, often drinking a fair amount. She'd lost so much weight by then that she was, as she called herself, a cheap drunk, and we seemed to float back easily into the comfortable, desultory intimacy we'd had when I was home alone with her in high school. Once she asked me what came next for me in life. I asked her what she meant. "Oh, I don't know, darling," she said. "You just seem so content, I wonder if this is really . . . *it* for you."

"I don't know," I said honestly. I felt, at the moment, so peaceful that it wouldn't have bothered me if it was. "It seems to me I've chosen the right profession, certainly. I'm really much better at pretending than at being. You know, I used to have such contempt for Jacey, for what he wanted out of life, for the kinds of women he went after. But in fact he always really went after things. And he suffered with it, but he's all right in the end. I like him. Whereas I haven't done that. I'm happy, but . . . Well, that's all that really counts, I guess. I am happy. I'm actually very happy."

"I know what you mean," she said. "I've been happy, too, and glad I didn't have the messes that some of my friends made of their lives. But sometimes I've worried that I lived a little like a nun, you know. Sort of a *pinched* life, in the end."

We sat. The only sound was the occasional faint noise of the old house shifting somewhere in the cold fall air.

Then I said, "Why didn't you ever remarry, Mother? Surely there were possibilities."

"Fewer than you'd think," she said. "Everyone always thinks things are more possible than they are. I mean, single men don't stay in Haley if they've got any starch. Who was there my age who was eligible? Drew Carter was always around, but he's a washout. And now there's a few old widowers who smell like their dogs." She laughed. "I'm getting mean," she said. "And then I was a schoolteacher for all those years. You don't meet men in a job like that. No, the only time I ever met anyone was in Chicago, a friend of Beatrice Goulding's. I used to go up and visit him every summer, stay with him for five or six days. Surely you remember that. I always told you I was staying with Beatrice." I nodded. I remembered those visits. "He was a wonderful man. Wonderful." And then, with that deft way my mother had of casting the entire story she was telling in a new light, she said, "A little boring, but really, very wonderful."

"Well, why didn't you marry him? Move us all up there?"

"Oh, I couldn't have done that to John," she said instantly. "He'd had such a terrible early childhood, and he was so happy at that stage. Remember? He was playing ball and had a good job and was chasing around after that middle Abbott girl. No." She shook her head. "All this life in Haley had gotten to be too important to him then. I can't imagine having asked him to give it up. I never would have forgiven myself. No, it was better for me to go on as I had been. And besides, I was still really in love with Charlie. With my memory of him. And I've enjoyed my life. I have," she said wistfully.

"Well, it's not over yet," I said.

But it nearly was. Jacey came out for the eight or ten days before she died. We took care of her at home, as she'd wanted, with a visiting nurse to help us out. She was very uncomfortable the last few days, though not in actual pain, and I think we were both relieved when her struggle stopped, when we didn't have to listen to her trying to breathe anymore in the night.

There wasn't really a funeral, because she'd been cremated and because she didn't want a service. She had requested that we have a hymn to sing, and she had written down three or four of her favorites she wanted us to be sure to do. Jacey and I discussed the plans the morning after she'd died. We were washing the last of her dishes, putting things away in the kitchen. "Isn't it like her," he said, tears sitting in his eyes, "to take charge even of the way we let her go." He shook his head in proud amazement, and I thought how differently we knew her, understood her.

So we gathered, around twenty or so of her friends, mostly women, and Jacey and I, and some young people who were former students, and sang "Guide Me, Oh Thou Great Jehovah" and "Fight the Good Fight" and "Amazing Grace" and "For All the Saints." It seemed so insufficient, as any service does, I suppose, that we went on singing too long, to compensate, and Jacey and I were both hoarse the next day.

But there were still things to pack up, and so we went to the old center of town to get some boxes. It was a cold, bright day, and the town looked small and shabby in the raw light, as though nothing important could ever have happened there. We were loading the trunk and the back seat of the car in front of the liquor store when I saw a woman walking toward us down the street whom I recognized instantly as Mrs. Abbott. She didn't look very different from the way she had at all those parties. Her hair, dyed now, I supposed, was still a pale arranged blonde; her lipstick was a girlish pink. She saw Jacey, and I could tell that for a moment she was thinking of walking past us without acknowledging us. Her step wavered marginally, but then she straightened up. We both assumed, I think, that she would speak to us of our mother's death, which is what every conversation we'd had in the last few days had started with.

But whether she didn't know what we were both in town for or whether her own emotions of the moment drove it out of her mind, that's not what she spoke of. A brilliant social smile flickered quickly across her face and was gone. Then, standing an uncomfortable distance from us on the sidewalk, she made for a minute or two the kind of small talk she'd made all those years ago under the tents in her backyard — a comment on the weather, on how we'd changed, on how busy young people's lives were, they could hardly ever get home anymore. As she spoke she nodded repeatedly, an odd birdlike motion of her head. There was an awkward silence when she finished — I know I couldn't imagine what an appropriate response would be — and then she said with brittle cheer to Jacey alone, "Well, I've no more daughters for you." And though she'd been talking about his loss rather than her own, she smiled again, and walked on.

For a moment we stood motionless on the sidewalk, watching her diminishing figure. Then I turned to Jacey, expecting, I suppose, some comment, and ready to be angry along with him, on his behalf. But he didn't even look at me. Instead, he bent down and started to load the empty boxes that would hold my mother's belongings into the car, as though what Mrs. Abbott had said and done had all happened with the rest of it, years before, when he was a child.

MADISON SMARTT BELL

The Lie Detector

FROM THE CRESCENT REVIEW

My APARTMENT in Hoboken had a water circulation heating system. There was a boiler in a closet by the stairs, which heated the water and pumped it into pipes that ran above my ceiling, under the roof, and finally the water got dumped into the radiators in my apartment, one in the kitchen, one in the bedroom. The pipes were not insulated and the fact that they ran through the ceiling made the whole system very inefficient. The boiler ran on electricity paid for by me, and I had been warned by the previous tenants that it could kick up the utility bill as much as a hundred dollars a month. For that reason I wasn't altogether sorry when I found out that I was going to be evicted from the place, even though the base rent was very low and I knew I would never find another place quite so cheap.

Mr. Evans, the landlord, came by to see me one rainy morning, on the first of October. It took him a long time to get me to come down to the door. I was lying on my mattress looking at the ceiling and listening to the water drip on the roof, and I wasn't expecting anyone to come over. The entrance door was at the bottom of a crooked staircase that went down from the second floor to the street. The previous tenants had made a doorbell by running a string through a slot in the door up to a set of chimes that hung inside the apartment. Someone in the street could pull the string and the chimes would ring and you would know that someone wanted to see you. But I didn't really know anyone in Hoboken and the Spanish kids in the neighborhood kept pulling the string, which annoyed me, so I cut the string and the chimes were silenced. The kids would sometimes throw firecrackers through the slot too, but they could never get them very far up the stairs, so that didn't bother me so much.

Mr. Evans banged on the door for a while and finally he gave up and let himself in with the key. He came into the stairwell and started calling. I heard him and went to the head of the stairs. Mr. Evans looked more like a doctor or a professor than a slumlord, and in fact he wasn't much of a slumlord. He owned only a few buildings, and probably it had been a nicer area when he bought them. He was about sixty, a fairly tall man with salt-and-pepper hair and practical black glasses. He had a nagging cough. On this rainy day he was wearing a trench coat, but his hair was damp and his glasses had steamed. When I came to the head of the stairs he had taken his glasses off and was wiping them with his handkerchief.

Mr. Evans heard me arrive and he looked up and put his glasses back on. He had come to tell me some bad news, he said. He was so sorry, but he had sold the building, and I was going to have to move out. I nodded my head to him. There was no light in the stairwell, except for a little dirty illumination that came in over the transom. I couldn't see Mr. Evans very well, and I'm not sure if he could see me at all. But he went on being very pleasant and polite. He told me I could have the month to move, and he warned me that he would be coming with the buyer to look the place over again. Then I thanked him for coming out and doing it the nice way. We exchanged a few compliments and apologies, and Mr. Evans said goodbye and went out and shut the door.

I listened to the lock clicking shut as Mr. Evans turned his key. Then I walked back into my apartment and went to the window. I could see him walking away down the broken sidewalk in the gray rain. It was too bad to lose the place, but I thought Mr. Evans had handled it very nicely. He could have just told me in a note or a phone call, and he didn't have to give me a month's notice at all, because I wasn't holding a lease on the place. At the moment I was even touched that he had come out in the rain to talk to me, but that was before I found out that he was going to cheat me out of my security deposit.

It was cold in the apartment. I went into the kitchen and put some water on to boil. Since I didn't want to run the circulation system, I used to try to warm up the place a little by boiling water on the stove. Sometimes it seemed to help. Anyway I could steam my hands over the pot. It was unusually cold for October and that had taken me by surprise. I had been thinking about moving to some place with furnished heat by November. I had been thinking about a lot of things and not doing any of them, and I thought now that the eviction might be a blessing in disguise, because it would force me to go out and deal with people again.

For the past few months I had done practically nothing and seen practically no one. I was recuperating from a bad love affair, and I spent the summer and early fall in suspended animation, watching my brain turn itself inside out. Time went by and my mind slowly filled itself with the salsa music and the Spanish voices that came drifting out of the rows of tenements, across the streets full of broken glass, and my memory of the lost woman diffused itself into the heavy air and the concrete of sidewalks and buildings. By the time it got cold this mental rotation was more or less complete, but I had become fixed in a routine that demanded nothing from me other than that I read the *New York Post* and eat something occasionally and watch my fingernails grow. I had the habit of inertia, but Mr. Evans's visit had broken that.

On Wednesday I got up at four and went into New York, so I could be in Sheridan Square by five, when the *Voice* came out. I picked up the paper and walked down Bleecker Street through the cold morning fog and went into a twenty-four-hour Greek diner, where I bought a cup of coffee and a piece of crumb cake for breakfast. I ate the crumb cake and started reading the ads in the back of the paper. *Voice* ads are about the only way to find a place to live without paying a broker's fee, and I didn't have any extra money to give to brokers.

I was considering moving into Manhattan, but there wasn't anything that looked too promising there. I didn't want to live in the worse parts of the Lower East Side, and I didn't think I would be very popular in Harlem. But there were a few nonspecific ads, and I thought that I would call those places, just for luck. I drank my coffee and smoked my cigarette. When I paid the check I bought a couple of dollars' worth of dimes.

The sun was beginning to eat up the fog by the time I left the diner, and I appreciated that. I had on a cloth coat that wasn't too warm, but it was all I had at the moment. It was a little before seven and there was no one else around except some garbage men. The cafés and boutiques along Bleecker Street hadn't opened yet. Really it was even too early to start making business calls, so I decided to walk over to Second Avenue. It would kill time and there was a quiet Russian deli over there, with a pay phone on the wall.

By noon that day I was shaking from coffee, I had about five of my dimes left, and I knew I wasn't going to live in Manhattan. I was sitting on a concrete island in the middle of Houston Street, looking down on a flock of pigeons which were trying to work up the nerve to come peck my shoelaces. I folded the *Voice* to another page and started reading the Brooklyn ads. Then I spent some more time on the telephone.

The next day I was in Williamsburg, a Brooklyn neighborhood I had never even heard of, on the far side of the bridge at the end of Delancey Street. I went over to look at a small apartment in a small row house out there, but by the time I arrived the woman who owned the place had already rented it to some friend of hers. She was sorry I had made the trip for nothing. She would have called me if she had known my number. If I was interested I could walk around the corner to the Galería del Sol and talk to Rick, who sometimes knew of apartments.

The Galería del Sol was supposed to be an art gallery, but it wasn't on an artsy block, and there were so few pictures that the place looked more like some kind of front. Rick was very drunk, although it was still early in the morning, and since his English was blurry it took us some time to discover that we couldn't make a deal. Rick moonlighted as a loft broker, but his lofts were too expensive for me. He didn't deal in apartments, but if I wanted to I could go down to 185 Broadway and talk to Benson, the super. Rick would have the kid go with me to show me where it was.

The kid was sitting on a trash can in front of the Galería del Sol. He had a heavy black beard and a briefcase-sized radio. Rick shouted some Spanish at him and he jumped up and set the radio on his shoulder, next to his left ear. I followed him down the street. He stayed about five yards ahead of me and never looked around. When we got to the building he unlocked the outside door and pointed me toward an apartment in the back. Then he went back in the street and sat down on another trash can, which was padlocked to a light pole, like all the trash cans in Williamsburg.

Eugenio Benson was a short coffee-colored man with square even teeth and tight knots of hair on his head. He was wearing blue coveralls with paint all over them, and when I told him what I was looking for he put on a Windbreaker and led me out around the corner, where we entered the building again through another door. There was a smell of fresh plaster in the entry, and Benson began telling me how he was repairing the walls. He showed me the elevator shaft and said that he hoped the elevator would work again sometime soon, but that wasn't a job he could do himself; Lubin, the landlord, would have to hire a mechanic, and Lubin was very slow about doing that kind of thing. But anyway the empty apartment was on the second floor. So Benson took me up to the second floor, where the replastering had not yet taken place and the walls were chipped and covered with layers of spray-painted graffiti. Benson's face folded over his smile; he folded his arms over his chest and stared at the walls. I waited for him to say something, but he didn't. In the quiet I could hear voices echoing down the staircase from six floors up and a dog barking in the light well at the center of the building.

Benson remembered me, turned around, and unlocked the apartment. We went in and walked around. The place was small but airy. I tried out the sinks, flushed the toilet, turned on the shower. Everything seemed to work. The paint was bad and there were some small holes in the wallboard, but Benson said he would fix those things, and I already believed he would do what he said. There were three steam radiators: heat furnished by the landlord. The rent was something more than I had been paying across the river, but I thought I could handle it. It could have been worse.

"I like it," I told Benson.

"Good," Benson said. "Good if you move in here, I like some more American people come in here. I don't like so many Spanish people in this building. I want some of them to go out." That seemed strange to me, because Benson was clearly Spanish himself, a Dominican as I would later learn, and my surprise must have showed on my face. Benson, who liked to communicate in gestures, took me back out in the hallway.

"Look," he said, jerking a thick arm. "Over here I want to be some American people, in here a Greek maybe, over there some Spanish people, okay, a few of them, and there some people from someplace else. I don't care who is who, but let everybody be different." Light began to dawn on me and I started to laugh. Benson looked up at me and grinned and went on. "All the Spanish people in here, they get too familiar, they in and out of all the apartments tearing everything up, they making noise all night long, till you can't live. You can't live that way." Benson started down the stairs, repeating "you can't live" like a refrain. It was a habit of his, I eventually found out.

We went back around the corner and Benson took me into his apartment. He pulled a chair out from the kitchen table for me to sit down, and called something into the back of the place. His wife came into the kitchen and her eyes widened and she nodded in my direction. Then she turned around to the stove and started making espresso. She was a large untidy woman, at least three times Benson's size. She had on a limp printed cotton dress under a loose sweater, and she was pregnant. When she had loaded the coffee pot and turned on the stove she looked back at Benson and spoke to him in Spanish. Benson hung his Windbreaker over the back of a chair and sat down opposite me.

"My wife she don't speak English," he said. "But she want to say you are welcome."

Then we started to talk about the money. It was the usual deal; a month's security deposit and a month's rent up front. I visualized my bank account, and did arithmetic in my head. I thought I could swing that and perhaps have enough left over to move and buy new sponges to clean the apartment, things like that. But I was definitely going to need a job in the near future, and that was something else to start thinking about.

"Who say for you to come here?" Benson asked me. He set his hands down on either side of the glass cup his wife had placed in front of him, and I told him about the Galería del Sol.

"This man want money from everybody he send here," Benson said, frowning. "He want one month rent."

I fell right out of the good mood I had been in. I didn't have that much money and if I did I wouldn't give it to Rick. I couldn't do it.

"I can't do it," I said.

"No," Benson said. "It's too much. Too much to ask from somebody. We don't tell him you moving in here. After while he going to forget about you."

"Will it work?" I said.

"Yes," said Benson. "When you want to move in?" I had already paid for October in Hoboken so Benson and I decided I would wait till the end of the month. I would bring the money for the deposit and advance and he would hold the apartment and my rent would start in November. I started to feel better again. The coffee pot began to gurgle and Benson's wife picked it up and poured us coffee. She offered me sugar and I refused it. She giggled and said something to Benson and giggled again.

"She say you should take some sugar," Benson said. "She say you too thin and you need it."

Benson's wife went into the main room and sat down in a wooden rocker, facing the television, which was not turned on. A three-year-old girl came out of the bedroom, stumped across the floor, and climbed into her mother's lap. Benson's wife put a hand on the girl's head and went on looking at the blank screen. She pressed her slipper against the floor and began to rock. The girl wormed her head under her mother's arm and looked at me, a sharp direct glance. She looked exactly like Benson, though she was darker and had longer hair, braided in cornrows. Her stare unnerved me a bit and I looked away from her, at the rocker and then at the other furniture in the room. There was another, similar rocker and two armchairs, all apparently hand-carved from some light wood I couldn't identify. I let my eyes coast along the wall, crossing a cabinet which looked as though it had been made by the same person, and back to the surface of the table we were sitting at. I looked up at Benson, and he heard the question I hadn't asked.

"My friend make me all these things," he said. "Man I knew when I used to be living in Santo Domingo. He make me this table you see and these chairs we sitting on and the bed in my bedroom. For me, when I get married. It nice, no?"

I nodded. I thought it was very nice.

"If I stay in Santo Domingo, I think he going to make me just one thing. The chairs maybe, or the bed. But after I get married I'm going to come in America." Benson tilted his chair and looked up. There was an ugly fluorescent tube up there and the ceiling was low, but I had a feeling it was transparent to Benson.

"Few days before I get married he take me in his house and show me all these things," Benson said. "He say to me, 'I'm giving you this present so you not ever able to forget me, mon.' "

I drank some coffee and burned my mouth. It sounded like a good trick to me. Benson would remember his friend whenever he sat down or ate something or went to bed or woke up. I wondered if I would ever forget him myself. I finished my coffee and gave Benson a twenty dollar bill to help him remember the deal until I could get back with the rest of the deposit.

It was about an hour before sunset when I got out of the PATH train in Hoboken, and it wasn't too cold, so I decided to walk down by the docks for a while before I went home. I picked my way among the gates of the different shipping yards until I found a place where I could get through to the water, on a dock below the bluffs where Stevens Institute is. I walked out to the end of the pier and sat down on an old tire. There was red light on the river from the sunset, and rainbows in the water from spilled oil. When the sun had gone down some mosquitoes came out of the water and started to bite me, so I left the pier and walked around to Elysian Park, which is up on the bluff at the corner of the Institute. I sat down on a bench near the fence and looked out across the river to where the lights of the city were getting turned on. When you look at New York from a plane or the Circle Line or the New Jersey Turnpike or just some high point on the other side of the river, the city is beautiful and coherent. When you are there it is more likely to be ugly and terrifying. I sat looking at it until the lights in the park began to come on, shutting me into their own little circle of light. Then I walked home.

I got to my building, walked up the first flight of stairs, hesitated in the dark, and climbed the second flight into the total darkness under the door at the top. I felt for the padlock there and lifted it out of the hasp, and pushed on the warped door till it opened. I could see again. I was on the roof. It was night now and I could look down and see the lights of the bars and storefront restaurants streaming up First Street toward the train station. In the other direction it was much darker, because most of the buildings down there were vacant and gutted. It was a dull, overcast night and the streetlights had a foggy aura around them. No one was out on the street. I stood there for half an hour and saw one man come out of a bar on the opposite corner and go down a side street, while I looked down at the top of his head. It was cold again and I went down into my apartment and turned on a light and put some water on to boil. I picked up my battered copy of the *Voice*, opened it to the back, and started looking for a job.

For the next couple of weeks I sniffed around for work. I passed up a few jobs because I didn't want to get locked into anything if I could help it. There wasn't much around except dishwashing and security, and those jobs would still be there when I needed them, so I tried to hold out for something better. The deposit on the Brooklyn apartment cleaned out my bank account, so I had to stop eating for a while. I called up all my contacts, trying to find some kind of free-lance work that might bag me a few dollars, but I didn't have any luck. I called up Mr. Evans and told him I was moving out and would he please return my security deposit. Mr. Evans congratulated me on finding an apartment and told me he would mail the check the same day.

I got a cashier's check made up for Benson and took it out to him sometime in the middle of October. Since I didn't have keys to the building yet I had to wait on the steps and hope he would come out. There were some ten-year-old kids playing on the sidewalk and after a while I asked them where Benson might be.

"Super?" one kid said. "Super go around to the store." He pointed. I went up the first side street and found Benson coming out of the bodega on the corner. I told him I had the money, and we walked back to the building together.

"Good you bring the money," Benson said. "That way I going to get the man to come down here. Only way to get him to come down is if you got some money." The man was Lubin, the landlord. He was a Hasidic Jew and he lived at the other end of the neighborhood in one of the last big Hasidic enclaves in Brooklyn. People who knew said the area reminded them of the Warsaw ghetto. Benson opened two glass doors and we went into the hallway of the building.

"I want to get him down here," Benson said, "because I got some people need new tiles in they kitchen and the man he don't want to buy for them. He sitting up in his office saying don't give no more tiles or no more paint. But he don't ever come down here. I have to live with the people. Somebody see a nice kitchen floor, then they going to want some new tiles, and why not? That not too much to ask for."

Benson looked up and down the newly plastered hall. "You see, down here where I fix it, the building is nice. But up there on the high floors, mon, this building is one big mess. Because I been away from this building for two years. I was here a long time before, but the man he don't never want to give the money for fixing, and one day I just get tired. Then I walk out and I go get a job in a factory. And Lubin, he get another guy in here, and this guy he don't do nothing. He just let the building go down."

Benson shrugged his shoulders. "So Lubin he starts calling me. Asking me to come back in the building. I say I'm not coming, but I don't like to work in the factory. Make more money than here maybe, but it too much the same thing. Every day the same. So then I tell Lubin, okay, if he give the money to fix the building and the apartments, and if he let me pick the people for renting the apartments, then I'm coming back. So we make the deal. And here I am back. Running all around this building."

Benson did a little catwalk on the hall floor, picking his feet up high and grinning at me from the side of his mouth. Then he got serious, and stared over my shoulder through the glass doors.

"It too much work right now. But when the place be fixed right, then I'm going to keep it that way. And when people come to me asking for something, then how do I tell them no, I can't do? The man sits up there and says don't give nothing, and he don't come down here, and he can say he don't have the money for the things. I can't be that way. I got to live down here, and when I say something then that thing is me. When I say *I,* then people know they can believe it. That way, when something go wrong in the building, everybody come around saying, 'What happened? What happened?' Because I tell them the truth."

Benson looked at me and I could see his eyes coming back into focus.

"Anyway," he said, "I'm going to call the man right now. Tell him I got this money and he can come on down if he want it. Because when I get him to walk in my house, he not going to say in my face he don't have money for tiles and paint. But you come with me now and I give you the key."

I went with Benson into his apartment and gave him the check. He wrote me a receipt and gave me keys to the outside doors of the building.

"I don't give you a key for the apartment now," Benson said, "because I going to put in a new lock for you. So nobody visit you when you not home." We laughed together at that.

I left Benson and went down under the el tracks to a dairy restaurant where there were some pay phones. You could hardly hear anything with the trains going by overhead but I got lucky in spite of that and landed a day of work with Greenberg-Mellon Productions. The next morning I was out at six, driving actors to a location upstate where they were shooting a commercial for some new product that was supposed to clean mildew off boats and beach umbrellas. It was a long boring day but I got forty-five dollars at the end of it. I went to Chinatown after I dumped the van and had Three-Kinds Lo Mein and jasmine tea in a restaurant. I bought a case of noodles and some duck sauce to eat for the next two weeks and put the rest of the cash in the night depository, so I could rent a car to move my mattress to Brooklyn.

By the last week of October, I still didn't have a job or a check from Evans. I had eaten almost all the noodles already, and I was starting to look very hard at the money I had saved to rent the car. All this was making me nervous, and I went out to see Benson to make sure everything was still okay. Everything wasn't.

"I got some bad news for you," Benson said. I finally found him in the stairwell at the east end of the building. He was putting a new pane in the window on the landing. "We got a little problem."

"Tell me about it," I said. Benson put down his putty knife and turned around, propping his elbows on the windowsill.

"Lubin took a deposit from some people," he said. "On the apartment you going to live in."

"No, I don't want to hear it," I said. "Don't tell me. What happened?" Benson pushed himself off the windowsill and turned around facing the wall.

"He took it before I had the money from you," he said. "The people went up to him and handed him the money and I didn't know. I told him not to do this. I told him I was going to find the people for the apartments, and if it can't be that way then I'm leaving like before." Benson put his fingers on the wall.

"I tell him not to and he do it anyway," he said, "so me and Lubin, we had a fight. Because I don't want these people in here. It is people taking welfare, and I don't want them, because sooner or later I know I have some trouble with them. So you going to get the apartment."

"So what is the problem," I said. Benson turned back to the window.

"What it is," Benson said. "The man don't want to give these people back they money. And somebody got to give it to them."

"Lubin's got to give it to them," I said. "He's got one deposit. From me."

"Yes," Benson said. "I tell him that and he tell me I'm holding the apartment empty for a month and he could have rented it to the other people." Benson turned back toward me. "The man, when he get a hand on the money, he don't turn it loose."

"How much," I said.

"A hundred dollars," Benson said.

"I can't," I said. "I don't have a hundred dollars." Truer words were never spoken. I didn't have a hundred dollars. I didn't have fifty dollars. Benson leaned back into the light well, looking up the central shaft.

"Then I don't know what we going to do," he said.

"I know what I'm going to do," I said. "I'm going to talk to Lubin."

"You can talk to him," Benson said. "I don't think he going to change."

Lubin's office was on the fourth floor of another building on Broadway, near the el train tracks. The sign on the door said Marcus and Neumann Realty. The hallway was painted institutional green and there was a mezuzah attached to the door frame of the office. I knocked, and a man cracked the door open and peered out. He had on thick glasses, a yarmulke, and a black coat with white tassels peeping out from under it. His face was pale, milky, and childish.

"Mr. Lubin?" I said.

"Out," said the face behind the crack. The mouth was red and spoke as if it were full of something unpleasant. "Come back two-thirty." The door slammed. I waited in the hallway, smoking cigarettes and stubbing them out, with a degree of malicious pleasure, on the freshly painted walls. I was on the point of grinding the last one into the mezuzah when Lubin finally walked out of the elevator.

He was an older man with a long whitening beard. He wore a wide-brimmed hat down the hallway, and when he took it off there was, of course, a yarmulke underneath it. I sat down in front of his desk and told him my name and the number of the apartment, and waved my copy of the cashier's check under his nose. Lubin started leafing through some papers and I looked out the window. I could see a train coming down off the bridge and turning onto the el track. Every car was covered with graffiti and the train was as colorful as a king snake.

"Yes," Lubin said, reading from a computer print-out. "You pay your deposit. You pay your one month rent. So what is the problem?"

"The problem is that somebody wants some more money," I said. "According to what I hear, you rented this apartment to two different people."

Lubin looked up at the ceiling, where there were a couple of dead flies hanging in a spider web. The whole office was about half the size of a subway car. Lubin broke abruptly into a long loud tirade about apartments standing empty, people not paying rent, damage to buildings, losses of money.

"Look," I said. "I'm not interested in these things. You got my money anyway. I don't care what your problems are."

"I took the deposit," Lubin said. "But that doesn't mean I have to give you the apartment. I could give back the deposit."

"Sure," I said. "Give it back."

"Wait," Lubin said. "Wait. You want the apartment?"

"Sure I want the apartment," I said. "That's why I paid for it."

"Yes," Lubin said. "Wait and I will talk to Benson. I'm not sure I know what it is you're talking about. Come back again tomorrow."

I went out and walked around the block, thinking it over. It seemed fairly certain that someone was trying to clip me, but I wasn't quite sure who it was. I also couldn't decide whether it was worth fighting it or not. If I could come up with the hundred dollars it would save me trouble and headaches. Evans owed me two hundred, which would be free money if only I could get it. I came back around the corner onto Broadway and went to the wall phone in the dairy restaurant. I slung the receiver over my shoulder and started unloading pieces of paper out of my wallet, looking for Evans's number. A tape came on the line and started telling me, "Please hang up, there appears to be a receiver off the hook, please hang up . . . " etcetera, etcetera, before I found the right scrap. Since it was a call to Jersey it cost me forty cents. But Evans answered on the third ring.

I mentioned my name and Evans burst into a coughing fit, which sounded genuine, and bad. When it was over I said,

"Look, Mr. Evans, I've been waiting to get that deposit back, and I was just wondering if it might have been lost in the mail."

"I didn't mail it," Evans said through the phlegm. A train came down on the tracks overhead and I lost the rest of what he was saying.

"What was that?" I said.

"I said what about the piano?" Evans said. "What about the refrigerator, and the broken furniture, and all the stuff on the stairs? The place is a wreck, I can't give you the deposit back. Not until the place is clean."

"Wait a second," I said. "None of that stuff is my stuff. Most of that stuff has been there for years. I never put it there. It was there when I took the place."

"I never put it there either," Evans said. "You're the tenant and you're responsible. Please understand, I can't return the deposit with the place in that condition." Even while ripping me off, Evans still had nice manners.

"I don't understand at all," I said. "I don't see what you're complaining about. Some of those things are worth money. I'm giving it to you all for nothing. You're the first landlord I ever heard complain about an extra refrigerator. That refrigerator *works*, Mr. Evans."

Mr. Evans coughed some more. "Well, the refrigerator," he said. "But what about the piano? I can't turn the place over to my buyer with things like that sitting around."

"Why not?" I said. "It's a nice piano. The guy can have his wife play him music at night." But I knew that was the wrong approach. "You could sell the piano," I said. "Make some extra cash on the whole deal."

"I'm not a junk man," Evans said. "I don't sell pianos. If it's worth anything, then you sell it. And all the rest has got to go too. I'm sorry, but that's my last word. Clean the apartment, you get your deposit. I wrote the check and it's sitting in my desk."

"Wait a second," I said. But the operator came on asking for more change and I didn't have any more change, so the connection was broken.

So I went on the street again and walked up and down, trying to think of a good idea. But as far as I could determine, I was in an airtight box. To make matters worse, it was raining in Brooklyn, right down the back of my neck. And if it was only a tiny bit colder, the rain would be sleet. And if something didn't give, I was going to be sitting out in the weather by the first of the month. I didn't have any illusions that Evans would let me coast into November. If I didn't move to Brooklyn, I would be moving into Grand Central Station. Therefore, I decided, something had to give. Since I didn't know which wall of the box was the weakest, I was going to bang on them all.

That let me in for a busy week. The same afternoon I invested about half of the remains of my petty cash in subway tokens, which I stored in the lining of my coat. When I got back to Hoboken I started calling Evans on the telephone. I was very polite to him, but I called him back every hour, from six until midnight. By the third call Evans was beginning to sound annoyed, which pleased me greatly — I wanted to make a nuisance of myself. At midnight he took his phone off the hook and I went to bed and lay there hoping that he would lose a lot of sleep listening to the telephone company pleading with him to put his receiver back on his phone, and in the morning I got up and rode out to Brooklyn, picking up the latest *Voice* when I changed trains, so that while I was taking a break from trying to drive Benson and Lubin out of their respective minds, which was how I planned to spend the rest of the week, I could keep looking for a job.

I decided to hit Benson first, since I knew Lubin wouldn't be in till two-thirty and I didn't feel like talking to the mush-mouthed mole that shared his office, so I walked down to 185 Broadway and let myself into the building and rang Benson's bell. His wife came to the door, gave me a bright smile full of gold teeth, and said, "Super no here," her only English phrase. She shut the door and I sat down on the stairs across the hall to wait for Benson and mark ads in the newspaper. I was down to the restaurant and security jobs. Free-lancing couldn't save me now; I was going to have to do straight time, forty hours a week and the check on Friday. In an hour Benson still hadn't come back and I had circled many ads, so I walked up to the dairy restaurant and got on the telephone, trying to find a place that would hire me immediately or at least before the end of the week. I called the security places first on the theory that that kind of job might be somewhat less dismal than a job in a restaurant. One place, a retail store in Manhattan, said they would take me at once if I fit their bill, so I made an appointment with the manager for the following day. None of the uniformed guard suppliers could promise me anything before the end of November, by which time I would already be dead, but I made appointments with them too, for the next week, and wrote them all down in my date book so as not to forget. Then I called Evans once for luck, getting nowhere again, and went back down Broadway to look for Benson.

I rang his bell and his wife came to the door and turned around and called into the apartment, "Lo Americano, Americano." Benson came out in the hall and we had a conversation in which I learned that the hypothetical other people were named Martinez and they would not take less than a hundred dollars and they would not take it on the instalment plan and it would be no use for me to go see them myself since none of them spoke English. While we were standing in the hall about a dozen people came up to talk to Benson about things that weren't working, until Benson finally turned his palms up in the air at me and ran off to fix a few things. I went back up to Lubin's office and had a replay of my previous day's meeting with him and then I went back to 185 Broadway and followed Benson around some more and then I went back to Hoboken and called Evans every hour and listened to him cough and choke over the phone until it was bedtime.

The next day I got up and put on my clean shirt and my tie and my jacket with the barely noticeable hole in the left elbow and went to keep my appointment at the store, which turned out to be a sort of budget boutique in the East Village. I went in a donut shop across the street and sat in front of one cup of coffee for around forty minutes, to be sure I arrived at exactly the right time, and then I went over and talked to the floor manager. I filled out the standard application and discussed the duties of the job with the manager and told him all about how I loved the store and the job and the manager himself and how eager I was to get the job and start working right away, with overtime if possible. I must have made the right impression, because the manager, who was actually a little twit, said that he wanted to take me, only first I had to take a polygraph test, because that was routine for all employees. So he called up a snoop shop in midtown and made an appointment between me and the machine for Friday; he couldn't get it any sooner.

So I wrote the appointment in my date book like a good little businessman, and I got out of there. I went around the corner and stepped into a doorway and changed my clothes out of the shoulder bag I was carrying, so I wouldn't look like I was worth mugging when I went out to Brooklyn, which was what I planned to do next. Then I went to Brooklyn and rang Benson's bell and his wife came and said, "Super no here," and I hung around in the hallways till I caught him, and we talked more about the Martinez family, and I visited Lubin again and I went home and called Evans all night, and this went on for the rest of the week, and nothing gave an inch.

During this time I formed the idea that if I could somehow catch Benson and Lubin together I might be able to break them down. Or at least I could find out which one of them was trying to con me, which was something I wanted to know more and more, if only for the satisfaction of knowing. But of course Lubin wouldn't come down to the building, and Benson wouldn't go up to the office. Patience was the obvious answer, but I had too little time to waste it on patience. But I still hadn't got them together when Friday came and I had to go keep my appointment at O.Q.R. Security Systems.

O.Q.R. was a typical operation of its kind. They ran uniformed guards out the front door and private eyes out the back and somewhere in the middle they had a polygraph machine to keep tabs on both ends of the business. I walked into their waiting room and talked to the receptionist through a hole in the wall the size of a matchbox. She pushed a twenty-page questionnaire through the hole at me and told me to sit down and fill it out and wait. I took the form to a chair and looked it over, and it was asking a lot of questions I really couldn't afford to answer. I hadn't expected anything like it. I had expected to be asked about drug addiction and felony convictions, two problems I happened not to have, and here were all these questions about problems that I did have. But I was up there already so I decided to try it. I filled out the form with what I wished was the truth and waited for them to call me. I sat there hoping that polygraph tests really are as unreliable as statistics say they are.

Then the examiner came for me. He was a young man on the make and he was wearing a Qiana shirt, open wide enough to show his gold chains, and he had a cute little pistol clipped to the back of his belt, right under the small of his back. We went in the examination room and we shook hands and he showed me the machine and asked me a lot of irrelevant questions that were supposed to help me relax, and then he had to go take a phone call, so I got a chance to look around the room. It looked like the inside of a refrigerator. There weren't any windows, but there was a big mirror. I went to the mirror and cupped my hands around my eyes so I could see into the little closet behind it, but no one was there. I sat back down.

The examiner came back and started plugging me into the apparatus. He put an air-pressure sleeve on my arm to read my heart rate, and clips on my fingers for my galvanic skin response, and two tubes around my chest for my breathing. Then he warned me not to move. If I moved the machine would get upset, he told me. He went back to the control panel and flipped some switches and four needles began to trace all my thoughts and feelings onto a large rotating spool of paper. I was then asked a lot of questions. I answered some of them truthfully and lied my face off on others. It all took about twenty minutes. When it was over the examiner got me untangled from the equipment and I stood up and asked him how I did. He apologized and said that professional ethics forbade him to tell me that, but he wished me the best. So I wished him the best, and we smiled and shook hands some more, and I went out of the office and got into the elevator.

Back in the street it was beginning to get dark. Everyone was getting off work, and I walked into a crowd and let it carry me all around the midtown area. Eventually the crowd spat me out in Herald Square, which is a concrete triangle where Broadway meets Sixth Avenue. There are benches there and winos and drug dealers and a big subway nexus and Macy's is right across the street. I sat down on a bench next to a guy who was passed out. His coat had fallen open and he didn't have anything on underneath it. I decided he was dead and moved to another bench. It should have been dusk, but twilight doesn't happen in midtown Manhattan; all the city lights go on and push the lingering daylight up into the stratosphere or down below 14th Street. At one end of the square there was a statue of Horace Greeley. At the other end there was a clock. It was twenty to six. They had told me at the store that I could call after six and find out if I got the job or not, but I was already sure I had flunked the polygraph test. I decided I was dead. But even a snake will keep on squirming after it's been cut in half. I picked up a scrap of newspaper to read while I waited for after six to come. It was a Spanish paper and after I had looked at it for a few minutes I realized it was some sort of Dear Abby column. I could make out verbs and prepositions but not the nouns, so I wasn't quite sure what the Spanish people's problems were, or how they were going to get solved. But because the column was impossible to understand it kept me amused for a nice long time.

Then it was after six and I got up and started looking for a good pay phone. Herald Square was littered with them, but I didn't want to call the store from the street, because then they would know I was on the street. I walked down Sixth Avenue, looking into coffee shops, but none of them had phones for some reason, so I went into a bar. It was quiet enough and I made the call and the girl who answered the phone told me that I had the job. Nothing about the polygraph test, just that I had the job and I should show up on Monday. I hung up the phone. There were only a couple of people in the bar, watching television. My heart was breaking for a drink, but luckily I had nothing in my pockets but tokens and a few dimes. I went to Brooklyn.

This time I didn't even ring Benson's bell. I just sat down on the steps opposite his door, with my chin in my hands and my elbows on my knees. I wasn't sure if I wanted to see Benson or not and I thought I would let luck decide. Some time went by and luck sent Benson in through the double front doors.

"How you doing good?" Benson said. He was an optimist, in his own way.

"Got a job," I said. Benson gave me congratulations. I asked him why he had a suit on, and he said he was coming from church.

"I got a job," I said, after we had had some conversation. "I start it Monday. I'm not sure I'm going to have time to be a Ping-Pong ball for you and Lubin anymore."

"Well," said Benson. "You going to kick it out?"

"Maybe," I said. "Who do I give it to? Lubin?"

"Don't give it to Lubin," Benson said. "Lubin keep it if you do. It got to go to the people."

"The people," I said.

"Martinez," Benson said.

"How do I give money to these people," I said. "I never even saw them."

"Bring it to me," Benson said. "I get it to them."

I looked at Benson. I was sitting on the first landing and Benson was standing on the hall floor and he looked very small down there. He stared back at me for something like a minute. Then he turned aside and looked out through the double glass doors. Benson smiled as though he had recognized someone, and I craned my head to see who it was, but the street was empty.

"One time," Benson said to the glass doors, "I lie to someone. To a man. A long time ago." Then he was silent for another minute. I looked at the street and noticed that it was raining again. The pavement was black and glossy with the rain.

"I never told him," I heard Benson say. "Not for a long time. And the lie came back at me. All the time, it coming back at me. Because if you lie, you have to live with it all by yourself, with your lie. And I don't like to live all by myself."

The pavement was so wet that I could see a traffic light reflecting in it. First it was red and then it was green. The colors swirled in the water.

"So then I went to the man," Benson said. "To tell him. And he laughed at me, because by then it was years, and he said, 'All this time passing, and you coming here now to tell me this?' He don't know why, but I had to tell him. So I don't have it with me no more."

A car came down the street and broke up the reflected light and water splashed on the outer door.

"I had to tell him," Benson said. I had the feeling he didn't know I was there anymore, so I lit a cigarette and kept quiet until I finished it.

"I'll bring the money," I said. "By Sunday, if I can."

"Good," Benson said. "You find me here on Sunday." I went out through the doors and walked up to the train, hugging the buildings so I wouldn't get too wet. I had decided, now. I didn't really believe in the Martinez family but now I thought that maybe I could believe in Benson. That would make it Lubin's play somehow, but I didn't even want to think about it; I was tired of thinking about it and of not trusting anyone. I went home and by Sunday there I was with my hundred bucks and a rented van containing my mattress and etceteras. I bought the key from Benson and moved my stuff into my apartment. Benson had patched the walls and painted and the place was clean and white. I pushed my mattress up against the radiator and lay down on it and let the steam heat sing me to sleep.

Then on Monday I started the job, and I couldn't get off on a weekday till the following week, so I couldn't get up to Lubin's office to sign my lease. The delay didn't bother me much. Now that I was in the place no piece of paper was going to get me out. But I did want to see Lubin again to nag him about the hundred dollars, so I went up there the first chance I got. From my new position of security, I was considering holding back a piece of the next month's rent.

So I went up to the office and there was no new trouble. Lubin and I each signed a few copies of the lease and I folded one up and put it in my coat pocket.

"So," Lubin said. "You like the apartment?" His English was thick and heavily accented. It was probably his third language, after Hebrew and Yiddish, and doubtless the least important to him. The Hasidim just don't believe that anybody else is really there.

"Too expensive," I said.

"So?" Lubin said. "You take it, you leave it." He smiled in his beard. "You took it."

"Not the rent," I said. "The kickback. A hundred dollars, that's expensive."

"What?" Lubin said. He sat up and looked very surprised. "Benson took a hundred dollars?" I looked at him. There was no doubting it. I had never seen Lubin look so sincere. Probably it was because he hadn't got a cut.

"It's too much," Lubin said. "Twenty dollars, thirty dollars, yes, but this is too much. I will speak with Benson."

I looked out the window. For just a minute I felt very upset. It was so simple to give the lie to Lubin, and now I couldn't do that. I had lost track of the lie now, and I might never find it again. Out beyond the window I could see the bright ribbon of train tracks curling away over the bridge, gleaming in the afternoon sun. So maybe the lie was out there too, I thought, even if I couldn't see it. It was just there, floating around with the other particles of the atmosphere, and everybody got a little piece of it, and it didn't belong to anyone. And that was fair for everybody, even for me. Because after all the hundred dollars didn't come from nowhere.

"Don't say anything to Benson," I told Lubin. "It's over now anyway. And I have to live with him."

I left Lubin's office and walked around my new neighborhood, looking into groceries and liquor stores and views and other matters of interest. And I thought a little bit about the hundred dollars, which, finally, I had squeezed out of Evans. I spent the whole Saturday before I started the job cleaning out the old apartment. I got rid of almost a truckload of junk and got a ticket for littering the street, which was a very funny thing to get a ticket for in Hoboken. Then in the evening I lured Evans out to the place to look at everything I had done. He was gratified, but he was still complaining about the piano and the refrigerator and all the broken furniture I hadn't been able to move.

So then I went into high gear. I gave Evans a recital of my sad situation, and I made a real tear-jerker out of it. It was very poetic and would have brought blood from a stone. It began with when I last ate and ended with when I expected to eat again, and there was a great deal of material in the middle. When it was over, Evans removed his glasses and wiped them and told me that he too knew what suffering was, because he had just found out he had cancer, and he was going into the hospital the following week and he didn't know if he would ever come back out. So then we commiserated with each other and Evans wrote me a new check, for the whole two hundred dollars. He gave it to me in exchange for my faithful promise that I would find some salvage company to remove all the stuff, but of course I never did anything of the kind.

I deposited Evans's check and held my breath till it cleared the bank. By that time it was no longer safe for me to go to Hoboken. I had been defaulting on my utility bills for quite some time, and I was afraid they were going to get me. The electric bill hadn't been paid for about a year before I even moved into the place, and I knew Evans would weep for real when he found out about that, as he was sure to eventually, when the building finally changed hands. But the most immediate problem was that I owed a big fine for littering. It was time to disappear, obviously, and that is just what I did.

I never went back to Hoboken, not even to drop off my key, and so I never knew if Evans lived or died. I still have the key, as a matter of fact, and sometimes I think about Evans, with his wet glasses and his nice professorial manners and his ruined buildings and his incurable cough. He wasn't a bad person, in his own way, and at least he didn't stop the check. Or maybe he died and didn't have a chance to stop it. I don't know, but sometimes I do wonder if he lived long enough to go back to the apartment and find out that I conned him. I'm sure he's dead by now either way, since you don't live too long without your lungs, so it really doesn't matter at all. But sometimes I still catch myself wondering.

ALICE MUNRO

Circle of Prayer

FROM THE PARIS REVIEW

TRUDY THREW A JUG across the room. It didn't reach the opposite wall, it didn't hurt anybody, it didn't even break.

This was the jug without a handle, cement-colored, with brown streaks in it, rough as sandpaper to the touch, that Dan made the winter he took pottery classes. He made six little handleless cups to go with it. The jug and the cups were supposed to be for sake, but the local liquor store doesn't carry sake. Once they brought some home from a trip, but they didn't really like it. So the jug Dan made sits on the highest open shelf in the kitchen, and a few odd items of value are kept in it. Trudy's wedding ring and her engagement ring, the medal Robin won for all-round excellence in grade eight, a long two-strand necklace of jet beads that belonged to Dan's mother, and was willed to Robin. Trudy won't let her wear it yet.

Trudy came home from work a little after midnight, she entered the house in the dark. Just the little stove light was on — she and Robin always left that on for each other. Trudy didn't need any other light. She climbed up on a chair without even letting go of her bag and got down the jug, fished around inside it.

It was gone. Of course. She had known it would be gone.

She went through the dark house to Robin's room, still with her bag over her arm, the jug in her hand. She turned on the overhead light. Robin groaned and turned over, pulled the pillow over her head. Shamming.

"Your grandmother's necklace," Trudy said. "Why did you do that? Are you insane?"

Robin shammed a sleepy groan. All the clothes she owned, it seemed, old and new and clean and dirty, were scattered on the floor, on the chair, the desk, the dresser, even on the bed itself. On the wall was a huge poster showing a hippopotamus, with the words underneath "Why Was I Born So Beautiful?" and another poster showing Terry Fox running along a rainy highway, with a whole cavalcade of cars behind him. Dirty glasses, empty yogurt containers, school notes, a Tampax still in its wrapper, the stuffed snake and tiger Robin had had since before she went to school, a collage of pictures of her cat Sausage, who had been run over two years ago. Red and blue ribbons that she had won for jumping, or running, or throwing basketballs.

"You answer me!" said Trudy. "You tell me why you did it!"

She threw the jug. But it was heavier than she'd thought, or else at the very moment of throwing it she lost conviction, because it didn't hit the wall, it fell on the rug beside the dresser, it rolled on the floor, undamaged.

You threw a jug at me that time. You could have killed me.

Not at you. I didn't throw it at you.

You could have killed me.

Proof that Robin was shamming:

She started up in a fright, but it wasn't the blank fright of somebody who'd been asleep. She looked scared, but underneath that childish scared look was another look — stubborn, calculating, disdainful.

"It was so beautiful. And it was valuable. It belonged to your grandmother."

"I thought it belonged to me," said Robin.

"That girl wasn't even your friend. Christ, you didn't have a good word to say for her, this morning."

"You don't know who is my friend!" Robin's face flushed a bright pink and her eyes filled with tears, but her scornful, stubborn expression didn't change. "I knew her. I talked to her. So get out!"

Trudy works at the Home for Mentally Handicapped Adults. Few people call it that. Older people in town still say "the Misses

Weir's house," and a number of others, including Robin, and presumably most of those her age, call it "the Half-wit House."

The house has a ramp now, for wheelchairs, because some of the mentally handicapped may be physically handicapped as well, and it has a swimming pool in the backyard, which caused a certain amount of discussion when it was installed at taxpayers' expense. Otherwise the house looks pretty much the way it always did — the white wooden walls, the dark-green curlicues on the gables, the steep roof and dark, screened side porch, and the deep lawn in front shaded by soft maple trees.

This month Trudy works the four to midnight shift. Yesterday afternoon she parked her car in front and walked up the drive thinking how nice the house looked, peaceful, as in the days of the Misses Weir, who must have served iced tea and read library books, or played croquet, whatever people did then.

Always some piece of news, some wrangle or excitement, once you get inside.

The men came to fix the pool but they didn't fix it, they went away again. It isn't fixed yet.

"We don't get no use of it, soon summer be over," Josephine said.

"It's not even the middle of June, you're saying summer'll be over," Kelvin said. "You think before you talk. Did you hear about the young girl that was killed, out in the country?" he said to Trudy.

Trudy had started to mix two batches of frozen lemonade, one pink and one plain. When he said that, she smashed the spoon down on the frozen chunk so hard that some of the liquid spilled over.

"How, Kelvin?"

She was afraid she would hear that a girl was dragged off a country road, raped in the woods, strangled, beaten, left there. Robin goes running along the country roads, in her white shorts and T-shirt, a headband on her flying hair. Robin's hair is golden, her legs and arms are golden. Her cheeks and limbs are downy, not shiny — you wouldn't be surprised to see a cloud of pollen delicately floating and settling behind her when she runs. Cars hoot at her and she isn't bothered. Foul threats are yelled at her, and she yells foul threats back.

"Driving a truck," Kelvin said.

Trudy's heart eased. Robin didn't know how to drive yet.

"Fourteen years old, she didn't know how to drive," Kelvin said. "She got in the truck and the first thing you know, she ran it into a tree. Where was her parents, that's what I'd like to know? They weren't watching out for her. She got in the truck when she didn't know how to drive and ran it into a tree. Fourteen. That's too young."

Kelvin goes uptown by himself, he hears all the news. He is fifty-two years old, still slim and boyish looking, well shaved, with soft, short, clean dark hair. He goes to the barbershop every day, because he can't quite manage to shave himself. Epilepsy, then surgery, an infected bone flap, many more operations, a permanent mild difficulty with feet and fingers, a gentle head fog. The fog doesn't obscure facts, just motives. Perhaps he shouldn't be in the Home at all, but where else? Anyway, he likes it. He says he likes it. He tells the others they shouldn't complain, they should be more grateful, they should behave themselves. He picks up the soft-drink cans, or beer bottles, that people have thrown into the front yard — though of course it isn't his job to do that.

When Janet came in just before midnight to relieve Trudy, she had the same story to tell.

"I guess you heard about that fifteen-year-old girl?"

When Janet starts telling you something like this, she always starts off with "I guess you heard." *I guess you heard Wilma and Ted are breaking up,* she says. *I guess you heard Alvin Stead had a heart attack.*

"Kelvin told me," Trudy said. "Only he said she was fourteen."

"Fifteen," Janet said. "She must've been in Robin's class at school. She didn't know how to drive. She didn't even get out of the lane."

"Was she drunk?" said Trudy. Robin won't go near alcohol, or dope, or cigarettes, or even coffee, she's so fanatical about what she puts into her body.

"I don't think so. Stoned, maybe. It was early in the evening. She was at home with her sister, their parents were out. Her sister's boyfriend came over, it was his truck, and he either gave her the keys to the truck or she took them. You hear different versions. You hear that they sent her out for something, they wanted to get rid of her, and you hear she just took the keys and went. Anyway she ran it right into a tree, in the lane."

"Jesus," said Trudy.

"I know. It's so idiotic. It's getting so you hate to think about your kids growing up. Did they all take their medication okay? What's Kelvin watching?"

Kelvin was still up, sitting in the living room watching TV.

"It's somebody being interviewed. He wrote a book about schizophrenics."

Anything he comes across about mental problems, Kelvin has to watch, or try to read.

"I think it depresses him, the more he watches that kind of thing. Do you know I found out today I have to make five hundred roses out of pink Kleenex, for my niece Laurel's wedding? For the car. She said, you promised you'd make the roses for the car. Well I didn't. I don't remember promising a thing. Are you going to come over and help me?"

"Sure," said Trudy.

"I guess the real reason I want him to get off the schizophrenics is I want to watch the old *Dallas*," Janet said. She and Trudy disagree about this. Trudy can't stand to watch those old reruns of *Dallas*, to see the characters with their younger, plumper, faces going through tribulations and bound up in romantic complications they and the audience have now forgotten all about. That's what's so hilarious, Janet says, it's so unbelievable it's wonderful. All that happens and they just forget about it and go on. But to Trudy it doesn't seem so unbelievable that the characters would go from one thing to the next thing — forgetful, hopeful, photogenic, forever changing their clothes. That it's not so unbelievable is what she really can't stand.

Robin, the next morning, said, "Oh, probably. All those people she hung around with drink. They party all the time. They're self-destructive. It's her own fault. Even if her sister told her to go she didn't have to go. She didn't have to be so stupid."

"What was her name?" Trudy said.

"Tracy Lee," said Robin with distaste. She stepped on the

pedal of the garbage pail, lifted rather than lowered the container of yogurt she had just emptied, and dropped it in. She was wearing bikini underpants and a T-shirt that said, "If I Want to Listen to an Asshole, I'll Fart."

"That shirt still bothers me," Trudy said. "Some things are disgusting but funny, and some things are more disgusting than funny."

"What's the problem?" said Robin. "I sleep alone."

Trudy sat outside in her wrapper, drinking coffee while the day got hot. There is a little brick-paved space by the side door that she and Dan always called the patio. She sat there. This is a solar-heated house, with big panels of glass in the south-sloping roof, the oddest-looking house in town. It's odd inside, too, with the open shelves in the kitchen, instead of cupboards, and the living room up some stairs, looking out over the fields at the back. She and Dan, for a joke, gave parts of it the most conventional, suburban-sounding names — the patio, the powder room, the master bedroom. Dan always had to joke about the way he was living. He built the house himself — Trudy did a lot of the painting, and staining — and it was a success. Rain didn't leak in around the panels, and part of the house's heat really did come from the sun. Most people who have the ideas, or ideals, that Dan has aren't very practical. They can't fix things, or make things, they don't understand wiring, or carpentry, or whatever it is they need to understand. Dan is good at everything — at gardening, cutting wood, building a house. He is especially good at repairing motors. He used to travel around, getting jobs as an auto mechanic, a small engines repairman. That's how he ended up here. He came here to visit Marlene, got a job as a mechanic, became a working partner in an auto repair business, and before he knew it — married to Trudy, not Marlene — he was a small-town businessman, a member of the Kinsmen. All without shaving off his sixties beard or trimming his hair any more than he wanted to. The town was too small. Dan was too smart, for that to be necessary.

Now Dan lives in a townhouse in Richmond Hill, with a girl named Genevieve. She is studying law. She was married when she was very young, and had three little children. Dan met her

three years ago, when her camper broke down a few miles outside of town. He told Trudy about her that night. The rented
camper, the three little children, hardly more than babies, the
lively little divorced mother with her hair in pigtails. Her brav-
ery, her poverty, her plans to enter law school. If the camper
hadn't been easily fixed, he was going to invite her and her
children to spend the night. She was on her way to her parents'
summer place at Pointe au Baril.

"Then she can't be all that poor," Trudy said.

"You can be poor and have rich parents," Dan said.

"No you can't."

Last summer, Robin went to Richmond Hill for a month's
visit. She came home early. She said it was a madhouse. The
oldest child has to go to a special reading clinic, the middle one
wets the bed. Genevieve spends all her time in the law library,
studying. No wonder. Dan shops for bargains, cooks, looks after
the children, grows vegetables, drives a taxi on Saturdays and
Sundays. He wants to set up a motorcycle repair business in the
garage, but he can't get a permit, the neighbors are against it.

He told Robin he was happy. Never happier, he said. Robin
came home firmly grown-up — severe, sarcastic, determined.
She had some slight, steady grudge she hadn't had before.
Trudy couldn't worm it out of her, couldn't tease it out of her
— the time when she could do that was over.

Robin came home at noon and changed her clothes. She put
on a light, flowered cotton blouse and ironed a pale blue cotton
skirt.

She said that some of the girls from the class might be going
around to the Funeral Home after school.

"I forgot you had that skirt," said Trudy.

If she thought that was going to start a conversation, she was
mistaken.

The first time Trudy met Dan, she was drunk. She was nineteen
years old, tall and skinny — as she still is — with a wild head of
curly black hair (it is cropped short now and showing the gray
as black hair does). She was very tanned, wearing jeans and a
tie-dyed T-shirt. No brassiere and no need. This was in Muskoka, in August, in a hotel bar where they had a band. She was

camping with girlfriends. He was there with his fiancée, Marlene. He had taken Marlene home to meet his mother, who lived in Muskoka on an island in an empty hotel. When Trudy was nineteen, he was twenty-eight. She danced around by herself, giddy and drunk, in front of the table where he sat with Marlene, a meek-looking blonde with a big pink shelf of bosom all embroidered in little fake pearls. Trudy just danced in front of him until he got up and joined her. At the end of the dance he asked her name, and took her back and introduced her to Marlene.

"This is Judy," he said. Trudy collapsed, laughing, into the chair beside Marlene's. Dan took Marlene up to dance. Trudy finished off Marlene's beer and went looking for her friends.

"How do you do?" she said to them. "I'm Judy!"

He caught up with her at the door of the bar. He had ditched Marlene when he saw Trudy leaving. A man who could change course quickly, see the possibilities, flare up with new enthusiasm. He told people later that he was in love with Trudy before he even knew her real name. But he told Trudy that he cried when he and Marlene were parting.

"I have feelings," he said. "I'm not ashamed to show them."

Trudy had no feelings for Marlene at all. Marlene was over thirty, what could she expect? Marlene still lives in town, works at the hydro office, is not married. When Trudy and Dan were having one of their conversations about Genevieve, Trudy said, "Marlene must be thinking I got what's coming to me."

Dan said he had heard that Marlene had joined the Fellowship of Bible Christians. The women weren't allowed makeup and had to wear a kind of bonnet to church on Sundays.

"She won't be able to have a thought in her head but forgiving."

Trudy said, "I bet."

This is what happened at the Funeral Home, as Trudy got the story from both Kelvin and Janet:

The girls from Tracy Lee's class all showed up together after school. This was during what was called the visitation, when the family waited beside Tracy Lee's open casket to receive friends. Her parents were there, her married brother and his wife, her sister, and even her sister's boyfriend, who owned the truck. They stood in a row and people lined up to say a few words to them. A lot of people came. They always do, in a case like this. Tracy Lee's grandmother was at the end of the row, in a brocade-covered chair. She wasn't able to stand up for very long.

All the chairs at the Funeral Home are upholstered in this white and gold brocade. The curtains are the same, the wallpaper almost matches. There are little wall-bracket lights behind heavy pink glass. Trudy has been there several times, she knows what it's like. But Robin, and most of these girls, had never been inside the place before. They didn't know what to expect. Some of them began to cry as soon as they got inside the door.

The curtains were closed. Soft music was playing, not exactly church music but it sounded like it. Tracy Lee's coffin was white with a gold trim, matching all the brocade and the wallpaper. It had a lining of pleated pink satin. A pink satin pillow. Tracy Lee had not a mark on her face. She was not made up quite as usual, because the undertaker had done it. But she was wearing her favorite earrings, turquoise-colored triangles and yellow crescents, two to each ear. (Some people thought that was in bad taste.) On the part of the coffin that covered her from the waist down there was a big heart-shaped pillow of pink roses.

The girls lined up to speak to the family. They shook hands, they said sorry-for-your-loss, just the way everybody else did. When they got through that, when all of them had let the grandmother squash their cool hands between her warm, swollen, freckled ones, they lined up again, in a straggling sort of way, and began to go past the coffin. Many were crying now, shivering. What could you expect? Young girls.

But they began to sing as they went past. With difficulty at first, shyly, but with growing confidence in their sad, sweet voices, they sang.

> "Now, while the blossom still clings to the vine,
> I'll taste your strawberries, I'll drink your sweet wine —"

They had planned the whole thing, of course, beforehand, they had got that song off a record. They believed that it was an old hymn.

So they filed past, singing, looking down at Tracy Lee, and it was noticed that they were dropping things into the coffin. They were slipping the rings off their fingers and the bracelets from their arms, and taking the earrings out of their ears. They were undoing necklaces and bowing to pull chains and long strands of beads over their heads. Everybody gave something. All this jewelry went flashing and sparkling down on the dead girl, to lie beside her in her coffin. One girl pulled the bright combs out of her hair, let those go.

And nobody made a move to stop this. How could anyone interrupt? It was like a religious ceremony. The girls behaved as if they'd been told what to do, as if this was what was always done on such occasions. They sang, they wept, they dropped their jewelry. The sense of ritual made every one of them graceful.

The family wouldn't stop it. They thought it was beautiful.

"It was like church," Tracy Lee's mother said, and her grandmother said, "All those lovely young girls loved Tracy Lee. If they wanted to give their jewelry to show how they loved her, that's their business. It's not anybody else's business. I thought it was beautiful."

Tracy Lee's sister broke down and cried. It was the first time she had done so.

Dan said, "This is a test of love."

Of Trudy's love, he meant. Trudy started singing.

"Please release me, let me go —"

She clapped a hand to her chest, danced in swoops around the room, singing. Dan was near laughing, near crying. He couldn't help it, he came and hugged her and they danced together, staggering. They were fairly drunk. All that June (it was two years ago) they were drinking gin, in between and during their scenes. They were drinking, weeping, arguing, explaining, and Trudy had to keep running to the liquor store. Yet she can't remember ever feeling really drunk or having a hangover. Except that she felt so tired all the time, as if she had logs chained to her ankles.

She kept joking. She called Genevieve "Jenny the Feeb."

"This is just like wanting to give up the business and become a potter," she said. "Maybe you should have done that. I wasn't really against it. You gave up on it. And when you wanted to go to Peru. We could still do that."

"All those things were just straws in the wind," Dan said.

"I should have known when you started watching *The Ombudsman* on TV," Trudy said. "It was the legal angle, wasn't it? You were never so interested in that kind of thing before."

"This will open life up for you too," Dan said. "You can be more than just my wife."

"Sure. I think I'll be a brain surgeon."

"You're very smart. You're a wonderful woman. You're brave."

"Sure you're not talking about Jenny the Feeb?"

"No, you. You, Trudy. I still love you. You can't understand that I still love you."

Not for years had he had so much to say about how he loved her. He loved her skinny bones, her curly hair, her roughening skin, her way of coming into a room with a stride that shook the windows, her jokes, her clowning, her tough talk. He loved her mind and her soul. He always would. But the part of his life that had been bound up with hers was over.

"That is just talk, that is talking like an idiot!" Trudy said. "Robin, go back to bed!" For Robin in her skimpy nightgown was standing at the top of the steps.

"I can hear you yelling and screaming," Robin said.

"We weren't yelling and screaming," Trudy said. "We're trying to talk about something private."

"What?"

"I told you, it's something private."

When Robin sulked off to bed, Dan said, "I think we should tell her. It's better for kids to know. Genevieve doesn't have any secrets from her kids. Josie's only five, and she came into the bedroom one afternoon —"

Then Trudy did start yelling and screaming. She clawed through a cushion cover. "You stop telling me about your sweet fucking Genevieve and her sweet fucking bedroom and her asshole kids, you shut up, don't tell me any more! You're just a big dribbling mouth without any brains, I don't care what you do, just shut up!"

*

Dan left. He packed a suitcase, he went off to Richmond Hill. He was back in five days. Just outside of town he had stopped the car to pick Trudy a bouquet of wild flowers.

He told her he was back for good, it was over.

"You don't say?" said Trudy.

But she put the flowers in water. Dusty pink milkweed flowers that smelled like face powder, black-eyed Susans, wild sweet peas, and orange lilies that must have got loose from old disappeared gardens.

"So, you couldn't stand the pace?" she said.

"I knew you wouldn't fall all over me," Dan said. "You wouldn't be you if you did. And what I came back to is you."

She went to the liquor store and this time bought champagne. For a month — it was still summer — they were back together being happy. She never really found out what had happened at Genevieve's house. Dan said he'd been having a middle-aged fit, that was all, he'd come to his senses. His life was here, with her and Robin.

"You're talking like a marriage-advice column," Trudy said.

"Okay. Forget the whole thing."

"We better," she said. She could imagine the kids, the confusion, the friends, old boyfriends maybe, that he hadn't been prepared for. Jokes and opinions that he couldn't understand. That was possible. The music he liked, the way he talked, even his hair and his beard might be out of style.

They went on family drives, picnics. They lay out in the grass behind the house at night, looking at the stars. The stars were a new interest of Dan's, he got a map. They hugged and kissed each other frequently and tried out some new things — or things they hadn't done for a long time — when they made love.

At this time the road in front of the house was being paved. They'd built their house on a hillside at the edge of town, past the other houses, but trucks were using this street quite a bit now, avoiding the main streets, so the town was paving it. Trudy got so used to the noise and constant vibration she said she could feel herself jiggling all night, even when everything was quiet. Work started at seven in the morning. They woke up at the bottom of a river of noise. Dan dragged himself out of bed then, losing the hour of sleep that he loved best. There was a smell of diesel fuel in the air.

She woke up one night to find him not in bed. She listened to hear noises in the kitchen or the bathroom, but she couldn't. She got up and walked through the house. There were no lights on. She found him sitting outside, just outside the door, not having a drink or a glass of milk or a coffee, sitting with his back to the street.

Trudy looked out at the torn-up earth and the huge stalled machinery.

"Isn't the quiet lovely?" she said.

He didn't say anything.

Oh. Oh.

She realized what she'd been thinking when she found his side of the bed empty and couldn't hear him anywhere in the house. Not that he'd left her, but that he'd done worse. Done away with himself. With all their happiness and hugging and kissing and stars and picnics, she could think that.

"You can't forget her," she said. "You love her."

"I don't know what to do."

She was glad just to hear him speak. She said, "You'll have to go and try again."

"There's no guarantee I can stay," he said. "I can't ask you to stand by."

"No," said Trudy. "If you go, that's it."

"If I go, that's it."

He seemed paralyzed. She felt that he might just sit there, repeating what she said, never be able to move or speak for himself again.

"If you feel like this, that's all there is to it," she said. "You don't have to choose. You're already gone."

That worked. He stood up stiffly, he came over and put his arms around her. He stroked her back.

"Come back to bed," he said. "We can rest for a little while yet."

"No. You've got to be gone when Robin wakes up. If we go back to bed it'll just start all over again."

She made him a thermos of coffee. He packed the bag he had taken with him before. All Trudy's movements seemed skillful and perfect, as they never were, usually. She felt serene. She felt as if they were an old couple, moving in harmony, in wordless love, past injury, past forgiving. Their goodbye was hardly a ripple. She went outside with him. It was between four-thirty and five o'clock, the sky was beginning to lighten and the birds to wake, everything was drenched in dew. There stood the big harmless machinery, stranded in the ruts of the road.

"Good thing it isn't last night, you couldn't have got out," she said. She meant that the road hadn't been navigable. It was just yesterday that they had graded a narrow track, for local traffic.

"Good thing," he said.

Goodbye.

"All I want is to know why you did it. Did you just do it for show? Like your father, for show. It's not the necklace so much. But it was a beautiful thing. I love jet beads, it was the only thing we had of your grandmother's. It was your right but you have no right to take me by surprise like that, I deserve an explanation, I always loved jet beads. Why?"

"I blame the family," Janet says. "It was up to them to stop it. Some of the stuff was just plastic, those junk earrings and bracelets, but what Robin threw in, that was a crime. And she wasn't the only one. There were birthstone rings and gold chains. Somebody said a diamond cluster ring, but I don't know if I believe that. They said the girl inherited it, like Robin. You didn't ever have it evaluated, did you?"

"I don't know if jet is worth anything," Trudy says.

They are sitting in Janet's front room, making roses out of pink Kleenex.

"It's just stupid," Trudy says.

"Well. There is one thing you could do," says Janet. "I don't hardly know how to mention it."

"What?"

"Pray."

Trudy had the feeling, from Janet's tone, that Janet was going to tell her something serious and unpleasant, something about herself — Trudy — that was affecting her life and that every-body knew except her. Now she wants to laugh, after bracing herself. She doesn't know what to say.

"You don't pray, do you?" Janet says.

"I haven't got anything against it," Trudy says. "I wasn't brought up to be religious."

"It's not strictly speaking religious," Janet says. "I mean, it's not connected with any church. This is just some of us that pray. I can't tell you the names of anybody in it but most of them you know. It's supposed to be secret. It's called the Circle of Prayer."

"Like at high school," Trudy says. "At high school there were secret societies, you weren't supposed to tell who was in them. Only I wasn't."

"I was in everything going." Janet sighs. "This is actually more on the serious side. Though some people in it don't take it seriously enough, I don't think. Some people, they'll pray that they'll find a parking spot, or they'll pray they get good weather for their holidays. That isn't what it's for. But that's just individual praying, what the Circle is really about is, you phone up somebody that is in it, and tell them what it is you're worried about, or upset about, and ask them to pray for you. And they do. And they phone one other person that's in the Circle, and they phone another and it goes all around, and we pray for one person, all together."

Trudy throws a rose away. "That's botched. Is it all women?"

"There isn't any rule it has to be. But it is, yes. Men would be too embarrassed. I was embarrassed at first. Only the first person you phone knows your name, who it is that's being prayed for, but in a town like this nearly everybody can guess. But if we started gossiping and ratting on each other it wouldn't work, and everybody knows that. So we don't. And it does work."

"Like, how?" Trudy says.

"Well, one girl banged up her car, she did eight hundred dollars damage, and it was kind of a tricky situation, where she wasn't sure her insurance would cover it, and neither was her husband, he was raging mad, but we all prayed, and the insurance came through without a hitch. That's only one example."

"There wouldn't be much point in praying to get the necklace back when it's in the coffin and the funeral's this morning," says Trudy mildly.

"It's not up to you to say that. You don't say what's possible or impossible. You just ask for what you want. Because it says in the Bible, ask and it shall be given. How can you be helped if you won't ask? You can't, that's for sure. What about when Dan left, what if you'd prayed then? I wasn't in the Circle then, or I could have said something to you. Even if I knew you'd resist it, I would have said something. A lot of people resist. Now even, it doesn't sound too great with that girl, how do you know, maybe even now it might work. It might not be too late."

"All right," says Trudy in a calm, slow voice. "All right." She pushes all the floppy flowers off her lap. "I'll just get down on my knees right now and pray that I get Dan back. I'll pray that I get the necklace back and I get Dan back and why do I have to stop there? I can pray that Tracy Lee never died. I can pray that she comes back to life. Why didn't her mother ever think of that?"

Good news. The swimming pool is fixed. They'll be able to fill it tomorrow. But Kelvin is depressed. Early this afternoon — partly to keep them from bothering the men who were working on the pool — he took Marie and Josephine uptown. He let them get ice cream cones. He told them to pay attention and eat the ice cream up quickly, because the sun was hot, and it would melt. They ignored him. They licked at their cones now and then, as if they had all day. Ice cream was soon dribbling down their chins and down their arms. Kelvin had grabbed a handful of paper napkins but he couldn't wipe it up fast enough. They were a mess. A spectacle. They didn't care. Kelvin told them they weren't so pretty that they could afford to look like that.

"Some people don't like the look of us anyway," he said. "Some people don't even think we should be allowed uptown. People just get used to seeing us and not staring at us like freaks and you make a mess and spoil it."

They laughed at him. He could have cowed Marie if he had her alone, but not when she was with Josephine. Josephine was one who needed some old-fashioned discipline, in Kelvin's opinion. Kelvin had been in places where people didn't get away with anything like they got away with here. He didn't agree with hitting. He had seen plenty of it done, but he didn't agree with it, even on the hand. But a person like Josephine could be shut up in her room, she could be made to sit in a corner, she could be put on bread and water, and it would do a lot of good. All Marie needed was a talking-to, she had a weak personality. But Josephine was a devil.

"I'll talk to both of them," Trudy says. "I'll tell them to say they're sorry."

"I want for them to *be* sorry," Kelvin says. "I don't care if they say they are. I'm not taking them ever again."

Later, when all the others are in bed, Trudy gets him to sit down to play cards with her on the screened verandah. They play crazy eights. Kelvin says that's all he can manage tonight, his head is sore.

Uptown, a man said to him, "Hey, which one of them two is your girlfriend?"

"Stupid," Trudy says. "He was a stupid jerk."

The man talking to the first man said, "Which one you going to marry?"

"They don't know you, Kelvin. They're just stupid."

But they did know him. One was Reg Hooper, one was Bud DeLisle. Bud DeLisle that sold real estate. They knew him, they had talked to him in the barbershop, they called him Kelvin. Hey, Kelvin, which one you going to marry?

"Nerds," says Trudy. "That's what Robin would say."

"You think they're your friend but they're not," says Kelvin. "How many times I see that happen."

Trudy goes to the kitchen to put on coffee. She wants to have fresh coffee to offer Janet when Janet comes in. She apologized this morning, and Janet said all right, I know you're upset. It really is all right. Sometimes, you think they're your friend, and they are.

She looks at all the mugs hanging on their hooks. She and Janet shopped all over to find them. A mug with each one's name. Marie, Josephine, Arthur, Kelvin, Shirley, George, Dorinda. You'd think Dorinda would be the hardest name to find, but actually, the hardest was Shirley. Even the people who can't read have learned to recognize their own mugs, by color and pattern.

One day two new mugs appeared, bought by Kelvin. They said Trudy and Janet.

"I'm not going to be too overjoyed seeing my name in that line-up," Janet said. "But I wouldn't hurt his feelings for a million dollars."

For a honeymoon, Dan took her to an island on the lake where the hotel was. The hotel was closed down, but his mother still lived there. Dan's father was dead. His mother lived there alone. She took the boat with the outboard motor across the water to get her groceries. She sometimes made a mistake and called Trudy Marlene.

The hotel wasn't much. It was a white wooden box in a clearing by the shore. Some little boxes of cabins stuck behind it. Dan and Trudy stayed in one of the cabins. Every cabin had a wood stove. Dan built a fire at night to take off the chill. But the blankets were damp and heavy when he and Trudy woke up in the morning.

Dan caught fish and cooked them. He and Trudy climbed the big rock behind the cabins and picked blueberries. He asked her if she knew how to make a pie crust, and she didn't. So he showed her, rolling out the dough with a whiskey bottle.

In the morning there was a mist over the lake, just as you see in the movies or in a painting.

One afternoon Dan stayed out longer than usual, fishing. Trudy kept busy for a while in the kitchen, rubbing the dust off things, washing some jars. It was the oldest, darkest kitchen she had ever seen, with wooden racks for the dinner plates to dry in. She went outside and climbed the rock by herself, thinking she would pick some blueberries. But it was already dark under the trees, the evergreens made it dark, and she didn't like the idea of wild animals. She sat on the rock looking down on the roof of the hotel, the old dead leaves and broken shingles. She heard a piano being played. She scrambled down the rock and followed the music, around to the front of the building. She walked along the front verandah and stopped at a window, looking into the room that used to be the lounge. The room with the blackened stone fireplace, the lumpy leather chairs, the horrible mounted fish.

Dan's mother was there, playing the piano. A tall, straight-backed old woman, with her gray-black hair twisted into such a tiny knot. She sat and played the piano, without any lights on, in the half-dark, half-bare room.

Dan had said that his mother came from a rich family. She had taken piano lessons, dancing lessons, she had gone around the world, when she was a young girl. There was a picture of her on a camel. But she wasn't playing a classical piece, the sort of thing you'd expect her to have learned. She was playing "It's Three O'Clock in the Morning." When she got to the end she started in again. Maybe it was a special favorite of hers, something she had danced to in the old days. Or maybe she wasn't satisfied yet that she had got it right.

Why does Trudy now remember this moment? She sees her young self looking in the window at the old woman playing the piano. The dim room, with its oversize beams and fireplaces and the lonely leather chairs. The clattering, faltering, persistent piano music. Trudy remembers that so clearly and it seems she stood outside her own body, which ached, then, from the punishing pleasures of love. She stood outside her own happiness, in a tide of sadness. And the opposite thing happened the morning Dan left. Then she stood outside her own unhappiness in a tide of what seemed unreasonably like love. But it was the same thing, really, when you got outside. What are those times that stand out, clear patches in your life — what do they have to do with it? They aren't exactly promises. Breathing spaces. Is that all?

She goes into the front hall and listens for any noise from upstairs.

All quiet there, all medicated.

The phone rings right beside her head.

"Are you still there?" Robin says.

"I'm still here."

"Can I run over and ride home with you? I didn't go for my run earlier because it was too hot."

You threw the jug. You could have killed me.

Yes.

*

Kelvin, waiting at the card table under the light, looks bleached and old. There's a pool of light whitening his brown hair. His face sags, waiting. He looks old, sunk into himself, wrapped in a thick bewilderment, nearly lost to her. Nearly lost.

"Kelvin, do you pray?" says Trudy. Her voice sounds harsh, even panicky, though she didn't mean it to. Also, she didn't know she was going to ask him that. "I mean, it's none of my business. But like, for anything specific?"

He's got an answer for her, which is rather surprising. He pulls his face up, as if he might have felt the tug he needed to bring him to the surface.

"If I was smart enough to know what to pray for," he says, "then I wouldn't have to."

He smiles at her with some oblique notion of conspiracy, offering his halfway joke. It's not meant as comfort, particularly. Yet it radiates — what he said, the way he said it, just the fact that he's there again, radiates, expands the way some silliness can when you're very tired. In this way, when she was young, and high, a person or a moment could become a lily floating on the cloudy river water, perfect and familiar.

Dreams of Distant Lives

FROM HARPER'S

THE OTHER VICTIM the summer my wife left me was my dream life, which, like a mirage, dried up completely as we came to the absolute end of us. In the fourteen years we were married I was a ferocious dreamer, drawing all I knew or feared or loved about the waking world into my sleep life. If I saw a neighbor's animal — Les Fletcher's horse, say, or Newt Grider's collie dog — I would see dozens of them in my dreams that night, beasts whose language I understood and respected, animals whose stories I heard and wept over just as one day I would weep over my own misfortune.

In the early morning hours after our first son was born, I watched a flock of pigeons from my wife's hospital room. There were hundreds, mindless as only those swivel-eyed birds can be, flapping and swirling in a hurly-burly over the air conditioners, their bird chatter an unhappy, loud whirring as constant as party talk. It was a noise I heard distinctly hours later, when I fell asleep at home. They were yammering, those dream birds; and what they said to each other, and would say to others yet to arrive, seemed so sensible to me in my sleep that I awoke smiling, as if I had heard secrets vital enough to live by. I had been where they had been: north and south, in good weather and bad, into trees and onto ledges, on rooftops and in parks. I was, in the few hours I dozed, a pigeon.

Another time, on a vacation to Disneyland, I became the folks we met on the road: those who pumped our gas, or cooked burgers for us, or stood behind the desks at the Holiday Inns we stayed in. I was the boy who bused our table in Phoenix, the blond woman outside the entrance of the San Diego zoo whose child was colicky or too well fed; I was the motorists we passed at sixty miles an hour, and I was the citizens whose communities we circled in the atlas: Santa Barbara, Laguna Beach, San Mateo. I paid their utility bills, shopped and ate and hollered for them. At the end of our four weeks, driving south from San Francisco to our home in Las Cruces, I was even the pilots overhead, whose babble was as remarkable and private as that of birds.

But when Karen left, my dreams stopped. Not abruptly, as if the tape that was my inner life had finally run out, but gradually, as if the world inside me were subject to erosion by the common elements of wind and water, and by the uncommon elements of lovelessness and despair. My first night alone I was a general, a George Armstrong Custer. I had blond heroic hair and heavy gold braid on the tight broadcloth tunic that flattened the lazy man's belly I have. My dream voice was stern, my vocabulary as fancy and important as one in any schoolbook. In that dream I issued orders that were happily and swiftly obeyed, and had my name called so often that when my alarm rang, I woke saying, "Yes, how may I help?" I remember standing — at attention, I suppose — at my bedside, alert as a sentinel, wondering what personal emergency had fetched me into daylight again. "Karen?" I said. "What is it?" Though I was awake, the part of me Karen had left behind when she went to her sister's in El Paso believed that she was still here, if not in the bathroom next door then in the kitchen.

Searching for her, I opened Danny's door, and then Mark's. Their bedrooms seemed empty, not abandoned. Beds were made, closets organized, toys put away. Still, hearing her name over and over in my memory, I looked for her. Her plants were here (the Boston fern, the overwatered rhododendron), as were her books and most of her clothes, but she was not. It was only when I opened the patio door and stood in the backyard, studying the rose bushes she'd planted the year before, that I snapped to. I had been slugged, I felt. I was actually staggered, thrown backward by a force like horror. "Karen?" I said again, but by then I did not mean it. Her name was only a word given

to an object that wasn't here anymore. It was a word that stood
for an absence, like darkness itself, that had made way for the
waking life.

In the weeks that followed, my dreams still came quickly, but
with parts missing or poorly joined. They had no beginnings,
and their endings seemed less like conclusions than interrup-
tions. They were like slide exhibits, flashing picture shows
thrown together by the weary, unthinking heart of me. The
family came and went: my boys were born, grew, and swept into
adulthood in minutes. My father, dead many years, now appeared, dressed for golf, in the checkerboard plus fours he
favored, and in his snappy Panama hat. He did not speak, nor
did I see him, as I often had, camped in front of the TV, his
banker's expression fixed and baleful. Instead, he was swinging
his Walter Hagen driver, in slide after slide, his stroke an envi-
able display of mind and muscle. I saw my mother, too. In every
frame that rose out of the night, she sat at the shallow end of
the country club pool, her bathing suit an unflattering one-piece
affair whose wide shoulder straps hung down her arms and
whose skirt seemed more appropriate to a child. She was fluttering her feet in the water, again and again and again, and pointing, in obvious joy, to a soaked figure in the baby pool, a skinny,
clumsily diapered toddler. One night I saw the few friends I
had as a youngster — Mike Runyan, John Risner, Jimmy Bul-
lard; and I saw the first house we lived in, 111 West Gallagher,
behind which was a cotton field where we raced our Schwinn
bicycles and, later, a rusted two-door Ford. I saw the Texas
college I could not graduate from, the cramped dorm room I
lived in, the Lake Dallas oil man's house I was violently drunk
in once — all of which became too sad and perplexing to sleep
through.

Often, too often to be unimportant, I saw faces and events
placed side by side, as if between them I were to make compar-
isons; as if between, on the left, my wife at home in her night-
wear and, on the right, me in the caddy room at the country
club, I were somehow to see a connection. I saw nothing. No
meaning, no significance. I was uninvolved, as distant from
what was being shown to me asleep as from what I had once

seen awake. I would climb into bed after KTFM's ten o'clock news and, before setting the alarm and switching off the bed-stand light, ask myself what silliness, what oddball's concoction of delight and misery, I would dream. Nothing of my job as a ninth-grade math teacher came to me, nor did I recognize any-one from the present — not Herb Swetman, my principal and best pal; not Emily Probert, his secretary; not any of the young-sters I coach on the soccer team. I began to conceive of my unconscious, the thing we are told our dreams spill from, as a fishing net whose weave was too wide for the current world.

By September, my dreams had put me to work. Night after night, I picked up leaves from trees I don't have, one by one, and stacked them in piles as high as my ears. I wrote my name, with one hand and then the other, in ink and in pencil, on ruled and on unlined paper. One time, after a phone call from Karen, whose last words were so impersonal they could have been ut-tered by a Martian, I sleepwalked. My dream concerned thirst, and when the alarm went off, on my nightstand I found not one but five glasses of water; and I report to you now that I drank each of them, slowly and seriously, as if I dared not, as if the penalty for neglecting what our dreams bid us do is not less than death itself. Yes, I drank them; and after each, in the icy silence between the putting down of one and the taking up of another, I had a vision of myself as I was when Karen and I married — a wise guy ignorant of what time can do to love.

The last of my dreams was almost a year later, after our divorce was final and I knew I had to go forward again. This was several years ago, when I regularly played stud poker in the men's locker at the country club. There were five of us, all married but me, and the most you could lose in our quarter-limit game was twenty dollars. We would drink and order roast beef sand-wiches from the second-floor snack bar and, if we expected to be late, we could shower or dive into the pool or go out to the driving range to be crazy. On the night of this dream, I was the last to leave. The sight of my winnings, folding money and change, didn't impress me. There was no place to go. Ed had driven home to Bonnie, Max to Jean, the rest to their own wives; and I was there, in a chair, a drink at my elbow, listening to the dripping showers and the satisfying *whoosh-whoosh* the outdoor sprinklers made. I went to the pool and tumbled in, clothes and lace-up shoes and all, and, as I had as a kid, I pulled straight for the deep end, down fifteen feet to the drain, where the pressure and heavy silence of the water overhead had once seemed as reassuring as gravity. Several times I plunged down, suspending myself as long as I could before crawling up for air. I felt good. I had a wife who lived elsewhere, sons who would not be too much damaged by what had happened, and a job I was fine enough at; more important, I had the night to myself — a spread of stars whole nations could wish upon, and clouds that say rain is on the way, and breezes that bring with them the smells of what we plant hereabouts in the Mesilla Valley. I think I sang; and now I hear that singing again, as if I am out on the course at night and saying to myself, as a stranger, that there is a man singing over yonder, in a scratchy voice with some liquor and cigarettes in it, and that man is happy.

I folded my soggy clothes over the chain-link fence and considered the place. I studied the buildings — the pro shop, the ballroom, the women's locker a floor above our own — and, beyond them, the third of my town that wasn't asleep or had no work to do. I could see Hiebert's Drive-in, the Rocket Theater, and the curve of North Main Street that swept by the Loretto Shopping Center. I could hear cars, faint and steady, and I wondered who was out there. I imagined moving the one hill in front of me and being able to point out the house I own as well as those I pass every day on my way to Alameda Middle School. I was putting together my world as my dreams had once put me together, and everywhere I looked I spotted something — a willow tree, someone's Lincoln Continental, a garage — that might look better over there. Or there. Or there. Naked, common sense stripped away by the Jack Daniel's I like, I saw the world I could construct for the sixty thousand souls I share it with. A house became a castle; a streetlight, a tower. As if I were solving a math problem for my class, I put X with Y, A with B, and by the time, an hour later, I sat down in a ratty chaise by the pool, this largest town in Doña Ana County had become as quaint and patchwork as those we yearn for from olden times that never were. Joy — and mirth and bliss and virtue — had many faces that night; for I put in pockets or hearts or minds whatever over time had been stolen or broken or made sad. Then I dreamed.

We are told, I believe, too many truisms about our inner lives. In books and magazines and on TV we hear too much about the selves we are. We are good, we hear, or we are bad; like dogs, or not; like angels, or not; flawed or perfected. Our swamis tell us — preachers and teachers, politicians and doctors, all the tattling experts running loose among us. But it is in dreams — of pigeons, of the past, of people long gone — that we attend to the inner life itself, hear it in its own words and at its own pitch.

My last dream featured the desert we have around Las Cruces, the thousands of square miles of sand and rock and scrawny brush that doomsayers tell us will one day be your home too. It was a flat world, infertile as a skillet, with lightning flashing at the rim. It was a world of red and yellow and green skies, all the colors poets love, a place whose light was liquid and melting all around. I was in it, I dreamed, at an unmarked crossroads, the age I am now, thirty-nine, and in good health. I could go left, or right, or straight, but to the man I was then the choice made no real difference. I was to see something, I knew, and soon enough it appeared in the shimmering, collapsed distance. I was seeing myself out there, black against white, absurdly tall in a diminished land. "All right," I said. "All right." My inner life, the world constructed from what I'd been and done, was speaking to me, patiently and calmly. I would hear what it had to say, and I would understand. And so I came to myself, observed the man I am now walk forward to the man I was then and take him, as a father takes his children, into his arms. The one held the other — the future cradling the present — and the one who had been left, the one whose interior hooks and hasps and snaps had come undone, gave himself up utterly. They were both there, in dreamland, under heaven and over hell, two versions of the same man, clasped in an embrace that would end when the world came up again.

Men under Water

FROM THE ATLANTIC

THE PETER PAN DINER, 10:30 A.M. breakfast with Gunther.

"You're depressed again," Gunther says to me. "I can tell." He has the catsup bottle in one fist like a chisel or a caulking gun, and with the heel of his other hand he's hammering catsup over his hash browns and scrambled eggs. He's getting some on the bacon and toast, too.

"I'm not depressed," I say.

"You're not eating."

"Gunther, I eat at home, remember? At breakfast time. I never eat here."

He slips into his pouting voice. "You used to," he says.

This is a bad sign. It means that Gunther is especially needy and delusional today. I haven't ordered anything but coffee in the Peter Pan since the first week I worked for him, more than six months ago.

I look at him, busying himself with breakfast on the other side of the booth. Lately I've spent more time with Gunther than I've spent with my wife, and still there are times — this moment is one of them — when I see him as I saw him the day we met, times when I cannot get beyond the amazing epidermal surface of the man. Gunther is one of the largest people I've ever known, but it's more than that, more than his general enormousness, the smooth expanse of his completely bald head, the perfect beardlessness of his broad face. Gunther has no eyebrows, no body hair whatsoever as far as I know; even the large nostrils of his great, wide nose are pink, hairless tunnels run-

ning up into his skull. His velour pullover is open to his sternum, and the exposed chest is precisely the complexion of all
the rest of him — the shrimplike color of new Play-Doh, the
substance from which Gunther sometimes seems to be made.
Under the movie lights he likes to muck around with, his skin
goes translucent and you can watch the blood vessels keeping
him alive.

"If you're not depressed," he says around a mouthful of catsup and eggs, "what are you?"

"Subdued," I say.

"Oh," he says. "Well, would you mind knocking off being
subdued? You're not putting out any energy. I can't do it all by
myself."

"Do what?"

"Write this goddamn screenplay," he says.

"Oh. Which screenplay is this?"

"You know perfectly well which screenplay. The sci-fi one
with the giant radioactive crayfish and the girl scientist who
understands them, and who's also the love interest for the guy
scientist. The one we've been working on all week."

"Oh, that one," I say. "I forgot. I thought maybe you meant
the kung fu screenplay. I guess that was last week."

"You want to work on that one? Hey, we could even do a
hybrid of the two. Say these huge, radioactive crayfish attack
mankind with a sort of lobster version of kung fu, bopping
people with their big claws. The guy scientist also happens to be
a martial-arts master. In the end he conquers the lobsters by
building robots programmed to hit them in their pressure
points. But before that there's a scene where the lobsters grab
the girl and he has to take a couple of them down with his bare
hands."

"No, Gunther." I sip my coffee and stare out the window
above the personal jukebox mounted on the wall of our booth.
The jukebox is playing Roy Orbison's "Pretty Woman," Gunther's favorite song. He put it on to cheer me up.

Outside, a light gray ash is falling from the sky like rain.
Cleveland has a lot of smokestack industry, and the Peter Pan is
one of the vulnerable old smokestack-area diners. That's why
we come here to eat. Not because we work in the plants our-

selves — our work, like God, is everywhere and nowhere — but because this is where reality is, the life and labor of the folk, the source of all art. Someday, after he's made the two or three commercial pictures that will establish him as one of the major film forces of our time, Gunther wants to celebrate his native city in a cinematic tone-poem about the ballet of heavy manufacture, the romance of rubber and steel.

I show him my wristwatch. "What about the Puerto Rican couple on Liberty Place? With the gas leak in their stove? Or the nursing students on Meadow with no hot water. You told them today for sure. And your answering service. I'll bet you didn't call your answering service. You'll call it at three this afternoon, and then we'll have to work until nine tonight."

Gunther throws his fork onto his plate. People at the counter turn on their stools to look at us. "This is your whole problem," he says. He clangs his coffee cup with his spoon to get the attention of our waitress. It's Alice today, a good woman. If Gunther gets too abusive, she'll pour coffee in his lap. She's done it before. She comes over now and fills our cups.

"I try to foster a creative spirit," Gunther says to me. Alice flashes him a look, the coffee pot poised in the air. He stops talking and stares at the table until she's gone on her way. "I try to pay you for your imagination," he says, "not just for dumb monkey work I could get anybody to do. I try to treat you like an artist. And all you want to do is fix toilets." He picks up the cream and sugar and pours a long stream of each into his cup. Then he starts the singsongy voice. "Yes, for a certain number of hours each week we have to do some essentially noncreative work, things that are not really what artists like us should be doing — painting apartments, replacing water heaters, fixing toilets. But it keeps us humble, I say. I try to be philosophical about it. I don't go into a mood just because I can't work on my movies every minute of every day."

"I left my house three hours ago, Gunther."

"Here we go again," he says.

He doesn't start paying my hourly wages until we leave the diner. But if I don't go over to Gunther's house each morning and wake him up and, while he takes a shower, watch parts of movies he's videotaped, and then listen to him rant about screenplays over breakfast at the Peter Pan, we won't go to work at all, and I won't be paid anything.

He turns to the jukebox and speaks to Roy Orbison. "Roy," he says, "what am I going to do with this guy? Sensitive and gifted, yes, but he has real limitations. He actually wants to work for wages." He turns back to me. "You're not being flexible," he says. "That's a major character flaw, you should watch that. How many times have I explained this to you? You're working for — and will soon be the partner of — an important motion-picture producer who happens at the moment to be trapped inside a landlord's body."

"That's not how it was advertised," I say. "It was advertised: 'Handyman and general helper, no experience necessary.' That's the ad I responded to. You changed it to scriptwriter after I was hired."

"After I discovered the talent I can't let you throw away, even if you want to. A good part of each week is ours to be talented together, you and me. We toss some ideas back and forth" — he slaps my shoulder — "and in a couple of weeks we have a screenplay. I round up some investors, we start shooting the movie, we're on our way. We could have made some progress on this movie right here at breakfast, but no, you're subdued. You think that just because we have to go fix a toilet today, that's all we are, two guys who have to fix a toilet, and you let it get you down."

"What toilet?" I say. "You're keeping something from me."

"Weren't you the one who wanted me to call my answering service?"

He stands up and tosses his wadded napkin onto his plate, smiling and bobbing his head from side to side like Hardy to Laurel. He leans toward me over the table as if to confide a great truth, a truth that will be true long after everything else is dust. "Rock band," he says, and strides away from the booth. Then he comes back, doing his wicked leer. "The horror, the horror," he adds.

We pay our bill and stroll out of the Peter Pan into the sunlight and ashes, me in my paint-spattered carpenter's pants and sweatshirt, Gunther swaggering in his red-and-yellow-striped velour pullover and racing shades. It's 11:30 A.M., almost time for lunch. The rest of the world has already accomplished much since waking, and laid down foundations for the accomplishment of much more. We have accomplished nothing. But neither have we yet lost everything, I remind myself. We still have much of what we had when the day began. I have my job with Gunther — twenty dollars an hour under the table, starting now — and Gunther has his small real estate empire, his Ford Bronco, the ability to pay me twenty dollars for each hour I ride around in it with him, and an unflagging, magical belief in the rightness of his life and methods despite all evidence to the contrary.

And he has me. We have each other.

Tina, my wife, cannot believe I continue to hold this job. We need the money, but Tina has had enough. She can't take any more stories about Gunther. She can't take what working for Gunther is doing to me. I'm no longer the man she married, Tina says. My inability to leave Gunther has raised serious questions about the deep structure of my personality, and now Tina wants us both to go in for counseling. She says she's become a kind of co-alcoholic, living through my experiences with this man. She's had to go through it all with me, even though it's not her life, and now in some perverse way she feels that she works for Gunther too.

Every night when I get home I must drink for one full hour and rail to Tina about Gunther. I tell her what Gunther has done to me that day, what he's done to his tenants, the lies he's made me tell the tenants about those things, the movie-script ideas he's forced me to invent. After an hour or so I'm able to take a shower and have dinner. But it's growing longer now, up to two hours sometimes. At first it was exotic and Tina enjoyed it. Every night I would bring home amazing new stories. Tina would listen and shake her head in wonder, marveling over the character of Gunther, the shamelessness of the business world, the length and breadth of the illusions men can entertain about themselves.

But then, late last winter, I came home one night with the Pakistani-baby story. Tina teaches in a day-care center, and the Pakistani-baby story pushed her over the edge. I'd been shoveling snow at Gunther's garden-apartment buildings when a Pakistani woman came out into the parking lot in her flowing ocher robes, weeping and screaming because she had no heat and her baby was freezing. I went inside to have a look, something I'm not supposed to do on my own. I'm supposed to refer tenants to Gunther's answering service, nothing more. In the apartment I could see my breath more clearly than I could outside. The woman's baby was swaddled in many blankets; only its nose and lips were sticking out, and they were blue. Sitting at the dinette table in his overcoat was the woman's husband, a little brown man with mournful eyes, eating a bowl of curry and shivering. Something big snapped inside me when I saw their lives. I showed them how to call the tenants'-rights division of Legal Aid, and then I gave them Gunther's unlisted home number, the most forbidden thing there is. Gunther and I had our biggest fight over the Pakistani family. When I got home, Tina spent the whole evening trying to calm me down. I quit for two entire weeks that time, finally going back for three dollars more an hour.

But now I must quit this job forever, Tina says — really quit, not just quit the way I do every week.

Every Friday, when Gunther pays me what I'm owed, I put the cash in my pocket and say sayonara. After a full week of Gunther I can't envision one more day. He shakes his head, looks at the ground, asks me what he's done wrong. Nothing, Gunther, I always say, not a thing, you're a prince. I just can't take the real estate life anymore.

You lack vision, he always says. You're turning your back on a brilliant future. The real estate is only a stop along the way, Reggie. Next stop, Hollywood!

No can do, Gunther, I say. We shake hands and go our separate ways forever. Sunday morning I buy the paper and read the ads. Again each week, in return for two thirds of a person's waking life, the free market offers enough money to rent a shed and eat a can of beans every day. "I'm currently holding the best job in Cleveland," I tell Tina. She puts her hands over her ears. Then Sunday afternoon Gunther calls to offer me an hourly increase of fifty cents over what I made the previous week. I accept his new offer. I started at four dollars an hour.

I'm up to twenty now. In his big house on a hill above town, Gunther has shown me where he hides his gun. When I reach fifty dollars an hour, he wants me to kill him.

Gunther's real estate holdings consist of two three-story brick garden-apartment buildings down near the projects, eight or nine rambling wooden Victorians scattered all over the rest of town, and miscellaneous. Miscellaneous includes some garages Gunther rents to people for their cars, and a couple of apartments he has the nerve to rent over the garages. Of the enormous Victorians, three are divided vertically into two-families, and another five or six — the ones in the better areas — have been partitioned into warrens of small studios and one-bedrooms for which Gunther charges outrageous rents. A massage parlor is in one of those; when Gunther's feeling uninspired, we go there and pretend we have to check on things. Only one of the Victorians — the biggest one, in the worst neighborhood — has its original structure and gets rented as one place, to one party.

Acid Rain, the rock band, lives there.

Now Gunther hits the gravel of Acid Rain's horseshoe drive going fast, and then jumps on the brake so that we slide sideways the last thirty feet to the house. Three old Chevy vans are parked around the drive, all painted with the band's name and logo — a thundercloud with a skull and crossbones in it — along with seven huge Harley-Davidsons. In the backyard is a big Doberman and an even bigger shepherd, both on frail-looking chains. They start howling at us. The washing machine and dryer are still out there, their doors torn off, birds and squirrels living in them, and enough old hibachi grills to make a rusty bridge to Barbecueland. Here and there stray concrete blocks and bricks are making dead rectangular voids in the two-foot-high crabgrass.

Gunther loads my arms with equipment from the back of the Bronco — coils of pipe, rolls of solder, garnet paper, a plumber's snake, a portable light, extension cords, a large toolbox. He leads the way with the propane torch, me following him to the house like a pack mule. Luke, the leader of Acid Rain, greets us.

"Why the fuck don't you call your answering service?" Luke says.

"Now, Luke," Gunther says, "I don't think you should be the one to start casting stones. I could say hurtful things to you too. I could say, for instance, Why don't you stop trying to flush each other down the toilets? It clogs them up."

"Ha, ha," Luke says. Then he doesn't say anything else, because he doesn't know where Gunther's breaking point is. Luke is not dumb, but you can see in his face that he can't figure Gunther out. He understands that Gunther didn't go from being a poor, snot-nosed son of a drunked-up electrician to owning a small real estate empire by taking unlimited abuse from people like him. But then sometimes Gunther seems a jolly fellow who doesn't always act in his own best interest. It's confusing for Luke. I sympathize.

And then there's the way Gunther looks, the massive pink presence of him.

Luke reports that all three of the toilets in the house are broken. I look at Gunther and narrow my eyes. He looks away, sheepish. On the ride over here, Gunther let slip that Acid Rain first called about their toilet a week ago. It was just the first-floor toilet then.

We make our way through the house. Acid Rain's place was an opulent Cleveland mansion once, and great cut-glass chandeliers still hang in the downstairs rooms above the drums and amplifiers and dismantled motorcycles. The glass pendants are gray blobs now, coated with greasy dust. The residents have decorated the chandeliers with pantyhose, pictures from motorcycle magazines, tennis balls, guitar strings. We head upstairs to begin with the topmost toilet. The law of gravity. Various tattooed men are wandering around with women in black leather. Catastrophic metal music is playing in all the rooms on the second floor.

I'd like to mention here that I'm a great lover of music, and so is Tina. We believe that music transcends all the differences between people, and we like to get out when we can to hear a band and dance and have fun. Even after all the things I had witnessed here, we still had perfectly open minds the night we went to see Acid Rain play at The Glo-Worm, over on the other side of the beltway. That's all I can say. When Tina finds out I was here again today, she'll go crazy. Maybe I won't even go home tonight.

Otis, the keyboard player, appears in a doorway. Otis is completely blind, and two of Acid Rain's roadies — all the roadies and many other people live in the house with the band — are blind in one eye apiece. People can be blind for many reasons, and you don't ordinarily think of blindness as caused by the blind person, the result of something he did to himself. But with Acid Rain the thought leaps to mind. Over the months I've watched to see if other ones become blind too — from drinking rubbing alcohol, say, or fighting among themselves over food or females, the way squirrels do. So far, it's only the same three.

"Is that my landlord?" Otis says. "Do I hear my landlord's voice?"

"My man Otis," Gunther says. "How you doing, Otis?"

"How am I doing? I'm going to the bathroom in the backyard, motherfucker. That's how I'm doing."

"It's under control now, Otis," Gunther says, stepping quietly around him and motioning for me to follow. But I'm draped with the coils of pipe, the extension cords, the plumber's snake, and I clank when I move.

Otis grabs me. "The dude who mows the lawn, right?" he says. "The landlord's sidekick?"

"I just work for the guy, Otis," I say. "You think it's a picnic? You think he doesn't do the same to me? Every day's a nightmare with this bozo, Otis."

Otis smiles and holds out his palm. "Hey," he says.

I slap his hand. "Renters of the world unite. Death to landlords."

"Right on!" Otis says, slapping me back. "Let's do it now!"

"No, Otis," I say. "Let him fix the toilets first."

"Good point," Otis says. "Okay. I'll be waiting right here."

We head up the last flight of stairs. "You overdid it a little," Gunther says, "but I was still impressed. You were convincing, and I liked the way you improvised under pressure. I thought you were just a writer. Now I find out you have natural acting ability. I'm giving you a screen test when we get back home."

On the third floor Gunther sees the toilet from the hallway.

His face becomes an image of the human capacity for sadness. "I think I just got a blown mind-gasket," he says. He lights up the propane torch and shoots little bursts of blue flame into the bathroom. "Firing retro rockets," he says. "Leaving doomed planet."

"Two words, Gunther," I say. "Just two little words."

"I know," he says. "You quit."

"No," I say. "Roto-Rooter."

"That's one word," he says. We back away from the bathroom. Gunther grips the banister and looks down into the spacious stairwell as though he might plunge himself into it. Then his head snaps up and he slaps me in the belly. "I just had an incredible idea," he says.

"No, Gunther," I say. "Whatever it is. Please, no."

"Everything just fell together for me," he says. "Oh, man, this is good."

Back down on the landing Otis is waiting. "Otis," Gunther says. "It's bigger than we thought. We have to call Roto-Rooter."

"You lie," Otis says, producing a length of chain from his leather vest.

"No, Otis," I say. "He's telling the truth this one time. It was my idea to call Roto-Rooter. There's no way this clown can fix these toilets."

"Okay," Otis says. "I believe you, brother. But if you lie, I kill you too."

"Don't worry, Otis," I say.

We head downstairs. In the kitchen we find Luke and some of the women swigging on bottles of Colt 45.

"Luke," Gunther says. "My man. I want to ask you a question. You like movies, Luke?"

"I like going to the bathroom," Luke says, slamming his bottle on the table.

"We're calling Roto-Rooter on that, Luke. Okay? Roto-Rooter, like on TV? The guys in the big yellow truck with the little sissy uniforms? You'll be able to make poo-poo right here tonight. Now sit down. I want you to answer my question. You like movies?"

"Yeah, sure."

"Okay. When was the last time you saw a really great movie

about an American rock-and-roll band? I mean a movie that had it all — bar scenes, motorcycle scenes, dressing-room scenes, rehearsal scenes, groupie love scenes, and the monster victory-concert scene at the end when the band comes back to its home town after making it big. A movie that captured all the suffering and the glory, the whole incredible life of a great, semifamous cult rock band in a medium-sized American city. Luke, when was the last time you saw a movie like that?"

"I never saw no such movie," Luke says.

"That's right!" Gunther says.

The Peter Pan Diner, 2:00 P.M. Alice comes over with the menus. "You guys really making a big day of it, huh?" she says.

"We're celebrating, Alice," Gunther says. "Two meatloaf specials, one for me and one for my lucky charm here. Gravy on everything. That's the password today, Alice. Gravy."

Alice flashes me a look — can I handle him by myself? I nod and she takes the menus away.

Gunther is on an inspirational roll. "This is it!" he says, gripping my shoulder. "My movie! Plot, characters, myth, fantasy! Commercial potential! It was right under my nose! But that's the way it always is in the art game, eh, Roscoe?" He pulls a legal pad out of his briefcase. "So what do you think? I say we start with the Luke character — let's call him Luke — we start with him as an inner-city kid, you know, getting his first guitar, getting beat up on by his alcoholic father because he practices guitar instead of getting a job. Plays good pool and B-ball, but he's better on guitar. Everybody's against him. His fellow gang members think guitar is for queers. And we need the bad father, right? We've got to give Luke something big to rebel against. I mean, he can't *like* his father."

"Cliché, Gunther. Cliché, cliché, cliché."

"You always say that. Well I say life's a cliché! I'm not letting that stop me!"

"Scratch the childhood," I say. "It begins with music, the band rehearsing in this tenement while the titles roll up the screen. Helicopter shot of the building, close in on the window of their apartment, music getting louder and louder until we're right in there with them. Then the landlord bursts in, demanding the rent. They don't have any money, so they beat the landlord to death with their guitars."

"Sounds like a cliché to me!" Gunther says, chortling and writing it all down. "But it's not bad! We might be able to use that! Okay, no childhood. Maybe we can put it back later. Or maybe — how about this? — Luke can go back and see his old dad in the hospital after he's famous. The old dad has the big C in his liver now, but together they watch Luke in concert on the tube in his hospital room. Just before he dies, he recognizes how wrong he always was."

"And he apologizes for the way things were. And it straightens Luke's head out about his life."

"Right!"

"Perfect."

"And the record biz, hey? We need a big scene with these parasitic record-producer types who want to tell Luke how to play, what kinds of clothes to wear. They want to make Luke like everybody else so they can use him to get all this money to put up their own noses. But Luke has a dream. He tells everybody to screw themselves. In the end they all want to kiss his ass."

"That's good," I say. "That's original." The meatloaf specials arrive. We dive into gravy. "Gunther," I say after a few bites, "it takes millions of dollars to make a real movie. You realize that, right? Millions."

"I have a little surprise for you," he says in the nursery-rhyme voice.

"No, Gunther, please, whatever it is, no."

"We're going to my place after lunch," he says. "Hollywood's paying your salary for the rest of the day. Before, I was going to leave you with the toilets and do the heavy business on my own. And I was worried, I admit it, because I didn't have the killer idea to show the big boys. But it came to me when I needed it. We're partners now, Ricardo. I always said you wouldn't be sorry if you stuck with me."

"Big boys?" I say. "What big boys?"

At Gunther's house a silver Mercedes with vanity plates is parked at the top of the drive. Gunther downshifts the Bronco and creeps toward the silver car as though he can't believe it's actually there. "This is really happening," he says.

For a year now he's been running an ad in the paper to attract investors to his film-production company. Every month a few cranks respond; that's all, nobody with money. But yesterday when he called his answering service he found a message from these guys. They've invested in movies before. He told me about it on the way over here.

He parks the Bronco and gets out. The two men getting out of the Mercedes look like they want to get back in when they see him. The driver is a thin young guy with a spiky haircut, blue-green iridescent jacket, Hawaiian shirt, black jeans, red shoes. The passenger is a small man in his early sixties, salt-and-pepper hair brushed back, business suit. Gunther introduces himself and shakes hands. He motions for me to come over. "Gentlemen," he says, "this is my associate, Flip. Flip is the co-author of my new screenplay."

I shake hands too. The driver's name is Willie. He's into the whole sullen James Dean thing. The passenger is Joseph, kindly and soft-spoken, with an Eastern European accent. His voice makes me see scenes for a movie version of our horrible century — bombings and occupations, pogroms, refugee camps, a boy in shabby knickers calling out the prices of fruit on the streets of the New World.

Both men are looking at my clothes. I brush the front of myself, but none of the paint spatters come off. "We like to be comfortable," I say.

Willie licks his lips, dubious, but Joseph smiles and nods. We go inside. Willie and Joseph look around. Gunther's place looks good. It's a big old house that didn't look so good when I first saw it, but often, while his tenants suffer, Gunther has me work around here. I've painted every room, sanded and finished the floors. One week in the winter we tore out the whole kitchen and put in a new one. Sometimes Gunther even has me clean the bathrooms for MaryLou, his wife, while he sits on a hassock in the hall telling me about screenplay ideas.

"You're prospering, Gunther," Joseph says.

"I guess I'm doing all right," Gunther says. He's more nervous than I thought. He tries to wink at me but botches it and looks like he's just been poked in the eye. "Flip, would you show Joseph and Willie into the living room? Gin and tonics, gentlemen?"

"Very good," Joseph says.

"Flip? Or would you prefer one of those good English ales?"

"Gin and tonic is fine, Gunther," I say. I take the men into the living room. The furnishings are trim and tasteful, vaguely Scandinavian. They were chosen by MaryLou. Gunther would have chosen a lot of chrome bars and Naugahyde. The living room makes me realize in a sudden, sweet way just how completely MaryLou holds Gunther's life together for him, what an impossible piece of luck or inspiration it was that he married her. If she ever left him he'd have to die, but she never will. She's a loving soul, from people even poorer than his, her head not easily turned from grateful devotion. Gunther put her through college while he worked, and never made it to college himself. She teaches grammar school now and thinks his carryings-on are what you put up with when you're married to a genius.

We sit down. French doors open from the living room into the dining room, now the office of the production company, where the big, useless 16 mm Movieola is poised like an old burro grazing among the bundles of screenplay drafts stacked everywhere. I've written whole scenes of them while Gunther's tenants acted out their martyrdom. Joseph and Willie are peering in there from the sofa. They don't know what to make of it all. I hear Gunther clinking glassware in the distant kitchen.

In a voice as soft as Joseph's I say, "Gunther is an unusual person." It's hardly an outlandish statement. They nod, meaning that they've noticed, and wait for me to go on. "He's actually rather amazing. Four, five years ago he had nothing. Now he owns properties all over town. Everything he has he built up for himself, with no help from anyone. His drive to succeed is unstoppable. All his life he's dreamed of making movies. He works on screenplays in his sleep." I lean forward and lower my voice even further. "His father was an electrician who drank himself to death, beat the kids, and smashed up the house all the time when Gunther was growing up. Now Gunther supports his old mother, bought a nice little house for her to live in across town.

He put his wife through college. You'll see him come in here with a Coke for himself. He never touches a drink, straight as an arrow. You understand what I'm saying. I'm talking about character, what motivates a man."

Everything I'm telling Willie and Joseph is true. Yes, I'm casting it in a certain light, even perceiving it as I say it, but I'm not telling a single lie.

"A lot of people have had it tough," Willie says.

But Joseph waves his hand. "I appreciate what you say," he says.

Gunther comes in with the drinks on a tray, three gin and tonics, and a Coke for himself. He sits down in a big chair. "Well," he says. Then he's about to say something else, but nothing comes out. We sip our drinks, waiting.

"So, Gunther," Joseph says, "you want to make a movie."

Gunther nods without expression. To the untrained eye he looks as enigmatic as Buddha, full of secret knowledge. But I've learned to read the fantastic face. He wants to speak, but his body has locked up on him. He never really believed that a man like Joseph would come to his house someday. His stage fright is as immense and immovable as he is.

"Joseph," I say. "Willie. Have you ever noticed that beyond the basic animal requirements there are very few things that all human beings must have, and that these few things are not physical but rather metaphysical, things of the spirit? Faith of some kind is the obvious example. Can you think of another?"

Willie looks at Joseph. "This is kind of a weird thing to be talking about," Willie says. But Joseph thinks it over and says, "Love, of course."

"Oh, good," I say. "Right. The big one. And how about learning, some systematic acquisition of knowledge?"

"Yes," Joseph says, nodding his head.

"Now I'm thinking of one more," I say. "One more nonphysical thing that all people must have, a thing that is always present whenever human beings gather together in grief or in joy."

Willie looks at his watch. Part of his job is to protect Joseph's precious time. "This is kind of like Twenty Questions," he says. "This might be fun at a party."

"Party is a clue," I say.

Joseph straightens up on the sofa. "Music!" he says.

I nod my head and smile. "Yes, Joseph, music."

"The nonphysical part fooled me," Willie says.

"Now, friends," I say, "the movie we're going to make is about music. Joseph, I'll bet there's a tape machine in your car out there. I'm going to guess what's on it at this very moment. Mozart."

"Wrong!" Joseph says, clapping his hands. "Mozart is in the glove compartment, I'll grant you that! But on the machine is Prokofiev. We listened to it on the way over here." he wags his finger at me. "You were wrong, smart boy!"

"Ha, ha!" I say. "But still I've made my point. You take your favorite music with you wherever you go. *And*," I say, "the second part of my point — it's music that Willie doesn't like."

"Right!" Joseph says. "He complains every day. But that part was easy, smart boy. Look at Willie's clothes, look at his hair."

"Sure," I say. "But look further, Joseph. Look at Willie and see the American moviegoer. We practically have Mister Entertainment, sitting right here. And that, Joseph, is why — for the crucial question — we must now defer to Willie."

I sip my drink. "Willie," I say. "I have a question for you. When was the last time you saw a really great movie about an American rock-and-roll band? I mean a movie that had it all — bar scenes, motorcycle scenes, dressing-room scenes, rehearsal scenes, groupie love scenes, and the monster victory-concert scene at the end when the band comes back to its home town after making it big. A movie that captured all the suffering and the glory, the whole incredible life of a great, semifamous cult rock band in a medium-sized American city. Willie, when was the last time you saw a movie like that?"

"I never saw any such movie," Willie says.

"That's right," I say.

Gunther's kitchen, 5.00 P.M. Gunther on the floor on his hands and knees.

"Gunther, get up," I say, looking in the refrigerator for those good English ales he was talking about. "Stop doing that. Show some self-respect. Where are those ales, you charlatan, you complete fraud? What if I'd decided to have one?"

"There wouldn't have been any left," he says, continuing to

do what he's been doing — crawling on all fours, nudging MaryLou's silver serving tray around the floor with his nose the way a dog nudges its bowl. Periodically he howls like a dog too, and when he does, tears spring from his eyes, which he takes care not to let drip upon the small slip of blue paper resting on the silver tray.

"I'm making a movie!" he keeps bawling between howls.

The slip of blue paper is the check Joseph wrote to Gunther before driving away in the silver Mercedes ten minutes ago. It's for an amount so large I can't bring myself to say it. When he wrote it, Joseph called it good-faith money. He has more, and he knows other investors.

I finish making another gin and tonic. "Gunther," I say. "I have to tell you something, and I want you to brace yourself. I'm not doing this movie with you."

He clambers up from the floor, Joseph's check in his hand. "Flip," he says. "Don't even joke about things like that, Flip."

"I'm not joking. Where did you get 'Flip,' by the way?"

"It just came to me. But I like it. That's you from now on. Flip, my man Flip."

"It's not bad," I say. "But you'll have to find somebody else."

"There is nobody else! Nobody like you! Nobody with your talent! Hey! A third of this money's yours! Half of it's yours! It's all yours, Flip!"

"I already have to go to a marriage counselor on account of you," I say. "If I throw in on this movie, Tina divorces me."

"She won't!" Gunther says. "Not when she hears about the money! I'll talk to her. Call her right now, I'll talk to her. No! We'll bring her in! Can she write? Can she act? Can she sing?"

"No, Gunther. She can't do anything. She's a vegetable now. The only thing she can do is say the word *quit,* over and over. If you ask me again, I'm leaving, and I still have most of a drink here." I raise my glass. "Congratulations, pal."

"Thanks, Flip. Flip! We have to celebrate somehow! We have to do something fun together!"

"I can't think of anything, Gunther."

"It's hot out. It's muggy. Flip! You've never been in my pool!"

"I didn't bring my suit today."

"You can use one of my suits."

"Really, Gunther."

He pounds upstairs. When he comes back down, he's in his trunks, a total embodiment of what it is to be flesh. He tosses me an extra pair. They're like a hot-air balloon or a parachute. I put them on in the bathroom and come out holding a yard of excess suit behind me. Gunther has the stapler from his desk. He staples the trunks until they stay up by themselves.

We go out the back door and into the yard. Gunther's pool is a big one, with all the fixtures — three ladders, two diving boards, ropes with colorful floats. The blue water sparkles with points of early-evening light. "Just a quick dip in the low end here, Gunther," I say. "I have to get home for dinner."

"Flip," he says. "Did I tell you I started taking real scuba-diving lessons? From a registered diving teacher at the Y? He's been showing the class all this neat stuff, special things you have to do in case of emergencies. I have to show you a couple of these things. I can teach you the basics of diving in about two minutes."

"Gunther, no, really. I've always had a slight fear of the water, to tell you the truth. I was swept out into the ocean once when I was a kid, and lifeguards had to save me with a motorboat."

"You never told me that," he says. "That would make a great scene. You should be a little more forthcoming with your experiences. It would help you rise above them." He starts getting the scuba stuff out of the equipment shed. "Now, look, these are what we call weight belts. They keep you from floating to the top." He hands me one and starts putting one on himself.

I drop it on the grass. "See you, Gunther. It's been, you know, nice."

He grabs my shoulder. "MaryLou goes diving with me, Flip, and she can't even drive a stick shift. Are you telling me you're afraid to do this? I know, you have to go home. Hey, it's been a special day. I'm asking you to take a little dive with me to celebrate. Ten lousy minutes for a little fun, and then you can go home."

I pick up the weight belt and put it on. Gunther is tying a heavy rope around his waist. About twenty feet of rope is left when he's finished, and he proceeds to tie the other end around me. "Like mountain climbers," he says.

"Divers don't do that, Gunther. No diver ties himself to another diver."

"Yes, they do, Flip. In certain kinds of salvage operations they do. It's a special knot that comes undone when you pull on it." He pulls on the knot and the rope drops off my waist onto the grass. "Okay?" He reties the rope for me. "I have this neat maneuver I want to show you — what divers do when one diver for some reason loses his tank or runs out of air. We have to do this particular maneuver if we want to have some fun here today, because I have only one tank with air in it."

"Oh, Christ."

"Put on your flippers, Flip," he says, putting on the only tank with air in it.

I put on the flippers and we slap across the lawn to the concrete apron along the edge of the pool. Gunther explains that we're going to fall into the deep end on our backs, get ourselves oriented under water, and then start sharing the one mouthpiece. I'm going to love it, he says. It'll be much more interesting than simply having my own tank. He shows me how to put the mouthpiece in and take it out without swallowing water. "Granted, it's a little different up here on land," he says. "Ready? Lower your mask."

I lower my mask. Then, without even giving me a signal, Gunther topples backward like a bomb leaving a plane. The splash he makes comes right over my head, and then the rope runs out and snaps me into the vortex behind him.

Under water it's white and opaque, with millions of tiny bubbles, and I can't see anything. Then I make out Gunther, his legs and arms wafting gently like seaweed fronds. I watch him swim for a few seconds, fascinated by how graceful he is under water, the way whales are said to be. I can see him smiling around the mouthpiece. He waves goodbye to me as I sink. The weight belt is doing much more to me than to Gunther; soon I'm directly beneath him and panicking. I try to swim upward, but I don't know how to use the flippers and can't kick with them on. I pull on the special knot, but it doesn't work now that it's wet. I try to undo the weight belt, but it's jammed by the rope. I'm about to start crying, despite the unexpected thought that crying under water would be absurd.

Then I feel myself rising toward the surface. Arm over arm, Gunther is hauling me up by the umbilical rope. When he gets me to his level, he pushes the mouthpiece into my face. I'm afraid to breathe through it. *Breathe!* he says with his hands. I breathe. The air from the tank is the most wonderful thing I've ever known, physical ecstasy and my life to do over again. After a few breaths I'm all calmed down.

Gunther points to me and moves his arms and legs. *You're supposed to hold yourself up,* he's saying. I point to myself and make some gestures: *I can't.* He gestures, *Try,* takes the mouthpiece away, and lets go of the rope. I try again and sink stupidly, all the way down. He hauls me back up, collects the excess rope, and ties it all into one big bow between us, so that I can't sink too far away.

We fall into a rhythm with the tank, two breaths each time, passing the hose back and forth peace-pipe fashion. Peace is what it is, an amazing, liquid peace. Each sharing of the air is the deepest cooperation between comrades, something solid and good that would never be withheld. We hear nothing but the gurgling of the tank and somewhere, very distant, the persistent *OM* of the pool filter. Random thoughts and memories bubble through me like Aqualung air, one notion after another in bubbly succession, each considered for a globular instant and then allowed to bubble away forever. I've never envied anything Gunther has, but maybe I've misunderstood it all, because I envy this. If I had a lot of money, a swimming pool and a scuba tank would be the first things I'd buy, so that I could leave the earth this way for an hour or two every evening.

A small kick or motion of the arm sends us orbiting slowly around each other in the water like space walkers. Behind Gunther's face mask his eyes are closed. He might almost be sleeping. I see that this is the essential Gunther — who he really is and who he'd be on land, too, if he didn't have to do what he does up there because of what his father did to him.

He opens his eyes and sees me staring at him. He smiles and gestures at the blueness around him as if to say, *Aren't you glad you stayed to check this out?* I nod and give him the okay sign. He points to the surface of the water, shrugs his shoulders, and flops his arms. He actually laughs, and a bubble floats out of his mouth with the message, *You really saved me up there.*

I tap my chest, meaning, *I know I did, you huge oaf.*

But the rock-and-roll movie was my idea! he says, slapping his own chest defiantly. *And I'm not a bad man!* he says, kicking his feet. *Not as bad as you make out, that's for sure. You're such a judgmental person. My tenants don't need to talk to me about every goddamn leaky faucet.*

What about that Pakistani baby? I signal, imitating the mother's flowing robes and jutting out my chin self-righteously.

Okay, he nods, *that was wrong. I admit it.*

I make a signal to my heart, meaning, *That really upset my wife. You almost destroyed my marriage.*

He shakes his head with great irritation. He lashes his pink fists through the blue water. *Me destroy your marriage! Did you ever think that maybe you shouldn't complain to your wife so much? I'll bet she doesn't bring home every single stupid thing that happens to her every day and inflict it on you. You're such a baby!*

I nod sadly. *Okay, you have a point.*

He rolls onto his back and starts paddling both of us around the depths of the pool. I let myself be towed along, staring up at the silvery surface of the water, taking my turns on the scuba tank. The water's surface reminds me of the silver screen of a movie theater, and as a game I try to see a movie in it. At first I don't see anything, and then after a while I begin to see the rock-and-roll movie. I see precisely how it ought to go, what scenes it ought to have, all the things about life that you could make people understand while you had their attention with the music. I see that the world really needs this great, honest, full-of-heart movie about an American band, and that if I don't do it with Gunther, he'll screw it up and it won't be the movie I'm seeing. Or Joseph will bring in somebody else to take my place. Somebody else will get to give the world all the pleasure and instruction of the great rock-and-roll movie, and then the world will give that person the swimming pool and scuba tank in return. Why shouldn't it be me?

RAYMOND CARVER

Boxes

FROM THE NEW YORKER

MY MOTHER IS packed and ready to move. But Sunday afternoon, at the last minute, she calls and says for us to come eat with her. "My icebox is defrosting," she tells me. "I have to fry up this chicken before it rots." She says we should bring our own plates and some knives and forks. She's packed most of her dishes and kitchen things. "Come on and eat with me one last time," she says. "You and Jill."

I hang up the phone and stand at the window for a minute longer, wishing I could figure this thing out. But I can't. So finally I turn to Jill and say, "Let's go to my mother's for a goodbye meal."

Jill is at the table with a Sears catalogue in front of her, trying to find us some curtains. But she's been listening. She makes a face. "Do we have to?" she says. She bends down the corner of a page and closes the catalogue. She sighs. "God, we been over there to eat two or three times in this last month alone. Is she ever actually going to leave?"

Jill always says what's on her mind. She's thirty-five years old, wears her hair short, and grooms dogs for a living. Before she became a groomer, something she likes, she used to be a housewife and mother. Then all hell broke loose. Her two children were kidnapped by her first husband and taken to live in Australia. Her second husband, who drank, left her with a broken eardrum before he drove their car through a bridge into the Elwha River. He didn't have life insurance, not to mention property-damage insurance. Jill had to borrow money to bury him, and then — can you beat it? — she was presented with a bill for the bridge repair. Plus, she had her own medical bills. She can tell this story now. She's bounced back. But she has run out of patience with my mother. I've run out of patience, too. But I don't see my options.

"She's leaving day after tomorrow," I say. "Hey, Jill, don't do any favors. Do you want to come with me or not?" I tell her it doesn't matter to me one way or the other. I'll say she has a migraine. It's not like I've never told a lie before.

"I'm coming," she says. And like that she gets up and goes into the bathroom, where she likes to pout.

We've been together since last August, about the time my mother picked to move up here to Longview from California. Jill tried to make the best of it. But my mother pulling into town just when we were trying to get our act together was nothing either of us had bargained for. Jill said it reminded her of the situation with her first husband's mother. "She was a clinger," Jill said. "You know what I mean? I thought I was going to suffocate."

It's fair to say that my mother sees Jill as an intruder. As far as she's concerned, Jill is just another girl in a series of girls who have appeared in my life since my wife left me. Someone, to her mind, likely to take away affection, attention, maybe even some money that might otherwise come to her. But someone deserving of respect? No way. I remember — how can I forget it? — she called my wife a whore before we were married, and then called her a whore fifteen years later, after she left me for someone else.

Jill and my mother act friendly enough when they find themselves together. They hug each other when they say hello or goodbye. They talk about shopping specials. But Jill dreads the time she has to spend in my mother's company. She claims my mother bums her out. She says my mother is negative about everything and everybody and ought to find an outlet, like other people in her age bracket. Crocheting, maybe, or card games at the Senior Citizens Center, or else going to church. Something, anyway, so that she'll leave us in peace. But my mother had her own way of solving things. She announced she was moving back to California. The hell with everything and everybody in this town. What a place to live! She wouldn't continue to live in this town if they gave her the place and six more like it.

Within a day or two of deciding to move, she'd packed her things into boxes. That was last January. Or maybe it was February. Anyway, last winter sometime. Now it's the end of June. Boxes have been sitting around inside her house for months. You have to walk around them or step over them to get from one room to another. This is no way for anyone's mother to live.

After a while, ten minutes or so, Jill comes out of the bathroom. I've found a roach and am trying to smoke that and drink a bottle of ginger ale while I watch one of the neighbors change the oil in his car. Jill doesn't look at me. Instead, she goes into the kitchen and puts some plates and utensils into a paper sack. But when she comes back through the living room I stand up, and we hug each other. Jill says, "It's okay." What's okay, I wonder. As far as I can see, nothing's okay. But she holds me and keeps patting my shoulder. I can smell the pet shampoo on her. She comes home from work wearing the stuff. It's everywhere. Even when we're in bed together. She gives me a final pat. Then we go out to the car and drive across town to my mother's.

I like where I live. I didn't when I first moved here. There was nothing to do at night, and I was lonely. Then I met Jill. Pretty soon, after a few weeks, she brought her things over and started living with me. We didn't set any long-term goals. We were happy and we had a life together. We told each other we'd finally got lucky. But my mother didn't have anything going in her life. So she wrote me and said she'd decided on moving here. I wrote her back and said I didn't think it was such a good idea. The weather's terrible in the winter, I said. They're building a prison a few miles from town, I told her. The place is bumper-to-bumper tourists all summer, I said. But she acted as if she never got my letters, and came anyway. Then, after she'd been in town a little less than a month, she told me she hated the place. She acted as if it were my fault she'd moved here and my fault she found everything so disagreeable. She started calling me up and telling me how crummy the place was. "Laying guilt trips," Jill called it. She told me the bus service was terrible and the drivers unfriendly. As for the people at the Senior Citizens — well, she didn't want to play casino. "They can go to hell," she said, "and take their card games with them." The clerks at the supermarket were surly, the guys in the service station didn't give a damn about her or her car. And she'd made up her mind about the man she rented from, Larry Hadlock. King Larry, she called him. "He thinks he's *superior* to everyone because he has some shacks for rent and a few dollars. I wish to God I'd never laid eyes on him."

It was too hot for her when she arrived, in August, and in September it started to rain. It rained almost every day for weeks. In October it turned cold. There was snow in November and December. But long before that she began to put the bad mouth on the place and the people to the extent that I didn't want to hear about it anymore, and I told her so finally. She cried, and I hugged her and thought that was the end of it. But a few days later she started in again, same stuff. Just before Christmas she called to see when I was coming by with her presents. She hadn't put up a tree and didn't intend to, she said. Then she said something else. She said if this weather didn't improve she was going to kill herself.

"Don't talk crazy," I said.

She said, "I mean it, honey. I don't want to see this place again except from my coffin. I hate this g.d. place. I don't know why I moved here. I wish I could just die and get it over with."

I remember hanging on to the phone and watching a man high up on a pole doing something to a power line. Snow whirled around his head. As I watched, he leaned out from the pole, supported only by his safety belt. Suppose he falls, I thought. I didn't have any idea what I was going to say next. I had to say something. But I was filled with unworthy feelings, thoughts no son should admit to. "You're my mother," I said finally. "What can I do to help?"

"Honey, you can't do anything," she said. "The time for doing anything has come and gone. It's too late to do anything. I wanted to like it here. I thought we'd go on picnics and take drives together. But none of that happened. You're always busy. You're off working, you and Jill. You're never at home. Or else if you are at home you have the phone off the hook all day. Anyway, I never see you," she said.

"That's not true," I said. And it wasn't. But she went on as if she hadn't heard me. Maybe she hadn't.

"Besides," she said, "this weather is killing me. It's too damned cold here. Why didn't you tell me this was the North Pole? If you had, I'd never have come. I want to go back to California, honey. I can get out and go places there. I don't know anywhere to go here. There are people back in California. I've got friends there who care what happens to me. Nobody gives a damn here. Well, I just pray I can get through to June. If I can make it that long, if I can last to June, I'm leaving this place forever. This is the worst place I've ever lived in."

What could I say? I didn't know what to say. I couldn't even say anything about the weather. Weather was a real sore point. We said goodbye and hung up.

Other people take vacations in the summer, but my mother moves. She started moving years ago, after my dad lost his job. When that happened, when he was laid off, they sold their home, as if this were what they should do, and went to where they thought things would be better. But things weren't any better there, either. They moved again. They kept on moving. They lived in rented houses, apartments, mobile homes, and motel units even. They kept moving, lightening their load with each move they made. A couple of times they landed in a town where I lived. They'd move in with my wife and me for a while and then they'd move on again. They were like migrating animals in this regard, except there was no pattern to their movement. They moved around for years, sometimes even leaving the state for what they thought would be greener pastures. But mostly they stayed in Northern California and did their moving there. Then my dad died, and I thought my mother would stop moving and stay in one place for a while. But she didn't. She kept moving. I suggested once that she go to a psychiatrist. I even said I'd pay for it. But she wouldn't hear of it. She packed and moved out of town instead. I was desperate about things or I wouldn't have said that about the psychiatrist.

She was always in the process of packing or else unpacking. Sometimes she'd move two or three times in the same year. She talked bitterly about the place she was leaving and optimistically about the place she was going to. Her mail got fouled up, her benefit checks went off somewhere else, and she spent hours

writing letters, trying to get it all straightened out. Sometimes
she'd move out of an apartment house, move to another one a
few blocks away, and then, a month later, move back to the place
she'd left, only to a different floor or a different side of the
building. That's why when she moved here I rented a house for
her and saw to it that it was furnished to her liking. "Moving
around keeps her alive," Jill said. "It gives her something to
do. She must get some kind of weird enjoyment out of it, I
guess." But enjoyment or not, Jill thinks my mother must be
losing her mind. I think so, too. But how do you tell your
mother this? How do you deal with her if this is the case?
Crazy doesn't stop her from planning and getting on with her
next move.

She is waiting at the back door for us when we pull in. She's
seventy years old, has gray hair, wears glasses with rhinestone
frames, and has never been sick a day in her life. She hugs Jill,
and then she hugs me. Her eyes are bright, as if she's been
drinking. But she doesn't drink. She quit years ago, after my
dad went on the wagon. We finish hugging and go inside. It's
around five in the afternoon. I smell whatever it is drifting out
of her kitchen and remember I haven't eaten since breakfast.
My buzz has worn off.
    "I'm starved," I say.
    "Something smells good," Jill says.
    "I hope it tastes good," my mother says. "I hope this chicken's
done." She raises the lid on a fry pan and pushes a fork into a
chicken breast. "If there's anything I can't stand, it's raw
chicken. I think it's done. Why don't you sit down? Sit anyplace.
I still can't regulate my stove. The burners heat up too fast. I
don't like electric stoves and never have. Move that junk off the
chair, Jill. I'm living here like a damned gypsy. But not for much
longer, I hope." She sees me looking around for the ashtray.
"Behind you," she says. "On the windowsill, honey. Before you
sit down, why don't you pour us some of that Pepsi? You'll have
to use these paper cups. I should have told you to bring some
glasses. Is the Pepsi cold? I don't have any ice. This icebox won't
keep anything cold. It isn't worth a damn. My ice cream turns
to soup. It's the worst icebox I've ever had."

She forks the chicken onto a plate and puts the plate on the table along with beans and coleslaw and white bread. Then she looks to see if there is anything she's forgetting. Salt and pepper! "Sit down," she says.

We draw our chairs up to the table, and Jill takes the plates out of the sack and hands them around the table to us. "Where are you going to live when you go back?" she says. "Do you have a place lined up?"

My mother passes the chicken to Jill and says, "I wrote that lady I rented from before. She wrote back and said she had a nice first-floor place I could have. It's close to the bus stop and there's lots of stores in the area. There's a bank and a Safeway. It's the nicest place. I don't know why I left there." She says that and helps herself to some coleslaw.

"Why'd you leave then?" Jill says. "If it was so nice and all." She picks up her drumstick, looks at it, and takes a bite of the meat.

"I'll tell you why. There was an old alcoholic woman who lived next door to me. She drank from morning to night. The walls were so thin I could hear her munching ice cubes all day. She had to use a walker to get around, but that still didn't stop her. I'd hear that walker *scrape, scrape* against the floor from morning to night. That and her icebox door closing." She shakes her head at all she had to put up with. "I had to get out of there. *Scrape, scrape* all day. I couldn't stand it. I just couldn't live like that. This time I told the manager I didn't want to be next to any alcoholics. And I didn't want anything on the second floor. The second floor looks out on the parking lot. Nothing to see from there." She waits for Jill to say something more. But Jill doesn't comment. My mother looks over at me.

I'm eating like a wolf and don't say anything, either. In any case, there's nothing more to say on the subject. I keep chewing and look over at the boxes stacked against the fridge. Then I help myself to more coleslaw.

Pretty soon I finish and push my chair back. Larry Hadlock pulls up in back of the house, next to my car, and takes a lawn-mower out of his pickup. I watch him through the window behind the table. He doesn't look in our direction.

"What's he want?" my mother says and stops eating.

"He's going to cut your grass, it looks like," I say.

"It doesn't need cutting," she says. "He cut it last week. What's there for him to cut?"

"It's for the new tenant," Jill says. "Whoever that turns out to be."

My mother takes this in and then goes back to eating.

Larry Hadlock starts his mower and begins to cut the grass. I know him a little. He lowered the rent twenty-five a month when I told him it was my mother. He is a widower — a big fellow, mid-sixties. An unhappy man with a good sense of humor. His arms are covered with white hair, and white hair stands out from under his cap. He looks like a magazine illustration of a farmer. But he isn't a farmer. He is a retired construction worker who's saved a little money. For a while, in the beginning, I let myself imagine that he and my mother might take some meals together and become friends.

"There's the king," my mother says. "King Larry. Not everyone has as much money as he does and can live in a big house and charge other people high rents. Well, I hope I never see his cheap old face again once I leave here. Eat the rest of this chicken," she says to me. But I shake my head and light a cigarette. Larry pushes his mower past the window.

"You won't have to look at it much longer," Jill says.

"I'm sure glad of that, Jill. But I know he won't give me my deposit back."

"How do you know that?" I say.

"I just know," she says. "I've had dealings with his kind before. They're out for all they can get."

Jill says, "It won't be long now and you won't have to have anything more to do with him."

"I'll be so glad."

"But it'll be somebody just like him," Jill says.

"I don't want to think that, Jill," my mother says.

She makes coffee while Jill clears the table. I rinse the cups. Then I pour coffee, and we step around a box marked "Knick-knacks" and take our cups into the living room.

Larry Hadlock is at the side of the house. Traffic moves slowly on the street out in front, and the sun has started down over the trees. I can hear the commotion the mower makes. Some crows leave the phone line and settle onto the newly cut grass in the front yard.

"I'm going to miss you, honey," my mother says. Then she says, "I'll miss you, too, Jill. I'm going to miss both of you."

Jill sips her coffee and nods. Then she says, "I hope you have a safe trip back and find the place you're looking for at the end of the road."

"When I get settled — and this is my last move, so help me — I hope you'll come and visit," my mother says. She looks at me and waits to be reassured.

"We will," I say. But even as I say it I know it isn't true. My life caved in on me down there, and I won't be going back.

"I wish you could have been happier here," Jill says. "I wish you'd been able to stick it out or something. You know what? Your son is worried sick about you."

"Jill," I say.

But she gives her head a little shake and goes on. "Sometimes he can't sleep over it. He wakes up sometimes in the night and says, 'I can't sleep. I'm thinking about my mother.' There," she says and looks at me. "I've said it. But it was on my mind."

"How do you think I must feel?" my mother says. Then she says, "Other women my age can be happy. Why can't I be like other women? All I want is a house and a town to live in that will make me happy. That isn't a crime, is it? I hope not. I hope I'm not asking too much out of life." She puts her cup on the floor next to her chair and waits for Jill to tell her she isn't asking for too much. But Jill doesn't say anything, and in a minute my mother begins to outline her plans to be happy.

After a time Jill lowers her eyes to her cup and has some more coffee. I can tell she's stopped listening. But my mother keeps talking anyway. The crows work their way through the grass in the front yard. I hear the mower howl and then thud as it picks up a clump of grass in the blade and comes to a stop. In a minute, after several tries, Larry gets it going again. The crows fly off, back to their wire. Jill picks at a fingernail. My mother is saying that the secondhand-furniture dealer is coming around the next morning to collect the things she isn't going to send on the bus or carry with her in the car. The table and chairs, TV, sofa, and bed are going with the dealer. But he's told her he doesn't have any use for the card table, so my mother is going to throw it out unless we want it.

"We'll take it," I say. Jill looks over. She starts to say something but changes her mind.

I will drive the boxes to the Greyhound station the next afternoon and start them on the way to California. My mother will spend the last night with us, as arranged. And then, early the next morning, two days from now, she'll be on her way.

She continues to talk. She talks on and on as she describes the trip she is about to make. She'll drive until four o'clock in the afternoon and then take a motel room for the night. She figures to make Eugene by dark. Eugene is a nice town — she stayed there once before, on the way up here. When she leaves the motel, she'll leave at sunrise and should, if God is looking out for her, be in California that afternoon. And God *is* looking out for her, she knows he is. How else explain her being kept around on the face of the earth? He has a plan for her. She's been praying a lot lately. She's been praying for me, too.

"Why are you praying for him?" Jill wants to know.

"Because I feel like it. Because he's my son," my mother says. "Is there anything the matter with that? Don't we all need praying for sometimes? Maybe some people don't. I don't know. What do I know anymore?" She brings a hand to her forehead and rearranges some hair that's come loose from a pin.

The mower sputters off, and pretty soon we see Larry go around the house pulling the hose. He sets the hose out and then goes slowly back around the house to turn the water on. The sprinkler begins to turn.

My mother starts listing the ways she imagines Larry has wronged her since she's been in the house. But now I'm not listening, either. I am thinking how she is about to go down the highway again, and nobody can reason with her or do anything to stop her. What can I do? I can't tie her up, or commit her, though it may come to that eventually. I worry for her, and she is a heartache to me. She is all the family I have left. I'm sorry she didn't like it here and wants to leave. But I'm never going back to California. And when that's clear to me I understand something else, too. I understand that after she leaves I'm probably never going to see her again.

I look over at my mother. She stops talking. Jill raises her eyes. Both of them look at me.

"What is it, honey?" my mother says.

"What's wrong?" Jill says.

I lean forward in the chair and cover my face with my hands. I sit like that for a minute, feeling bad and stupid for doing it. But I can't help it. And the woman who brought me into this life, and this other woman I picked up with less than a year ago, they exclaim together and rise and come over to where I sit with my head in my hands like a fool. I don't open my eyes. I listen to the sprinkler whipping the grass.

"What's wrong? What's the matter?" they say.

"It's okay," I say. And in a minute it is. I open my eyes and bring my head up. I reach for a cigarette.

"See what I mean?" Jill says. "You're driving him crazy. He's going crazy with worry over you." She is on one side of my chair, and my mother is on the other side. They could tear me apart in no time at all.

"I wish I could die and get out of everyone's way," my mother says quietly. "So help me Hannah, I can't take much more of this."

"How about some more coffee?" I say. "Maybe we ought to catch the news," I say. "Then I guess Jill and I better head for home."

Two days later, early in the morning, I say goodbye to my mother for what may be the last time. I've let Jill sleep. It won't hurt if she's late to work for a change. The dogs can wait for their baths and trimmings and such. My mother holds my arm as I walk her down the steps to the driveway and open the car door for her. She is wearing white slacks and a white blouse and white sandals. Her hair is pulled back and tied with a scarf. That's white, too. It's going to be a nice day, and the sky is clear and already blue.

On the front seat of the car I see maps and a thermos of coffee. My mother looks at these things as if she can't recall having come outside with them just a few minutes ago. She turns to me then and says, "Let me hug you once more. Let me love your neck. I know I won't see you for a long time." She puts an arm around my neck, draws me to her, and then begins to cry. But she stops almost at once and steps back, pushing the heel of her hand against her eyes. "I said I wouldn't do that, and I won't. But let me get a last look at you anyway. I'll miss you, honey," she says. "I'm just going to have to live through this. I've already lived through things I didn't think were possible. But I'll live through this, too, I guess." She gets into the car, starts it, and runs the engine for a minute. She rolls her window down.

"I'm going to miss you," I say. And I *am* going to miss her. She's my mother, after all, and why shouldn't I miss her? But, God forgive me, I'm glad, too, that it's finally time and that she is leaving.

"Goodbye," she says. "Tell Jill thanks for supper last night. Tell her I said goodbye."

"I will," I say. I stand there wanting to say something else. But I don't know what. We keep looking at each other, trying to smile and reassure each other. Then something comes into her eyes, and I believe she is thinking about the highway and how far she is going to have to drive that day. She takes her eyes off me and looks down the road. Then she rolls her window up, puts the car into gear, and drives to the intersection, where she has to wait for the light to change. When I see she's made it into traffic and headed toward the highway, I go back in the house and drink some coffee. I feel sad for a while, and then the sadness goes away and I start thinking about other things.

A few nights later my mother calls to say she is in her new place. She is busy fixing it up, the way she does when she has a new place. She tells me I'll be happy to know she likes it just fine to be back in sunny California. But she says there's something in the air where she is living, maybe it's pollen, that is causing her to sneeze a lot. And the traffic is heavier than she remembers from before. She doesn't recall there being so much traffic in her neighborhood. Naturally, everyone still drives like crazy down there. "California drivers," she says. "What else can you expect?" She says it's hot for this time of the year. She doesn't think the air-conditioning unit in her apartment is working right. I tell her she should talk to the manager. "She's never around when you need her," my mother says. She hopes she hasn't made a mistake in moving back to California. She waits before she says anything else.

I'm standing at the window with the phone pressed to my ear, looking out at the lights from town and at the lighted houses closer by. Jill is at the table with the catalogue, listening.

"Are you still there?" my mother asks. "I wish you'd say something."

I don't know why, but it's then I recall the affectionate name my dad used sometimes when he was talking nice to my mother — those times, that is, when he wasn't drunk. It was a long time ago, and I was a kid, but always, hearing it, I felt better, less afraid, more hopeful about the future. *"Dear,"* he'd say. He called her "dear" sometimes — a sweet name. "Dear," he'd say, "if you're going to the store, will you bring me some cigarettes?" Or "Dear, is your cold any better?" "Dear, where is my coffee cup?"

The word issues from my lips before I can think what else I want to say to go along with it. "Dear." I say it again. I call her "dear." "Dear, try not to be afraid," I say. I tell my mother I love her and I'll write to her, yes. Then I say goodbye, and I hang up.

For a while I don't move from the window. I keep standing there, looking out at the lighted houses in our neighborhood. As I watch, a car turns off the road and pulls into a driveway. The porch light goes on. The door to the house opens and someone comes out on the porch and stands there waiting.

Jill turns the pages of her catalogue, and then she stops turning them. "This is what we want," she says. "This is more like what I had in mind. Look at this, will you." But I don't look. I don't care five cents for curtains. "What is it you see out there, honey?" Jill says. "Tell me."

What's there to tell? The people over there embrace for a minute, and then they go inside the house together. They leave the light burning. Then they remember, and it goes out.

BHARATI MUKHERJEE

The Tenant

FROM THE LITERARY REVIEW

MAYA SANYAL has been in Cedar Falls, Iowa, less than two weeks. She's come, books and clothes and one armchair rattling in the smallest truck that U-Haul would rent her, from New Jersey. Before that she was in North Carolina. Before that, Calcutta, India. Every place has something to give. She is sitting at the kitchen table with Fran, drinking bourbon for the first time in her life. Fran Johnson found her the furnished apartment and helped her settle in. Now she's brought a bottle of bourbon, which gives her the right to stay and talk for a bit. She's breaking up with someone named Vern, a pharmacist. Vern's father is also a pharmacist and owns a drugstore. Maya has seen Vern's father on TV twice already. The first time on the local news was when he spoke out against the selling of painkillers like Advil and Nuprin in supermarkets and gas stations. In the matter of painkillers, Maya is a universalist. The other time he was in a barbershop quartet. Vern gets along all right with his father. He likes the pharmacy business, as business goes, but he wants to go back to graduate school and learn to make films. Maya is drinking her first bourbon tonight because Vern left today for San Francisco State.

"I understand totally," Fran says. She teaches Utopian Fiction and a course in Women's Studies and worked hard to get Maya hired. Maya has a Ph.D. in Comparative Literature and will introduce writers like R. K. Narayan and Chinua Achebe to three sections of sophomores at the University of Northern Iowa. "A person has to leave home. Try out his wings."

Fran has to use the bathroom. "I don't feel abandoned." She pushes her chair away from the table. "Anyway, it was a sex thing totally. We were good together. It'd be different if I'd loved him."

Maya tries to remember what's in the refrigerator. They need food. She hasn't been to the supermarket in over a week. She doesn't have a car yet and so she relies on a corner store — a longish walk — for milk, cereal, and frozen dinners. Someday these exigencies will show up as bad skin and collapsed muscle tone. No folly is ever lost. Maya pictures history as a net, the kind of safety net traveling trapeze artists of her childhood fell into when they were inattentive, or clumsy. Going to circuses in Calcutta with her father is what she remembers vividly. It is a banal memory, for her father, the owner of a steel company, is a complicated man.

Fran is out in the kitchen long enough for Maya to worry. They need food. Her mother believed in food. What is love, anger, inner peace, etc., her mother used to say, but the brain's biochemistry. Maya doesn't want to get into that, but she is glad she has enough stuff in the refrigerator to make an omelet. She realizes Indian women are supposed to be inventive with food, whip up exotic delights to tickle an American's palate, and she knows she should be meeting Fran's generosity and candor with some sort of bizarre and effortless countermove. If there's an exotic spice store in Cedar Falls or in neighboring Waterloo, she hasn't found it. She's looked in the phone book for common Indian names, especially Bengali, but hasn't yet struck up culinary intimacies. That will come—it always does. There's a six-pack in the fridge that her landlord, Ted Suminski, had put in because she'd be thirsty after unpacking. She was thirsty, but she doesn't drink beer. She probably should have asked him to come up and drink the beer. Except for Fran she hasn't had anyone over. Fran is more friendly and helpful than anyone Maya has known in the States and she came to North Carolina ten years ago, at nineteen. Fran is a Swede, and she is tall, with blue eyes. Her hair, however, is a dull, darkish brown.

"I don't think I can handle anything that heavy duty," Fran says when she comes back to the room. She means the omelet. "I have to go home in any case. She lives with her mother and her aunt, two women in their mid-seventies, in a drafty farm-house. The farmhouse now has a computer store catty-corner from it. Maya's been to the farm. She's been shown photographs of the way the corner used to be. If land values ever rebound, Fran will be worth millions.

Before Fran leaves she says, "Has Rab Chatterji called you yet?"

"No." She remembers the name, a good, reliable Bengali name, from the first night's study of the phone book. Dr. Rabindra Chatterji teaches Physics.

"He called the English office just before I left." She takes car keys out of her pocketbook. She reknots her scarf. "I bet Indian men are more sensitive than Americans. Rab's a Brahmin, that's what people say."

A Chatterji has to be a Bengali Brahmin — last names give ancestral secrets away — but Brahminness seems to mean more to Fran than it does to Maya. She was born in 1954, six full years after India became independent. Her India was Nehru's India: a charged, progressive place.

"All Indian men are wife beaters," Maya says. She means it and doesn't mean it. "That's why I married an American." Fran knows about the divorce, but nothing else. Fran is on the Hiring, Tenure, and Reappointment Committee.

Maya sees Fran down the stairs and to the car that is parked in the back in the spot reserved for Maya's car, if she had owned one. It will take her several months to save enough to buy one. She always pays cash, never borrows. She tells herself she's still recovering from the U-Haul drive halfway across the country. Ted Suminski is in his kitchen watching the women. Maya waves to him because waving to him, acknowledging him in that way, makes him seem less creepy. He seems to live alone, though a sign THE SUMINSKIS hangs from a metal horse's head in the front yard. Maya hasn't seen Mrs. Suminski. She hasn't seen any children either. Ted always looks lonely. When she comes back from campus, he's nearly always in the back, throwing darts or shooting baskets.

"What's he like?" Fran gestures with her head as she starts up her car. "You hear these stories."

Maya doesn't want to know the stories. She has signed a year's lease. She doesn't want complications. "He's all right. I keep out of his way."

"You know what I'm thinking? Of all the people in Cedar Falls, you're the one who could understand Vern best. His wanting to try out his wings, run away, stuff like that."

"Not really." Maya is not being modest. Fran is being impulsively democratic, lumping her wayward lover and Indian friend together as headstrong adventurers. For Fran, a utopian and feminist, borders don't count. Maya's taken some big risks, made a break with her parents' ways. She's done things a woman from Ballygunge Park Road doesn't do, even in fantasies. She's not yet shared stories with Fran, apart from the divorce. She's told her nothing of men she picks up, the reputation she'd gained, before Cedar Falls, for "indiscretions." She has a job, equity, three friends she can count on for emergencies. She is an American citizen. But.

Fran's Brahmin calls her two nights later. On the phone he presents himself as Dr. Chatterji, not Rabindra or Rab. An old-fashioned Indian, she assumes. Her father still calls his closest friend "Colonel." Dr. Chatterji asks her to tea on Sunday. She means to say no but hears herself saying, "Sunday? Fivish? I'm not doing anything special this Sunday."

Outside, Ted Suminski is throwing darts in his garage door. The door has painted-on rings: orange, purple, pink. The bull's-eye is gray. He has to be fifty at least. He is a big, thick lonely man about whom people tell stories. Maya pulls the phone cord as far as it'll go so she can look down more directly on her landlord's large, bald head. He has his back to her as he lines up a dart. He's in black running shoes, red shorts, he's naked to the waist. He hunches his right shoulder, he pulls the arm back; a big lonely man shouldn't have so much grace. The dart is ready to cut through the September evening. But Ted Suminski doesn't let go. He swings on worn rubber soles, catches her eye in the window (she has to have imagined this), takes aim at her shadow. Could she have imagined the noise of the dart's metal tip on her windowpane?

Dr. Chatterji is still on the phone. "You are not having any mode of transportation, is that right?"

Ted Suminski has lost interest in her. Perhaps it isn't interest at all; perhaps it's aggression. "I don't drive," she lies, knowing it sounds less shameful than not owning a car. She has said this so often she can get in the right degree of apology and Asian upper-class helplessness. "It's an awful nuisance."

"Not to worry, please." Then, "It is a great honor to be meeting Dr. Sanyal's daughter. In Calcutta business circles he is a legend."

On Sunday she is ready by four-thirty. She doesn't know what the afternoon holds; there are surely no places for "high tea" — a colonial tradition — in Cedar Falls, Iowa. If he takes her back to his place, it will mean he has invited other guests. From his voice she can tell Dr. Chatterji likes to do things correctly. She has dressed herself in a peach-colored nylon georgette sari, jade drop-earrings, and a necklace. The color is good on dark skin. She is not pretty, but she does her best. Working at it is a part of self-respect. In the mid-seventies, when American women felt rather strongly about such things, Maya had been in trouble with her women's group at Duke. She was too feminine. She had tried to explain the world she came out of. Her grandmother had been married off at the age of five in a village now in Bangladesh. Her great-aunt had been burned to death over a dowry problem. She herself had been trained to speak softly, arrange flowers, sing, be pliant. If she were to seduce Ted Suminski, she thinks as she waits in the front yard for Dr. Chatterji, it would be minor heroism. She has broken with the past. But.

Dr. Chatterji drives up for her at about five-ten. He is a hesitant driver. The car stalls, jumps ahead, finally slams to a stop. Maya has to tell him to back off a foot or so; it's hard to leap over two sacks of pruned branches in a sari. Ted Suminski is an obsessive pruner and gardener.

"My sincerest apologies, Mrs. Sanyal," Dr. Chatterji says. He leans across the wide front seat of his noisy, very old, very used car and unlocks the door for her. "I am late. But then, I am sure you're remembering that Indian Standard Time is not at all the same as time in the States." He laughs. He could be nervous — she often had that effect on Indian men. Or he could just be chatty. "These Americans are all the time rushing and rushing but where it gets them?" He moves his head laterally once, twice. It's the gesture made famous by Peter Sellers. When Peter Sellers did it, it had seemed hilarious. Now it suggests that Maya and Dr. Chatterji have three thousand years plus civilization, sophistication, moral virtue, over people born on this continent. Like her, Dr. Chatterji is a naturalized American. His wallet is on the seat between them. She can see his citizenship card overlapping his driver's license.

"Call me Maya," she says. She fusses with the seat belt. She does it because she needs time to look him over. He seems quite harmless. She takes in the prominent teeth, the eyebrows that run together. He's in a blue shirt and a beige cardigan with the K-Mart logo that buttons tightly over the waist. It's hard to guess his age because he has dyed his hair and his mustache. Late thirties, early forties. Older than she had expected. "Not Mrs. Sanyal."

This isn't the time to tell about ex-husbands. She doesn't know where John is these days. He should have kept up at least. John had come into her life as a graduate student at Duke, and she, mistaking the brief breathlessness of sex for love, had married him. They had stayed together two years, maybe a little less. The pain that John had inflicted all those years ago by leaving her had subsided into a cozy feeling of loss. This isn't the time, but then she doesn't want to be a legend's daughter all evening. She's not necessarily on Dr. Chatterji's side is what she wants to get across early; she's not against America and Americans. She makes the story — of marriage outside the Brahminic pale, the divorce — quick, dull. Her unsentimentality seems to shock him. His stomach sags inside the cardigan.

"We've each had our several griefs," the physicist says. "We're each required to pay our karmic debts."

"Where are we headed?"

"Mrs. Chatterji has made some Indian snacks. She is waiting to meet you because she is knowing your cousin-sister who studied in Scottish Church College. My home is okay, no?"

Fran would get a kick out of this. Maya has slept with married men, with nameless men, with men little more than boys, but never with an Indian man. Never.

*

The Chatterjis live in a small blue house on a gravelly street. There are at least five or six other houses on the street; same size but in different colors and with different front yard treatments. More houses are going up. This is the cutting edge of suburbia.

Mrs. Chatterji stands in the driveway. She is throwing a large plastic ball to a child. The child looks about four, and is Korean or Cambodian. The child is not hers because she tells it, "Chung-Hee, ta-ta, bye-bye. Now I play with guest," as Maya gets out of the car.

Maya hasn't seen this part of town. The early September light softens the construction pits. In that light the houses too close together, the stout woman in a striped cotton sari, the child hugging a pink ball, the two plastic lawn chairs by a tender young tree, the sheets and saris on the clothesline in the back, all seem miraculously incandescent.

"Go home now, Chung-Hee. I am busy." Mrs. Chatterji points the child homeward, then turns to Maya, who has folded her hands in traditional Bengali greeting. "It is an honor. We feel very privileged." She leads Maya indoors to a front room that smells of moisture and paint.

In her new, deliquescent mood, Maya allows herself to be backed into the best armchair — a low-backed, boxy Goodwill item draped over with a Rajasthani bedspread — and asks after the cousin Mrs. Chatterji knows. She doesn't want to let go of Mrs. Chatterji. She doesn't want husband and wife to get into whispered conferences about their guest's misadventures in America as they make tea in the kitchen.

The coffee table is already laid with platters of mutton croquettes, fish chops, onion pakoras, ghugni with puris, samosas, chutneys. Mrs. Chatterji has gone to too much trouble. Maya counts four kinds of sweetmeats in Corning casseroles on an end table. She looks into a see-through lid; spongy, white dumplings float in rosewater syrup. Planets contained, mysteries made visible.

"What are you waiting for, Santana?" Dr. Chatterji becomes imperious, though not unaffectionate. He pulls a dining chair up close to the coffee table. "Make some tea." He speaks in Bengali to his wife, in English to Maya. To Maya he says, grandly,

"We are having real Indian Green Label Lipton. A nephew is bringing it just one month back."

His wife ignores him. "The kettle's already on," she says. She wants to know about the Sanyal family. Is it true her great-grandfather was a member of the Star Chamber in England?

Nothing in Calcutta is ever lost. Just as her story is known to Bengalis all over America, so are the scandals of her family, the grandfather hauled up for tax evasion, the aunt who left her husband to act in films. This woman brings up the Star Chamber, the glories of the Sanyal family, her father's philanthropies, but it's a way of saying, I know the dirt.

The bedrooms are upstairs. In one of those bedrooms an unseen, tormented presence — Maya pictures it as a clumsy ghost that strains to shake off the body's shell — drops things on the floor. The things are heavy and they make the front room's chandelier shake. Light bulbs, shaped like tiny candle flames, flicker. The Chatterjis have said nothing about children. There are no tricycles in the hallway, no small sandals behind the doors. Maya is too polite to ask about the noise, and the Chatterjis don't explain. They talk just a little louder. They flip the embroidered cover off the stereo. What would Maya like to hear? Hemanta Kumar? Manna Dey? Oh, that young chap, Manna Dey! What sincerity, what tenderness he can convey!

Upstairs the ghost doesn't hear the music of nostalgia. The ghost throws and thumps. The ghost makes its own vehement music. Maya hears in its voice madness, self-hate.

Finally the water in the kettle comes to a boil. The whistle cuts through all fantasy and pretense. Dr. Chatterji says, "I'll see to it," and rushes out of the room. But he doesn't go to the kitchen. He shouts up the stairwell. "Poltoo, kindly stop this nonsense straightaway! We're having a brilliant and cultured lady guest and you're creating earthquakes?" The kettle is hysterical.

Mrs. Chatterji wipes her face. The face that had seemed plump and cheery at the start of the evening now is flabby. "My sister's boy," the woman says.

So this is the nephew who has brought with him the cartons of Green Label tea, one of which will be given to Maya.

Mrs. Chatterji speaks to Maya in English as though only the

alien language can keep emotions in check. "Such an intelligent boy! His father is government servant. Very highly placed."

Maya is meant to visualize a smart, clean-cut young man from south Calcutta, but all she can see is a crazy, thwarted, lost graduate student. Intelligence, proper family, guarantee nothing. Even Brahmins can do self-destructive things, feel unsavory urges. Maya herself had been an excellent student.

"He was first class first in B.Sc. from Presidency College," the woman says. "Now he's getting master's in ag science at Iowa State."

The kitchen is silent. Dr. Chatterji comes back into the room with a tray. The teapot is under a tea cozy, a Kashmiri one embroidered with the usual chinar leaves, loops, and chains. *"Her* nephew," he says. The dyed hair and dyed mustache are no longer signs of a man wishing to fight the odds. He is a vain man, anxious to cut losses. "Very unfortunate business."

The nephew's story comes out slowly, over fish chops and mutton croquettes. He is in love with a student from Ghana.

"Everything was A-okay until the Christmas break. Grades, assistantship for next semester, everything."

"I blame the college. The office for foreign students arranged a Christmas party. And now, *baapre baap!* Our poor Poltoo wants to marry a Negro Muslim."

Maya is known for her nasty, ironic one-liners. It has taken her friends weeks to overlook her malicious, un-American pleasure in others' misfortunes. Maya would like to finish Dr. Chatterji off quickly. He is pompous; he is reactionary; he wants to live and work in America but give back nothing except taxes. The confused world of the immigrant — the lostness that Maya and Poltoo feel — that's what Dr. Chatterji wants to avoid. She hates him. But.

Dr. Chatterji's horror is real. A good Brahmin boy in Iowa is in love with an African Muslim. It shouldn't be a big deal. But the more she watches the physicist the more she realizes that "Brahmin" isn't a caste; it's a metaphor. You break one small rule, and the constellation collapses. She thinks suddenly that John Cheever — she is teaching him as a "world writer" in her classes, cheek by jowl with Africans and West Indians — would have understood Dr. Chatterji's dread. Cheever had been on her mind ever since the late afternoon light slanted over Mrs.

Chatterji's drying saris. She remembers now how full of a soft Cheeverian light Durham had been the summer she had slept with John Hadwen, and how after that, her tidy graduate student world became monstrous, lawless. All men became John Hadwen; John became all men. Outwardly, she retained her poise, her Brahminic breeding. She treated her crises as a literary event; she lost her moral sense, her judgment, her power to distinguish. Her parents had behaved magnanimously. They had cabled from Calcutta: WHAT'S DONE IS DONE. WE ARE CONFIDENT YOU WILL HANDLE NEW SITUATIONS WELL. ALL LOVE. But she knows more than do her parents. Love is anarchy.

Poltoo is Mrs. Chatterji's favorite nephew. She looks as though it is her fault that the Sunday has turned unpleasant. She stacks the empty platters methodically. To Maya she says, "It is the goddess who pulls the strings. We are puppets. I know the goddess will fix it. Poltoo will not marry that African woman." Then she goes to the coat closet in the hall and staggers back with a harmonium, the kind sold in music stores in Calcutta, and sets it down on the carpeted floor. "We're nothing but puppets," she says again. She sits at Maya's feet, her pudgy hands on the harmonium's shiny black bellows. She sings, beautifully, in a virgin's high voice, "Come, goddess, come, muse, come to us hapless people's rescue."

Maya is astonished. She has taken singing lessons at Dakshini Academy in Calcutta. She plays the sitar and the tanpur, well enough to please Bengalis, to astonish Americans. But stout Mrs. Chatterji is a devotee, talking to God.

A little after eight, Dr. Chatterji drops her off. It's been an odd evening and they are both subdued.

"I want to say one thing," he says. He stops her from undoing her seat belt. The plastic sacks of pruned branches are still at the corner.

"You don't have to get out," she says.

"Please. Give me one more minute of your time."

"Sure."

"Maya is my favorite name."

She says nothing. She turns away from him without making her embarrassment obvious.

"Truly speaking, it is my favorite. You are sometimes lonely, no? But you are lucky. Divorced women can date, they can go to bars and discos. They can see mens, many mens. But inside marriage there is so much loneliness." A groan, low, horrible, comes out of him.

She turns back toward him, to unlatch the seat belt and run out of the car. She sees that Dr. Chatterji's pants are unzipped. One hand works hard under his Jockey shorts; the other rests, limp, penitential, on the steering wheel.

"Dr. Chatterji — *really!*" she cries.

The next day, Monday, instead of getting a ride home with Fran — Fran says she *likes* to give rides, she needs the chance to talk, and she won't share gas expenses, absolutely not — Maya goes to the periodicals room of the library. There are newspapers from everywhere, even from Madagascar and New Caledonia. She thinks of the periodicals room as an asylum for homesick aliens. There are two aliens already in the room, both Orientals, both absorbed in the politics and gossip of their far-off homes.

She goes straight to the newspapers from India. She bunches her raincoat like a bolster to make herself more comfortable. There's so much to catch up on. A village headman, a known Congress-Indira party worker, has been shot at by scooter-riding snipers. An Indian pugilist has won an international medal — in Nepal. A child drawing well water — the reporter calls the child "a neo-Buddhist, a convert from the now-outlawed untouchable caste" — has been stoned. An editorial explains that the story about stoning is not a story about caste but about failed idealism; a story about promises of green fields and clean, potable water broken, a story about bribes paid and wells not dug. But no, thinks Maya, it's about caste.

Out here, in the heartland of the New World, the India of serious newspapers unsettles. Maya longs again to feel what she had felt in the Chatterji's living room: virtues made physical. It is a familiar feeling, a longing. Had a suitable man presented himself in the reading room at that instant, she would have seduced him. She goes on to the stack of *India Abroad*s, reads through matrimonial columns, and steals an issue to take home.

Indian men want Indian brides. Married Indian men want Indian mistresses. All over America, "handsome, tall, fair" engineers, doctors, data processors — the new pioneers — cry their eerie love calls.

Maya runs a finger down the first column; her fingertip, dark with newsprint, stops at random.

Hello! Hi! Yes, you *are* the one I'm looking for. You are the new emancipated Indo-American woman. You have a zest for life. You are at ease in USA and yet your ethics are rooted in Indian tradition. The man of your dreams has come. Yours truly is handsome, ear-nose-throat specialist, well-settled in Connecticut. Age is 41 but never married, physically fit, sportsmanly and strong. I adore idealism, poetry, beauty. I abhor smugness, passivity, caste system. Write with recent photo. Better still, call!!!

Maya calls. Hullo, hullo, hullo! She hears immigrant lovers cry in crowded shopping malls. Yes, you who are at ease in both worlds, you are the one. She feels she has a fair chance.

A man answers. "Ashoke Mehta speaking."

She speaks quickly into the bright red mouthpiece of her telephone. He will be in Chicago, in transit, passing through O'Hare. United counter, Saturday, two P.M. As easy as that.

"Good," Ashoke Mehta says. "For these encounters I, too, prefer a neutral zone."

On Saturday at exactly two o'clock the man of Maya's dreams floats toward her as lovers used to in shampoo commercials. The United counter is a loud, harassed place, but passengers and piled-up luggage fall away from him. Full-cheeked and fleshy-lipped, he is handsome. He hasn't lied. He is serene, assured, a Hindu god touching down in Illinois.

She can't move. She feels ugly and unworthy. Her adult life no longer seems miraculously rebellious; it is grim, it is perverse. She has accomplished nothing. She has changed her citizenship but she hasn't broken through into the light, the vigor, the *hustle* of the New World. She is stuck in dead space.

"Hullo. Hullo!" Their fingers touch.

Oh, the excitement! Ashoke Mehta's palm feels so right in the small of her back. Hullo, hullo, hullo. He pushes her out of the reach of anti-Khomeini Iranians, Hare Krishnas, American fascists, men with fierce wants, and guides her to an empty gate. They have less than an hour.

"What would you like, Maya?"

She knows he can read her mind, she knows her thoughts are open to him. *You,* she's almost giddy with the thought, with simple desire. "From the snack bar," he says, as though to clarify. "I'm afraid I'm starved."

Below them, where the light is strong and hurtful, a Boeing is being serviced. "Nothing," she says.

He leans forward. She can feel the nap of his scarf — she recognizes the Cambridge colors — she can smell the wool of his Icelandic sweater. She runs her hand along the scarf, then against the flesh of his neck. "Only the impulsive ones call," he says.

The immigrant courtship proceeds. It's easy, he's good with facts. He knows how to come across to a stranger who may end up a lover, a spouse. He makes over a hundred thousand. He owns a house in Hartford and two income properties in Newark. He plays the market but he's cautious. He's good at badminton but plays handball to keep in shape. He watches all the sports on television. Last August he visited Copenhagen, Helsinki, and Leningrad. Once upon a time he collected stamps but now he doesn't have hobbies, except for reading. He counts himself an intellectual, he spends too much on books. Ludlum, Forsyth, MacInnes; other names she doesn't catch. She suppresses a smile, she's told him only she's a graduate student. He's not without his vices. He's a spender, not a saver. He's a sensualist: good food — all foods, but easy on the Indian — good wine. Some temptations he doesn't try to resist.

And I, she wants to ask, do I tempt?

"Now tell me about yourself, Maya." He makes it easy for her. "Have you ever been in love?"

"No."

"But many have loved you, I can see that." He says it not unkindly. It is the fate of women like her and men like him. Their karmic duty, to be loved. It is expected, not judged. She feels he can see them all, the sad parade of need and demand. This isn't the time to reveal all.

And so the courtship enters a second phase.

When she gets back to Cedar Falls, Ted Suminski is standing on the front porch. It's late at night, chilly. He is wearing a down vest. She's never seen him on the porch. In fact there's no chair to sit on. He looks chilled through. He's waited around a while.

"Hi." She has her keys ready. This isn't the night to offer the six-pack in the fridge. He looks expectant, ready to pounce.

"Hi." He looks like a man who might have aimed the dart at her. What has he done to his wife, his kids? Why isn't there at least a dog? "Say, I left a note upstairs."

The note is written in Magic Marker and thumb-tacked to her apartment door. DUE TO PERSONAL REASONS, NAMELY REMAR-RIAGE, I REQUEST THAT YOU VACATE MY PLACE AT THE END OF THE SEMESTER.

Maya takes the note down and retacks it to the kitchen wall. The whole wall is like a bulletin board, made of some new, crumbly building material. Her kitchen, Ted Suminski had told her, was once a child's bedroom. Suminski in love: the idea stuns her. She has misread her landlord. The dart at her window speaks of no twisted fantasy. The landlord wants the tenant out.

She gets a glass out of the kitchen cabinet, gets out a tray of ice, pours herself a shot of Fran's bourbon. She is happy for Ted Suminski. She is. She wants to tell someone how moved she'd been by Mrs. Chatterji's singing. How she'd felt in O'Hare, even about Dr. Rab Chatterji in the car. But Fran is not the person. No one she's ever met is the person. She can't talk about the dead space she lives in. She wishes Ashoke Mehta would call. Right now.

Weeks pass. Then two months. She finds a new room, signs another lease. Her new landlord calls himself Fred. He has no arms, but he helps her move her things. He drives between Ted Suminski's place and his twice in his station wagon. He uses his toes the way Maya uses her fingers. He likes to do things. He pushes garbage sacks full of Maya's clothes up the stairs.

"It's all right to stare," Fred says. "Hell, I would."

That first afternoon in Fred's rooming house, they share a chianti. Fred wants to cook her pork chops but he's a little shy about Indians and meat. Is it beef, or pork? Or any meat? She says it's okay, any meat, but not tonight. He has an ex-wife in Des Moines, two kids in Portland, Oregon. The kids are both normal; he's the only freak in the family. But he's self-reliant. He shops in the supermarket like anyone else, he carries out the garbage, shovels the snow off the sidewalk. He needs Maya's help with one thing. Just one thing. The box of Tide is a bit too heavy to manage. Could she get him the giant size every so often and leave it in the basement?

The dead space need not suffocate. Over the months, Fred and she will settle into companionship. She has never slept with a man without arms. Two wounded people, he will joke during their nightly contortions. It will shock her, this assumed equivalence with a man so strikingly deficient. She knows she is strange, and lonely, but being Indian is not the same, she would have thought, as being a freak.

One night in spring, Fred's phone rings. "Ashoke Mehta speaking." None of this "do you remember me?" nonsense. The god has tracked her down. He hasn't forgotten. "Hullo," he says, in their special way. And because she doesn't answer back, "Hullo, hullo, hullo." She is aware of Fred in the back of the room. He is lighting a cigarette with his toes.

"Yes," she says, "I remember."

"I had to take care of a problem," Ashoke Mehta says. "You know that I have my vices. That time at O'Hare I was honest with you."

She is breathless.

"Who is it, May?" asks Fred.

"You also have a problem," says the voice. His laugh echoes. "You will come to Hartford, I know."

"Yes," she says.

When she moves out, she tells herself, it will not be the end of Fred's world.

JOY WILLIAMS

The Blue Men

FROM ESQUIRE

BOMBER BOYD, age thirteen, told his new acquaintances that summer that his father had been executed by the state of Florida for the murder of a sheriff's deputy and his drug-sniffing German shepherd.

"It's a bummer he killed the dog," a girl said.

"Guns, chair, or lethal injection?" a boy asked.

"Chair," Bomber said. He was sorry he had mentioned the dog in the same breath. The dog had definitely not been necessary.

"Lethal injection is fascist, man; who does lethal injection?" a small, fierce-looking boy said.

"Florida, Florida, Florida," the girl murmured. "We went to Key West once. We did sunset. We did Sloppy's. We bought conch-shell lamps with tiny plastic flamingos and palm trees inside lit up by tiny lights." The girl's hair was cut in a high Mohawk that rose at least half a foot in the air. She was pale, her skin flawless except for one pimple artfully flourishing above her full upper lip.

"Key West isn't Florida," a boy said.

There were six of them standing around, four boys and two girls. Bomber stood there with them, waiting.

May was in her garden looking through a stack of a hundred photographs that her son and daughter-in-law had taken years before when they had visited Morocco. Bomber had been four at the time and May had taken care of him all that spring. There were pictures of camels, walled towns, tiled staircases, and large vats of colored dyes on rooftops. May turned the pictures methodically. There were men washing their heads in a marble ablutions basin. On a dusty road there was the largest pile of carrots May had ever seen. May had been through the photographs many many times. She slowly approached the one that never ceased to trouble her, a picture of her child in the city of Fez. He wore khaki pants and a polo shirt and was squatting beside a blanket upon which teeth were arranged. It had been explained to May that there were many self-styled dentists in Morocco who pulled teeth and then arranged them on plates and sold them. In the photograph, her son looked healthy, muscular, and curious, but there was something unfamiliar about his face. It had begun there, May thought, somehow. She put the photographs down and picked up a collection of postcards from that time, most of them addressed to Bomber. May held one close to her eyes. Men in blue burnouses lounged against their camels, the desert wilderness behind them. On the back was written, *The blue men! We wanted so much to see them but we never did.*

May and Bomber were trying out their life together in a new town. They had only each other, for Bomber's mother was resting in California, where she would probably be resting for quite some time, and May's husband, Harold, was dead. In the new town, which was on an island, May had bought a house and planted a pretty little flower garden. She had two big rooms upstairs that she rented out by the week to tourists. One was in yellow and one was in gray. May liked to listen to the voices in the rooms, but as a rule her tourists didn't say much. Actually, she strained to hear at times. She was not listening for sounds of love, of course. The sounds of love were not what mattered, after all.

Once, as she was standing in the upstairs hallway, polishing a small table there, her husband's last words had returned to her. Whether they had been spoken again by someone in the room, either in the gray room or the yellow room, she did not quite know, but there they were. *That doctor is so stuck on himself* . . . The same words as Harold's very last ones.

The tourists would gather seashells and then leave them behind when they left. They left them on the bureaus and on the windowsills and May would pick them up and take them back to the beach. At night when she could not sleep she would walk downtown to a bar where the young people danced called the Lucky Kittens and have a glass of beer. The Lucky Kittens was a loud and careless place where there was dancing all night long. May sat alone at a table near the door, an old lady, dignified and out of place.

Bomber was down at the dock, watching tourists arrive on the ferry. The tourists were grinning, and ready for anything, they thought. Two boys were playing catch with a tennis ball on the pier, a young boy and an older one in a college sweat shirt. The younger one sidled back and forth close to the pier's edge, catching in both hands the high, lobbed throws the other boy threw. The water was high and dark and flecked with oil and they were both laughing like lunatics. Bomber believed they were brothers and he enjoyed watching them.

A girl moved languidly across the dock toward him. She was the pale girl with the perfect pimple and she touched it delicately as she walked. Her shaved temples had a slight sheen of baby powder on them. Her name was Edith.

"I've been thinking," Edith said, "and I think that what they should do, like, a gesture is enough. Like for murderers they could make them wear black all the time. They could walk around but they'd have to be always in black and they'd have to wear a mask of some sort."

Sometimes Bomber thought of what had happened to his father as an operation. It was an operation they had performed. "A mask," he said. "Hey." He crossed his arms tight across his chest. He thought Edith's long, pale face beautiful.

She nodded. "A mask," she said. "Something really amazing."

"But that wouldn't be enough, would it?" Bomber asked.

"They wouldn't be able to take it off," Edith said. "There'd be no way." There was a pale vein on her temple, curving like a piece of string. "We didn't believe what you told us, you know," she said. "There was this kid, his name was Alex, and he had a boat. And he said he took this girl water-skiing he didn't like, and they were water-skiing in this little cove where swans were and he steered her right in the middle of the swans and she just creamed them, but he wasn't telling the truth. He's such a loser."

"Which one's Alex?" Bomber asked.

"Oh, he's around," Edith said.

They were silent as the passengers from the ferry eddied around them. They watched the two boys playing catch, the younger one darting from side to side, never looking backward to calculate the space, his eyes only on the softly slowly falling ball released from his brother's hand.

"That's nice, isn't it?" Edith said. "That little kid is so trusting it's kind of holy, but if his trust were misplaced it would really be holy."

Bomber wanted to touch the vein, the pimple, the shock of dark, waxed hair, but he stood motionless, slouched in his clothes. "Yeah," he said.

"Like, you know, if he fell in," Edith said.

One Sunday, May went to church. It was a denomination that, as she gratefully knew, would bury anyone. She sat in a pew behind three young women and studied their pretty blond hair, their necks and their collars and their zippers. One of the girls scratched her neck. A few minutes later, she scratched it again. May bent forward and saw a small tick crawling on the girl. She carefully picked it off with her fingers. She did it with such stealth that the girl did not even know that May had touched her. May pinched the tick vigorously between her fingernails for some time, then dropped it to the floor, where it vanished from her sight.

After the service, there was a coffee hour. May joined a group around a table that was dotted with plates of muffins, bright cookies, and glazed cakes. When the conversation lagged, she said, "I've just returned from Morocco."

"How exotic!" a woman exclaimed. "Did you see the Casbah?" The group turned toward May and looked at her attentively.

"There are many casbahs," May said. "I had tea under a tent on the edge of the Sahara. The children in Morocco all want aspirin. *'Boom-boom la tête,'* they say, *'boom-boom la tête.'* Their little hands are dry as paper. It's the lack of humidity, I suppose."

"You didn't go there by yourself, did you?" a fat woman asked. She was very fat and panted as she spoke.

"I went alone, yes," May said.

The group hummed appreciatively. May was holding a tiny blueberry muffin in her hand. She couldn't remember picking it up. It sat cupped in the palm of her hand, the paper around it looking like the muffin itself. May had been fooled by such muffins in public places in the past. She returned it to the table.

"I saw the blue men," May said.

The group looked at her, smiling. They were taller than she and their heads were tilted toward her.

"Most tourists don't see them," May said. "They roam the deserts. Their camels are pale beige, almost white, and the men riding them are blue. They wear deep-blue floating robes and blue turbans. Their skin is even stained blue where the dye has rubbed off."

"Are they wanderers?" someone asked. "What's their purpose?"

May was startled. She felt as though the person were regarding her with suspicion.

"They're part of the mystery," she said. "To see them is to see part of the mystery."

"It must have been a sight," someone offered.

"Oh yes," May said, "it was."

After some moments, the group dispersed and May left the church and walked home through the town. May liked the town, which was cut off from other places. People came here only if they wanted to. You couldn't find this place by accident. The town seemed to be a place to visit and most people didn't stay on. There were some, of course, who had stayed on. May liked the clear light of the town and the trees rounded by the wind. She liked the trucks and the Jeeps with the dogs riding in them. When the trucks were parked, the dogs would stare solemnly down at the pavement as though there were something astounding there.

May felt elated, almost feverish. She had taken up lying rather late in life and she had taken it up with enthusiasm. Bomber didn't seem to notice, even though he had, in May's opinion, a hurtful obsession with the truth. When May got back to her house, she made herself a cup of tea and changed from her good dress into her gardening dress. She looked at herself in the mirror. I'm in charge of this person, she thought. "You'd better watch out," she said to the person in the mirror.

Bomber's friends never drank or smoked or ate meat. They were bony and wild. In the winter, a psychiatrist came into their classrooms and said, *You think that suicide is an escape and not a permanent departure, but the truth is it is a permanent departure.* They know that! Their eyes watered with boredom. Their mothers used to lie to them when they were little about dead things, but they knew better now. It's stupid to wait for the dead to do anything new. But one of their classmates had killed himself, so the psychiatrist would come back every winter.

"They planted a tree," Edith said, "you know, in this kid's memory at school and what this kid had done was hung himself from a tree." Edith rolled her eyes. "I mean, this school. You're not going to believe this school."

Edith and Bomber sat on opposite sides of May's parlor, which was filling with twilight. Edith wore a pair of men's boxer shorts, lace-up boots, and a lurid Hawaiian shirt. "This is a nice house," Edith said. "It smells nice. I see your granny coming out of the Kittens sometimes. She's cute."

"A thing I used to remember about my dad," Bomber said, "was that he gave me a tepee once when I was little and he pitched it in the middle of the living room. I slept in it every night for weeks right in the middle of the living room. It was great. But it actually wasn't my dad who had done that at all, it was my gramma."

"Your granny is so cute," Edith said. "I know I'd like her. Do you know Bobby?"

"Which one's Bobby?" Bomber asked.

"He's the skinny one with the tooth that overlaps a little. He's the sort of person I used to like. What he does is he fishes. There's not a fish he can't catch."

"I can't do that," Bomber said.

"Oh, you don't have to do anything like that now," Edith said.

The last things May had brought her son were a dark suit and a white shirt. They told her she could if she wished, and she had.

She had brought him many things in the two years before he died — candy and cigarettes and batteries, books on all subjects — and lastly she had brought these things. She had bought the shirt new and then washed it at home several times so it was soft and then she had driven over to that place. It was a cool, misty morning and the air smelled of chemicals from the mills miles away. Dew glittered on the wires and on the tips of grasses and the fronds of palms. She sat opposite him in the tall, narrow, familiar room, its high windows webby with steel, and he had opened the box with the shirt in it. Together they had looked at it. Together, mutely, they had bent their heads over it and stared. Their eyes had fallen into it as though it were a hole. They watched the shirt and it seemed to shift and shrink as though to accommodate itself to some ghastly and impossible interstice of time and purpose.

"What a shirt," her child said.

"Give it back," May whispered. She was terribly frightened. She had obliged some lunatic sense of decorum, and dread — the dread that lay beyond the fear of death — seized her.

"This is the one, I'm going out in this one," her child said. He was thin, his hair was gray.

"I wasn't thinking," May said. "Please give it back, I can't think about any of this."

"I was born to wear this shirt," her child said.

In the Lucky Kittens, over the bar, was a large painting of kittens crawling out of a sack. The sack was huge, out of proportion to the sea and the sky behind it. When May looked at it for a time, the sack appeared to tremble. One night, as she was walking home, someone brushed against her, almost knocking her down, and ran off with her purse. Her purse had fifteen dollars in it and in it too were the postcards and pictures of Morocco. May continued to walk home, her left arm still feeling the weight of the purse. It seemed heavier now that it wasn't there. She pushed herself down the street, looking, out of habit, into the lighted rooms of the handsome homes along the way. The rooms were artfully lit, as though on specific display for the passerby. No one was ever seen in them. At home, she looked at herself in the mirror for bruises. There were none, although her face was deeply flushed.

"You've been robbed," she said to the face.

She went into her parlor. On the floor above, in either the gray room or the yellow room, someone shifted about. Her arm ached. She turned off the light and sat in the dark, rubbing her arm.

"The temperature of the desert can reach one hundred seventy-five degrees," she said aloud. "At night, it can fall below freezing. Many a time I awoke in the morning to find a sheet of ice over the water in the glass beside my bed." It was something that had been written on one of the cards. She could see it all, the writing, the words, plain as day.

Sometime later, she heard Bomber's voice. "Gramma," he said, "why are you sitting in the dark?" The light was on again.

"Hi!" May said

"Sometimes," Bomber said, "she lies out in the garden and the fog rolls in, and she stays right out there."

"The fog will be swirling around me," May said, "and Bomber will say, 'Gramma, the fog's rolled in and there you are!' " She was speaking to a figure beside Bomber with a flamboyant crest of hair. The figure was dressed in silk lounging pajamas and a pair of black work boots with steel toes.

"Gramma," Bomber said, "this is Edith."

"Hi!" Edith said.

"What a pretty name," May said. "There's a hybrid lily called Edith that I like very much. I'm going to plant an Edith bulb when fall comes."

"Will it come up every year?" Edith asked.

"Yes," May said.

"That is so cool," Edith said.

A few days after she had been robbed, May's purse was returned to her. It was placed in the garden, just inside the gate. Everything was there, but the bills were different. May had had a ten and a five and the new ones were singles. The cards were there. May touched one and looked at the familiar writing on the back. *It never grows dark in the desert*, the writing said. *The night sky is a deep and intense blue as though the sun were shut up behind it.* Her child had been a thoughtful tourist once, sending messages home, trying to explain things she would never see.

He had never written from the prison. The thirst for explanation had left him. May thought of death. It was as though someone were bending over her, trying to blow something into her mouth. She shook her head and looked at her purse, turning it this way and that. "Where have you been?" she said to the purse. The pictures of Morocco were there. She looked through them. All there. But she didn't want them anymore. Things were never the same when they came back. She closed the purse up and dropped it in one of her large green trash cans, throwing some clipped, brown flowers over it so that it was concealed. It was less than a week later that everything was returned to her again, once more placed inside the gate. People went through the dump, she imagined, people went through the dump all the time to see what they could find. In town, the young people began calling her by name. "May," they'd say, "good morning!" They'd say, "How's it going, Gramma!" She was the condemned man's mother, and Bomber was the condemned man's son, and it didn't seem to matter what they did or didn't do, it was he who had been accepted by these people, and he who was allowing them to get by.

Edith was spending more and more time at May and Bomber's house. She ate dinner there several times a week. She had dyed her hair a peculiar brown color and wore scarves knotted around her neck.

"I like this look," Edith said. "It looks like I'm concealing a tracheotomy, doesn't it?"

"Your hair's good," Bomber said.

"You know what the psychiatrist at school says?" Edith said. "He says you think you want death when all you want is change."

"What is with this guy?" Bomber asked. "Is there really a problem at that place or what?"

"Oh there is, absolutely," Edith said. "You look a little like your granny. Did your dad look like her?"

"A little, I guess," Bomber said.

"You're such a bad boy," Edith said. "Such a sweet, sweet bad boy. I really love you."

The summer was over. The light had changed, and the leaves

on the trees hung very still. At the Lucky Kittens, the dancing went on, but not so many people danced. When May went there, they wouldn't take her money and May submitted to this. She couldn't help herself, it seemed.

Edith helped around the house. She washed the windows with vinegar and made chocolate desserts. One evening she said, "Do you still, like, pay income tax?"

May looked at the girl and decided to firmly lie. "No," she said.

"Well, that's good," Edith said. "It would be pretty preposterous to pay taxes after what they did."

"Of course," May said.

"But you're paying in other ways," Edith said.

"Please, dear," May said, "it was just a mistake. It doesn't mean anything in the long run," she said, dismayed at her words.

"I'll help you pay," Edith said.

With the cool weather, the tourists stopped coming. When school began, Edith asked if she could move into the yellow room. She didn't get along with her parents, she had been moving about, staying here and there with friends, but she had no real place to live, could she live in the yellow room?

May was fascinated by Edith. She did not want her in the house, above her, living in the yellow room. She felt that she and Bomber should move on, that they should try their new life together somewhere else, but she knew that this was their new life. This was the place where it appeared they had gone.

"Of course, dear," May said.

She was frightened and this surprised her, for she could scarcely believe she could know fright again after what happened to them, but there it was, some thing beyond the worst thing — some disconnection, some demand. She remembered telling Edith that she was going to plant bulbs in the garden when fall came, but she wasn't going to do it, certainly not. "No," May said to her garden, "don't even think about it." Edith moved into the yellow room. It was silent there, but May didn't listen either.

Something happened later that got around. May was driving,

it was night, and the car veered off the road. Edith and Bomber were with her. The car flipped over twice, miraculously righted itself and skidded back onto the road, the roof and fenders crushed. This was observed by a policeman who followed them for over a mile in disbelief before he pulled the car over. None of them was injured and at first they denied that anything unusual had happened at all. May said, "I thought it was just a dream, so I kept on going."

The three seemed more visible than ever after that, for they drove the car in that damaged way until winter came.

KENT HARUF

Private Debts/Public Holdings

FROM GRAND STREET

WHEN JESSIE BURDETTE became public property in Holt that spring, it was a matter of community honor. Her husband, Jack Burdette, had disappeared in January with a suitcase full of new clothes that he hadn't paid for. It wasn't this particular fact that bothered us, however. On the contrary, most of us were rather amused by it.

Jack had been the manager of the Farmers Co-op Elevator for about seven years. He had grown up here, we all liked him and were willing to accept a local boy's temporary indiscretion. But after he had been gone for about a month, we discovered that, besides shirts and pants and three packages of blue underwear, he had stolen $150,000 too. This money belonged to the Co-op Elevator, and since the elevator was owned in shares by half the county, we were naturally mad as hell about it. But none of us knew where he was anymore; the police couldn't find him; all of the all-points bulletins failed to turn him up; we grew increasingly outraged and hostile. In his absence, then, we sought our revenge on someone whose whereabouts we did know. We turned on his accomplice: old Charlie Soames.

Charle Soames was a local accountant, a seventy-year-old man with wire glasses and a paunch, and we all knew him, just as we had thought we had known Jack Burdette. But at about the same time we discovered the facts about Jack's embezzlement of co-op funds, we also learned that it was Charlie Soames who had helped him: Charlie had juggled the books. He had been doing this for about three years. And now Charlie had pretty good reason to be mad himself — Jack hadn't told Charlie he was leaving either, so Charlie was still in town. Consequently, he was apprehended almost immediately and put in jail. And that contented us for a while. We looked forward to gaining something satisfying out of him at least.

But then in March when Charlie was temporarily released on his own recognizance to await the trial, the first thing that old man did was, he climbed up into the attic of his house on Birch Street and shot himself in the head with a .22 single-shot rifle. And it didn't kill him. It merely scrambled his brains in such a way that any thought of further prosecution or eventual imprisonment was out of the question. So we felt doubly cheated then. It was as if we'd been deceived by two of the people in town we had always believed we could trust.

As a result of these events and these feelings, we declared a kind of open season on Jack Burdette's wife. She was the only person left to us who might offer a sense of local redress. She seemed to understand that too. At times she even seemed to welcome it. Anyway, she stayed in Holt.

It began in April. At the beginning of April that year she apeared one afternoon at the elevator beside the railroad tracks. She walked up the steps into the outer office and scale room and told Bob Thomas she wanted to see Doyle Francis. This surprised Bob Thomas. It was just after lunch and no doubt Bob had eaten too much as usual and was half asleep. He was slouched at the desk behind the counter, shuffling through some shipping receipts. When he looked up there she was. "What?" he said. "What'd you say?"

"I'd like to see Doyle Francis, please. I believe he's still working here."

"I'll go get him. No, I'll go tell him. Hell. You wait here."

She had her information right: Doyle Francis was in fact still working at the elevator. In the months after her husband had left town the board of directors had begun to advertise for a new manager, but they hadn't hired a permanent replacement yet because in the intervening months they had become suspicious of their fellow man. Deeply, excessively suspicious. They had begun to insist on researching each applicant's past — and not just his work experience, as is customary when hiring some-body new, but his ethical and moral and religious history as well. It was as if they had begun to suspect everybody, to believe every man in the world who applied for the manager's job at the elevator wanted only to take their money, to skip town with it. In the end, however, what they really only wanted to ask these men was: "Goddamn it, if we hire you now, how long are you going to be here working for us before you think you have to add to what we pay you, before you turn out to be another son of a bitch like Jack Burdette did? You ought to at least be able to tell us that much."

We didn't blame them for this attitude, this new profound mistrust of others; we felt similarly ourselves. But, because of their suspicions, Doyle Francis, who had been the manager be-fore Jack, was still there in April, still waiting for the board to hire someone else so he could relax into retirement again. That afternoon he was still in his old office when Bob Thomas burst in.

"She's here," Bob said. "She wants to see you."

"Who does?"

"Her. That son of a bitch's wife. She's out there in the scale room."

"What does she want?"

"How the hell do I know? She just said she wanted to see you. That's all she said."

"Well," Doyle said. "Show her in, Bob. Or are you scared, if you get too close to her, she might steal your pocketbook or something?"

"By God," Bob said. "I don't trust none of them no more. That's a fact."

"Never mind," Doyle said. "Ask her to come back here. Go on now, try to act like a gentleman for once in your life."

"I don't need to act like no gentleman. Not with her, I don't."

He turned and went back out to get Jessie. She was still stand-ing at the counter.

"He said he'd see you. Come on, I'll show you where he's at."

"Thank you," Jessie said, "but I know where the manager's office is."

"Well, don't take too long. Some of us got to work for a liv-ing."

Jessie walked around the counter and down the narrow hallway past the toilet and the storage room. She was wearing slacks
and a loose green blouse. When she entered, Doyle Francis
stood up. He was one of the few men in town then, at least of
those connected to the elevator, who still treated her with respect and minimal courtesy. He offered her a wood chair with
arm rests.

She sat down, heavily, a little carefully — she was still pregnant then, still carrying that little girl of hers that Jack had left
her with; she was in her seventh month. She set her purse on
her shortened lap, in front of her stomach.

"Now then," Doyle said. "What can I do for you, Jessie?"

"I don't want anything. If that's what you think."

"No," he said. "I don't think that. They don't pay me enough
to worry about what other people think."

"Well, I don't," Jessie said. "I didn't come here to ask for
anything. I came here to give you something."

"Oh?" he said. "What is it you want to give me?"

"Not you. The board of directors. The elevator. All these
people."

"What is it?"

"Here." She opened her purse and withdrew a legal document. She pushed it across the desk toward him. Doyle picked
it up, looked at it.

"Wait a minute," he said. "Hold on now. This is some kind of
a deed, isn't it?"

"They said it was legal."

"Who said it was legal? What are you talking about?"

"The people down at the bank. They said I could sign it over
to whoever I wanted to, even if Jack wasn't here to co-sign it.
They said considering the circumstances it would be all right."

"Did they now?" Doyle said. "I'll bet they did too."

He looked at the document again, read it this time. It was a
quitclaim deed transferring the title of a house and property
over to the board of directors of the Holt County Farmers Co-
op Elevator. Her signature was at the bottom in fresh ink.

"All right then," he said, "I suppose it is legal. I wouldn't
know; I'm not a lawyer. But then I don't suppose anybody
around here would protest it very much, would they? Even if it
wasn't legal?"

"No, they wouldn't protest it."

Doyle laid the deed down on the desk. He folded his hands over it. He said: "How old are you, Jessie?"

"I'm twenty-six."

"And you have two boys?"

"Yes."

"How old are they?"

"They've just turned four and three. But why are you asking me these —"

"And you're going to have another one pretty soon, aren't you?"

"In June," she said. "But —"

"Do you believe in hell?" he said. "Is that it?"

She stared back at him.

"Is that why you're doing this? Because, let me tell you, I don't think there is any hell. No, I don't. And I don't think there's any heaven either. We just die, that's all. We just stop breathing after a while and then everybody starts to forget about us and pretty soon they can't even remember what it is we think we did to them."

"I don't know what I believe," she said.

"Then why are you doing this? Will you tell me that?"

"Because," she said.

"Because? That's all. Just because."

She continued to stare back at him, to watch him, her eyes steady and deep brown. Finally Doyle said:

"All right, you're not going to tell me. You don't have to tell me; I think I know anyway. But listen, now. Listen: let an old man ask you this. Don't you think you're going to need that house anymore? I mean, if you give it up like you're proposing to do, just where in hell are you and these kids going to live afterwards?"

"That's my concern," she said. "Isn't it."

"Yes, of course it is, but —"

"And you agree it's legal, don't you?"

"Yes, as far as I can tell."

"So will you please give that piece of paper to the board? You can tell them we'll be out of the house by the first of May."

"But listen," he said. "Damn it, wait a minute now —"

Because Jessie had already stood up. She was already leaving. And Doyle Francis was still leaning toward the chair she had been sitting in. Those good intentions of his were still swimming undelivered in his head and his arms were still resting on that quitclaim deed on his desk. She walked out through the hallway and on outside.

In the scale room Bob Thomas watched her leave. When she had driven away he went in to see Doyle. "Well," he said, "she was here long enough. What'd she want?"

"What?"

"I said, 'What did she want?' Burdette's wife."

"Nothing. She didn't want anything."

"I don't believe that."

"I don't care what you believe. That woman doesn't want a goddamn thing from any one of us."

"What do you mean she doesn't want anything? She's a Burdette, isn't she?"

"I mean," Doyle Francis said, "get the hell out of here and leave me alone. Goddamn it, Bob, go find something else to do with yourself."

For some of us that was enough. I suppose we felt about it a little like Doyle Francis did, that she deserved the magnanimity of our good intentions. Privately, we understood that she was innocent, or at least we knew that she was ignorant — it wasn't her fault, we told ourselves; she wasn't involved. We could afford to be nice to her. Anyway, we could refrain from actually wishing her harm.

For others, though, who were more vocal and more active, it still wasn't sufficient. These people argued that the house didn't amount to enough. It didn't matter that it was all that she had, that it was the sum total of her collateral and disposable property. It was merely an old two-bedroom house in the middle of town. It needed tin siding and new shingles; it needed painting. Besides, there was still a fifteen-year lien against it when she signed it over, so that when the board of directors became the fee owners of the house and then sold it at public auction, it didn't even begin to make a dent in that $150,000 that Jack had taken. No, they weren't satisfied. A house wasn't alive and capable of bleeding, like a human was. It wasn't pregnant, like Jessie was.

Anyway, by the first of May she and the two boys had moved out of the house as Jessie said they would — they had begun to rent the downstairs apartment in the old Fenner place on Hawthorne Street at the west edge of town — and it was Doyle Francis who helped them move. They used his pickup. Jessie accepted that much assistance from him at least, although afterward she sent him a freshly baked chocolate cake on a platter, to square things, to keep that balance sheet of hers in the black.

Well, it was a nice enough apartment: they had five rooms — a kitchen, a living room, two small bedrooms, and a bathroom with a shower off the kitchen. They also had use of the front porch, a wide old-style porch with a wooden rail around it and with a swing suspended from hooks in the ceiling. From the porch, they could look west diagonally across the street toward open country, since that was where Holt ended then, at Hawthorne Street: there was just Harry Smith's pasture west of them, a half section of native grass in which Harry kept some horses. So it was a good place for her boys to grow up: they would have all that open space available to them across the street.

When they had settled in and after new curtains had been hung over the windows — heavier ones to block any view from the street — Jessie began to take care of the money end of it as well. She began to earn a living. She took a job at the Holt Café on Main Street. Six days a week she worked as a waitress, rising each morning to feed TJ and Bobby and to play with them until just before noon when the sitter, an old neighbor lady — Mrs. Nyla Waters, a kindly woman, a widow — came to watch the boys while Jessie worked through the noon rush hour and the afternoon and the dinner hour, and then returned again each evening about seven o'clock to bathe and put the boys to bed and to read them stories. She often sang to them a little too, before they slept.

And working in this way — being pregnant and having to spend that many hours away from her children — was not the optimum solution to all her problems either, of course, but she didn't have many alternatives. She refused to consider welfare.

Accepting Aid to Dependent Children, or even food stamps, was not a part of her schedule of payments — that local balance sheet of hers, I mean — since any public assistance of this kind came from taxes. A portion of that public tax money would have originated, at least theoretically, in Holt County. She knew that. And she didn't want anything from us. Not if she hadn't paid for it, she didn't. Doyle Francis was right about that.

But then, toward the end of spring that year, she discovered a way to make the final payment. She began to go out dancing at the Holt Legion on Saturday nights.

But no one would dance with her at first. She came down the stairs that first Saturday night early in May and walked over to the bar, lifted herself onto a bar stool, ordered a vodka Collins, and waited. And nothing happened. Maybe it got a little quieter for a moment, but not very much, so she couldn't be certain that she'd even been noticed. She looked lovely too: she had made herself up and had put on a deep blue dress that was loose enough that her stomach showed only a little, as if she were merely in the first months of pregnancy; she was wearing nylons and heels; her brown hair was pulled away from her face in a way that her eyes appeared to be even larger and darker than they were ordinarily. Sitting there, she waited; no one talked to her; nothing happened; finally she ordered another drink. On either side of her, men on bar stools were talking to one another, so she swung around to look at the couples in the nearby booths. They were laughing loudly and rising regularly from the booths to dance. Maybe they looked at her, maybe they didn't — she didn't know. So that first night she sat there at the bar, waiting, for almost two hours. Then she went home.

The second time, that second Saturday — this would have been about the middle of May now — she drank a small glass of straight vodka at home in the kitchen before she went out. Also, she was dressed differently this time. There was more blue makeup over her eyes and she was wearing a dark red dress with a low neckline that showed a good deal of her full breasts, a dress that made no pretense at disguising her pregnancy: it was stretched tight across her stomach and hips. Preparing to go out, she combed her hair close against her cheeks, partially obscuring her face, and then she entered the Legion again, walked down the steps into that noise and intense Saturday-night revelry a second time. And as before, she mounted a bar stool, ordered a drink, and then she turned around, with that short red dress hiked two inches above the knees of her crossed legs, with a look of expectation, of invitation almost, held permanently on her beautiful face.

Well, it was pathetic in its lack of subtlety. But subtlety and pathos are not qualities that are much appreciated at the Legion on Saturday nights, so she only had to sit there for an hour this second time before Vince Higgims, Jr., asked her to dance. Vince is one of our permanent Holt County bachelors, a lank, black-haired man, a man considered by many of us to be well educated in the ways of strong drink and ladies in tight dresses. "Come on, girl," Vince said. "They're playing my song."

They were playing Lefty Frizzell's "I Love You in a Thousand Ways," with its promise of change, the end of blue days — a song with a slow enough tempo to allow Vince, Jr., to work his customary magic. He led Jessie out onto the crowded floor and pulled her close against his belt buckle; then he began to pump her arm, to walk her backward in that rocking two-step while she held that permanent look of invitation on her face and he went on smiling past her hair in obvious satisfaction. They danced several dances that way, including a fast one or two so that Vince could demonstrate his skill at the jitterbug — he twirled her around and performed intricate movements with his hands — then they cooled off again with a slow song.

And that's how it began: innocently enough, I suppose, because unlike some of the others, at least Vince Higgims meant Jessie Burdette no harm. I doubt that Vince even had hopes of any post-dance payoff. It was merely that he was drunk and that he liked to dance. The same cannot be said about the others, however. These other men were still remembering the grain elevator.

They all began to dance with her. It was as if Vince had broken some taboo, some barrier of accepted behavior, so that now it was not only acceptable to dance with Jack Burdette's pregnant wife, it was required; it was a matter of community honor and retribution. And so, ten or fifteen men took their turns with her that night. They danced her hard around the floor. They swung her violently around; they held her clenched against themselves, forcing their own slack stomachs against her swollen hard one. From that point on they danced every song with her. And all that time Jessie seemed to welcome it, to smile and speak pleasantly to all the men who held her. When it was over, though, when the band finally stopped playing and the lights were turned on once again, she was very pale; she was sweating and her dress looked wrinkled, worn out, stained, as if it had been cheapened. She went home exhausted.

But the local routine was established now — that three-week-long Holt County system of payment was initiated and accepted. And so the third time, that third Saturday night in May, it was just the same — only it was worse. This time the men not only danced with her in the same fierce vindictive manner but they also insisted on buying her drinks. She was wearing that same red dress too, washed and pressed again but showing the additional week of pregnancy. If anything it looked tighter on her now, riper, as if the seams would burst at any moment, while above the deep neckline the blue veins in her full breasts showed clearly. Nevertheless, she danced with every man who asked her. They danced and danced — waltzes, jitterbugs, country two-steps, a kind of local hard-clenched fox trot — anything and everything the men thought they knew how to do, regardless of the violence and energy it required. And this dancing, if you can call it that, this intense communal jig, stopped only when the band stopped. Then, during those ten minutes of brief rest between sets, the men bought her drinks. They sat her on a bar stool and three or four of them stood around her, telling jokes and buying drinks — taking turns with this too, ordering her double shots of Scotch or whiskey or vodka — it didn't matter what the combination or how unlikely the mix — they ordered liquor for her to drink and insisted that she drink it. And she did that too. She accepted it all, seemed to welcome it all, as if she were privately obliged to honor any demand.

Of course, by the evening's end she was even more exhausted this time than she had been the previous Saturday night. Also, she was very close to being drunk. When the lights came on at last, when the last man stopped dancing with her, she could barely walk off the dance floor. She was weak on her feet; there was a drunken waver in her step. She didn't say anything, though. Nothing in the way of complaint, I mean. And when that last man thought to ask her if she were coming back again the next week, she said: "You want me to, don't you?"

"Why course," he said. "Don't you know I'll be here? We'll all be here."

"Then I will too," she said.

And she was. Only, by this time, many of the women and at least some of the men were growing a little uneasy, a little uncomfortable with this particular form of weekly gambol and amusement. So not everyone showed up the following week, that last Saturday in May. Jessie did, though. It was the last time that she went to the Legion for a long time.

But again it was the same. She was wearing that same red dress, as if it were a uniform now, an essential part of the routine, and there was the same excessive amount of makeup on her face. She was drinking too — it was obvious that she'd been drinking heavily even before she arrived at the Legion. She entered the bar-and-dance room about nine o'clock and didn't even bother this time to lift herself onto a bar stool. She merely waited inside the door, with the music and smoke and laughter already at full strength around her. She didn't have to wait long: two or three men discovered her at the same moment and ushered her in.

"What are you drinking?" one of them said.

"Don't you want to dance first?"

"No, let's have a drink. I'm buying."

"All right," she said. "A whiskey sour then."

"Make it a double," he said.

She drank it fast, as if it were no more than water or lemonade, like she was no more conscious of what she drank than she was of the banter around her. When she had finished it, she set the glass down and said: "Now who's going to ask me to dance? I thought you boys knew how to dance."

"I'll show you how to dance," one of them said. "Come on."

This was Alden Haines, a man of forty-three who was only recently divorced and who farmed a couple of irrigated circles of corn east of town. He was not a bad man really, but he was still angry at the time about the divorce: his wife had been the one to initiate the legal proceedings. More to the point, he was a shareholder in the Farmers Co-op Elevator. "See if you can keep up with this," he said.

He took her out onto the dance floor. Pushing roughly through the other couples, he began immediately to swing her about the floor in circles and abrupt spins. Jessie kept up with him, moving back and forth or circling at the end of his outstretched arm. As we watched, she seemed almost feverish with intensity, as if she were resolved to test some private limits. When the dance ended, she and Haines were both sweating. The band played a slower song next and Haines pulled her close to himself, clenching his hands behind her back while she held tightly to his neck. He rocked her backward across the floor in time to the slow music. Neither of them talked. When the song ended, someone else cut in, and so it began again, with the same intensity, with the same feverish resolve. It went on in that way until the end of the set.

Then the band broke for ten minutes and the local men bought her drinks again at the bar. While they stood around her, not speaking to her very much but merely talking and joking among themselves while still paying close attention to the level of liquor in her glass, the rest of us in the Legion that night were also ordering fresh drinks. The two or three barmaids were kept busy carrying trays of glasses and bottles out to us in the booths. Across the room somebody started throwing ice cubes at one of the barmaids to get her attention. "Stop that," she called. "I see you — I'll be there in a minute."

Then the ten-minute break was over. The band resumed their places at the far end of the room and began to play. And Alden Haines led Jessie out onto the floor again. It was a fast song, the band's rendition of "That'll Be the Day." He swung her violently out at the end of his arm — and that was the end of it. Almost before it had begun, it was finished, completed. I suppose it was the ice cubes on the floor. Or perhaps during the break one of us had spilled beer or liquor in the dance area. We weren't certain what it was. In any case, her foot slipped on something wet and she went down. She tried to catch herself when she fell but she couldn't; she fell forward, hard, and didn't get up immediately. Afterward she lay there in her red dress while the rest of us around her stopped dancing. She turned onto her side, pulling her legs upward against herself. Haines leaned over her.

"You all right?" he said. "Can you get up?"

He lifted under her arm, helping her to stand. She was very pale. She was sweating again now, her face shining like wet chalk in the dim light. In the center of the dance floor she stood unsteadily on her feet while Alden Haines held her arm and people watched. "I think I need to go to the rest room," she said.

"You want me to walk you upstairs?"

"No. I want to be alone."

Later it was obvious to us that the pains had already begun while she was still on the dance floor — we remembered seeing her eyes focus peculiarly, a kind of brief intermittent stare — but she refused any assistance. She walked off the dance floor by herself, past the bar and up the stairs to the rest room near the front entrance. She went inside, into one of the toilet stalls, and sat down. We waited for her to come back. When she was still there ten minutes later, a couple of the women went in to check on her. She was still seated on the toilet, still conscious but quiet and very white. She was bent forward over her knees. There were clots of blood in the toilet. One of the women came outside into the hallway and told us to call the ambulance.

The ambulance got there in five or six minutes. The attendants went in and brought her back out in a wheelchair, tipping it backward to get down the front steps, and then they pushed the chair up a ramp into the ambulance and drove to the hospital. None of that took very long — the hospital is only three or four blocks east of the Legion — but it wouldn't have mattered if it had taken an hour.

When they arrived at the hospital, they wheeled her into the emergency room and Dr. Martin laid her down on a bed and examined her. He lifted her dress and noticed the blood. Then he listened for fetal heart tones. He couldn't hear anything, though: the little girl inside her was already dead. Afterward he said the placenta and uterine walls had separated. When she fell she had gone immediately into labor, and because its source of oxygen had been cut off, the baby had died within the first five minutes — probably during the time Jessie was still in the rest room. He didn't tell her that, though. He didn't want to upset her: she still had to deliver the baby.

They gave her Pitocin to help stimulate the contractions of the uterus. But she was in labor for nearly ten hours and there was additional loss of blood and she might have died. But finally she delivered the baby late on Sunday evening.

Afterward they held it up so she could look at it for a moment. The little girl was ashen but otherwise it looked quite normal. Jessie reached up and touched one of its feet. Then they took it away and one of the nurses said: "I'm so sorry, Mrs. Burdette."

So we thought she would cry then. We thought she would break down at last. I suppose we wanted her to do that. But she didn't. Perhaps she had gone past the point where human tears make any difference in such cases, because instead, she turned her face away and shut her eyes and after a while she went to sleep.

She stayed in the hospital for most of that next week. Mrs. Waters, her neighbor, took it upon herself to care for TJ and Bobby during that period. The old woman brought the boys in to see their mother as soon as she was able to have company, and Jessie talked to the little boys every day and held their hands and brushed the hair off their foreheads. She refused, however, to talk to any of the hospital staff about the little girl she had delivered and she refused absolutely to talk to a local minister when he came to her room to visit her. She preferred to lie quietly, looking out the window. When the week was over, they released her and she went home again, to the old Fenner House on Hawthorne Street. And then in another week she returned to work at the Holt Café. In the following months she continued to refill our cups with coffee and to bring us steaks and potatoes from the kitchen.

And so I don't know what monetary value people place on baby girls in other areas, but here we learned in May that year that $150,000 — less the resale value of a two-bedroom house in the middle of town — was a figure that seemed appropriate.

CHARLES BAXTER

How I Found My Brother

FROM INDIANA REVIEW

I WAS SEPARATED from my biological mother when I was four months old. Everything from that period goes through the wash of my memory and comes out clean, blank. The existing snapshots of my mother show this very young woman holding me, a baby, at arm's length, like a caught fish, outside in the blaring midday summer sunlight. She's got clothes up on the clothesline in the background, little cotton infant things. In one picture a spotted dog, a mongrel combination of Labrador and Dalmatian, is asleep beside the bassinet. I'd like to know what the dog's name was, but time has swallowed that information. In another picture, a half-empty bottle of Grain Belt beer stands on the lawn near a wading pool. My mother must have figured that if she could have me, at the age of seventeen, she could also have the beer.

My mother's face in these pictures is having a tough time with daylight. It's a struggle for her to bask in so much glare. She squints and smiles, but the smile is all on one side, the right. The left side stays level, except at the edge, where it slips down. Because of the sunlight and the black-and-white film, my mother's face in other respects is bleached, without details, like a sketch for a face. She's a kid in these pictures and she has a kid's face, with hair pulled back with bobby pins and a slight puffiness in the cheeks, which I think must be bubble gum.

She doesn't look like she's ever been used to the outdoors, the poor kid. Sunlight doesn't become her. It's true she smiled, but then she did give me up. I was too much serious work, too much of a squalling load. Her girlish smile was unsteady and finally didn't include me. She gave me away — this is historical record — to my adoptive parents, Harold and Ethel Harris, who were older and more capable of parental love. She also gave them these photographs, the old kind, with soft sawtooth borders, so I'd be sure to know how she had looked when the unfamiliar sunlight hit her in a certain way. I think her teenaged boyfriend, my father, took these pictures. Harold and Ethel Harris were my parents in every respect, in love and in their care for me, except for the fact of these pictures. The other children in the family, also adopted, looked at the snapshots of this backyard lady with curiosity but not much else.

My biological father was never a particle of interest to me compared to my adoptive father, Harold Harris, a man who lived a life of miraculous calm. A piano tuner and occasional jazz saxophonist, Harold liked to sit at home, humming and tapping his fingers in the midst of uproar and riot, kids shouting and plaster falling. He could not be riled; he never made a fist. He was the parental hit of any childhood group, and could drive a car competently with children sitting on his shoulders and banging their hands on the side of his head. Genetic inheritance or not, he gave us all a feeling for pitch. Ask me for an F-sharp, I'll give you one. I get the talent from Harold.

I went to high school, messed around here and there, did some time in the Navy, and when I was discharged I married my sweetheart of three years, the object of my shipboard love letters, Lynda Claire Norton. We had an apartment. I was clerking at Meijer's Thrifty Acres. I thought we were doing okay. Each night I was sleeping naked next to a sexual angel. At sunrise she would wake me with tender physical comfort, with hair and fingertips. I was working to get a degree from night school. Fourteen months after we were married, right on the day it was due, the baby came. A boy, this was. Jonathan Harold Harris. Then everything went to hell.

I was crazy. Don't ask me to account for it. I have no background or inclination to explain the human mind. Besides, I'm not proud of the way I acted. Lynda moved right out, baby and all, the way any sensible woman would have, and she left me two empty rooms in the apartment in which I could puzzle myself out.

I had turned into the damnedest thing. I was a human monster movie. I'd never seen my daddy shouting the way I had; he had never carried on or made a spectacle of himself. Where had I picked up this terrible craziness that made me yell at a woman who had taken me again and again into her arms? I wrote long letters to the world while I worked at home on my model ships, a dull expression on my face. You will say that liquor was the troublemaker here and you would be correct, but only so far. I had another bad ingredient I was trying to track down. I broke dishes. My mind, day and night, was muzzy with bad intentions. I threw a light bulb against a wall and did not sweep up the glass for days. Food burned on the stove and then I ate it. I was committing outrageous offenses against the spirit. Never, though, did I smash one of the model ships. Give me credit for that.

I love oceans and the ships that move across them. I believe in man-made objects that take their chances on the earth's expanses of water. And so it happened that one weekday afternoon I was watching a rerun of *The Caine Mutiny*, with my workboard set up in front of me with the tiny pieces of my model *Cutty Sark* in separated piles, when the phone rang. For a moment I believed that my wife had had second thoughts about my behavior and was going to give me another chance. To tell the truth, whenever the phone rang, I thought it would be Lynda, announcing her terms for my parole.

"Hello? Is this Andy Harris?" a man's voice asked.

"This is him," I said. "Who's this?"

"This is your brother." Just like that. Very matter-of-fact. This is your brother. Harold and Ethel Harris had had two other adopted sons, in addition to me, but I knew them. This voice was not them. I gripped the telephone.

Now — and I'm convinced of this — every adopted child fears and fantasizes getting a call like this announcing from out of the blue that someone in the world is a relative and has tracked you down. I know I am not alone in thinking that anyone in the world might be related to me. My biological mother and father were very busy, urgent lovers. Who knows how much procreation they were capable of, together and separately? And maybe they had brothers and sisters, too, as urgent in their own way as my mother and father had been in theirs, filling up the adoption agencies with their offspring. I could never go into a strange city without feeling that I had cousins in it.

Therefore I gripped the telephone, hoping for reason, for the everyday. "This is not my brother," I said.

"Oh yes, it is. Your mother was Alice Barton, right?"

"My mother was Ethel Harris," I said.

"Before that," the voice said, "your mother was Alice Barton. She was my mother, too. This is your brother, Kurt. I'm a couple of years younger than you." He waited. "I know this is a shock," he said.

"You can't find out about me," I said. The room wasn't spinning, but I had an idea that it might. My mouth was open halfway and I was taking short sweaty breaths through it. One shiver took its snaky way down and settled in the lumbar region. "The records are sealed. It's all private, completely secret."

"Not anymore, it isn't," he said. "Haven't you been keeping up? In this country you can find out anything. There are no secrets worth keeping anymore; nobody *wants* privacy, so there isn't any."

He was shoving this pile of ideas at me. *My* thoughts had left me in great flight, the whole sad flock of them. "Who are you?" I asked.

"Your brother Kurt," he said, repeating himself. "Listen, I won't bore you to explain what I had to do to find you. The fact is that it's possible. Easy, if you have money. You pay someone and someone pays someone and eventually you find out what you want to know. Big surprise, right?" He waited, and when I didn't agree with him, he started up again, this time with small talk. "So I hear that you're married and you have a kid yourself." He laughed. "And I'm an uncle."

"What? No. Now you're only partly right," I said, wanting very hard to correct this man who said he was my brother. "My wife left me. I'm living here alone now."

"Oh. I'm sorry about that." He offered his sympathies in a shallow, masculine way: the compassion offered by princes and salesmen. "But listen," he said, "you're not alone. It's happened before. Couples separate all the time. You'll get back. It's not the end of the world. Andy?"

"What?"

"Would you be willing to get together and talk?"

"Talk? Talk about what?"

"Well, about being brothers. Or something else. You can talk about anything you please." He waited for me to respond, and I didn't. This was my only weapon — the terrible static of telephone silence. "Look," he said, "this is tough for me. *I'm not a bad person.* I've been sitting by this phone for an hour. I don't know if I'm doing the right thing. My wife . . . you'll meet her . . . she hasn't been exactly supportive. She thinks this is a mistake. She says I've gone too far this time. I dialed your number four times before I dialed it to the end. I make hundreds of business calls but this one I could not do. It may be hard for you, also: I mean, I take a little getting used to. I can get obsessive about little things. That's how I found you."

"By being obsessive."

"Yeah. Lucille . . . that's my wife . . . she says it's one of my faults. Well, I always wanted a brother, you know, blood related and everything, but I couldn't have one until I found you. But then I thought you might not like me. It's possible. Are you following me?"

"Yes, I am." I was thinking: here I am in my apartment, recently vacated by my wife, talking to a man who says he's my brother. Isn't there a law against this? Someone help me.

"You don't have to like me," he said, his brusque voice starting to stumble over the consonants. That made me feel better. "But that isn't the point, is it?" Another question I didn't have to answer, so I made him wait. "I can imagine what's in your head. But let's meet. Just once. Let's try it. Not at a house. I only live about twenty miles away. I can meet you in Ann Arbor. We can meet in a bar. I *know* where you live. I drove by your building. I believe I've even seen your car."

"Have you seen me?" This brother had been cruising past my house, taking an interest. Do brothers do that? What *do* they do?

"Well, no, but who cares about looks where brothers are concerned? We'll see each other. Listen, there's this place a couple of miles from you, The Wooden Keg. Could we meet there? Tomorrow at three? Are you off tomorrow?"

"That's a real problem for me," I said. "Booze is my special poison."

"Hell, that's all right," he said. "I'll watch out for you. I'm your brother. Oh. There's one other thing. I lied. I look like you. That's how you'll recognize me. I have seen you."

I held on to the telephone a long time after I hung up. I turned my eyes to the television set. José Ferrer was getting drunk and belligerent at a cocktail party. I switched off the set.

I was in that bar one hour before I said I would be, and my feelings were very grim. I wasn't humming. I didn't want him to be stationed there when I came in. I didn't want to be the one who sauntered in through the door and walked the long distance to the bar stool. I didn't want some strange sibling checking out the way I close the distance or blink behind my glasses while my eyes adjusted to the light. I don't like people watching me when they think they're going to get a skeleton key to my character. I'm not a door and I won't be opened that easily.

Going into a bar in the midsummer afternoon takes you out of the steel heat and air-hammer sun; it softens you up until you're all smoothed out. This was one of those wood sidewall bars with air that hasn't recirculated for fifty years, with framed pictures of thoroughbreds and cars on the walls next to the chrome decorator hubcaps. A man's bar, smelling of cigarettes and hamburger grease and beer. The brown padded light comes down on you from some recessed source, and the leather cushions on those bar stools are as soft as a woman's hand, and before long the bar is one big bed, a bed on a barge eddying down a sluggish river where you've got nothing but good friends lined up on the banks. This is why I am an alcoholic. It wasn't easy drinking Coca-Cola in that place, that dim halfway house between the job and home, and I was about to slide off my wagon and order my first stiff one when the door cracked open behind me, letting in a trumpet blast of light, and I saw, in the doorframe outline, my brother coming toward me. He was taking his own time. He had on a hat. When the door closed and my eyes adjusted, I got a better look at him, and I saw what he said I would see: I saw instantly that this was my brother. The elves had stolen my shadow and given it to him. A version of my face was fixed on a stranger. From the outdoors came this example of me, wearing a coat and tie.

He took a bar stool next to mine and held out his hand. I held

out mine and we shook like old friends, which we were a long
way from becoming. "Hey," we both said. He had the eyes, the
cheek, and the jaw in a combination I had seen only in the
mirror. "Andy," he said, refusing to let my hand go. "Good to
meet you."

"Kurt," I said. "Likewise." Brother or no brother, I wasn't
giving away anything too fast. This is America, after all.

"What're you drinking?" he asked.

"Coke."

"Oh. Right." He nodded. When he nodded, the hat nodded.
After he saw me looking at it, he said, "Keeps the sun out of my
eyes." He took it off and tried to put it on the bar, but there
wasn't enough room for it next to the uncleared beer glasses
and the ashtrays, so he stood up and dropped it on a hook over
by the popcorn machine. There it was, the only hat. He said,
"My eyes are sensitive to light. What about yours?" I nodded.
Then he laughed, hit the bar with the broad flat of his hand,
and said, "Isn't this great?" I wanted to say, yes, it's great, but
the true heart of the secret was that, no, it was not. It was
horrifyingly strange without being eventful. You can't just get a
brother off the street. But before I could stop him from doing
it, he leaned over and put his right arm, not a large arm but an
arm all the same, over my shoulders, and he dropped his head
so that it came sliding in toward my chest just under the chin.
Here was a man dead set on intimacy. When he straightened
up, he said, "We're going to have ourselves a day today, that's
for sure." His stutter took some of the certainty out of the
words. "You don't have to work this afternoon, right?"

"No," I said, "I'm not scheduled."

"Great," he said. "Let me fill you in on myself."

Instead of giving me his past, he gave me a résumé. He tried to
explain his origins. My biological mother, for all the vagueness
in her face, had been a demon for good times. She had been
passionate and prophylactically carefree. Maybe she had had
twenty kids, like old Mother Hubbard. She gave us away like
presents to a world that wanted us. This one, this Kurt, she had
kept for ten months before he was adopted by some people
called Sykes. My brother said that he understood that we — he

and I — had two other siblings in Laramie, Wyoming. There might be more he didn't know about. I had a sudden image of Alice Barton as a human stork, flying at tree level and dropping babies into the arms of waiting parents.

Did I relax as my brother's voice took me through his life? Were we related under the skin, and all the way around the block? He talked; I talked. The Sykes family had been bookish types, lawyers, both of them, and Kurt had gone to Michigan State University in East Lansing. He had had certain advantages. No falling plaster or piano tuning. By learning the mysterious dynamics of an orderly life, he had been turned out as a salesman, and now he ran a plastics factory in Southfield, north of Detroit. "A small business," he said in a friendly, smug way. "Just fifteen employees." I heard about his comfortably huge home. I heard about his children, my nephews. From the wallet thick with money and credit cards came the line-up of photos of these beautiful children.

So what was he doing, this successful man, sitting on a bar stool out here, next to his brother, me, the lowly check-out clerk?

"Does anybody have enough friends?" he asked me. "Does anyone have enough *brothers?*" He asked this calmly, but the questions, as questions, were desperate. "Here's what it was," he said. "Two or three times a week I felt like checking in with someone who wasn't a wife and wasn't just a friend. Brothers are a different category, right there in the middle. It's all about *relatedness,* you know what I mean?" I must have scowled. "We can't rush this," he said. "Let's go have dinner somewhere. My treat. And then let's do something."

"Do what?" I asked.

"I've given that a lot of thought," he said. "What do you do the first time out with your brother? You can't just eat and drink. You can't shop; women do that." Then he looked me square in the eye, smiled, and said, "It's summer. Maybe we could go bowling or play some softball." There was a wild look in his eye. He let out a quick laugh.

We went in his Pontiac Firebird to a German restaurant and loaded up on sauerbraten. I had a vague sense he was lowering himself to my level but did not say so. He ordered a chest-sized decorated stein of beer but I stayed on the cola wagon. I tried to talk about my wife, but it wouldn't come out: all I could say was that I had a problem with myself as a family man. That wasn't me. The crying of babies tore me up. Feeding time gave me inexplicable jitters. I had acted like Godzilla. When I told him this, he nodded hard, like a yes man. It was all reasonable to him.

"Of course," he said. "Of course you were upset and confused." He was understanding me the way I wanted to be understood. I talked some more. Blah blah blah. Outside, it was getting dark. The bill came, and he paid it: out came the thick wallet again, and from a major-league collection of credit cards came the white bank plastic he wanted. I talked more. He agreed with everything I said. He said, "You're exactly right." Then I said something else, and he responded, "Yes, you're exactly right."

That was when I knew I was being conned. In real life people don't say that to you unless they're trying to earn your love in a hurry. But here he was, Kurt Sykes, visibly my brother, telling me I was exactly right. It was hard to resist, but I was holding on, and trying.

"Here's how," he said. He lifted his big stein of beer into the air, and I lifted my glass of Coke. Click. A big blond waitress watched us, her face disciplined into a steel-helmet smile.

After that, it was his idea to go outside and play catch. This activity had all sorts of symbolic meanings for him, but what was I going to do? Go home and watch television? I myself have participated in a few softball leagues and the jock way of life is not alien to me, but I think he believed he could open up if we stayed at my level, throwing something back and forth, grunting and sweating. We drove across town to Buhr Park, where he unloaded his newly purchased baseball, his two brand-new gloves, and a shiny new bat. Baseball was on the agenda. We were going to play ball or die. "We don't have to do any hitting," he said. While I fitted the glove to my left hand — a perfect fit, as if he had measured me — he locked the car. I have never had a car worth locking; it was not a goal.

The sun having set, I jogged out across a field of darkening grass. The sky had that blue tablecloth color it gets at dusk just before the stars come out. I had my jeans, sweat shirt, and sneakers on, my usual day-off drag. I had not dressed up for this event. In fact, I was almost feeling comfortable, except for some growing emotional hot spot I couldn't locate that was making me feel like pushing the baseball into my brother's face. Kurt started to toss the ball toward me and then either noticed his inappropriate dress-for-success formality or felt uncomfortable. He went back to the car and changed into his sweat clothes in the half-dark. He could have been seen, but wasn't, except by me. (My brother could change his clothes out in the open, not even bothering to look around to see who would see. What did this mean?)

Now, dressed down, we started to hustle, keeping the rhythms up. He threw grounders, ineptly, his arm stiff and curious. I bent down, made the imaginary play, and pivoted. He picked up the bat and hit a few high flies toward me. Playing baseball with me was his way of claiming friendship. Fine. Stars came out. We moved across the field, closer to a floodlit tennis court, so we had a bit of light. I could see fireflies at the edge of where we were playing. On the court to my right, a high school couple was working their way through their second set. The girl let out little cries of frustration now and then. They were pleasurable to hear. Meanwhile, Kurt and I played catch in the near-dark, following the script that, I could see, he had written through one long sleepless night after another.

As we threw the ball back and forth, he talked. He continued on in his résumé. He was married but had two girlfriends. His wife knew about them both. She did not panic because she expected imperfection in men. Also, he said, he usually voted Republican. He went to parent-teacher-organization meetings.

"I suppose you weren't expecting this," he said.

No, I thought, I was *not* expecting you. I glanced at the tennis court. Clouds of moths and bright bugs swarmed in insect parabolas around the high-voltage lights. The boy had a white Huron high school T-shirt on, and white shorts and tennis shoes, and a blue sweatband around his thick damp hair. The girl was dressed in an odd assortment of pink and pastel blue clothes. She was flying the colors and was the better player. He had the force, but she had the accuracy. Between his heat and her coolness, she piled up the points. I let myself watch her; I allowed myself that. I was having a harder and harder time keeping my eyes on my brother.

"You gonna play or look at them?" Kurt asked.

I glanced at him. I thought I'd ignore his question. "You got any hobbies?" I asked.

He seemed surprised. "Hobbies? No. Unless you count women and making money."

"How's your pitch?"

"You mean baseball?"

"No. Music. How's your sense of pitch?"

"Don't have one."

"I do," I said. "F-sharp." And I blew it at him.

He leaned back and grimaced. "How do you know that's F-sharp?"

"My daddy taught me," I said. "He taught me all the notes on the scale. You can live with them. You can become familiar with a note."

"I don't care for music," he said, ending that conversation. We were still both panting a bit from our exertions. The baseball idea was not quite working in the way he had planned. He seemed to be considering the possibility that he might not like me. "What the hell," he said. "Let's go back to that bar."

Why did I hit my brother in that bar? Gentlemen of the bottle, it is you I address now. You will understand when I tell you that when my brother and I entered the bar, cool and smoky and filled with midsummer ballplayers, uniformed men and women, and he thoughtlessly ordered me a Scotch, you will understand that I drank it. Drank it after I saw his wad of money, his credit cards, his wallet-rubbed pictures of the children, my little nephews. He said he would save me from my alcoholism but he did not. Gentlemen, in a state of raw blank irritation I drank down what God and nature have labeled "poison" and fixed with a secret skull and crossbones. He bought me this drink, knowing it was bad for me. My mind withdrew in a snap from my brain. The universe is vast, you cannot predict it. From the great resources of anger I pulled my fund, my honest share. But I do not remember how, or exactly why, I said something terrible, and hit my brother.

He staggered back, and he looked at me.

His nose was bleeding and my knuckles hurt. I was sitting in the passenger side of his car. My soul ached. My soul was lying face down. He was taking me back to my apartment, and I knew that my brother would not care to see me from now on. He would reassert his right to be a stranger. I had lost my wife, and now I had lost him, too.

We stumbled into my living room. I wobbled out to the kitchen and, booze-sick, filled a dish towel with ice cubes and brought it to him. My right hand felt swollen. We were going to have ugly bruises, but his were facial and would be worse. Holding the ice to his damaged face, he looked around. Above the ice his eyes flickered on with curiosity. "Ships," he said. Then he pointed at the worktable against the wall. "What's all that?"

"It's my hobby," I said. The words came slow and wormlike out of my puzzled mouth.

He squinted above the ice. "Bottles? And glue?"

"I build ships in bottles." I sounded like a balloon emptying itself of air. I pointed at the decorator shelf on the west wall, where my three-masted clipper ship, the *Thermopylae*, was on display.

"How long have you done this?" he asked.

"So long I can't remember."

"How do you do it?"

He gave me a chance. Even a bad drunk is sometimes forced to seize his life and to speak. So I went over to the worktable. "You need these." I held up the surgical forceps. I could hardly move my fingers for the pain. Alcoholic darkness sat in a corner with its black bag waiting to cover me entirely. I went on talking. "And these. Surgical scissors." Dried specks of glue were stuck to the tips. "Some people cheat and saw off the bottom of the bottle, then glue it back on once the ship is inside. I don't do it that way. It has to grow inside the bottle. You need a challenge. I build the hull inside. I have used prefab hulls. Then you've got to lay the deck down. I like to do it with deck furnishings already in place: you know, the cabin doors and hatch covers and cleats and riding bits already in place on the deck. You put the glue on and then you put the deck in, all in one piece, folded up, through the neck, then you fold it out. With all that glue on, you only have one shot. Then you do the rigging inside the bottle. See these masts? The masts are laid down inside the bottle with the bottom of the mast in a hole."

I pointed to the *Cutty Sark,* which I was working on. I did not care if my hands were broken; I would continue this, the only lecture in my head, even if I sounded like a chattering magpie.

"You see, you pull the mast up inside the bottle with a string attached to the mast, and there's a stop in the hole that'll keep the mast from going too far forward. Then you tie the lines that are already on the mast off on the belaying pins and the bits and the cleats." I stopped. "These are the best things I do. I make ships in bottles better than anything else I do in my life."

"Yes." He had been standing over my worktable, but now he was lying on the sofa again.

"I like ships," I said. "When I was growing up, I had pictures on the wall of yachts. I was the only person in the Harris family who was interested in ships."

"Hmm."

"I like sailboats the most." I was talking to myself. "They're in their own class."

"That's interesting," he said. "That's all very interesting, but I wonder if I could lie down here for a while."

"I think you're already doing it."

"I don't need a pillow or a blanket," Kurt said, covered with sweat. "I can lie here just as is."

"I was going to turn on the air conditioner."

"Good. Put it on low."

I went over to the rattletrap machine and turned it on. The compressor started with a mechanical complaint, a sound like *orrr orrr orrr,* and then faster, *orrorrorr.* By the time I got back into the living room, my brother's eyes were closed.

"You're asleep," I said.

"No," he said, "no, I'm not. My eyes are just closed. I'm bruised and taking a rest here. That's all. Why don't you talk to me for a minute while I lie here with this ice. Say anything."

*

So I talked against the demons chittering in the corners of the room. I told my brother about being on a carrier in the Navy. I talked about how I watched the blue lifting swells of the Pacific even when I wasn't supposed to and would get my ass kicked for it. I was hypnotized by sea water, the crazy majesty of horizontal lines. I sleepwalked on that ship, I was so happy. I told him about the rolling progress of oceanic storms, and how the cumulonimbus clouds rose up for what looked like three or four miles into the atmosphere. Straight-edged curtains of rain followed us; near the Straits of Gibraltar it once rained for thirty minutes on the forward part of the ship, while the sun burned down on the aft.

I talked about the ship's work, the painting and repairing I did, and I told him about the constant metallic rumble vibrating below decks. I told him about the smell, which was thick with sterile grease stink that stayed in your nostrils, and the smell of working men. Men away from women, men who aren't getting any, go bad, and they start to smell like metal and fur and meat.

Then I told him about the ships I built, the models, and the originals for them, about the masts and sails, and how, in the water, they had been beautiful things.

"What if they fell?" my brother said.

I didn't understand the question, but thought I would try to answer it anyway. It was vague, but it showed he was still awake, still listening. I wanted to ask, fell from where? But I didn't. I said if a man stood on the mainmast lookout, on a whaler, for example, he could lose his balance. If he tumbled from that height, he might slap the water like he was hitting cement. He might be internally damaged, but if he did come up, they'd throw him a lifebuoy, the white ones made out of cork and braided with a square of rope.

I brought one of the ships toward him. "I've got one here," I said, "tiny, the size of your fingernail."

He looked at it, cleated to the ship above the deck. He studied it and then he gazed at me. "Yes," he said. It was the most painful smile I'd ever seen in an adult human being, and it reminded me of me. I thought of the ocean, which I hadn't viewed for years and might not, ever again. "Yes," my brother said from under the icepack. "Now I get it."

*

Like strangers sitting randomly together in a midnight peeling-gray downtown bus depot smelling of old leather shoes, we talked until four in the morning, and he left, his face bruised dark, carrying one of my ships, the *Lightning,* under his arm. He came back a week later. We sat in the park this time, not saying much. Then I went to see him, and I met his wife. She's a pleasant woman, a tall blonde who comes fully outfitted with jewels I usually see under glass in display cases. My brother and I know each other better now; we've discovered that we have, in fact, no subjects in common. But it's love, so we have to go on talking, throwing this nonsense into the air, using up the clock. He has apologized for trying to play softball with me; he admits now that it was a mistake.

When I was small, living with Harold and Ethel Harris and the other Harris children, I knew about my other parents, the aching lovers who had brought me into my life, but I did not miss them. They'd done me my favor and gone on to the rest of their lives. No, the only thing I missed was the world: the oceans, their huge distances, their creatures, the tides, the burning water-light I heard you could see at the equator. I kept a globe nearby my boy's bed. Even though I live here, now, no matter where I ever was, I was always homesick for the rest of the world. My brother does not understand that. He thinks home is where he is now. I show him maps; I tell him about Turkey and the Azores; I have told him about the great variety and beauty of human pigmentation. He listens but won't take me seriously.

When my brother talks now, he fingers his nose, probably to remind me where I hit him. It's a delicate gesture, with a touch of self-pity. With this gesture he establishes a bit of history between us. He wants to look up to me. He's twenty-eight years old, hasn't ever seen Asia, and he says this to me seriously. Have you ever heard the sound of a man's voice from a minaret? I ask him, but he just smiles. He's already called my wife; he has a whole series of happy endings planned, scene by scene. He wants to sit in a chair and see me come into the room, perfected, thanking the past for all it has done for me.

TOBIAS WOLFF

The Other Miller

FROM THE ATLANTIC

FOR TWO DAYS now Miller has been standing in the rain with the rest of Bravo Company, waiting for some men from another company to blunder down the logging road where Bravo waits in ambush. When this happens, if this happens, Miller will stick his head out of the hole he is hiding in and shoot off all his blank ammunition in the direction of the road. So will everyone else in Bravo Company. Then they will climb out of their holes and get on some trucks and go home, back to the base.

This is the plan.

Miller has no faith in it. He has never yet seen a plan that worked, and this one won't either. He can tell. For one thing, the lieutenant who thought up the plan has been staying away a lot — "doing recon," he claims, but that's a lie. How can you do recon if you don't know where the enemy is? Miller's foxhole has about a foot of water in it. He has to stand on little shelves he's been digging out of the walls, but the soil is sandy and the shelves keep collapsing. That means his boots are wet. Plus his cigarettes are wet. Plus he broke the bridge on his molars the first night out while chewing up one of the lollipops he'd brought along for energy. It drives him crazy the way the broken bridge lifts and grates when he pushes it with his tongue, but last night he lost his will power and now he can't keep his tongue away from it.

When he thinks of the other company, the one they're supposed to ambush, Miller sees a column of dry, well-fed men marching farther and farther away from the hole where he stands waiting for them. He sees them moving easily under light packs. He sees them stopping for a smoke break, stretching out on fragrant beds of pine needles under the trees, the murmur of their voices growing more and more faint as one by one they drift into sleep.

It's the truth, by God. Miller knows it like he knows he's going to catch a cold, because that's his luck. If he were in the other company then they'd be the ones standing in holes.

Miller's tongue does something to the bridge, and a surge of pain shoots through him. He snaps up straight, eyes burning, teeth clenched against the yell in his throat. He fights it back and glares around him at the other men. The few he can see look stunned and ashen-faced. Of the rest he can make out only their poncho hoods. The poncho hoods stick out of the ground like bullet-shaped rocks.

At this moment, his mind swept clean by pain, Miller can hear the tapping of raindrops on his own poncho. Then he hears the pitchy whine of an engine. A jeep is splashing along the road, slipping from side to side and throwing up thick gouts of mud behind it. The jeep itself is caked with mud. It skids to a stop in front of Bravo Company's position, and the horn beeps twice.

Miller glances around to see what the others are doing. Nobody has moved. They're all just standing in their holes.

The horn beeps again.

A short figure in a poncho emerges from a clump of trees farther up the road. Miller can tell it's the first sergeant by how little he is, so little that the poncho hangs almost to his ankles. The first sergeant walks slowly toward the jeep, big blobs of mud all around his boots. When he gets to the jeep, he leans his head inside; he pulls it out again a moment later. He looks down at the road. He kicks at one of the tires in a thoughtful way. Then he looks up and shouts Miller's name.

Miller keeps watching him. Not until the first sergeant shouts his name again does Miller begin the hard work of hoisting himself out of the foxhole. The other men turn their ashen faces up at him as he trudges past their heads.

"Come here, boy," the first sergeant says. He walks a little distance from the jeep and waves Miller over.

Miller follows him. Something is wrong. Miller can tell, because the first sergeant called him "boy," instead of "shitbird." Already he feels a burning in his left side, where his ulcer is.

The first sergeant stares down the road. "Here's the thing," he begins. He stops and turns to Miller. "Hell's bells, I don't know. Goddamn it. Listen. We got a priority here from the Red Cross. Did you know your mother was sick?"

Miller doesn't say anything. He pushes his lips tight together.

"She must have been sick, right?" When Miller remains silent the first sergeant says, "She passed away last night. I'm real sorry." The first sergeant looks sadly up at Miller, and Miller watches the sergeant's right arm beginning to rise under the poncho; then it falls to his side again. Miller can see that the first sergeant wants to give his shoulder a man-to-man kind of squeeze, but it just won't work. You can only do that if you're taller than the other fellow, or maybe the same size.

"These boys here will drive you back to base," the first sergeant says, nodding toward the jeep. "You give the Red Cross a call, and they'll take it from there. Get yourself some rest," he adds. He turns away and walks off toward the trees.

Miller retrieves his gear. One of the men he passes on his way back to the jeep says, "Hey, Miller, what's the story?"

Miller doesn't answer. He's afraid that if he opens his mouth he'll start laughing and ruin everything. He keeps his head down and his lips tight as he climbs into the back seat of the jeep, and he doesn't look up again until the company is a mile or so behind. The fat Pfc. sitting beside the driver is watching him. He says, "I'm sorry about your mother. That's a bummer."

"Maximum bummer," says the driver, another Pfc. He shoots a look over his shoulder. Miller sees his own face reflected for an instant in the driver's sunglasses.

"Had to happen someday," he mumbles, and looks down again.

Miller's hands are shaking. He puts them between his knees and stares through the snapping plastic window at the trees going past. Raindrops rattle on the canvas overhead. He is inside, and everyone else is still outside. Miller can't stop thinking about the others standing around getting rained on, and the thought makes him want to laugh and slap his leg. This is the luckiest he has ever been.

"My grandmother died last year," the driver says. "But that's not the same thing as losing your mother. I feel for you, Miller."

"Don't worry about me," Miller tells him. "I'll get along."

The fat Pfc. beside the driver says, "Look, don't feel like you have to repress just because we're here. If you want to cry or anything just go ahead. Right, Leb?"

The driver nods. "Just let it out."

"No problem," Miller says. He wishes he could set these fellows straight, so they won't feel like they have to act mournful all the way to Fort Ord. But if he tells them what happened they'll turn right around and drive him back to his foxhole.

This is what happened. Another Miller in the battalion has the same initials he's got, W. P., and this Miller is the one whose mother has died. His father passed away during the summer and Miller got that message by mistake too. So he has the lay of the land now; as soon as the first sergeant started asking about his mother, he got the entire picture.

For once, everybody else is on the outside and Miller is on the inside. Inside, on his way to a hot shower, dry clothes, a pizza, and a warm bunk. He didn't even have to do anything wrong to get here; he just did as he was told. It was their own mistake. Tomorrow he'll rest up like the first sergeant ordered him to, go on sick call about his bridge, maybe go downtown to a movie after that. Then he'll call the Red Cross. By the time they get everything straightened out it will be too late to send him back to the field. And the best thing is, the other Miller won't know. The other Miller will have a whole other day of thinking his mother is still alive. You could even say that Miller is keeping her alive for him.

The man beside the driver turns around again and studies Miller. He has little dark eyes in a round, baby-white face covered with beads of sweat. His name tag reads KAISER. Showing little square teeth like a baby's, he says, "You're really coping, Miller. Most guys pretty much lose it when they get the word."

"I would too," the driver says. "Anybody would. Or maybe I should say almost anybody. It's *human,* Kaiser."

"For sure," Kaiser says. "I'm not saying any different. That's going to be my worst day, the day my mom dies." He blinks rapidly, but not before Miller sees his little eyes mist up.

"Everybody has to go sometime," Miller says. "Sooner or later. That's my philosophy."

"Heavy," the driver says. "Really deep."

Kaiser gives him a sharp look and says, "At ease, Lebowitz."

Miller leans forward. Lebowitz is a Jewish name. That means Lebowitz must be a Jew. Miller wants to ask him why he's in the Army, but he's afraid Lebowitz might take it wrong. Instead, he says, conversationally, "You don't see too many Jewish people in the Army nowadays."

Lebowitz looks into the rearview mirror. His thick eyebrows arch over his sunglasses, and then he shakes his head and says something Miller can't make out.

"At ease, Leb," Kaiser says again. He turns to Miller and asks him where the funeral is going to be held.

"What funeral?" Miller says.

Lebowitz laughs.

"Back off," Kaiser says. "Haven't you ever heard of shock?"

Lebowitz is quiet for a moment. Then he looks into the rearview mirror again and says, "Sorry, Miller. I was out of line."

Miller shrugs. His probing tongue pushes the bridge too hard and he stiffens suddenly.

"Where did your mom live?" Kaiser asks.

"Redding," Miller says.

Kaiser nods. "Redding," he repeats. He keeps watching Miller. So does Lebowitz, glancing back and forth between the mirror and the road. Miller understands that they expected a different kind of performance from the one he's given them, more emotional and all. They have seen other personnel whose mothers died and now they have certain standards that he has failed to live up to. He looks out the window. They are driving along a ridgeline. Slices of blue flicker between the trees on the left-hand side of the road; then they hit a space without trees and Miller can see the ocean below them, clear to the horizon under a bright cloudless sky. Except for a few hazy wisps in the treetops they've left the clouds behind, back in the mountains, hanging over the soldiers there.

"Don't get me wrong," Miller says. "I'm sorry she's dead."

Kaiser says, "That's the way. Talk it out."

"It's just that I didn't know her all that well," Miller says, and after this monstrous lie a feeling of weightlessness comes over him. At first it makes him uncomfortable, but almost immediately he begins to enjoy it. From now on he can say anything.

He makes a sad face and says, "I guess I'd be more broken up and so on if she hadn't taken off on us the way she did. Right in the middle of harvest season. Just leaving us like that."

"I'm hearing a lot of anger," Kaiser tells him. "Ventilate. Own it."

Miller got that stuff from a song, but he can't remember any more. He lowers his head and looks at his boots. "Killed my dad," he says, after a time. "Died of a broken heart. Left me with five kids to raise, not to mention the farm." Miller closes his eyes. He sees a field all plowed up with the sun setting behind it, a bunch of kids coming in from the field with rakes and hoes on their shoulders. As the jeep winds down through the switchbacks he describes his hardships as the oldest child in this family. He is at the end of his story when they reach the coast highway and turn north. All at once the jeep stops rattling and swaying. They pick up speed. The tires hum on the smooth road. The rushing air whistles a single note around the radio antenna. "Anyway," Miller says, "it's been two years since I even had a letter from her."

"You should make a movie," Lebowitz says.

Miller isn't sure how to take this. He waits to hear what else Lebowitz has to say, but Lebowitz is silent. So is Kaiser, who's had his back turned to Miller for several minutes now. Both men stare at the road ahead of them. Miller can see that they have lost interest in him. He is disappointed, because he was having a fine time pulling their leg.

One thing Miller told them was true: he hasn't had a letter from his mother in two years. She wrote him a lot when he first joined the Army, at least once a week, sometimes twice, but Miller sent all her letters back unopened and after a year of this she finally gave up. She tried calling a few times but Miller wouldn't go to the telephone, so she gave that up too. Miller wants her to understand that her son is not a man to turn the other cheek. He is a serious man. Once you've crossed him, you've lost him.

Miller's mother crossed him by marrying a man she shouldn't

have married: Phil Dove. Dove was a biology teacher in the high school. Miller was having trouble in the course, and his mother went to talk to Dove about it and ended up getting engaged to him. Miller tried to reason with her, but she wouldn't hear a word. You would think from the way she acted that she had landed herself a real catch instead of someone who talked with a stammer and spent his life taking crayfish apart.

Miller did everything he could to stop the marriage but his mother had blinded herself. She couldn't see what she already had, how good it was with just the two of them. How he was always there when she got home from work, with a pot of coffee already brewed. The two of them drinking their coffee together and talking about different things, or maybe not talking at all — maybe just sitting in the kitchen while the room got dark around them, until the telephone rang or the dog started whining to get out. Walking the dog around the reservoir. Coming back and eating whatever they wanted, sometimes nothing, sometimes the same dish three or four nights in a row, watching the programs they wanted to watch and going to bed when they wanted to and not because some other person wanted them to. Just being together in their own place.

Phil Dove got Miller's mother so mixed up that she forgot how good their life was. She refused to see what she was ruining. "You'll be leaving anyway," she told him. "You'll be moving on, next year or the year after" — which showed how wrong she was about Miller, because he would never have left her, not ever, not for anything. But when he said this she laughed as if she knew better, as if he wasn't serious. He was serious, though. He was serious when he promised he'd stay and he was serious when he promised he'd never speak to her again if she married Phil Dove.

She married him. Miller stayed at a motel that night and two more nights, until he ran out of money. Then he joined the Army. He knew that would get to her, because he was still a month shy of finishing high school, and because his father had been killed while serving in the Army. Not in Vietnam but in Georgia, killed in an accident. He and another man were dipping mess kits in a garbage can full of boiling water and somehow the can fell over on him. Miller was six at the time. Miller's mother hated the Army after that, not because her husband was dead — she knew about the war he was going to, she knew about snipers and booby traps and mines — but because of the way it happened. She said the Army couldn't even get a man killed in a decent fashion.

She was right, too. The Army was just as bad as she thought, and worse. You spent all your time waiting around. You lived a completely stupid existence. Miller hated every minute of it, but he found pleasure in his hatred, because he believed that his mother must know how unhappy he was. That knowledge would be a grief to her. It would not be as bad as the grief she had given him, which was spreading from his heart into his stomach and teeth and everywhere else, but it was the worst grief he had power to cause, and it would serve to keep her in mind of him.

Kaiser and Lebowitz are describing hamburgers to each other. Their idea of the perfect hamburger. Miller tries not to listen but their voices go on, and after a while he can't think of anything but beefsteak tomatoes and Gulden's mustard and steaming, onion-stuffed meat crisscrossed with black marks from the grill. He is on the point of asking them to change the subject when Kaiser turns and says, "Think you could handle some chow?"

"I don't know," Miller says. "I guess I could get something down."

"We were talking about a pit stop. But if you want to keep going, just say the word. It's your ball game. I mean, technically we're supposed to take you straight back to base."

"I could eat," Miller says.

"That's the spirit. At a time like this you've got to keep your strength up."

"I could eat," Miller says again.

Lebowitz looks up into the rearview mirror, shakes his head, and looks away again.

They take the next turnoff and drive inland to a crossroads where two gas stations face two restaurants. One of the restaurants is boarded up, so Lebowitz pulls into the parking lot of the Dairy Queen across the road. He turns the engine off and

the three men sit motionless in the sudden silence that follows.
It soon begins to fade. Miller hears the distant clang of metal on
metal, the caw of a crow, the creak of Kaiser shifting in his seat.
A dog barks in front of a rust-streaked trailer next door. A
skinny white dog with yellow eyes. As it barks the dog rubs itself,
one leg raised and twitching, against a sign that shows an out-
spread hand below the words KNOW YOUR FUTURE.

They get out of the jeep, and Miller follows Kaiser and Lebowitz across the parking lot. The air is warm and smells of oil.
In the gas station across the road a pink-skinned man in a swimming suit is trying to put air in the tires of his bicycle, jerking at
the hose and swearing loudly at his inability to make the pump
work. Miller pushes his tongue against the broken bridge. He
lifts it gently. He wonders if he should try eating a hamburger,
and decides that it can't hurt as long as he is careful to chew on
the other side of his mouth.

But it does hurt. After the first couple of bites Miller shoves
his plate away. He rests his chin on one hand and listens to
Lebowitz and Kaiser argue about whether people can actually
tell the future. Lebowitz is talking about a girl he used to know
who had ESP. "We'd be driving along," he says, "and out of the
blue she would tell me exactly what I was thinking about. It was
unbelievable."

Kaiser finishes his hamburger and takes a drink of milk. "No
big deal," he says. "I could do that." He pulls Miller's hamburger
over to his side of the table and takes a bite.

"Go ahead," Lebowitz says. "Try it. I'm not thinking about
what you think I'm thinking about," he adds.

"Yes, you are."

"All right, now I am," Lebowitz says. "but I wasn't before."

"I wouldn't let a fortune-teller get near me," Miller says. "The
way I see it, the less you know the better off you are."

"More vintage philosophy from the private stock of W. P.
Miller," Lebowitz says. He looks at Kaiser, who is eating the last
of Miller's hamburger. "Well, how about it? I'm up for it if you
are."

Kaiser chews ruminatively. He swallows and licks his lips.
"Sure," he says. "Why not? As long as Miller here doesn't mind."

"Mind what?" Miller asks.

Lebowitz stands and puts his sunglasses back on. "Don't worry about Miller. Miller's cool. Miller keeps his head when men all around him are losing theirs."

Kaiser and Miller get up from the table and follow Lebowitz outside. Lebowitz is bending down in the shade of a dumpster, wiping off his boots with a paper towel. Shiny blue flies buzz around him. "Mind what?" Miller repeats.

"We thought we'd check out the prophet," Kaiser tells him.

Lebowitz straightens up, and the three of them start across the parking lot.

"I'd actually kind of like to get going," Miller says. When they reach the jeep he stops, but Lebowitz and Kaiser walk on. "Now, listen," Miller says, and skips a little to catch up. "I have a lot to do," he says to their backs. "I want to go home."

"We know how broken up you are," Lebowitz tells him. He keeps walking.

"This shouldn't take too long," Kaiser says.

The dog barks once and then, when it sees that they really intend to come within range of its teeth, runs around the trailer. Lebowitz knocks on the door. It swings open, and there stands a round-faced woman with dark, sunken eyes and heavy lips. One of her eyes has a cast; it seems to be watching something beside her while the other looks down at the three soldiers at her door. Her hands are covered with flour. She is a gypsy, an actual gypsy. Miller has never seen a gypsy before, but he recognizes her just as he would recognize a wolf if he saw one. Her presence makes his blood pound in his veins. If he lived in this place he would come back at night with some other men, all of them yelling and waving torches, and drive her out.

"You on duty?" Lebowitz asks.

She nods, wiping her hands on her skirt. They leave chalky streaks on the bright patchwork. "All of you?" she asks.

"You bet," Kaiser says. His voice is unnaturally loud.

She nods again and turns her good eye from Lebowitz to Kaiser, and then to Miller. After she takes Miller in she smiles and rattles off a string of strange sounds, words from another language or maybe a spell, as if she expects him to understand. One of her front teeth is black.

"No," Miller says. "No, ma'am. Not me." He shakes his head.

"Come," she says, and stands aside.

Lebowitz and Kaiser mount the steps and disappear into the trailer. "Come," the woman repeats. She beckons with her white hands.

Miller backs away, still shaking his head. "Leave me alone," he tells her, and before she can answer he turns and walks away. He goes back to the jeep and sits in the driver's seat, leaving both doors open to catch the breeze. Miller feels the heat drawing the dampness out of his fatigues. He can smell the musty wet canvas overhead and the sourness of his own body. Through the windshield, covered with mud except for a pair of grimy half circles, he watches three boys solemnly urinating against the wall of the gas station across the road.

Miller bends down to loosen his boots. Blood rushes to his face as he fights the wet laces, and his breath comes faster and faster. "Goddamn laces," he says. "Goddamn rain. Goddamn Army." He gets the laces untied and sits up, panting. He stares at the trailer. Goddamn gypsy.

He can't believe those two fools actually went inside there. Yukking it up. Playing around. That shows how stupid they are, because anybody knows that you don't play around with fortune-tellers. There is no predicting what a fortune-teller might say, and once it's said, no way to keep it from happening. Once you hear what's out there it isn't out there anymore, it's here. You might as well open your door to a murderer as to the future.

The future. Didn't everybody know enough about the future already, without digging up the details? There is only one thing you have to know about the future: everything gets worse. Once you have that, you have it all. The specifics don't bear thinking about.

Miller certainly has no intention of thinking about the specifics. He peels off his damp socks and massages his white crinkled feet. Now and then he glances up toward the trailer, where the gypsy is pronouncing fate on Kaiser and Lebowitz. Miller makes humming noises. He will not think about the future.

Because it's true — everything gets worse. One day you are sitting in front of your house, poking sticks into an anthill, hearing the chink of silverware and the voices of your mother and father in the kitchen; then, at some moment you can't even remember, one of those voices is gone. And you never hear it again. When you go from today to tomorrow you're walking into an ambush.

A new boy, Nat Pranger, joins your Little League team. He lives in a boardinghouse a couple of streets over from you. The first day you meet Nat you show him the place under the bleachers where you keep the change you steal from your mother. The next morning you remember doing this, and you push your half-eaten breakfast away and run to the ball park, blindly, your chest hurting. The change is still in its hiding place. You count it. Not a penny is missing. You kneel there in the shadows, catching your breath.

All summer you and Nat throw each other grounders and develop plans to acquire a large sailboat for use in the South Seas — that is Nat's term, "the South Seas." Then school starts, your first year of junior high, and Nat makes other friends but you don't, because something about you turns people cruel. Even the teachers. You want to have friends, you would change if you knew what it was that needed changing, but you don't know. You see Nat struggling to be loyal and you hate him for it. His kindness is worse than cruelty. By December you know exactly how things will be in June. All you can do is watch it happen.

What lies ahead doesn't bear thinking about. Already Miller has an ulcer, and his teeth are full of holes. His body is giving out on him. What will it be like when he's sixty? Or even five years from now? Miller was in a restaurant the other day and saw a fellow about his own age in a wheelchair, getting fed soup by a woman who was talking to some other people at the table. This boy's hands lay twisted in his lap like gloves dropped there; his pants had crawled halfway to his knees, showing pale, wasted legs no thicker than bones. He could barely move his head. The woman feeding him did a lousy job because she was too busy blabbing to her friends. Half the soup went over the boy's shirt. Yet his eyes were bright and watchful.

Miller thought, *That could happen to me.*

You could be going along just fine and then one day, through no fault of your own, something could get loose in your bloodstream and knock out part of your brain. Leave you like that. And if it didn't happen now, all at once, it was sure to happen slowly later on. That was the end you were bound for.

Someday Miller is going to die. He knows that, and he prides himself on knowing it when other people only pretend to know it, secretly believing that they will live forever. This is not the reason that the future is unthinkable to Miller. There is something worse than that, something not to be considered, and he will not consider it.

He will not consider it. Miller leans back against the seat and closes his eyes, but his effort to trick himself into somnolence fails. Behind his eyelids he is wide awake and fidgety with gloom, probing against his will for what he is afraid to find, until, with no surprise at all, he finds it. A simple truth. His mother is also going to die. Just like him. And there is no telling when. Miller cannot count on her to be there to come home to, and receive his pardon, when he finally decides that she has suffered enough.

Miller opens his eyes and looks at the raw shapes of the buildings across the road, their outlines lost in the grime on the windshield. He closes his eyes again. He listens to himself breathe and feels the familiar, almost muscular ache of knowing that he is beyond his mother's reach. He has put himself where she cannot see him or speak to him or touch him in that thoughtless way of hers, resting her hand on his shoulder as she stops behind his chair to ask him a question or just stand for a moment, her mind somewhere else. This was supposed to be her punishment, but somehow it has become his own. He understands that it has to stop. It is killing him.

It has to stop now, and as if he has been planning for this day all along Miller knows exactly what he will do. Instead of reporting to the Red Cross when he gets back to base, he will pack his bag and catch the first bus home. No one will blame him for this. Even when they discover the mistake they've made they still won't blame him, because it would be the natural thing for a grieving son to do. Instead of punishing him they will probably apologize for giving him a scare.

He will take the first bus home, express or not. It will be full of Mexicans and soldiers. Miller will sit by a window and drowse.

Now and then he will come up from his dreams to stare out at the passing green hills and loamy plowland and the stations where the bus puts in, stations cloudy with exhaust and loud with engine roar, where the people he sees through his window will look groggily back at him as if they too have just come up from sleep. Salinas. Vacaville. Red Bluff. When he gets to Redding, Miller will hire a cab. He will ask the driver to stop at Schwartz's for a few minutes while he buys some flowers, and then he will ride on home, down Sutter and over to Serra, past the ball park, past the grade school, past the Mormon temple. Right on Belmont. Left on Park. Leaning over the seat, saying farther, farther, a little farther, that's it, that one, there.

The sound of voices behind the door as he rings the bell. Door swings open, voices hush. Who are these people? Men in suits, women wearing white gloves. Someone stammers his name, strange to him now, almost forgotten. "W-W-Wesley." A man's voice. He stands just inside the door, breathing perfume. Then the flowers are taken from his hand and laid with other flowers on the coffee table. He hears his name again. It is Phil Dove, moving toward him from across the room. He walks slowly, with his arms raised, like a blind man.

Wesley, he says. Thank God you're home.

ROBERT TAYLOR, JR.

Lady of Spain

FROM THE HUDSON REVIEW

WHEN THE Lady of Spain revealed herself to me, I was fourteen years old, the owner of an Allstate motor scooter and a large and shining Polina accordion. The accordion lessons had begun several years earlier with a tiny rented instrument and were held in the Sunday school room of the Britton Baptist Church. My teacher, a red-cheeked, dark-haired woman named Lorena Harris, wore little makeup and pinned her soft dark hair atop her head in a circle capped by a delicate net. I thought her the member of a strict religious sect, perhaps a Nazarene. The Nazarenes, my father once told me, had founded the town of Bethany, then a few miles away from Oklahoma City instead of surrounded by it, and to this day Bethany permitted neither the sale of tobacco nor the showing of movies. I also had the notion that the Nazarenes had no musical instruments in their church — that they only sang their hymns, and therefore would surely scorn Miss Harris's beautiful accordion, so lavishly trimmed in chrome and pearl. I entertained the idea that she might keep it a secret from them, lead two lives or more, like the spies on television who, throughout that innocent decade, kept track of communists, and this was a pleasant notion that bore much embellishment. Late at night when I grew bored with the radio broadcasts of the latest humiliation of the Oklahoma City Indians, I saw her take her accordion from its plush velvet case, strap it effortlessly to her chest, and begin to play, somewhere in smokeless, movieless Bethany, secret melodies, intricate versions of "Lady of Spain," "Dark Eyes," "La Golondrina." I always imagined her alone, by herself in a room, a version of myself, doomed to solitude but redeemed by strong feeling.

Closed up in my room with bunk beds, an old desk of my father's, and plastic model airplanes dangling above me from the ceiling, I played my accordion for Lorena Harris and for my mother. For Miss Harris I played "Blue Moon," "Sentimental Journey," "Are You Lonesome Tonight"; for my mother, "Whispering Hope," "Nearer My God to Thee," "Sweet Hour of Prayer." The accordion was costly, paid for in large part by money that my mother had managed to put aside from her grocery allowance. It had ten shifts on the treble, so that a single note might be made to sound at one moment rich and deep like an organ and in the next shrill and high like a piccolo. Three shifts lined the bass, and a marvelous black and white zigzag design decorated the front of the bellows. Its weight alone bespoke a vast and intricate interior, a secret realm of lever and wheel. What made the sound? A system of trembling reeds, Miss Harris told me. In my mind the word *reed* was highly significant. It was biblical. I remembered that among the reeds of the Nile the baby Moses had been hidden from the Pharaoh.

My father had to travel days at a time from one end of Oklahoma to the other, selling class rings and diplomas and band uniforms to reluctant school districts. I had heard stories of his tribulations. It was all politics, he said. His competitors were expert at politicking a superintendent. They did not permit their products to stand on merit. They sold their souls and robbed him of his rightful customers. I imagined smooth-talking, pallid men, plump in pinstriped suits and black and white wing-tipped oxfords. They drove big somber Buicks and their daughters were cheerleaders, their sons quarterbacks.

Such children I had nothing to do with. Anyway, they did not seek me out. My best friend Steve, who had only recently given up his accordion lessons in order to devote more time to baseball, was a quiet, nice church-going boy like myself. I knew he had betrayed something important when he quit his accordion lessons. His mother, I remember, attended all his lessons and had a small beginners' accordion of her own that she practiced on, using Steve's music. I heard her play on several occasions, late afternoons when, out of a need for companionship, I played catch with Steve. The songs floated forth from her bedroom as if from a phonograph record, distant and dreamy. Even the bright polkas sounded plaintive and sweet. Several years older than my mother, Steve's mother wore dresses rich with eyelets and lace. Her husband scowled a lot, though he was cheerful enough when spoken to. He was a U.S. marshal. Once I saw his picture in the *Daily Oklahoman*. He was handcuffed to the notorious murderer of entire families, Billy Cook, and although considerably shorter than the killer he looked like he meant business.

My father was surely cut out for better things than measuring the breadth of the fingers of high school juniors for their class rings, the length of their legs for band uniforms. I knew that given the opportunity he would do nothing at all, or else be an artist. A high school teacher of his had urged him to pursue a career in commercial art, but he had graduated from high school in 1932 and had had to take what he could get. Selling, he once told me, was the backbone of the country. But there was no conviction in his voice.

During this time his was a quiet presence in the house. He enjoyed a cigar with his evening paper. Then he went out to the office that he had built a few summers ago adjoining our garage, where he worked evenings and sometimes well into the night on his designs for class rings. I liked going out there and was always pleased when asked to deliver a telephone message from a customer, usually some superintendent or principal canceling an appointment. After relaying the message, I sat on a small sofa just behind the desk, lingering amidst an amazing clutter of papers — what could they have been — orders, bills, magazines, unfinished designs. I remember liking to find copies of the newsletter put out by the company that he worked for, Star Engraving Company of Houston, Texas, a mimeographed pamphlet really, printed on a dozen or so pastel sheets stapled together, its chief function to report on the volume of business done by the sales force, ranking the top salesmen in various categories (rings, caps and gowns, diplomas, invitations, and the like). Finding my father's name most often near the top of each list, I was proud. Sometimes there were notes written by the sales manager or even the president of the company congratulating selected men, the week's leaders.

My father worked diligently at his broad desk, a cigar gone

out in the ashtray, a crooked-neck fluorescent lamp glowing and humming softly above his head. Frequently he used a magnifying glass, holding it steady a few inches from the sketch, which might have been a representation of a lion's head or the entranceway to a high school, an Indian's profile or a crouching tiger, or a coiled rattler. Once he had drawn (not for a ring design, of course) a picture of my mother, a pencil sketch of her head in profile, a good likeness and life-size, her long hair upswept in front and cascading into tiny curls on the side and in the back. It was done, I had been told by her, when she was pregnant with me. She looked stern, even a little angry, but a certain serenity also came through. The picture hung in a white frame above their bed and I thought it a very romantic thing to have drawn and wished that I had such a gift.

What do you think of this, he said, pausing to show me what he worked on. Pretty good, eh. There's nothing in McDowell's line to compete with this.

I believed him an excellent artist, but except for these moments of pride in a new design he spoke disparagingly of his talent. It had been compromised, he said, spoiled before it could properly be developed.

The Allstate motor scooter was the cheapest offered by Sears, its engine only slightly larger than the one on my father's power mower. It had a foot brake and tires the diameter of hubcaps. On it I was nonetheless enabled to crisscross Oklahoma City, circle it, ride out Western Avenue until on either side of me the plains stretched endless, the trees disappeared, and the strong wind in my face smelled of hay and occasionally of cattle or horses. Back in town, I paid visits to girls and took them for rides. They had to ride behind me on the tractor-style seat, their legs straddling my hips, their arms wrapped tightly around my chest. Often I could feel their hair brush against the back of my neck, and I shivered and wished, as we crept up a slight rise, the throttle wide open, for more speed, more power.

That summer I worked as a carhop at the Orange Julius stand on May Avenue, near the Lakewood and Lakeside shopping centers. Sometimes carloads of teenaged girls came in. These girls, mightily rouged and perfumed, their dark mascaraed eyes flashing, hinted in no uncertain terms of the wonderful pleasures one might have in the back seat of their father's Pontiac or Olds 88. I flirted mercilessly and cultivated a swagger, a nonchalant wink, a rakish grin. They told me I was cute, oh so much cuter than the boys their own age, and I began to fancy that I would always have a taste for older women. It did not surprise me that the girls seldom left a tip. Wasn't the feeling that we had so briefly shared beyond the realm of appetite and commerce?

Steve, who also worked at the Orange Julius stand, said that if he ever had the chance, he would be in that back seat in a jiffy. I feared for his soul, but suspected that he wasn't as likely as I was to be put to the test. My attraction, I believed, was somehow connected to playing the accordion, and Steve had left his accordion playing to his mother.

What would you do, I asked him, if you were in the back seat of one of those cars with girls in them.

We were picking up trash on the lot during a lull in customers, stabbing at paper cups and wadded napkins with our spears, as we called the broomsticks with nails in the end.

I would know, Steve said. I'd know what to do all right.

What.

It all depends.

If they let you kiss them then, what would you do?

It still all depends.

On what.

It was not the ethics of the situation that concerned me. I was after reliable information, and suspected that Steve might have known something that I didn't. I knew precious little, it seemed to me. My two sisters were younger than I was and no help. My curiosity was not just academic. Having kissed a girl before, I was keen on repeating the experience. Was it as pleasant for the girl, though? That's what I couldn't imagine. A memory that I cherished was of a party given by my cousin and a few of her girlfriends at which kissing was the object of several games. These girls were a year older than I was, dazzling in their promise, with such smooth red lips and soft warm cheeks, the air surrounding them thick with the scent of a variety of perfumes.

A boy was mysteriously chosen and led into a darkened room where one of the girls awaited him, kissed him before he could properly see her, and then he was sent back out to the lighted room, to be greeted by giggles and jeers. I wanted to stay in that darkened room. Let them laugh — in there I wouldn't hear a thing.

That night on the lot of the Orange Julius stand, Steve seemed annoyed by my question, but at last said that what you did after a girl let you kiss her depended on whether she let you kiss her on the cheek or on the mouth.

On the mouth, I said.

Then you just keep kissing her until she says quit it.

What if she doesn't say quit.

They always say quit.

A car came in then — my customer. The girl in this car sat very close to her date, and her hand rested on his thigh. I was the one she looked at — there was no mistaking it — and in that look I suddenly seemed to see all I needed to know. I vowed to memorize her eyes, and also the shape of that hand resting securely on her date's thigh. It was a small hand, the fingernails long and red. Her scent, I told myself, was like fresh almonds, her voice like a love song. She said, I could drink a pint. And her date said, Two pints, thick, no straws. When I picked up their tray after they were finished, she winked at me. Her boyfriend, a big guy in a letter jacket, left no tip. He sprayed gravel getting out of the lot and laid down rubber on May Avenue. Wherever he was taking her, he was in a big hurry. Too big a hurry, I concluded. I knew now that I would treat her different. I'd take my time.

This was the summer that my accordion teacher got married. I saw the man briefly one day as I was leaving my lesson. Leaning against the fender of her car, he smoked a cigarette and seemed on the verge of sleep. Tall and lanky, long-necked and tightly jeaned, he had a head shaped like the grill of an Edsel, with hair congealing into dark ribbonlike strands that curved over his head and curled at the upper reaches of his neck. I could not imagine him with a regular job, or even with one such as my father had. He would stand around like that all day, smoking, contemplating the trees, leaning on some fender. The money from my lessons — I saw it in a flash — would make possible his squalid languor.

Have a good lesson? my mother asked.

It was okay, I said, keeping my eye on the new husband as Mother pulled the car onto Britton Road.

I hope you did, she said. I certainly hope you had a good lesson. It means a lot to have a good lesson.

That was Mr. Cox back there, wasn't it.

Mr. Cox?

Miss Harris's husband.

I didn't see anyone.

He was right there. Leaning against her car.

I must not have noticed.

I'm sure it was him.

Well, maybe it was.

It was him all right.

Maybe it was. I wouldn't know the man if I saw him. I've got other things on my mind.

What could she see in a man like that.

I said I didn't see him.

Where are we going.

Home.

We don't usually go this way.

We had passed Western Avenue and now were in Britton, which was like a small town, though really part of Oklahoma City, on the very edge of it. There was a Main Street with a T. G. & Y. store, a C. R. Anthony Department Store, a Western Auto, and a drugstore that had a good soda fountain. Western Avenue connected it to the city, to supermarkets and shopping centers and subdivisions such as Nichols Hills, where we lived. I rode here often on my motor scooter and liked to imagine that I had come to a town far away from Oklahoma City, perhaps in Texas or New Mexico. In the drugstore I purchased cherry Cokes and then examined the rack of paperback books near the cash register to see if there were any new titles among the westerns and detective thrillers and to read the covers avidly. I picked up a copy of *Playboy*, then a bold new magazine, and discreetly flipped to the centerfold photograph, careful not to linger too long on it before putting it down and then feigning interest in *Field and Stream* or, even duller, *Sports Illustrated*.

At the drugstore my mother pulled into a parking space.

You drive, she said.

Since I had never driven a car before — aside from backing and pulling forward on the driveway — this command came as a surprise.

You've got to learn sometime, she said. She took a deep breath and opened the door. I realized that I was to trade places with her, and I managed to do as she did, get out and cross to the other side, the driver's side.

Have I said that my mother was a beautiful woman? She was. I found this somewhat of an embarrassment, another instance of how my family was not right. Mothers were supposed to be plump and gray, slightly younger versions of grandmothers, but mine was trim and dark, with auburn hair and hazel eyes that flashed brilliantly. Around the house during the summer she wore shorts and high-heeled wedge sandals, usually with a halter top. When she picked me up at my accordion lesson she was on her way home from the volunteer work that she did every Thursday at the big Veterans' Hospital on NE 13th Street, and so she always wore what she called her gray lady uniform, in fact a gray dress rather like a nurse's uniform except for the gray color. But on this Thursday she wore a scooped-necked blouse, white with bright red and green trim around the neckline, and a flowing full skirt, also white, trimmed with the same bright colors as the blouse. So preoccupied with scorn of my music teacher's husband, I had not even noticed this bold departure from her usual Thursday style of dress until, seated at the wheel of her DeSoto, I watched her get in beside me, the engine running smoothly, air conditioner humming.

Push the lever to R, she said. You know how to back up. Just watch where you're going.

Where are we going?

I don't know. For God's sake, I don't know. Nowhere. Anywhere. Will you just go, please.

But I had been struck by two unnerving realizations: first, that I was scared to death to back into the traffic that was steadily coursing through Britton, and second, that my mother was upset. Tears were in her eyes, and she began to rummage through her purse, at last pulling forth a crumpled tissue. It did not seem the right time for a driving lesson. The car loomed large and lethal, but at the same time was dangerously vulnerable. I kicked at the brake pedal and pretended to have trouble finding R on the gear-shift column.

I don't know, I said. Maybe there's too much traffic.

You just have to watch where you're going, she said, wiping at her eyes with the tattered, lipstick-stained tissue. It will be all right. Just go.

And so I backed the big DeSoto out onto Britton Road ever so slowly, looking from one side to the other. Sure enough, a car had to stop in order to allow me onto the street. Mortified, I pressed the accelerator. The immediate surge forward took my breath away. I gripped the wheel firmly and vowed to remain calm. One only had to concentrate, watch the road ahead, glance now and then into the rearview mirror. Would I have to stop? No, I had traveled this route often on my motor scooter and knew that there was no stoplight or sign between us and the open highway. Once outside Britton — a matter of only several blocks — traffic would fall off, the wide flat prairie land on either side of us, the highway stretching straight ahead as far as the eye could see. The knowledge of this ahead was comforting, and as we crept past the last of the storefronts, and then at last the frame houses on their small treeless lawns gave way to the full breadth of the sky and the land leveled out into immensity, I was certain that I could drive this DeSoto to the end of the continent if need be.

My mother began to sob, softly at first, so that I could easily enough pretend not to notice, and in fact I succeeded quite well in not noticing, such fun it was to see the highway ahead, to feel the power of the big engine, a hundred times greater than that of my motor scooter, that strange sense of limitlessness, as if this were my life itself opening up before me, a straight line to eternity.

I glanced at the speedometer. We were going sixty-five miles per hour, yet scarcely seemed to move, so vast was the land that we moved across. The sobbing had grown louder, and, in the quickest of glances, I saw that she covered her face in her hands. The crumpled tissue had fallen to her lap.

It's no good, she said. Everything's all wrong. Every time you think things are getting better, they only get worse.

I didn't know what to say. Really she didn't seem to be addressing me, but rather talking to herself. Perhaps she didn't mean for me to have heard. The road was smooth. Soon we would come to the Edmond turnoff. A few distant trees bent to the strong wind and now and then a red sworl of dust whipped across the highway. The sky was pale blue, cloudless. I was absolutely confident.

Keep going, my mother said. I can't go back yet. I don't care if we end up in Tulsa. I'll tell you when to stop.

I drove and drove. We skirted the city, staying always on the edge of it, away from the traffic, making an almost complete circle by the end. It is one of the most dreamlike memories that I have, those dizzying plains all around, the red soil badly eroded, the tufts of sharply pointed weeds bordering the highway, now and then the skyline of the city appearing, those twin bank buildings rising like grand gray monuments tall and eternal from the sealike vastness, now to the west, now to the north, at last again to the south, and then windmills in the middle of nowhere or oil derricks thumping steadily into the depths of a land that looked as dry as the dust ever blowing across it. The car rolled along, heavy and smooth and quiet. My mother's tears subsided. She told me about the sorrow of her life, and her voice might have been the very sound of the landscape. I cannot imagine that place, that straight highway, those gullies and the red flat land, without hearing again her voice as it came to me across the car, the grief in it as pure as any I have ever known.

The reason for my mother's not wearing her gray lady uniform on that particular afternoon was that there had been a special party on the ward. The veterans had seemed to languish of late, and the women who gave their own time to cheer up the men had agreed that something extraordinary had to be done. Thus the party. It was to be, my mother said, a *real* party. Everyone was to dress up for the occasion in his best clothes. There was to be music, dancing, entertainment, refreshments, the ward decorated with bright-colored streamers and balloons. The balloons would contain messages and the veterans were to be encouraged to puncture those balloons and find the messages, which would be cheerful, optimistic phrases from *The Prophet* and *The Power of Positive Thinking*. My mother did not care for this last idea. It was treating them like children, she argued, when what they needed was to be treated as responsible adults. How else were they to regain their pride and dignity. She was overruled. The men of the ward were *not* like other men. In many ways they were like little boys — boys who had been asked to assume the responsibilities of manhood before they were ready. They needed to find their lost childhoods. My mother saw that there was no arguing with the other women. At least they had accepted her suggestion that uniforms be put aside in favor of nicer clothes, even though one of them said quite vehemently that to do so was to invite trouble. Wasn't that silly, my mother said to me, and of course I agreed, having no idea what such trouble would mean.

I was never to find out exactly what did happen at that Thursday's party to make her so unhappy, though she talked to me often of her work with the veterans, of how much that work meant to her and at last of the one veteran who she took a very special interest in. Sometimes we went for long drives similar to that first one, drives that she spoke of to my sisters and father as instruction, but increasingly that instruction occurred late at night in my room, when I lay in the top bunk of my bed only half awake. Sometimes she actually slept in the bottom bunk — other times she returned to her own bed before dawn. I confess that sometimes, tired from a particularly busy night carhopping at the Orange Julius stand, I fell asleep as she talked. Nonetheless, I remember with absolute clarity the underlying sorrow, the sense of lamentation and attendant relief, the strange feeling of shared grief, the notion that I had become for her a confidante, as much sister as son.

I constructed in my own mind a version of the Thursday party, seemed at last to see it as though I had been there. I put this version together as I rode out the highways that crossed wheat fields and prairies, rutted soil and pasture, the same territory we covered in the DeSoto for my instruction. The special veteran would have been waiting for her. He was a lot like me, she had told me, not in looks of course, but in temperament. *Sensitive* was the word she used. Shy. Kept to himself and thought a lot. Liked to read, and read everything he could get his hands on. She brought him books, paperbacks that she purchased at Rector's downtown, and he received them eagerly, gratefully.

He never had a chance, she said. His father mistreated him and then he was drafted and sent to Korea. Something bad happened to him over there. Maybe something bad happens to them all, but some can't forget it. Some are haunted by what they had to go through. Can you imagine? It's hard for us to imagine.

I could imagine.

She would have had a book for him on that Thursday, a mystery novel with a lurid cover, carried in her large straw handbag. He would stand to one side of a group of talkative men, somewhat taller than most of them, his face in shadow. Music comes from a portable record player, one similar to my sisters', the size of one of my father's suitcases, with the speaker across the front. It is lively music, music to jitterbug to, to rhumba or samba to. Xavier Cugat, Tommy Dorsey, Bob Crosby. Occasionally a ballad sung by Jo Stafford or Margaret Whiting, a love song, not too sad. Records the women would have brought from home, records such as my parents had, in booklike albums, six big 78s per album, each in its own slot within. Some of the men bat at the balloons. Others dance — this part was harder to imagine. I was no dancer myself, and I concluded that neither would her veteran be. But the others — I had little to go on, junior high school formals, to which the girls wore stiff gauzy dresses.

She would encourage him to dance, for she was a good dancer herself. I had heard my father say so, and even remember seeing him dance with her in our living room. They reminded me of Fred Astaire and Ginger Rogers, whose movies my sisters loved to watch on television, my father spinning her and twirling her, drawing her close, dancing cheek to cheek, twirling again so that her full skirt fanned outward and she began to laugh, saying, That's enough now. You'll knock something over.

This room is too small, the way you dance! Oh, my father said, you always spoil the fun. Just like your mother! Come on. Let's show the kids what real dancing is like.

But she had had enough, and so the best I could do was picture something like that, incomplete but lovely while it lasted. For the others though, not for my mother and the veteran whom she wished to help. Off to the side the two of them stand. She looks pretty in her white dress, so pretty that the other women are envious.

You should dance, she says. Dancing is good for you.

No, he says, I don't feel like dancing.

Well, would you like a cup of punch then?

No, thanks.

I've brought you a book.

I'm tired of reading.

And with that he turns and leaves her, making his way across the crowded dance floor, through the crepe paper streamers and the floating balloons and at last down a long narrow hallway and into the tiny room where she would not be permitted to follow him. The room would have bunk beds — made of black metal, though, not varnished maple like mine — and a single curtainless window with bars on the outside. He would throw himself upon the bottom bunk and glower at the mattress springs above him, his jaw clenched tightly. Then his terrible memories overcome him and he closes his eyes, sinks into the nightmare of war, bombs flashing and exploding all around him, friends shrieking and dying everywhere.

My mother makes her apologies to the other women.

I have to take my son to his music lesson, she says. He can't carry that heavy accordion on his motor scooter.

She sought understanding from me. While I pretended to understand, much in fact escaped me. I believe I learned to become a good listener, and perhaps, after all, that is a kind of understanding. Coming home late from the Orange Julius stand, my lungs filled with the sweet night air, I sat on the living room floor of the silent house and counted my earnings, then went to bed and awaited my mother's arrival in the bunk beneath me. Sometimes I heard a sound from my parents' bedroom first, the raised voice of my father, and then their door opening, shutting, and her soft footsteps in the hall. I imagine her pausing to look into my sisters' bedroom, seeing them deep in their own dreams, motionless in their twin beds. Why had she not chosen one of them to confide in? One was too young surely, only seven at this time, but the other was just a year younger than I was. This one, however, Carolyn, the elder of the two, was considerably more spirited than I, even scrappy, and often argued long and hard with her mother over issues that I would have let pass as trivial. She seemed to me in fact to go out of her way to pick a fight, and both girls got along better with their daddy, though even he could become the focus of their tempers. There is something with mothers and daughters, finally and significantly, that does not exist with mothers and sons: fundamental antagonism, no doubt a rivalry. Whatever, I was chosen and not one of my sisters.

She came to my doorway and I heard her breathing, even now hear it, and smell again the scent of her perfume, a smell in memory more carnal than floral. Are you asleep, she asks. I know that an answer is not required. She enters my room, and I hear her pull back the bedspread, the sheets, and then feel the bedframe move slightly as she eases herself into the bunk beneath mine. Are you awake, she asks. This time I say yes.

Once she said this: I knew nothing about men, not the first thing about love. My mother told me nothing. I was married to another man before your father. I was too young and though I cared deeply for him and he loved me that marriage failed. I thought that I would never marry again.

All my life, she said another time, has been a sacrifice for others. I didn't finish high school because my father needed me to bring in an extra paycheck to help support the family. I was the oldest, and happy to help. I know that he was grateful. I worked in Baker's Shoe Store downtown, selling hosiery, and then at the jewelry counter of John A. Brown's. That's where I met your father, and when we were married another long sacrifice began. I learned what it meant to be a mother as well as a wife, to be responsible for a home. Please understand. I don't resent what I've been given. I love my children, all of you. But I have to ask — do you understand this — when my own time will come, when I can begin to live for myself. Is that so much to ask for, a life of my own?

I said no, that it certainly was not, but I really had no idea what it would mean for her to lead a life of her own. I responded on an abstract level, guided only by a sense of fairness. Life was short, she said, and was one's own. You could kill the life within you if you neglected it. The life within — that's what mattered, that's what must not be allowed to die. It had to be kept alive.

From their hidden homes in the big elm outside my window, the crickets whirred, and above the branches that I loved so much to climb upon in the daytime, the stars no doubt held their own in the broad night sky. Everywhere an eloquence that would not — no matter how much it insisted — be comprehended.

I did not practice my accordion often in the summer, but some mornings before the heat grew deadly I strapped the heavy instrument to my chest and labored mightily to perfect "Claire de Lune" or "Santa Lucia" or "*The Washington Post* March." My own favorite was something called "Sweet Sugar," a fox trot in the key, if I remember correctly, of B-flat. Dutifully, to please Lorena Harris (now Mrs. Cox), I worked on chromatic scales, on arpeggios, on bass runs. In the afternoons I rode my motor scooter or had my instruction in the DeSoto.

Before I knew it, August came. In that month heat was general, day and night. My father purchased a small air conditioner, still somewhat of a novelty in those days, and had it installed in a living room window. This room, shut off from the others in order to keep the chilled air effective, became a cool refuge. When the air conditioner was turned on in midmorning, we all sat around it, watching "Queen for a Day" or reruns of "My Little Margie" or the old movie musicals that my sisters were so fond of. Summer was my father's off-season, since the high schools that he called on were not in session, and so he often sat there in his big green chair, sometimes with a *Daily Oklahoman,* the cigar smoke puffing out from behind it. Mother kept busy in the kitchen or in the back of the house, claiming that the heat did not bother her, though frequently joining us by midafternoon — the heat of the day, as she called this time.

On milder mornings she might be found stretched out on a towel in the backyard, tanning her legs.

In our talks she came to speak less of her youth — of her overly stern mother and sweetly indulgent father — and more of her dissatisfaction with my father. They argued fiercely all during those years. This had become simply a fact of our family life. Why don't they get divorced, Carolyn wondered. How can two people live together and fight all the time. It made no sense to me either, but mine was not an inquiring mind in those days — if it *ever* has been! Maybe they still love each other, I said to Carolyn. In my heart I knew that this could not be true. Hadn't I heard her say as much.

She began to urge me to visit the ward with her.

I've told the men about you, she said. It would mean so much if you came to visit them.

She wanted me to play my accordion for them. "Lady of Spain," she kept saying. Wouldn't I play "Lady of Spain" for the men on the ward.

It was the last thing I would have chosen to do to end the summer, but there was no resisting her. She wanted "Lady of Spain." She would have it. I thought that she might have wanted "Whispering Hope" or perhaps my last recital piece, a complicated arrangement of "The Stars and Stripes Forever" that she had praised fervently, even though I'd made several mistakes and left out an entire section. But it made no difference to me. I'd played "Lady of Spain" almost from the start of my lessons — in increasingly difficult arrangements — and was fond enough of its quick pace and rollicking rhythm. In the sixth grade I'd played it for my girlfriend, who did a dance to it with castanets, on a program for the entire school. Perhaps it was that triumph that my mother remembered. Or perhaps the melody was a favorite of one of the men. Whatever, she had got it into her head that I would play "Lady of Spain."

All right, I said. When?

Thursday, she said.

This gave me five days to prepare myself. Once I had agreed, and the date was set, I began to feel intensely nervous, the way I always felt before those yearly recitals in the Baptist churches that Lorena Harris found for her students to perform in. The

more recitals I played in, the more nervous I became beforehand. What got me through was the thought that it would soon
be over.

The dynamics of "Lady of Spain" were crucial. So Lorena
Harris had taught me, and as I took out the accordion and slid
my shoulders into its cushioned straps I seemed to see her
clearly before me. She wore a sky-blue blouse of thin gauzy
material and a tiered skirt that made a soft swish when she
crossed her legs. A strand of her dark hair had come loose from
her hair net and the top button of her blouse was undone. Soft
here, she says, raising a finger to her lips. Now *crescendo!*

Sometimes the student who had his lesson after me did not
come, and my lesson continued overtime. We were surrounded
by tiny folding chairs and back of us hung a large bulletin board
filled with color pictures of Jesus at the important stages of his
life, from manger to cross. On a desk to one side of Lorena
Harris the Sunday school lesson books were stacked in three
even ranks. A banner across one wall displayed in large black
letters John 3:16, For God so loved the world that he gave his
only begotten son . . .

My mother would be waiting in the car, of course, but so
would the new husband of Lorena Harris. It was pleasant to
think that he was kept waiting. I imagined it while unsnapping
the bellows of the accordion, saw him as I listened to the air flow
through the mysterious corridors of that strange instrument.
He wore pink-soled suede shoes and leaned on the fender of
her little Plymouth, his palms pressed against the clean and
shining metal. He would have to wait. "Lady of Spain," I played.
Lady of Spain I adore you. And when I was finished, I played it
again.

I practiced hard for the men. As I have said, I was scared to
death. There was an edge to this fright that made it worse by
far than the usual recital nervousness. Who, after all, were these
men who were so eager to hear me play? What did a veteran
look like? They have feelings, my mother had told me, just the
same as you and me, only they've never been given a chance.
But what would they look like?

At the Orange Julius stand the lights that encircled the lot

bobbed back and forth in the strong wind, and I fancied them
eyes, the eyes of the veterans. With the girls who drove up in
their fathers' big cars, I flirted as usual, but my heart was not in
it.

I asked my father if sometime in the fall I might go along
with him on one of his sales trips. I must have been feeling
guilty for having agreed to play on the ward. Unlike those veterans, he had never been to war. When the Japanese bombed
Pearl Harbor, he had gone down to enlist, but was turned away
because he had recently became a father — I was the child, of
course.

Yes, he would take me along with him sometime. He did not
look up from the book he was reading — I think it must have
been Sandburg's *Young Abe Lincoln* — and did not remove the
cigar from his mouth. The floor lamp shone brightly on his
head, through his thinning hair and onto his pink scalp. When
my mother and I left for the Veterans' Hospital, he was not
home. I thought it just as well. He prided himself on her not
having to work outside the house and did not even approve of
her volunteer work. Perhaps also he was suspicious, a little jeal-
ous. He had good reason to be. Years later, when my mother at
last went through with her divorce, she told him she planned to
marry one of these veterans. And she did. I could not have
foretold such an event, but I sensed the reason in my father's
fear of her work.

I hope you know how much this means to me, she said to me
in the car.

I assured her I did.

It did not matter how well I played, she said. It was the gesture itself that counted.

I told her I understood.

I did not. Otherwise why would I be shaking so? When at last
it came time to strap on the instrument, I felt faint. The great
black thing was impossibly heavy.

The men milled about, tall and short, young and old. Some
wore blue pajamas with white trim at the sleeve and pants cuff.
Others dressed as if for a formal ball, white shirts and bow ties,
gleaming black shoes. Still others wore T-shirts and blue jeans.
I thought there were hundreds of them, but surely there could

not have been more than thirty. The room itself was small. Couches and chairs had been pushed back against the walls, and some of the older men, their mouths hanging open and eyelids half shut, slumped in the big cushions, clutched the arms of the chairs as if they expected sudden movement. Through the high oblong windows above the seated men, the glass so thick it was almost opaque, I saw the bars that I had imagined.

Gray ladies circulated among the men, carrying trays of paper cups and paper napkins. One of the women I had met before — she had come to our house on several occasions — but the others, perhaps there were six of them altogether, I had never seen. Yet they looked familiar. The gray dresses, of course, were identical, the same stiff uniform my mother wore. They smiled pleasantly, handing out the punch with ease. They might have been, I realized, the mothers of my friends.

My mother led me from group to group. *This is my son.* I shook innumerable hands, gripping firmly as my father had taught me. No, they invariably said, you couldn't have a son this big! They were all well-mannered, soft-spoken, polite. One man kissed my mother's hand.

I must have been brought there to meet the man my mother would later marry, though I remember no such meeting. The man I've come to know as my stepfather must have been one of the inconspicuous ones. He would have preferred watching me from a distance. My mother has explained to me that he cannot work because he refuses to be bossed around. They live on a government pension in an apartment complex near Will Rogers Field. Fearing robbery, they seldom go out. It is not an unfounded fear. Apartments all around them have been hit. He recently screwed shut their windows and during my last visit sat up all one night, his recliner turned to face the window, watching to be sure that no mischief was done to my poor, shabby car.

My father remarried — twice, but the first marriage was brief. She was a schoolteacher, a widow, and must have known right away that she had made a mistake. By then he had become a little wild, spending a lot of time in singles bars and not keeping track of where the money went. He lost his job — also more than once. Took to representing several companies, no longer handling profitable class rings and diplomas but textbooks, which he lugged around to the adopting school districts all over Oklahoma and the Texas panhandle. He no longer worked on his designs for class rings, of course. The house where he'd had his office was sold when he went into bankruptcy, not long after I started college. In the end he achieved a degree of stability. His last marriage lasted four years, until his death by heart failure quite suddenly last year. He was sixty-nine. He had begun to draw and paint again and was tolerably solvent.

That afternoon in the ward I played "Lady of Spain," and as I played, my fear passed away. In its place came a strange elation. The men listened, and their listening was of a different order from what I felt at recitals. They too might have played the tune, the sentimental quality of it giving way to a passion that went into the depths of all music and included my mother in it, drew her into it. *Lady of Spain!* When I saw her, that gray lady, that dark-eyed Nazarene atremble in the shadows of shades of men, it was as if I saw all the women I would love. This was music, this was the life within, this was the love I would sell my soul to possess. The air that set the reeds to quaver, God help me, might have been my own breath.

DANIEL STERN

The Interpretation of Dreams by Sigmund Freud: A Story

FROM THE ONTARIO REVIEW

"ALWAYS A THREESOME," she said. "Two men and a woman. Except that one man, the one with previous rights in the matter, is always dead."

"I hate this nickel analysis," he said.

"I can't help it. When it gets neat is when it feels true. You don't have to *do* anything about it. It's just that it's like a murder mystery with a series of imaginary murders. If you marry two widows there are two dead men in the background."

This is how it went after his second wife was bitten on the finger by a squirrel. Dickstein had a feeling things would change, and not for the better. It was a three-month situation: meeting, wooing, marrying, and up to New York for a new life. She was fourteen years younger than he and nothing besides falling in love and marriage had been decided; would she work at her music, at a job, have a baby, have two babies? In the meantime, it was a muggy August and against his wishes — though he hadn't examined them or actually expressed them — she had been marking time taking a course at the NYU summer school: Dream, Myth, and Metaphor.

The day had been warm and after class she'd lingered in a small rainbow of sunlight and offered one of the peanuts she was shucking and munching to a begging squirrel. She was a Georgia girl and the peanut habit died hard.

Fortunately, after the animal nipped her and drew blood

a sharp park attendant netted the squirrel. The rabies test was negative but they put the little bastard to sleep anyway. Leaving Sharon in bed for a few days with shock and a bandaged hand.

"You're mad at me," she said to Dickstein.

"Surprised," he said. "What happened to your country girl smarts? You don't feed New York squirrels from your hand."

"Well, how would I learn that in Chapel Hill?"

He snapped a portable dinner tray in place and tried a laugh. "I always thought that course was dangerous."

"How so?"

He shut up fast. There was no decent way he could tell her how he'd felt the day she came back from the class with a paperback copy of Freud's *Interpretation of Dreams*. Tell her what? That if he'd wanted to marry somebody who could rattle off about latent and manifest content, who could play peekaboo with symbols and wish fulfillment and repression, he wouldn't have waited until he was thirty-nine to remarry. He could have tied up with any of the smart-ass, overeducated, underserious women he'd spent most of his life with.

Sharon was wonderfully articulate without being glib. She had the southern gift for language flow without the little chunks of undigested information — okay, call it knowledge — that was the conversation he'd grown up with and hated. He couldn't tell her any of this because it would come out upside down. The truth of it was in intangibles: the intelligence of her smile, the quick wit that sparkled questions the night he'd lectured to a dozen students who'd swallowed a snowstorm just to hear him compare Schubert and Keats.

"They both go from major to minor keys and back again very quickly," she'd said. Not a question or academic comment: a fragment of a song. Just what he was in need of: idea-tossed, song-hungry. "I mean," he said, "that I expected you to start poking at yourself with the new tools of psychology."

"Instead," she said, "I'm poking at you."

"Can you have wine?" he asked. "I forgot what the doctor said."

Sharon shivered against her pillows. "He didn't say. I'll have a glass, thank you. Listen, you knew I was a widow, right off."

"You told me instantly. With all the appropriately Southern Gothic details."

"Gothic! It was a hunting accident. Everybody in our part of Georgia hunts. But you didn't tell me your first wife — Alma — was a widow until — for God's sake, last week!"

"It didn't seem important. It's all of three months, not our golden wedding anniversary. Both men died natural deaths — one, sickness, one a shooting accident — both men were considerably older than the women. Now you know what I know."

Dickstein filled the bowls with linguine and shared the wine.

"Two widows," she sighed.

"I'm damned if I know why I didn't tell you sooner. But you didn't notice anything odd until New York University and Sigmund Freud told you it was worthy of thinking about."

He set down an amazement of utensils, any which way on the trays. It was not like him and he noted it.

"It gave me the shivers . . ." she began.

"What did?"

"Reading the dream book. I think you have to read things at the right moment for them to get to you. I must have read Freud at school. I took all the right courses. I graduated. I took a year of graduate school."

"You were doing music, not psychology."

"But reading this now in class it gave me the eerie feeling that everything is connected."

"Overdetermined . . ."

"Please don't be just clever," she said. "I'm wounded and I'm trying to track something down. I got shaky in class and that's why I wasn't careful in the park . . . It wasn't a change in the way I think — I wasn't born yesterday. It was a weird change in the way I *feel* about the way I think."

"Let me see; is that oozing?"

"Looks the same. I've been bitten before."

"Not in Washington Square Park. City animals are more dangerous."

She ate carefully with her left hand.

"I'm talking about the sensation of strangeness — just thinking that causes and connections run through everything like the bloodstream through the body."

"Did you think everything was random, till yesterday?"

She laughed. "I *felt* that way till yesterday. Then, sitting on the bench with the bag of peanuts I got distracted, the wet heat, I'm used to more hot and dry in August, and I began to think about you and Alma and me and Joshua and widows and husbands and fathers and wives and mothers, and it was more like a dream than *thinking* and I fed this squirrel and I must have done it in a funny way because I've fed them a million times before and nothing ever happened and he bit me."

Dickstein didn't know why the memory appeared for delivery at that moment. It was not a buried one, was right at hand. Rather, it showed up at that instant to help deal with Sharon, who sounded shakier every minute.

"To give you a dose of strange," he told her, "you're not my second widow. You're my fourth. You're living with a regular Bluebeard in reverse."

And he told her of being puppy-young, meeting the war widow with the long legs at a fund-raising chamber music evening, and about his family's terror.

His father, Doctor Dickstein, the Gynecologist/Philosopher and his Big Moment in Paternal Wisdom!

"A woman whose husband has died and who marries a younger man puts too much of a burden on the boy. And don't forget: she'll always be comparing you to him."

So he was shipped out to Stanford instead of finishing at Columbia and fell in love, for a time, with a California aerospace widow. Nothing glamorous like a test-pilot crash; just an equipment explosion.

"It's not funny," Sharon said; she was purplish from trying not to laugh. His intent was distraction and seemed to be succeeding. She was slipping into her country accent as she did when she felt easier. She wasn't a modern West Side of New York Sharon; her full name was Rose-a-Sharon. "I grieved so much," she said, "when Joshua died. I was mad, too, 'cause I hated hunting."

"We're not talking about how it feels when your husband dies. We're talking about how much more connective tissue there is here than even you thought of."

She wasn't laughing anymore. "Four," she murmured. "A

daytime dream of *the* dream. The older man who possesses your woman, first, dies, but you didn't kill him. You just get to have *her*. Over and over again. My God. Doesn't that count as murder and possession of the spoils?"

What he couldn't bring himself to bring up was what would seem to be the underlying strategy. He saw all these men as brutal, himself as tender; they were heedless of their women, he was concerned; they took what they wanted, he asked or waited for the moment to ripen.

When Dickstein envisioned those hunting trips of Sharon's husband, Joshua, he imagined some kind of secret, violent sex mixed in with the country satisfactions of blood sport. He'd never asked her about such things and she'd not offered much beyond a black mustache, six-foot-three height and a paper mill business. Questions of fidelity were not included in the data. But when he recalled his father's caution, he welcomed the comparison. Not only were they dead and he alive; *he was molded to offer precisely what they lacked. That was his enterprise!*

But he wasn't going to bring up all that and reinforce this dream-book talk. Instead, he poured the wine more freely than usual and the astonishment turned festive. Sharon was pretty in what she called her sick-time-of-the-month robe, though only her finger bled. They laughed again at her fears of the "uncanny" connections in the mind. (Freud, he told her, had written a famous letter in which he claimed an absence of any such "uncanny" feelings; more about religion than psychology, though.) And she promised never to feed squirrels in the city again — and she grew coy and sensual, drinking more and eating less, holding her injured hand out into the air as she caressed him with the other and it seemed like a nice idea to eat dinner in the bedroom at times and afterward she asked him if she was the more precious of the prizes he'd won from the dream murder of all those father/lovers; and he kissed her mouth as answer and evasion and she grew most Southern and promised to at least consider dropping the class since something about it bothered him, if he would take her to Turkey at Christmas time. (He had absolutely no interest in things Turkish.)

She wondered aloud if they'd made a baby; and he wondered, silently, thinking he could be a husband and a father and could

die, like all the others, leaving his lovely Rose-a-Sharon for . . .
who?

Late that night he woke, his head frantic from too much wine.
In the bathroom he stared at the mirror and thought of his
father's face for the first time in many months: square immigrant tough where Dickstein's was second-generation soft-
nurtured; perfunctory and commanding with his sullen, witty
wife, where Dickstein was the one who provided attentions and
the occasions for laughter. He remembered the early childhood
Saturday visits to Dr. Dickstein's office, the women waiting patiently, obediently, and the chrome and stirrups . . . and remembered, too, years later, how amazed he was that the old
man should be at the mercy of the pain and fears that came
with final illness. He'd never seen his father at the mercy of
anything before.

Dickstein's eyes blazed in the bathroom mirror with the awful
knowledge that there were no more of these imposing older
men to die and leave him their women to take for his own. He
would be forty in three months, he thought and listened to
Sharon's regular hiss of breath. Now he was at the top of the
ladder: an uncomfortable, precarious position.

There she lay, the next widow, unsuspecting; in spite of her
squirrel-wisdom, in spite of NYU and Freud. Because she was
young and easy in her skin and had been bereaved only by a
rifle, not by time and entropy.

"Peasant pleasures," his father would have said, with irony,
about people who died in hunting accidents. He'd sent himself
through college and sold insurance to help pay for medical
school. These successes entitled him to a loftiness toward those
less educated and less successful. Including, on occasion, his
wife and son. But now Dickstein, staring into the mirror, saw
mirror images hard to ignore. He, too, had become a Doctor
Dickstein, though only a Ph.D. shadow of the real thing: no
chrome, no stirrups, not even a white coat.

Like his father he always had at least three major activities.
(The old man lectured, did the first television medical education
series along with his regular practice. Dickstein taught English,
lectured when asked, and edited a journal.) The income and

prestige were not comparable but the restless multiple activities had similar outlines.

He searched in the mirror for some of the older man's features he could recognize and endow with the qualities he admired. What he thought of as a Hungarian mouth, he saw, eloquent, romantic.

"The better for talking out of both sides at the same time," Doctor Dickstein had said, laughing his runaway laugh. Dickstein, too, laughed nonstop, large and loud. For years he'd felt his father's heavy laughter aimed at him. The truth was, he suspected, that it was aimed at everyone, the good doctor included.

But that was all gone. It was utterly quiet in the night. He sat on the closed commode and leaned his flushed face against the tile of the sink.

"The top of the ladder," he whispered. And now it was not some young woman waiting to greet him. It was his father, waiting where vanished fathers wait for sons.

The disturbing image mixed with the wine in his gut in a surprise of nausea. He vomited into the sink with an energetic heave. It lasted several minutes and then he fell asleep wedged against the sink, the water still running.

Sharon found him about ten minutes after dawn. He was slumped over the sink. When she touched his shoulder, instead of jumping he woke gradually, her lovely cloud of yellow-reddish hair swimming into vague then focused view. Her eyes and cheeks looked slept-in, striated, rumpled.

She had to pee and he tottered to his feet and waited. When she finished she washed the sink and sat him down again and washed his face with her good hand. He had the convalescent's quiet gladness that she was present, that she had found him, that he had found her.

She would undoubtedly survive him. That was in the natural order of things. But, first, for as long as possible, they would survive together. He would be her loving husband, father, friend, teacher: wise, sensual, patient; knowing that, like all teachers, he was temporary.

And for himself, he would learn to ward off the inevitable, to slow down the dance of death. It was time to become his own father: forgiving, intelligent, always remembering that he had once been young and lost and now was found.

A new arrangement.

The bathroom smelled of vomit and Sharon sprayed something lilac into the air and gave him something mint to rinse his mouth with and kissed him and stumbled back to bed and sleep.

Dickstein sat there a moment. He had never felt so lucky in his life.

It was like a dream.

RON CARLSON

Milk

FROM THE NORTH AMERICAN REVIEW

THEY ALMOST FINGERPRINT the children before I can stop them. Phyllis is making a rare personal appearance in my office to help with a motorcycle injury claim, and I want to squeeze every minute out of her, and I'm taking no calls. We all call Phyllis the Queen of Wrongful Death, which is the truest nickname in the firm. She likes being a hard case, and she's lording it over me a bit this morning, rereading a lot of the stuff that I'd summarized for her, when Tim buzzes and says Annie's on the line.

I almost wave it off. It's probably a lunch date and there's going to be no lunch today, because I want to get this motorcycle case buttoned up so we can take the twins on a picnic this weekend. Now that they can walk, our house is getting real small. But, it's not lunch. It's Community Fuel's Fingerprint Program. I listen to Annie tell the story and watch Phyllis frowning through the file. My mother read about the program in the paper and with so many children abducted and missing, etc. etc. etc. Annie closes with *I know what you think, but this is something we should do for your mother's sake.*

I don't say anything.

"Jim?" Annie says.

"Ann. You said it. You know what I think. *No way.* Not the twins. Not for my mother. Not for anybody."

"She's coming over to get us in half an hour."

"Ann," I say again. "Take her to lunch, but do not fingerprint the boys. Okay? Under no circumstances. That's all."

"It's no big deal . . . "

"Tell my mother that."

"I'm going to tell your mother that you're terrified and unable at this time to do the right thing."

When I hang up, Phyllis looks up. At thirty-four she wears those auspicious half glasses, which, drunk at last year's firm barbecue, she admitted to me are just part of her costume: "dress to win"; and I admit now that they intimidate me.

"Fingerprints?" she says. "Are the twins being booked?"

"It's that I.D. program at Community Fuel. My mother wants to take the kids."

"And . . . ?"

"My kids are not being fingerprinted. I'm not caving in to this raging paranoia. It's a better world than people think."

Phyllis takes off her awful glasses and lets them drop on their necklace against her breast. "And you're not scared in the least, are you?"

When I come home from work, Lee and Bobby laugh their heads off. It has become my favorite part of the day. I peek into the kitchen and say, "Oh-oh!" and they amble in stiffly in their tiny overalls, arms up for balance, and they start: "Oh-oh!" as I pick them up and they laugh and laugh as we do our entire repertoire of sounds — *Dadda, Momma, Baby,* and the eleven or twelve other syllables, as well as a good portion of growling, humming, meowing, mooing, and buzzing. When I whistle softly through my teeth, they hug me hard to make me stop.

They are fraternal twins. Bobby has a lot of hair and a full face. Lee, though he probably weighs the same — twenty-two pounds — seems slighter, more fragile. Ironically, Bobby cries more and easier. They can lie on a blanket with fists full of each other's hair, and only Bobby will fuss. They each have four and a half teeth and they call each other the same name: *Baby.*

Tonight I lift them up and the laughing intensifies as I tote them into the living room where Annie is picking up the blanket and toys.

She starts right in. "Well, boys, it's Daddy the Rulemaker."

"Annie . . ."

"The lawgiver." She holds the bundle in her arms and stands

to face me. She goes on in a gruff voice, *"No fingerprints. Not in this house! Not for anybody!"*

Bobby and Lee think this is wonderful and they laugh again. Each has a good hold on my hair and their laughing pulls my scalp in two directions. Annie comes right up to the boys and makes a mock frown, her nose against mine. She growls. *"Not even for my mother!"* She kisses me quickly and disappears into the boys' room. The boys snap around quickly and the hair pulling brings tears to my eyes.

Annie's got me. We've been married nine years, and it's been a good marriage; we've grown up together really, and only since the boys have arrived have I started with this rule stuff. Annie and I used to go crazy after visiting our friends Stuart and Ruth and their kids. Everything was rules. *No baseball in the backyard. No jackets in the basement. No magazines in the kitchen. No loud talking in the hall. No snacks during homework.* We promised then never to post rules. Driving home from their house, Annie and I would make up rules and laugh until we'd have to pull over. *No hair dryers in the bathtub. No looking out the window while someone is talking to you. No looking at the answers to the crossword puzzle. No shirt, no shoes, no service.* And Annie even gave Ruth one of our ridiculous lists, typed up as a joke (their lists were typed and posted on the refrigerator door), but Ruth did not think it was that funny. She said, "Wait until you have kids."

And now I have both kids in my arms when Annie comes back into the room. "Call your mother," she says, taking Lee from me and putting him in his high chair. "She wants to know why you're not looking out for the best interest of your children. Put Bobby in his chair before you call, okay?"

We've been through this all before, but I can see this week is going to be different. I saw the news programs on television and saw the troops of children being fingerprinted. I made it clear from the beginning that we did not want to do that. Annie was fine with that, but my mother wanted to know why, in light of all the missing children and the recent abductions, why wouldn't I do it *for their sake.*

"Because," I had explained to her at last, at the end of my patience. "Because the only use those prints will ever have is in

identifying *a body,* okay? *Do you see?* They use them to identify
the body. And my children will not need fingerprints, *because
nothing is going to happen to my children.* Is that clear?" I had
almost yelled at my mother. "We don't need fingerprints!"

Then my mother would be hurt for a few days and then silent
for a few days and then there'd be another news story and we'd
do it all again.

Annie would try to intervene, make peace. "It's not a big deal.
The boys will forget it. Your mother would feel better."

"No."

"Why not?"

I don't know how many times we had some version of that
conversation, but I do know that once I took Annie's wrist and
raged through the house like the sorry creature I can be at
times, pointing to the low surfaces. "Because, we've got fingerprints! Look!" I made her look at the entryway door and the
thousand hands printed there, at the car windows, and the front
of the fridge, and finally the television, where a vivid hand
printed in rice cereal made Tom Brokaw on the evening news
look like he was growing a beard. "We have fingerprints. And I
love these fingerprints. We don't need any others."

All Annie said was "Can I have this now?" She indicated her
arm. I let her go. She simply turned her back and went in to
check on the boys, shaking her head.

And there was the milk.

I wanted Annie to change milk. We had been getting the
Hilltop green half-gallon cartons. Then they started putting
children on the back panels, missing children. Under the bold
heading MISSING would be two green and white photographs of
the children with their statistics printed underneath: date of
birth, age, height, eyes, hair, weight, date missing, from . . . The
photographs themselves assumed a lurid, tabloid quality, and
every time I opened the fridge they cautioned me in a way I
didn't care for. I'd already seen ads for missing children on a
weekly mailer we receive that offers — on the flip side — discount coupons for curtain and rug cleaning, optical services and
fast food, primarily chicken. And in Roy's Drug one night I
dropped the *Archie* comic I was going to buy for the boys (to
keep them from ripping up our art books) when I saw two
missing children inside the front cover. It was all getting to me.

One night, late, I went into Smith's Food King and turned all the Hilltop milk to the back panel so sixty children stared out from the dairy case. I started it as a statement of some kind, but when I stepped back across the aisle and saw their group sadness, all those green and white poor-resolution smiles, wan even in the bright Food King light, I lost my breath. I fled the store and sulked home and asked Annie if we could buy another brand.

When I told her why, when I told her about the two kids taking a little starch out of the world for me when I opened the refrigerator at two A.M. to grab Bobby a bottle, those nights when he still fusses, Annie just said *no*.

Tonight after I have the fifteenth version of my fingerprint call with my mother, I am out of tolerance, reason, generosity, and any of their relatives. I never swear in the company of my mother, and as I sit down in the kitchen and watch Annie spoon the boys their macaroni and strained beef, I think perhaps I should. I might not have this knot in my neck. There on the table is the Hilltop milk with somebody's picture on the back.

I don't know why, but I start, "Annie, I don't want this milk in the house."

She's cool. "And is there a reason for that, oh powerful Rulemaker?"

"I've told you the reason. I'm not interested in being depressed or in having my children frightened by faces of lost souls in the refrigerator."

Annie says nothing. She spoons the macaroni into Bobby's open mouth. After each mouthful, he goes "mmmmmnnnnn!" and laughs. It's something I taught the boys with Milupa and bananas, but Lee's version is softer, almost a sigh of satisfaction.

"What is the point? There is no point in publishing these lurid photographs."

"They're not lurid."

"What's the point? I am supposed to study the carton, cruise the city, stop every child walking home from school: *Is he missing? Would he like to go home now?* Really, what? I see some girl playing tennis against the practice wall in Liberty Park, am I supposed to match her with my carton collection of missing children?" I've raised my voice a little, I can tell, because Annie looks narrow-eyed, stony.

She hands me the spoon for Lee, who is smiling at me for yelling. Annie rises and takes the milk and puts it in the refrigerator. "Missing children don't get to play tennis," she says quietly, wiping Bobby up and putting him on the floor. Bobby goes immediately to the one cupboard I haven't safety clipped, opens it, and pulls a large bottle of olives onto his foot.

He watches the bottle roll across the floor, and when it stops against the stove, he looks up into my face with his beautiful face and he starts to cry.

"Bobby's first," Annie says, plucking him from the floor. "Bobby's first in bed tonight!"

When she carts Bobby off, I let Lee out of his chair. I hand him his bottle out of the fridge and he takes it with both hands as if it were an award. He starts to walk off, then realizes, I guess, that Mom isn't here and he doesn't really know where to go. So, he looks up at me, a child who resembles an angel so much it is troubling. Then Annie is behind him, lifting him away, and I am left alone in the kitchen.

I wipe up the chairs and the floor and cap the macaroni and strained beef, but when I put them away, I see that green Hilltop milk carton.

"You want to close the fridge?" Annie is behind me.

"No look. Look at this."

"Close the fridge door."

"Look!" I point at the child, his green and white photograph so grim in the bright light of the fridge.

I take one carton of milk out and close the fridge. I read aloud: "MISSING: Name: Richard Tarrel. D.O.B.: 10/21/81. Age: 4. Height: 2 feet 8 inches. Eyes: blue. Hair: light brown. Weight: 27 pounds. Date missing: 6/24/83. From: Omaha . . ." I mean to make a point by reading it, but the "twenty-seven pounds" gets me a little, and by the time I read "Omaha," I stop and sit down and look across at Annie. She looks like she is going to cry. She looks a lot like I have made her cry again.

She firms her mouth once and shakes her head as she stands up to leave the room. "Nebraska," she whispers. "Omaha, Nebraska."

I sit at the kitchen table listening to Bobby and Lee murmuring toward sleep in their room, and I look at little twenty-seven-pound Richard Tarrel. Even in the poor-quality photograph he is beautiful, his eyes huge and dark, his lips pouted in a coy James Dean smile. There is no background in the photo, but I've been to Omaha. I can imagine the backyard somewhere out near 92nd Street, the swing set, the young peach tree Richard's father planted this summer, after the man at the nursery told him that though it was small, there would be peaches next fall.

The next morning, I've got the day trip to Denver, the quick deposition, and back on the nine o'clock. Annie is cordial to me in the morning — well, stern. I have a cup of coffee and pick at some of Bobby's scrambled eggs. Annie doesn't offer to have the whole gang drive me to the airport, which would have happened if we weren't fighting. I feel bad about it, kind of flat, but the boys will not have their fingerprints taken. I do not believe in it and it will not happen. Not my boys. It's a rule.

The flight over is rocky. The plane pitches heavily up the slope and then down, across the mountains to Denver. Sitting in the window seat of my row, one empty seat away, is a pale blond girl. I'm trying to head all the forms so I can maybe make the early plane tonight, but she stops me. I have to study her. She huddles to the window, her fragile face poised there, watching the unchanging grayness. Her Levi's are worn and the red plaid bag she clutches on her lap is years old. Her shirt is a blue-stripe dress shirt that could never, ever fit her; it is five sizes large. She sits in a linty, dark-blue serape. I can't stop myself from looking at her. Date of birth: 1969. Age: 17. Height: 5 feet 9 inches. Eyes: brown. Hair: light blond. Weight: 120. Date missing: . . .

The girl turns her face to me in the bouncing airplane and speaks, her lips barely moving. "Don't," she says. "Please. Just don't."

My deposition is a witness to a motorcycle accident, a sophomore in psychology, and I meet him at the University Union in Boulder just after noon. In our hour, I learn: both children moved to avoid the cycle, but they moved different ways and one, the victim, our client, was hit and injured. My witness was driving pizza delivery behind the motorcycle and saw it all. Daylight. Sun to his back. A simple story. After the witness leaves for class, I sit in the modular furniture, mesmerized for a while by the young people streaming around me.

There are children everywhere. All the way down the highway from Boulder to Denver, I see them alone and in groups, kicking along in the gravel. They all seem to need haircuts. I check my watch: two o'clock on a school day. Why isn't anybody where he's supposed to be? I think about our case; it's a given. I wonder what help the settlement will be to the parents of the hurt girl. I try to make the equation in my mind. We'll ask for six hundred thousand and get two. The girl's eleven years old and has one complete knee and six tenths of the other. Let's see: she'll have that limp for sixty-eight years, if she lives her statistic. That's three thousand dollars a year not to walk like everyone else, or play soccer, I guess, or tennis. I ditch my rental car at the Avis curb, and think: What a strange man I'm becoming. What's happening to me?

The six o'clock is full so I hit the little sky lounge near the gate and have a Manhattan. I used to love having an hour or two to ransack the magazines and have a Manhattan, my little joke living in the West, but now it's not much fun. There seems some urgency about getting home. I can't really settle down. I want to get home.

Sometimes, driving home alone in the last two blocks before our house, a feeling descends upon me like a gift. It is as if a huge door had opened and I can breathe differently, see the entire scope of our lives, and it makes me unreasonably happy. It makes me want to rush into the kitchen and sweep Annie up and cry, *Forgive me, forgive us, let's never quarrel again, we have everything.* I don't know where the feeling comes from or how real it is, but I have it tonight as I turn into the driveway.

My mother's white Seville is parked to one side, something I didn't really want to see, but there's our house standing like a house in a story, an entire happy little world. The kitchen windows are beautiful yellow squares, and a blue glow in the two small windows out front means they're watching television.

I vow to go in cheerfully and join them, open a beer, chat openly with the two women about everything. This fingerprint thing doesn't have to be such a big deal. We can agree. We can face the future without unreasonable fear.

In the kitchen, two blue Community Fuel folders spill across the table. On the cover of each is a large white fingerprint the size of a head of lettuce. Underneath the print it says, COMMUNITY I.D./PROJECT FINGERPRINT. I can hear the women talking in the other room under the television noises. I open the first folder and there it is in Annie's printing: Bobby Hensley. Date of Birth. Age. Weight. Hair. There is an empty square: place recent photograph here. And below: the ten smudges of Bobby's fingers.

I reach two bottles out of the fridge, one Nuk, one yellow nipple for Lee, and slip them inside my sportcoat. I tiptoe into the boys' room. Lee is asleep in a knot of blanket; Bobby lies on his side with his thumb loosely in his mouth experimenting with sounds: doya, doya, moya. He looks up at me calmly and smiles and then rolls to a crawl and stands in his crib. I pick him up and park him in a shoulder and then lift Lee like a melon under my forearm. I sweep the boys noiselessly through the kitchen and out to the car.

I am calm enough to strap them in their car seats, Lee asleep in the back and Bobby on the seat next to me in the front. I coast back down the driveway before starting the car, and I am on the road half a block before I pull the lights on.

"Ba . . . " Bobby says as we pass a city bus in front of East High. "Ba . . . "

"Bus," I say, the first word I've said aloud since my plane landed. "That's right. It's a bus."

The streets are luminous, wet and shiny, ticketed with early leaves, and our tires make the friction I have always loved to hear after rain. So the streets whisper darkly as we slow at each bright intersection, the flaring 7-Elevens, the flat white splash of a gas station. Then it is dark again, and we are driving.

Lee starts to squeak, which means he will babble for a while and then cry. He's a little tongue-tied and is gradually tearing the cord underneath by stretching his mouth in low squalls that become real crying after about a minute. I stop at the light at Fourth and State and give both boys their bottles.

We turn left onto State and head south, cruising by the jillion colored lights the kids love. In the rearview mirror, I can see Lee settled now in his seat. He has learned to balance the bottle on the car seat arm-tray, so his hands are free. Right now, they extend off to each side, palms up, and Lee opens and closes his hands slowly as he watches them and sucks on the bottle.

Bobby has his head tipped right to witness the spectacle of neon from the bars and motels, the bright dragon above the Double Hey Rice Palace, the pulsing tire in front of Big O. He has his bottle clutched in both hands and set hard in the side of his mouth like a cigar.

When I was a boy I remember that my father would always pick up babies in restaurants. We'd go to Harmon's on North Temple about every other Sunday as a treat. My brother and I always had the gorgeous shakes, strawberry and chocolate, too thick for the straw, my mother always wore one of her three pretty dresses and patted our faces with the corner of her napkin, and my father would always spot a baby three tables away. He would simply rise and go over to the little family and pick up their baby and bring it over to our table and talk to it, asking did it want to be ours and things like that, just loud enough for the parents to hear. I remember the parents always smiling, perhaps an older sister craning her neck to see where the baby had gone, and my father dipping a spoon into my strawberry shake for the child. Sometimes he'd keep the baby on his lap for half an hour, showing off; sometimes he would return it right away, the baby squirming in his arms, fighting for a last glance at my strawberry shake. My father gave forty kids their first taste of ice cream at our table, and no one seemed to be scared of anything.

"Namma," Bobby says, lifting his bottle over the seat and dropping it. He places one hand on the window and says it again, "Namma."

Somewhere out in this garish Disneyland of light, he has spotted a bear, and now he wants "Namma," his bear, actually a stuffed raccoon. Namma is the one who taught us all Peek a boo and Where's-your-nose. In my haste leaving the house, I have forgotten Namma.

In the back seat, Lee is again asleep, his arms limp at his sides, his bottle still protruding from his mouth.

"Namma," Bobby says turning to me.

"Namma," I say back to him and he smiles. We will have to go home. Namma is at home peeking out of a corner of the crib. Bobby is still smiling at me coyly, waiting for me to say something else, so I sing his favorite song: "The Lion Sleeps Tonight."

"A wimba-way, a-wimba-way, a-wimba-way . . . " I sing, nodding my head so Bobby will nod his too. "In the jungle, the quiet jungle, the lion sleeps tonight . . . "

Tired, he leans his head back against the car seat and watches me sing, his open-mouth grin never changing. I do a lot of extra "a-wimba-ways," and the song ends somewhere in Murray. Bobby has closed his mouth now; his eyes are next. I look at my watch: ten to twelve; and I realize that this is the latest I've been out since the boys were born, and people are everywhere. We better go home.

I do a U-turn in the bright, crowded parking lot of a 7-Eleven. A lone teenager leans against the phones, smoking a cigarette. He wears a Levi's jacket and a blue bandana around his neck. I look at his face, the eyebrows almost grown together, the pretty lower lip. Date of birth: 1971. Age: 15. Height: 5 feet 7 inches. Weight: 125. Eyes: blue. Hair: dark brown. Date missing: I don't know. On the milk carton there will be a date, but as I glance back at the boy, I can only see that it looks like he's been out in the night a long time.

Three blocks later, Bobby's asleep. It's late. The traffic is thick and bright. I pass a twenty-four-hour Safeway and the parking lot is full. Behind me the headlights teem. A man cruises by us smoking a cigarette in a large Chevrolet. Two couples on motorcycles, the girls holding on, their faces turned out of the wind into their boyfriends' backs. A new station wagon, three girls bouncing in the front seat. Two boys in a Volkswagen bug, their elbows out the windows as if summer weren't really over.

At home Annie has checked on the children by now and found them gone, and she has found my valise, and she has given my mother another drink and calmed her down. She knows I'm coming home. We have been safe all our lives. We've traveled: London, Tokyo, Paris, where we saw a diplomat shot down the block from us. Annie has broken her leg skiing. Our Cherokee was totaled by a street department truck two summers ago. We have always felt safe until the boys arrived, and now I am afraid of everything.

I start to sing. We're locked in, the windows are up. These are my boys. I sing softly. "A-wimba-way, a-wimba-way, a-wimba-way, a-wimba-way," and on, even at a stop light. I can feel people looking at me, and I lower my face onto the back of my hand on the steering wheel. It's so late. What is everybody doing up so late?

The Things They Carried

FROM ESQUIRE

FIRST LIEUTENANT Jimmy Cross carried letters from a girl named Martha, a junior at Mount Sebastian College in New Jersey. They were not love letters, but Lieutenant Cross was hoping, so he kept them folded in plastic at the bottom of his rucksack. In the late afternoon, after a day's march, he would dig his foxhole, wash his hands under a canteen, unwrap the letters, hold them with the tips of his fingers, and spend the last hour of light pretending. He would imagine romantic camping trips into the White Mountains in New Hampshire. He would sometimes taste the envelope flaps, knowing her tongue had been there. More than anything, he wanted Martha to love him as he loved her, but the letters were mostly chatty, elusive on the matter of love. She was a virgin, he was almost sure. She was an English major at Mount Sebastian, and she wrote beautifully about her professors and roommates and midterm exams, about her respect for Chaucer and her great affection for Virginia Woolf. She often quoted lines of poetry; she never mentioned the war, except to say, Jimmy, take care of yourself. The letters weighed ten ounces. They were signed "Love, Martha," but Lieutenant Cross understood that "Love" was only a way of signing and did not mean what he sometimes pretended it meant. At dusk, he would carefully return the letters to his rucksack. Slowly, a bit distracted, he would get up and move among his men, checking the perimeter, then at full dark he would return to his hole and watch the night and wonder if Martha was a virgin.

The things they carried were largely determined by necessity. Among the necessities or near necessities were P-38 can openers, pocket knives, heat tabs, wrist watches, dog tags, mosquito repellent, chewing gum, candy, cigarettes, salt tablets, packets of Kool-Aid, lighters, matches, sewing kits, Military Payment Certificates, C rations, and two or three canteens of water. Together, these items weighed between fifteen and twenty pounds, depending upon a man's habits or rate of metabolism. Henry Dobbins, who was a big man, carried extra rations; he was especially fond of canned peaches in heavy syrup over pound cake. Dave Jensen, who practiced field hygiene, carried a toothbrush, dental floss, and several hotel-size bars of soap he'd stolen on R&R in Sydney, Australia. Ted Lavender, who was scared, carried tranquilizers until he was shot in the head outside the village of Than Khe in mid-April. By necessity, and because it was SOP, they all carried steel helmets that weighed five pounds including the liner and camouflage cover. They carried the standard fatigue jackets and trousers. Very few carried underwear. On their feet they carried jungle boots — 2.1 pounds — and Dave Jensen carried three pairs of socks and a can of Dr. Scholl's foot powder as a precaution against trench foot. Until he was shot, Ted Lavender carried six or seven ounces of premium dope, which for him was a necessity. Mitchell Sanders, the RTO, carried condoms. Norman Bowker carried a diary. Rat Kiley carried comic books. Kiowa, a devout Baptist, carried an illustrated New Testament that had been presented to him by his father, who taught Sunday school in Oklahoma City, Oklahoma. As a hedge against bad times, however, Kiowa also carried his grandmother's distrust of the white man, his grandfather's old hunting hatchet. Necessity dictated. Because the land was mined and booby-trapped, it was SOP for each man to carry a steel-centered, nylon-covered flak jacket, which weighed 6.7 pounds, but which on hot days seemed much heavier. Because you could die so quickly, each man carried at least one large compress bandage, usually in the helmet band for easy access. Because the nights were cold, and because the monsoons were wet, each carried a green plastic poncho that could be used as a raincoat or ground sheet or makeshift tent. With its quilted liner, the poncho weighed almost two pounds, but it was worth every ounce. In April, for instance, when Ted Lavender was shot, they used his poncho to wrap him up, then to carry him across the paddy, then to lift him into the chopper that took him away.

They were called legs or grunts.

To carry something was to "hump" it, as when Lieutenant Jimmy Cross humped his love for Martha up the hills and through the swamps. In its intransitive form, "to hump" meant "to walk," or "to march," but it implied burdens far beyond the intransitive.

Almost everyone humped photographs. In his wallet, Lieutenant Cross carried two photographs of Martha. The first was a Kodachrome snapshot signed "Love," though he knew better. She stood against a brick wall. Her eyes were gray and neutral, her lips slightly open as she stared straight-on at the camera. At night, sometimes, Lieutenant Cross wondered who had taken the picture, because he knew she had boyfriends, because he loved her so much, and because he could see the shadow of the picture taker spreading out against the brick wall. The second photograph had been clipped from the 1968 Mount Sebastian yearbook. It was an action shot — women's volleyball — and Martha was bent horizontal to the floor, reaching, the palms of her hands in sharp focus, the tongue taut, the expression frank and competitive. There was no visible sweat. She wore white gym shorts. Her legs, he thought, were almost certainly the legs of a virgin, dry and without hair, the left knee cocked and carrying her entire weight, which was just over one hundred pounds. Lieutenant Cross remembered touching that left knee. A dark theater, he remembered, and the movie was *Bonnie and Clyde*, and Martha wore a tweed skirt, and during the final scene, when he touched her knee, she turned and looked at him in a sad, sober way that made him pull his hand back, but he would always remember the feel of the tweed skirt and the knee beneath it and the sound of the gunfire that killed Bonnie and Clyde, how embarrassing it was, how slow and oppressive. He remembered kissing her good night at the dorm door. Right then, he thought, he should've done something brave. He should've carried her up the stairs to her room and tied her to the bed and touched that left knee all night long. He should've risked it. Whenever he looked at the photographs, he thought of new things he should've done.

What they carried was partly a function of rank, partly of field specialty.

As a first lieutenant and platoon leader, Jimmy Cross carried a compass, maps, code books, binoculars, and a .45-caliber pistol that weighed 2.9 pounds fully loaded. He carried a strobe light and the responsibility for the lives of his men.

As an RTO, Mitchell Sanders carried the PRC-25 radio, a killer, twenty-six pounds with its battery.

As a medic, Rat Kiley carried a canvas satchel filled with morphine and plasma and malaria tablets and surgical tape and comic books and all the things a medic must carry, including M&M's for especially bad wounds, for a total weight of nearly twenty pounds.

As a big man, therefore a machine gunner, Henry Dobbins carried the M-60, which weighed twenty-three pounds unloaded, but which was almost always loaded. In addition, Dobbins carried between ten and fifteen pounds of ammunition draped in belts across his chest and shoulders.

As PFCs or Spec 4s, most of them were common grunts and carried the standard M-16 gas-operated assault rifle. The weapon weighed 7.5 pounds unloaded, 8.2 pounds with its full twenty-round magazine. Depending on numerous factors, such as topography and psychology, the riflemen carried anywhere from twelve to twenty magazines, usually in cloth bandoliers, adding on another 8.4 pounds at minimum, fourteen pounds at maximum. When it was available, they also carried M-16 maintenance gear — rods and steel brushes and swabs and tubes of LSA oil — all of which weighed about a pound. Among the grunts, some carried the M-79 grenade launcher, 5.9 pounds unloaded, a reasonably light weapon except for the ammunition, which was heavy. A single round weighed ten ounces. They typical load was twenty-five rounds. But Ted Lavender, who was scared, carried thirty-four rounds when he was shot and killed outside Than Khe, and he went down under an exceptional burden, more than twenty pounds of ammunition, plus the flak jacket and helmet and rations and water and toilet paper and tranquilizers and all the rest, plus the unweighed fear. He was dead weight. There was no twitching or flopping. Kiowa, who saw it happen, said it was like watching a rock fall, or a big sandbag or something — just boom, then down — not like the movies where the dead guy rolls around and does fancy spins and goes ass over teakettle — not like that, Kiowa said, the poor bastard just flat-fuck fell. Boom. Down. Nothing else. It was a bright morning in mid-April. Lieutenant Cross felt the pain. He blamed himself. They stripped off Lavender's canteens and ammo, all the heavy things, and Rat Kiley said the obvious, the guy's dead, and Mitchell Sanders used his radio to report one U.S. KIA and to request a chopper. Then they wrapped Lavender in his poncho. They carried him out to a dry paddy, established security, and sat smoking the dead man's dope until the chopper came. Lieutenant Cross kept to himself. He pictured Martha's smooth young face, thinking he loved her more than anything, more than his men, and now Ted Lavender was dead because he loved her so much and could not stop thinking about her. When the dust-off arrived, they carried Lavender aboard. Afterward they burned Than Khe. They marched until dusk, then dug their holes, and that night Kiowa kept explaining how you had to be there, how fast it was, how the poor guy just dropped like so much concrete. Boom-down, he said. Like cement.

In addition to the three standard weapons — the M-60, M-16, and M-79 — they carried whatever presented itself, or whatever seemed appropriate as a means of killing or staying alive. They carried catch-as-catch-can. At various times, in various situations, they carried M-14s and CAR-15s and Swedish Ks and grease guns and captured AK-47s and Chi-Coms and RPGs and Simonov carbines and black-market Uzis and .38-caliber Smith & Wesson handguns and 66 mm LAWs and shotguns and silencers and blackjacks and bayonets and C-4 plastic explosives. Lee Strunk carried a slingshot; a weapon of last resort, he called it. Mitchell Sanders carried brass knuckles. Kiowa carried his grandfather's feathered hatchet. Every third or fourth man carried a Claymore antipersonnel mine — 3.5 pounds with its firing device. They all carried fragmentation grenades — fourteen ounces each. They all carried at least one M-18 colored smoke grenade — twenty-four ounces. Some carried CS or tear-gas grenades. Some carried white-phosphorus grenades. They carried all they could bear, and then some, including a silent awe for the terrible power of the things they carried.

In the first week of April, before Lavender died, Lieutenant Jimmy Cross received a good-luck charm from Martha. It was a simple pebble, an ounce at most. Smooth to the touch, it was a milky-white color with flecks of orange and violet, oval-shaped, like a miniature egg. In the accompanying letter, Martha wrote that she had found the pebble on the Jersey shoreline, precisely where the land touched water at high tide, where things came together but also separated. It was this separate-but-together quality, she wrote, that had inspired her to pick up the pebble and to carry it in her breast pocket for several days, where it seemed weightless, and then to send it through the mail, by air, as a token of her truest feelings for him. Lieutenant Cross found this romantic. But he wondered what her truest feelings were, exactly, and what she meant by separate-but-together. He wondered how the tides and waves had come into play on that afternoon along the Jersey shoreline when Martha saw the pebble and bent down to rescue it from geology. He imagined bare feet. Martha was a poet, with the poet's sensibilities, and her feet would be brown and bare, the toenails unpainted, the eyes chilly and somber like the ocean in March, and though it was painful, he wondered who had been with her that afternoon. He imagined a pair of shadows moving along the strip of sand where things came together but also separated. It was phantom jealousy, he knew, but he couldn't help himself. He loved her so much. On the march, through the hot days of early April, he carried the pebble in his mouth, turning it with his tongue, tasting sea salts and moisture. His mind wandered. He had difficulty keeping his attention on the war. On occasion he would yell at his men to spread out the column, to keep their eyes open, but then he would slip away into daydreams, just pretending, walking barefoot along the Jersey shore, with Martha, carrying nothing. He would feel himself rising. Sun and waves and gentle winds, all love and lightness.

*

What they carried varied by mission.

When a mission took them to the mountains, they carried mosquito netting, machetes, canvas tarps, and extra bug juice.

If a mission seemed especially hazardous, or if it involved a place they knew to be bad, they carried everything they could. In certain heavily mined AOs, where the land was dense with Toe Poppers and Bouncing Betties, they took turns humping a twenty-eight-pound mine detector. With its headphones and big sensing plate, the equipment was a stress on the lower back and shoulders, awkward to handle, often useless because of the shrapnel in the earth, but they carried it anyway, partly for safety, partly for the illusion of safety.

On ambush, or other night missions, they carried peculiar little odds and ends. Kiowa always took along his New Testament and a pair of moccasins for silence. Dave Jensen carried night-sight vitamins high in carotin. Lee Strunk carried his slingshot; ammo, he claimed, would never be a problem. Rat Kiley carried brandy and M&M's. Until he was shot, Ted Lavender carried the starlight scope, which weighed 6.3 pounds with its aluminum carrying case. Henry Dobbins carried his girlfriend's pantyhose wrapped around his neck as a comforter. They all carried ghosts. When dark came, they would move out single file across the meadows and paddies to their ambush coordinates, where they would quietly set up the Claymores and lie down and spend the night waiting.

Other missions were more complicated and required special equipment. In mid-April, it was their mission to search out and destroy the elaborate tunnel complexes in the Than Khe area south of Chu Lai. To blow the tunnels, they carried one-pound blocks of pentrite high explosives, four blocks to a man, sixty-eight pounds in all. They carried wiring, detonators, and battery-powered clackers. Dave Jensen carried earplugs. Most often, before blowing the tunnels, they were ordered by higher command to search them, which was considered bad news, but by and large they just shrugged and carried out orders. Because he was a big man, Henry Dobbins was excused from tunnel duty. The others would draw numbers. Before Lavender died there were seventeen men in the platoon, and whoever drew the number seventeen would strip off his gear and crawl in head first with a flashlight and Lieutenant Cross's .45-caliber pistol.

The rest of them would fan out as security. They would sit down or kneel, not facing the hole, listening to the ground beneath them, imagining cobwebs and ghosts, whatever was down there — the tunnel walls squeezing in — how the flashlight seemed impossibly heavy in the hand and how it was tunnel vision in the very strictest sense, compression in all ways, even time, and how you had to wiggle in — ass and elbows — a swallowed-up feeling — and how you found yourself worrying about odd things — will your flashlight go dead? Do rats carry rabies? If you screamed, how far would the sound carry? Would your buddies hear it? Would they have the courage to drag you out? In some respects, though not many, the waiting was worse than the tunnel itself. Imagination was a killer.

On April 16, when Lee Strunk drew the number seventeen, he laughed and muttered something and went down quickly. The morning was hot and very still. Not good, Kiowa said. He looked at the tunnel opening, then out across a dry paddy toward the village of Than Khe. Nothing moved. No clouds or birds or people. As they waited, the men smoked and drank Kool-Aid, not talking much, feeling sympathy for Lee Strunk but also feeling the luck of the draw. You win some, you lose some, said Mitchell Sanders, and sometimes you settle for a rain check. It was a tired line and no one laughed.

Henry Dobbins ate a tropical chocolate bar. Ted Lavender popped a tranquilizer and went off to pee.

After five minutes, Lieutenant Jimmy Cross moved to the tunnel, leaned down, and examined the darkness. Trouble, he thought — a cave-in maybe. And then suddenly, without willing it, he was thinking about Martha. The stresses and fractures, the quick collapse, the two of them buried alive under all that weight. Dense, crushing love. Kneeling, watching the hole, he tried to concentrate on Lee Strunk and the war, all the dangers, but his love was too much for him, he felt paralyzed, he wanted to sleep inside her lungs and breathe her blood and be smothered. He wanted her to be a virgin and not a virgin, all at once. He wanted to know her. Intimate secrets — why poetry? Why so sad? Why that grayness in her eyes? Why so alone? Not lonely, just alone — riding her bike across campus or sitting off by herself in the cafeteria. Even dancing, she danced alone —

and it was the aloneness that filled him with love. He remembered telling her that one evening. How she nodded and looked away. And how, later, when he kissed her, she received the kiss without returning it, her eyes wide open, not afraid, not a virgin's eyes, just flat and uninvolved.

Lieutenant Cross gazed at the tunnel. But he was not there. He was buried with Martha under the white sand at the Jersey shore. They were pressed together, and the pebble in his mouth was her tongue. He was smiling. Vaguely, he was aware of how quiet the day was, the sullen paddies, yet he could not bring himself to worry about matters of security. He was beyond that. He was just a kid at war, in love. He was twenty-two years old. He couldn't help it.

A few moments later Lee Strunk crawled out of the tunnel. He came up grinning, filthy but alive. Lieutenant Cross nodded and closed his eyes while the others clapped Strunk on the back and made jokes about rising from the dead.

Worms, Rat Kiley said. Right out of the grave. Fuckin' zombie.

The men laughed. They all felt great relief.

Spook City, said Mitchell Sanders.

Lee Strunk made a funny ghost sound, a kind of moaning, yet very happy, and right then, when Strunk made that high happy moaning sound, when he went *Ahhooooo,* right then Ted Lavender was shot in the head on his way back from peeing. He lay with his mouth open. The teeth were broken. There was a swollen black bruise under his left eye. The cheekbone was gone. Oh shit, Rat Kiley said, the guy's dead. The guy's dead, he kept saying, which seemed profound — the guy's dead. I mean really.

The things they carried were determined to some extent by superstition. Lieutenant Cross carried his good-luck pebble. Dave Jensen carried a rabbit's foot. Norman Bowker, otherwise a very gentle person, carried a thumb that had been presented to him as a gift by Mitchell Sanders. The thumb was dark brown, rubbery to the touch, and weighed four ounces at most. It had been cut from a VC corpse, a boy of fifteen or sixteen. They'd found him at the bottom of an irrigation ditch, badly burned, flies in his mouth and eyes. The boy wore black shorts and sandals. At the time of his death he had been carrying a pouch of rice, a rifle, and three magazines of ammunition.

You want my opinion, Mitchell Sanders said, there's a definite moral here.

He put his hand on the dead boy's wrist. He was quiet for a time, as if counting a pulse, then he patted the stomach, almost affectionately, and used Kiowa's hunting hatchet to remove the thumb.

Henry Dobbins asked what the moral was.

Moral?

You know. *Moral.*

Sanders wrapped the thumb in toilet paper and handed it across to Norman Bowker. There was no blood. Smiling, he kicked the boy's head, watched the flies scatter, and said, It's like with that old TV show — Paladin. Have gun, will travel.

Henry Dobbins thought about it.

Yeah, well, he finally said. I don't see no moral.

There it *is,* man.

Fuck off.

They carried USO stationery and pencils and pens. They carried Sterno, safety pins, trip flares, signal flares, spools of wire, razor blades, chewing tobacco, liberated joss sticks and statuettes of the smiling Buddha, candles, grease pencils, *The Stars and Stripes,* fingernail clippers, Psy Ops leaflets, bush hats, bolos, and much more. Twice a week, when the resupply choppers came in, they carried hot chow in green Mermite cans and large canvas bags filled with iced beer and soda pop. They carried plastic water containers, each with a two-gallon capacity. Mitchell Sanders carried a set of starched tiger fatigues for special occasions. Henry Dobbins carried Black Flag insecticide. Dave Jensen carried empty sandbags that could be filled at night for added protection. Lee Strunk carried tanning lotion. Some things they carried in common. Taking turns, they carried the big PRC-77 scrambler radio, which weighed thirty pounds with its battery. They shared the weight of memory. They took up what others could no longer bear. Often, they carried each other, the wounded or weak. They carried infections. They carried chess sets, basketballs, Vietnamese-English dictionaries, insignia of rank, Bronze Stars and Purple Hearts, plastic cards imprinted with the Code of Conduct. They carried diseases, among them malaria and dysentery. They carried lice and ringworm and leeches and paddy algae and various rots and molds. They carried the land itself — Vietnam, the place, the soil — a powdery orange-red dust that covered their boots and fatigues and faces. They carried the sky. The whole atmosphere, they carried it, the humidity, the monsoons, the stink of fungus and decay, all of it, they carried gravity. They moved like mules. By daylight they took sniper fire, at night they were mortared, but it was not battle, it was just the endless march, village to village, without purpose, nothing won or lost. They marched for the sake of the march. They plodded along slowly, dumbly, leaning forward against the heat, unthinking, all blood and bone, simple grunts, soldiering with their legs, toiling up the hills and down into the paddies and across the rivers and up again and down, just humping, one step and then the next and then another, but no volition, no will, because it was automatic, it was anatomy, and the war was entirely a matter of posture and carriage, the hump was everything, a kind of inertia, a kind of emptiness, a dullness of desire and intellect and conscience and hope and human sensibility. Their principles were in their feet. Their calculations were biological. They had no sense of strategy or mission. They searched the villages without knowing what to look for, not caring, kicking over jars of rice, frisking children and old men, blowing tunnels, sometimes setting fires and sometimes not, then forming up and moving on to the next village, then other villages, where it would always be the same. They carried their own lives. The pressures were enormous. In the heat of early afternoon, they would remove their helmets and flak jackets, walking bare, which was dangerous but which helped ease the strain. They would often discard things along the route of march. Purely for comfort, they would throw away rations, blow their Claymores and grenades, no matter, because by nightfall the resupply choppers would arrive with more of the same, then a day or two later still more, fresh watermelons and crates of ammunition and sunglasses and woolen sweaters — the resources were stunning — sparklers for the Fourth of

July, colored eggs for Easter. It was the great American war chest — the fruits of science, the smokestacks, the canneries, the arsenals at Hartford, the Minnesota forests, the machine shops, the vast fields of corn and wheat — they carried like freight trains; they carried it on their backs and shoulders — and for all the ambiguities of Vietnam, all the mysteries and unknowns, there was at least the single abiding certainty that they would never be at a loss for things to carry.

After the chopper took Lavender away, Lieutenant Jimmy Cross led his men into the village of Than Khe. They burned everything. They shot chickens and dogs, they trashed the village well, they called in artillery and watched the wreckage, then they marched for several hours through the hot afternoon, and then at dusk, while Kiowa explained how Lavender died, Lieutenant Cross found himself trembling.

He tried not to cry. With his entrenching tool, which weighed five pounds, he began digging a hole in the earth.

He felt shame. He hated himself. He had loved Martha more than his men, and as a consequence Lavender was now dead, and this was something he would have to carry like a stone in his stomach for the rest of the war.

All he could do was dig. He used his entrenching tool like an ax, slashing, feeling both love and hate, and then later, when it was full dark, he sat at the bottom of his foxhole and wept. It went on for a long while. In part, he was grieving for Ted Lavender, but mostly it was for Martha, and for himself, because she belonged to another world, which was not quite real, and because she was a junior at Mount Sebastian College in New Jersey, a poet and a virgin and uninvolved, and because he realized she did not love him and never would.

Like cement, Kiowa whispered in the dark. I swear to God — boom-down. Not a word.

I've heard this, said Norman Bowker.

A pisser, you know? Still zipping himself up. Zapped while zipping.

All right, fine. That's enough.

Yeah, but you had to see it, the guy just —

I *heard*, man. Cement. So why not shut the fuck *up?*

Kiowa shook his head sadly and glanced over at the hole where Lieutenant Jimmy Cross sat watching the night. The air was thick and wet. A warm, dense fog had settled over the paddies and there was the stillness that precedes rain.

After a time Kiowa sighed.

One thing for sure, he said. The Lieutenant's in some deep hurt. I mean that crying jag — the way he was carrying on — it wasn't fake or anything, it was real heavy-duty hurt. The man cares.

Sure, Norman Bowker said.

Say what you want, the man does care.

We all got problems.

Not Lavender.

No, I guess not. Bowker said. Do me a favor, though.

Shut up?

That's a smart Indian. Shut up.

Shrugging, Kiowa pulled off his boots. He wanted to say more, just to lighten up his sleep, but instead he opened his New Testament and arranged it beneath his head as a pillow. The fog made things seem hollow and unattached. He tried not to think about Ted Lavender, but then he was thinking how fast it was, no drama, down and dead, and how it was hard to feel anything except surprise. It seemed un-Christian. He wished he could find some great sadness, or even anger, but the emotion wasn't there and he couldn't make it happen. Mostly he felt pleased to be alive. He liked the smell of the New Testament under his cheek, the leather and ink and paper and glue, whatever the chemicals were. He liked hearing the sounds of night. Even his fatigue, it felt fine, the stiff muscles and the prickly awareness of his own body, a floating feeling. He enjoyed not being dead. Lying there, Kiowa admired Lieutenant Jimmy Cross's capacity for grief. He wanted to share the man's pain, he wanted to care as Jimmy Cross cared. And yet when he closed his eyes, all he could think was Boom-down, and all he could feel was the pleasure of having his boots off and the fog curling in around him and the damp soil and the Bible smells and the plush comfort of night.

After a moment Norman Bowker sat up in the dark.

What the hell, he said. You want to talk, *talk.* Tell it to me. Forget it.

No, man, go on. One thing I hate, it's a silent Indian.

For the most part they carried themselves with poise, a kind of dignity. Now and then, however, there were times of panic, when they squealed or wanted to squeal but couldn't, when they twitched and made moaning sounds and covered their heads and said Dear Jesus and flopped around on the earth and fired their weapons blindly and cringed and sobbed and begged for the noise to stop and went wild and made stupid promises to themselves and to God and to their mothers and fathers, hoping not to die. In different ways, it happened to all of them. Afterward, when the firing ended, they would blink and peek up. They would touch their bodies, feeling shame, then quickly hiding it. They would force themselves to stand. As if in slow motion, frame by frame, the world would take on the old logic — absolute silence, then the wind, then sunlight, then voices. It was the burden of being alive. Awkwardly, the men would reassemble themselves, first in private, then in groups, becoming soldiers again. They would repair the leaks in their eyes. They would check for casualties, call in dust-offs, light cigarettes, try to smile, clear their throats and spit and begin cleaning their weapons. After a time someone would shake his head and say, No lie, I almost shit my pants, and someone else would laugh, which meant it was bad, yes, but the guy had obviously not shit his pants, it wasn't that bad, and in any case nobody would ever do such a thing and then go ahead and talk about it. They would squint into the dense, oppressive sunlight. For a few moments, perhaps, they would fall silent, lighting a joint and tracking its passage from man to man, inhaling, holding in the humiliation. Scary stuff, one of them might say. But then someone else would grin or flick his eyebrows and say, Roger-dodger, almost cut me a new asshole, *almost.*

There were numerous such poses. Some carried themselves with a sort of wistful resignation, others with pride or stiff soldierly discipline or good humor or macho zeal. They were afraid of dying but they were even more afraid to show it.

They found jokes to tell.

They used a hard vocabulary to contain the terrible softness. *Greased,* they'd say. *Offed, lit up, zapped while zipping.* It wasn't cruelty, just stage presence. They were actors and the war came at them in 3-D. When someone died, it wasn't quite dying, because in a curious way it seemed scripted, and because they had their lines mostly memorized, irony mixed with tragedy, and because they called it by other names, as if to encyst and destroy the reality of death itself. They kicked corpses. They cut off thumbs. They talked grunt lingo. They told stories about Ted Lavender's supply of tranquilizers, how the poor guy didn't feel a thing, how incredibly tranquil he was.

There's a moral here, said Mitchell Sanders.

They were waiting for Lavender's chopper, smoking the dead man's dope.

The moral's pretty obvious, Sanders said, and winked. Stay away from drugs. No joke, they'll ruin your day every time.

Cute, said Henry Dobbins.

Mind-blower, get it? Talk about wiggy — nothing left, just blood and brains.

They made themselves laugh.

There it is, they'd say, over and over, as if the repetition itself were an act of poise, a balance between crazy and almost crazy, knowing without going. There it is, which meant be cool, let it ride, because oh yeah, man, you can't change what can't be changed, there it is, there it absolutely and positively and fucking well *is.*

They were tough.

They carried all the emotional baggage of men who might die. Grief, terror, love, longing — these were intangibles, but the intangibles had their own mass and specific gravity, they had tangible weight. They carried shameful memories. They carried the common secret of cowardice barely restrained, the instinct to run or freeze or hide, and in many respects this was the heaviest burden of all, for it could never be put down, it required perfect balance and perfect posture. They carried their reputations. They carried the soldier's greatest fear, which was the fear of blushing. Men killed, and died, because they were embarrassed not to. It was what had brought them to the war in the first place, nothing positive, no dreams of glory or honor, just to avoid the blush of dishonor. They died so as not to die of embarrassment. They crawled into tunnels and walked point and advanced under fire. Each morning, despite the unknowns, they made their legs move. They endured. They kept humping. They did not submit to the obvious alternative, which was simply to close the eyes and fall. So easy, really. Go limp and tumble to the ground and let the muscles unwind and not speak and not budge until your buddies picked you up and lifted you into the chopper that would roar and dip its nose and carry you off to the world. A mere matter of falling, yet no one ever fell. It was not courage, exactly; the object not valor. Rather, they were too frightened to be cowards.

By and large they carried these things inside, maintaining the masks of composure. They sneered at sick call. They spoke bitterly about guys who had found release by shooting off their own toes or fingers. Pussies, they'd say. Candyasses. It was fierce, mocking talk, with only a trace of envy or awe, but even so, the image played itself out behind their eyes.

They imagined the muzzle against flesh. They imagined the quick, sweet pain, then the evacuation to Japan, then a hospital with warm beds and cute geisha nurses.

They dreamed of freedom birds.

At night, on guard, staring into the dark, they were carried away by jumbo jets. They felt the rush of takeoff. *Gone!* they yelled. And then velocity, wings and engines, a smiling stewardess — but it was more than a plane, it was a real bird, a big sleek silver bird with feathers and talons and high screeching. They were flying. The weights fell off, there was nothing to bear. They laughed and held on tight, feeling the cold slap of wind and altitude, soaring, thinking *It's over, I'm gone!* — they were naked, they were light and free — it was all lightness, bright and fast and buoyant, light as light, a helium buzz in the brain, a giddy bubbling in the lungs as they were taken up over the clouds and the war, beyond duty, beyond gravity and mortification and global entanglements — *Sin loi!* they yelled, *I'm sorry, motherfuckers, but I'm out of it, I'm goofed, I'm on a space cruise, I'm gone!* — and it was a restful, disencumbered sensation, just riding the light waves, sailing that big silver freedom bird over the mountains and oceans, over America, over the farms and great sleeping cities and cemeteries and highways and the golden arches of McDonald's. It was flight, a kind of fleeing, a kind of falling, falling higher and higher, spinning off the edge of the earth and beyond the sun and through the vast, silent vacuum where there were no burdens and where everything weighed exactly nothing. *Gone!* they screamed, *I'm sorry but I'm gone!* And so at night, not quite dreaming, they gave themselves over to lightness, they were carried, they were purely borne.

On the morning after Ted Lavender died, First Lieutenant Jimmy Cross crouched at the bottom of his foxhole and burned Martha's letters. Then he burned the two photographs. There was a steady rain falling, which made it difficult, but he used heat tabs and Sterno to build a small fire, screening it with his body, holding the photographs over the tight blue flame with the tips of his fingers.

He realized it was only a gesture. Stupid, he thought. Sentimental, too, but mostly just stupid.

Lavender was dead. You couldn't burn the blame.

Besides, the letters were in his head. And even now, without photographs, Lieutenant Cross could see Martha playing volleyball in her white gym shorts and yellow T-shirt. He could see her moving in the rain.

When the fire died out, Lieutenant Cross pulled his poncho over his shoulders and ate breakfast from a can.

There was no great mystery, he decided.

In those burned letters Martha had never mentioned the war, except to say, Jimmy, take care of yourself. She wasn't involved. She signed the letters "Love," but it wasn't love, and all the fine lines and technicalities did not matter.

The morning came up wet and blurry. Everything seemed part of everything else, the fog and Martha and the deepening rain.

It was a war, after all.

Half smiling, Lieutenant Jimmy Cross took out his maps. He shook his head hard, as if to clear it, then bent forward and began planning the day's march. In ten minutes, or maybe twenty, he would rouse the men and they would pack up and head west, where the maps showed the country to be green and inviting. They would do what they had always done. The rain might add some weight, but otherwise it would be one more day layered upon all the other days.

He was realistic about it. There was that new hardness in his stomach.

No more fantasies, he told himself.

Henceforth, when he thought about Martha, it would be only to think that she belonged elsewhere. He would shut down the daydreams. This was not Mount Sebastian, it was another world, where there were no pretty poems or midterm exams, a place where men died because of carelessness and gross stupidity. Kiowa was right. Boom-down, and you were dead, never partly dead.

Briefly, in the rain, Lieutenant Cross saw Martha's gray eyes gazing back at him.

He understood.

It was very sad, he thought. The things men carried inside. The things men did or felt they had to do.

He almost nodded at her, but didn't.

Instead he went back to his maps. He was now determined to perform his duties firmly and without negligence. It wouldn't help Lavender, he knew that, but from this point on he would comport himself as a soldier. He would dispose of his good-luck pebble. Swallow it, maybe, or use Lee Strunk's slingshot, or just drop it along the trail. On the march he would impose strict field discipline. He would be careful to send out flank security, to prevent straggling or bunching up, to keep his troops moving at the proper pace and at the proper interval. He would insist on clean weapons. He would confiscate the remainder of Lavender's dope. Later in the day, perhaps, he would call the men together and speak to them plainly. He would accept the blame for what had happened to Ted Lavender. He would be a man about it. He would look them in the eyes, keeping his chin level, and he would issue the new SOPs in a calm, impersonal tone of voice, an officer's voice, leaving no room for argument or discussion. Commencing immediately, he'd tell them, they would no longer abandon equipment along the route of march. They would police up their acts. They would get their shit together, and keep it together, and maintain it neatly and in good working order.

He would not tolerate laxity. He would show strength, distancing himself.

Among the men there would be grumbling, of course, and maybe worse, because their days would seem longer and their loads heavier, but Lieutenant Cross reminded himself that his obligation was not to be loved but to lead. He would dispense with love; it was not now a factor. And if anyone quarreled or complained, he would simply tighten his lips and arrange his shoulders in the correct command posture. He might give a curt little nod. Or he might not. He might just shrug and say Carry on, then they would saddle up and form into a column and move out toward the villages of Than Khe.

Contributors' Notes

LEE K. ABBOTT has recently published two collections of stories, *Love Is the Crooked Thing* (published by Algonquin) and *Strangers in Paradise* (Putnam's). He teaches at Case Western Reserve University in Cleveland.

▪ "Truth to tell and sad to say, Lee K. Abbott does not remember how 'Dreams of Distant Lives' came to be written. Over the years, his stories have announced themselves to him, in the voice he habitually hears, as sentences, ones that plant the 'stout stake of emotion' Henry James said the action should swirl against; and the sentence that opens this story — 'The other victim the summer my wife left me was my dream life . . .' — is the sort Mr. Abbott believes in, for it gives the reader what he is too often without, a reason to care. Where this line came from, however, remains too much a mystery of the afterlife to think about.

"Of more interest is how the story came to a finish. Originally, and unhappily, another section followed '. . . an embrace that would end when the world came up again'; semi-reconciled and sleepy. It — this superfluous block of type — was all wrong, but Mr. Abbott, antsy as he always is about the last of anything, just couldn't see that. Like a clanging cow bell in Windsor Palace, its tone was wrong; its drama, tiresome and stupid; its language, sleep-soaked. Yet he persisted, for months and months it seemed, in trying to fix it, going back again and again, like an unlucky gambler, in the belief that one word, one fancy 'move,' might save (as in *redeem*) the whole mess and leave him astonished by the perfected thing storytellers feel obliged to make. Then, fittingly frustrated but without the weepy, teeth-gnashing melodrama those in TV-land prefer in their scenes of self-discovery, he said, 'The hell with it,' and, well, he played a trick, one played by his betters before and since: he cut it. Zapped it. It had offended, and he put it out.

"This was a hard lesson learned the hard way — when to stop — but a lesson particularly important for a writer who, having found starting easy, loves to keep going and going. Madison Jones, the underpraised Alabama novelist and farmer, says that endings should fall off in the hand like ripe peaches from the tree; and Mr. Abbott, well taught by his experience with dreams and distant lives, now aims to be one peach picker who's eager to cut the stuff that keeps him too late in the orchard."

CHARLES BAXTER lives in Ann Arbor, Michigan. He is the author of two collections of stories, *Harmony of the World* and *Through the Safety Net*, and a novel, *First Light*. He teaches at Wayne State University.

▪ "Because of the nature of its story, I could never get 'How I Found My Brother' exactly right. The chronicle of its writing would be a tiresome account of desk pounding, swearing, and pages flung into wastebaskets. I finally gave up on the story and sent it out into the world, bandaged and patched and held up on crutches. But I couldn't quit and bedeviled the editor of the magazine where it appeared with last-minute cosmetic changes. I am grateful that he was a tolerant man.

"For me, the story is located in its details: in Andy's sorrowful lyricism in his description of the bar; in Kurt's hat hanging alone near the popcorn machine; in the couple playing tennis at night; in the little specks of glue stuck to the tip of Andy's surgical scissors. I remember nothing about how I thought of the story, but I remember the day (Sunday) and the time (afternoon) and the weather (pre-thunderstorm) when I thought of the specks of glue.

"I tried to give Andy's prose a jumpy and anxious sound, an eyes-darting-in-the-corners style, the prose of a man who drinks too much coffee. Beyond those details remains the story itself, which is somewhat mysterious to me and which will, I hope, give some sense of the mystery of relations to its readers."

MADISON SMARTT BELL is the author of four novels, most recently *The Year of Silence*, and a collection of short stories, *Zero db*. He is married to the poet Elizabeth Spires and currently teaches at the Iowa Writers' Workshop.

▪ " 'The Lie Detector' is around seven years old, so I think whatever story it tells probably should be over for me now. The temptation to start talking about it (ever sweet) might be one better resisted. It's sure enough that I'm no longer quite the same person who wrote it anymore. Seven years is even long enough to replace all the cells of the body, isn't it? Returning to the story as a relative stranger, I find that I like it well enough, though I still sometimes wish I could have made it just a little shorter.

"It was written at Hollins College, where I'd gone as a graduate student after spending a year in a section of the Brooklyn waterfront somewhat similar to the one that the story describes. I had had a good time for a year in the ghetto, but I left it discouraged, having written nothing for many months other than a few panicky letters to Richard Dillard, head of the Hollins writing program, pleading for reassurance that my deferred admission was still good, which it was. And, luckily from my point of view, the move there broke the ice. While I'd been sitting in the middle of it, the city might as well have been invisible to me: it was too much, too all-encompassing, irreducible to words and a page. At a greater distance it shrank a little and I began to see ways of reinventing it rather than trying to swallow it whole.

"Out of that change in perspective began my first novel and a few stories, of which 'The Lie Detector' is one. It now seems to me that what this particular story did was try to exploit all my technical weaknesses in writing as if they were strengths. I didn't have the confidence to make up whole lives for the neighborhood people in the story, so I projected both that lack of information and that hesitancy onto the narrator. I didn't know him quite well enough either, so I made him not exactly transparent but opaque, a sort of shadow cast on the action he describes. The upshot of all this is that the story is not really about either the person telling it or the people told about, only the way in which their fleeting contacts briefly define them to each other. Or at least that's what I think it's about, but it's well past time I left it to you. You can draw your own conclusions about it, and that, after all, is the point."

RON CARLSON is the author of two novels and a collection of stories, *The News of the World*, all published by W. W. Norton. He lives in Arizona.
▪ "I wrote 'Milk' in Salt Lake City soon after the arrival of my second child. It was an era of 'missing-children awareness,' and every day we saw shopping bags, posters, television programs (including the news), that featured photographs and statistics about missing children. All these children were missing. Fifty thousand children. Community services implored parents to fingerprint their children. We were down a few levels of sleep into that all-zone of high-wire fatigue, sleeping with our ears open, infants in the house, and we did not want to see the missing children. I did not want to see the missing children on the milk carton in the refrigerator at three in the morning. I'd stand there and read the statistics under the missing children's faces in the fridge light while I held one of my boys against my bare chest, waiting for the bottle to warm. I'd always thought of our refrigerator as a friendly, hospitable place, in many ways the hearth of our household, and these children

were getting to me. Then one night I was watching the news and there was another feature about joining the ranks of parents fingerprinting their children, and then when Tom Brokaw came on with the national news, I saw that he had a little beard of Milupa cereal on his chin, printed there by my son Nick (he was one and a half). It was a specific moment, seeing that handprint on Tom Brokaw's face, and it was the germ of the story. It looked like a goatee, and though I don't say so in the story, it looked pretty good on Tom Brokaw."

RAYMOND CARVER has published three books of short stories — *Will You Please Be Quiet, Please?*, *What We Talk About When We Talk About Love,* and *Cathedral* — as well as several collections of poems including, most recently, *Where Water Comes Together with Water* and *Ultramarine.* His work has been translated into more than twenty languages, and his stories have been widely anthologized. *Where I'm Calling From: New and Selected Stories* will appear in January 1988.

MAVIS GALLANT is the author of eleven books, which include two novels and seven collections of short stories. Nearly all her short fiction has appeared in *The New Yorker,* and she has published a number of essays and reviews. Born in Montreal, she has spent most of her life in France. Her most recent story collection is *Overheard in a Balloon* (Random House, 1987).

▪ "The beginning of any short story is always an image of somebody doing something — in this case, an elderly man buying an ice cream cone on a street corner in Helsinki. I don't mean that I actually saw this or that I remembered any person in particular. It was not the conscious memory of anything seen, but just a picture that appeared in my mind of a character in fiction. It was many years since I had been to Finland, and I do not know why 'Helsinki' was so definite and persistent. I discovered long ago that if one tries to change the names of the characters as they occur, or one locality for another, the story stops working.

"Very often as a story evolves, almost of its own accord, it seems to me that a number of coincidences take place — in one's reading, or the things one sees and hears — that have some bearing or effect on the story. Probably it happens because one's interest in anything but the story has become focused and selective. To put it another way, for a short time one's daily life and the parallel life — the story — run on two sets of rails that eventually have to merge into a single track: sometimes it is easy, occasionally impossible, and the story has to be thrown away.

"In this case, I happened to be reading a book, *Indo-European Philology,* by W. B. Lockwood, that contained the Lord's Prayer in Maltese, a language I do not know and have never heard spoken. The words 'missierna' (literally, 'father-our') and 'saltnatek' ('kingdom') seemed to move into the story I was writing, and to stick. I cannot explain why, but they seemed to be exactly right, and from there the story took on its final shape and I could finish it quickly.

"I am not sure that any of this is helpful. It makes the composition of fiction sound like an automatic or mechanical process, with the writer serving as a kind of transmitter, or conduit — which, of course, is not the case. In fact, I do not think it possible to describe the process of writing in any accurate or satisfactory way. The best I can say is that there is always a central image, a kind of nucleus, around which a story grows."

KENT HARUF's novel, *The Tie That Binds,* was published by Holt, Rinehart and Winston in 1984 and by Penguin in 1986, and was awarded a special citation by the PEN/Hemingway Foundation. His short fiction has appeared in *Puerto del Sol* and *Grand Street.* He is the recipient of a Whiting Foundation Writer's Award and lives with his family in Nebraska.

▪ " 'Private Debts/Public Holdings' came out of a longer story. I had in mind to write a full-length novel about Jessie Burdette, to tell how she came to marry her husband, to say what she did after he disappeared, and to show what happened to her when he came back. The first paragraphs, in fact, are a distillation of some of that material. In any case, I had the events described in 'Private Debts/Public Holdings' clearly in mind from the beginning. I also knew from the beginning that some of what would happen to her would happen in the Legion, since the Legion is a place in small towns where people are thrown together without regard to class or station — a fact that seems important to me in establishing the setting for these events.

"Beyond that, about this story I can only say that I don't know how it came to be written or why I wanted to write it. There is nothing mysterious in this admission and I don't mean to suggest that there is. I suppose it is merely the result of a fascination I have for people who are caught in the ways that Jessie Burdette is caught. I am interested in what people do in such circumstances. Perhaps it is a kind of test of character. Occasionally people act in astonishing (and even courageous and beautiful) ways when they are tested."

RALPH LOMBREGLIA's stories have appeared in several magazines, including *The Atlantic, The Iowa Review,* and *The Agni Review.* He studied in the Johns Hopkins Writing Seminars, held a Wallace Stegner Fellowship at Stanford, and then taught writing at Hobart and William Smith

Colleges and Skidmore College. The recipient of writing fellowships from Yaddo and the New York Foundation for the Arts, he now lives in Boston, where he is finishing a story collection and a novel with the support of the National Endowment for the Arts.

▪ "I wrote the first scene of 'Men under Water' in late autumn 1984, and then I abandoned the story. The scene was close to what exists there now, except that it didn't end by setting up the idea of a rock 'n' roll band living in a house somewhere with a bad bathroom; it didn't end by setting up anything. My men simply paid their breakfast bill and stepped out of the Peter Pan Diner — on their way, presumably, to some adventure, but with no particular place to go.

"Not too surprisingly, I had nowhere to go myself. I didn't have a clue about what would happen next. Part of the problem was *the tyranny of actuality*. This scene was based loosely upon 'real life' — years before, I'd worked for a man who lived by real estate but dreamed of making movies — and in the real-life situation nothing much ever happened, certainly nothing with the dramatic structure and dimension of art. I was going to have to make something up. No, more than that, I was going to have to make something up that embodied — in a new and delightful way that would be mine and nobody else's — the classic short story action I had in mind: a character in an ironic and exasperating situation unexpectedly learns something essential about himself and the world.

"I struggled for weeks before accepting defeat, then I put it away and out of my mind and started writing something else. At the same time, I was going about my usual collecting of notes and ideas for future projects; one of these happened to be the notion of a screenplay about a rock 'n' roll band, a legendary-but-still-local rock band in a medium-sized American city. I thought — still do think — that it was a good idea for a screenplay. My screenplay.

"Eight months went by and it was the summer of 1985. I hadn't written a story in a long time (instead I'd been teaching creative writing), and I was full of that golden yearning to make fiction, to wander my garden bestowing names on the creatures, things still good between me and God. I took out my abandoned scene only to find that I still didn't know how to develop it. And then, by the most simple-minded association possible, I thought of my rock 'n' roll screenplay, and a noble voice spoke to me. Give up your movie idea. Let them have it. I merely did what the voice told me to do, and that single act of largesse to my fictive children triggered, eventually, an entire succession of ideas for getting myself through their story.

"Or almost through it. For the very end, the 'real life' that I'd tossed away came boomeranging back. Joseph and Willie had driven off in the

Mercedes, Gunther had the money to make his film, and once again I was stuck. And then I recalled the man I'd actually worked for, the one whose wish to make movies had been the germ of my story. At his house one day he happened to tell me about the scuba lessons he was taking with his wife. They'd been practicing their diving maneuvers in his built-in pool, and he thought — since it was hot outside and we didn't have anything better to do, and his wife wasn't around just then — that I might like to see how some of these things were done . . . "

Sue Miller grew up in Chicago and now lives in Cambridge, Massachusetts. Her first novel, *The Good Mother,* was published in 1986. "The Lover of Women" appears as "Inventing the Abbotts" in a collection of that name published in May 1987 by Harper & Row.

▪ "In July of 1983, while I was helping my father repair his house in the mountains, I ran into a man who'd been my first sweetheart in that summer place, when I was fourteen. We sat around together for a long, black-fly-ridden New Hampshire evening, talking about the various complications and joys and wrinkles of the intervening twenty-five years or so. In the course of the evening, he told me a story of dating all three sisters in a family we both knew, of running into the mother years later, of her saying curtly to him, 'Well, I've no more daughters for you.' That line seemed expressive of so much — an understandable anger, a quick wit, a lingering pain — that it stayed in my mind.

"I was beginning a novel then, trying to pull away from the tightening impulses that usually govern my short story writing, that had governed an earlier, failed attempt at novel writing, trying to relax into an expansive first-person voice. I began 'The Lover of Women' as a kind of experiment, a dry run for the novel. Somehow, setting the story in the past, in an imaginary, distant town, having the narrator be more observer than participant in the action, and perhaps also slightly unreliable, all seemed ways of making myself write more discursively. I willed myself to meander, to linger, to speculate — but I always had that wonderful line as my final destination.

"I had an office that year, by good luck and a grant from the Bunting Institute. It overlooked a dining hall at Radcliffe, with a large grassy yard behind it. Over the time I was working on 'The Lover of Women,' this yard was the site of several parties, and the band music floating across Brattle Street into my windows seemed part of what helped me write.

"I wrote the story rather quickly by my standards, in less than a week, as I recall it (though I did a lot of revision later). Even now it seems a gift: the accident of meeting my old sweetheart, the wonderful line that triggered my imagination, the relative ease with which the details of the story came to me, the music that wound its way into it — all from the blue, apparently."

BHARATI MUKHERJEE is the author of two novels, *The Tiger's Daughter* and *Wife;* a collection of stories, *Darkness;* and co-author with Clark Blaise of two nonfiction works, *Days and Nights in Calcutta* and *The Sorrow and the Terror* (all published by Penguin). A new story collection will be brought out by Grove Press in 1988. She lives in Manhattan and teaches at Queens College.

▪ "When the writing is going well, all random encounters are story material. For the past several years, the lives of the India-born — and, increasingly, the Third World–born — in the New World have been my passion and my obsession.

"The germ for this story was planted in the snows of a New Jersey morning. A young woman approached me at my bus stop and asked, 'You're from India, aren't you?' For the India-born, New Jersey is a leafy suburb of Bombay or Calcutta; this encounter, like many others in a given week, was virtually mandated by propinquity. Twenty years ago we might have instinctively sought each other out and ignored inconvenient incongruities in our caste, language, religion, and class. Now we give each other a once-over and usually turn our heads.

"This woman, I quickly learned, had known my sister in India. Here she was studying for a graduate degree and working as a dishwasher in an ethnic restaurant. An Indian gentleman had recently exposed himself to her and begun masturbating. Then the bus arrived.

"Nothing in the life of this well-born, middle-class girl would have prepared her for the precariousness of immigration: her life as a shadowy visa-blaster with a fickle boyfriend, her vulnerability as an attractive woman without traditional protection. Had foresight been granted her, she might never have left the certainties of small-town India. *And yet.* It seemed to me then, listening to her, that such women and men are heroes, new conquerors, no different from earlier generations of immigrants. *But.*

"This story is a mix of the bizarre and the ordinary, strung along three of the shortest, simplest words in the English language: 'but' and 'and yet.' We — the new arrivals — now live among you and share your fate and want your approval. But. Our gods are different, we can bear to look at matrimonial ads and still believe. We still hope, and look beyond the immediate misery, and we would not go back to the securities we knew. We are wonderfully equipped by discipline and breeding and education to be Western, to be just like you. And yet.

"If I have anything so lofty as a literary agenda, it is to give voice to these new American lives and to fit them into a pioneering context that American readers and editors might begin to appreciate."

ALICE MUNRO was born in Wingham, Ontario, and attended the University of Western Ontario. She has published several books of fiction, two of which have received the Governor's Award in Canada. Her newest collection of short stories, *The Progress of Love,* was published in 1986 by Knopf. Ms. Munro lives in Clinton, Ontario.

▪ "Some stories are easy to trace. There's an anecdote or a bit of remembered experience — sometimes a whole chunk of it — that will account for them. But with 'Circle of Prayer' I have a hard time finding the clue. I suppose it is the 'Circle of Prayer' itself. I heard about that, heard some women talking about how it worked, and that linked up with the strong image of the young girls dropping their jewelry and with something I know of the feelings between mothers and daughters. This was in the fall of 1985, when I already had the stories ready for *Progress of Love,* so I hurried up and got this one ready to join them. Most of it — the hotel on the lake and so on — came out of thin air. Or so far as I can tell."

CRAIG NOVA's new book, *Glare,* will be published next year by Delacorte/Dell.

▪ "A few years ago I was trying to write a novel about venison, or a novel in which almost all the main events had to do with killing, eating, and trading in deer. I know a fair number of stories about this, and have been amazed at the commerce (especially illegal commerce) in venison. The book was called *Venison* and it began with a menu: 'Melon, Roast Stuffed Grouse, Wild Rice, Broccoli Flowers, Raspberry Sherbet, Crown Roast of Venison, Roast Potatoes, Glazed Carrots, Chocolate Souffle, Coffee, Brandy, Cigars.' I saw the book as a kind of *Canterbury Tales* in which each character had a story about venison. For instance, one of the stories had to do with a crown roast of venison turning up in an expensive whorehouse on the Upper East Side of New York City, and another had to do with a pregnant woman who demands that her husband kill a deer so she can have a little untainted meat for the child she is carrying. (As an aside, I should probably say that my wife, when she was pregnant with our last child, insisted that I go out and bring her some venison.) In any case, most of the stories I wrote for the book were set in New England, and the book was taking on a regional quality I didn't like, and because of this I started working on a chapter that was a long way from the abandoned orchards and river bottoms of Vermont and New Hampshire. As you can see, the deer in 'The Prince' are not much more than a vestige, although I like to think of their presence in this story as a kind of pang. As far as *Venison* is concerned, I put it aside, although every now and then I will use a story from it."

TIM O'BRIEN received the National Book Award for his novel *Going After Cacciato.* His other books are *If I Die in a Combat Zone, Northern Lights,* and *The Nuclear Age.* His short fiction has appeared in numerous anthologies, including *The Best American Short Stories 1977, Great Esquire Fiction, The Pushcart Prize (II* and *X), The Ploughshares Reader,* and *The O. Henry Prize Stories* (1976, 1978, and 1982). Mr. O'Brien lives in Boxford, Massachusetts.

SUSAN SONTAG is the author of two novels, *The Benefactor* and *Death Kit;* a collection of stories, *I, etcetera;* and five volumes of essays — all published by Farrar, Straus & Giroux. *A Susan Sontag Reader* appeared in 1982.

DANIEL STERN is a New Yorker who has also lived and written in Los Angeles and Paris. He is the author of nine novels, the latest being *An Urban Affair.* An earlier novel, *The Suicide Academy,* has recently been reissued. He is also a motion picture, television, and advertising executive and has been a Visiting Professor in Letters and English at Wesleyan University. "The Interpretation of Dreams by Sigmund Freud: A Story" will be included in his collection titled *Missing the Point and Other Stories.*

▪ "I wrote 'The Interpretation of Dreams by Sigmund Freud: A Story' (that statement is transformed from insanity to mere irony by the addition of the words 'a story') shortly after completing a seven-year psychoanalysis. This would seem, on the face of it, to be explanation and description of process enough. An understandable touch of *chutzpah* by adding my name and commentary to the Master's masterwork. We're in this together, Doctor Freud, you and Daniel Stern. *Punkt!*

"Not so near, however, are the ways of fiction. After so many years of self-examination I was working, as a writer, to escape from the narrow constrictions of the narrator who can be easily confused with the author — in my opinion a major American artistic malady. Dickstein the academic is certainly not the author (this author never attended college). But in exploring the motif of Fathers and Sons and certain personal encounters (with widows and others, too 'personal' to be explicit about), I found that I had, indeed, graduated. Not only from the couch, but from the sentimental to the comic mode as a writer.

"That alone seems to me to be worth the time, money, and pain. Actually, the Freud story was the second one I wrote after completing analysis. The first was called 'The Liberal Imagination by Lionel Trill-

ing: A Story.' It has a protagonist even further removed from my
personal character than the story reprinted here. And what I found
was that the further I got from the typical 'personal' voice, the more
strongly I could deal with deeply personal material.

"This would be no great news to Flaubert or Turgenev, but in America in 1987 it is, I think, of interest. And for me, personally, to be able
to deal with the death (and life) of one's father with distance did not
drain it of feeling-tone. In fact, the comedy of contrast gives emotional
subjects such as loss, age, and death the edge they need to avoid sub-
merging us and the reader in false emotion.

"I realized also that by dealing with Trilling and Freud in fiction, I
was reaching back in literary time the way one reaches back in autobio-
graphical time. Thus I proceeded to write all the stories to be in my
new book: 'Aspects of the Novel by E. M. Forster: A Story'; 'A Clean,
Well-lighted Place by Ernest Hemingway: A Story'; 'Brooksmith by
Henry James: A Story'; and others.

"The entire collection will be called *Missing the Point* — an irony, I
think, which is precisely to the point.

"It's been like a dream."

ELIZABETH TALLENT is the author of *Museum Pieces,* a novel. "Favor" is
included in a collection of short stories, *Time with Children,* to be published by Knopf.
▪ "Maybe the first detail that I had for 'Favor' was a smell, the faint,
familiar, grassy dustiness of an old denim jacket my husband had almost worn to pieces, and the fact that he once left a spice jar out on the
kitchen table, having rubbed his hunting gloves with cloves. Those
details seemed to belong together, and to suggest others, or to provoke
others to appear and fit into a kind of constellation that began to feel
not only right, but storylike. If I was a photographer, I would have
tried to get at the things I wanted to get at in 'Favor' by photographing
those doe-brown hunting gloves, their leather darkened to an almost
iridescent black at the fingertips and ball of the thumb, their palms
creased so intricately they suggested flexibility, suppleness, nimbleness,
grace. Left lying anywhere, those gloves inevitably, if imperfectly, mim-
icked the shapes of my husband's hands; they couldn't have been more
his, and something I felt about them interested me, though it was only
a small emotion and hardly turns up in the story at all.

"Still, I suppose that minor emotion connects to a theme of 'belonging' that I find in this and in some other stories I've written — especially
those set in New Mexico — which seem to me to be about how land or
a house belongs to someone, or how some*one* belongs to someone, and
what two people, if they 'belong together,' must exclude; not only that,

but how those two people interpret belonging, what responsibility it entails for them, and how it feels to them. That is the crux for me: how it feels to them. I sometimes imagine that writing a story is a way of setting up a field of details such that the feeling you are chasing can play over and through those details. Because 'Favor' is one of a series of stories that have this couple, Jenny and Sam, in them, the details are fanned out through several stories, and for me that has made them more alive. There were certain New Mexico images I wanted (and still want) to dwell on. The country of northern New Mexico is very generous that way. Though famous, it's not exhausted. It's a landscape you can fall for and then find yourself wildly grateful to for years."

ROBERT TAYLOR, JR., is the author of *Loving Belle Starr,* a collection of outlaw fiction, and *Fiddle and Bow,* a novel, both books from Algonquin. Co-editor of the literary journal *West Branch,* from Bucknell University, he will be a visiting professor at the University of Tennessee during 1987–88. His stories have appeared in magazines such as *The Georgia Review, Shenandoah, The Agni Review,* and *The Best American Short Stories 1983.*

▪ "Several years ago a friend asked: What was it like, growing up in Oklahoma? This was in a letter, and so I had time to think about a reply. What memories did I have? What feelings had lasted?

"Clearly, fiction was in the works. I wanted to find out what I had forgotten and know better what I remembered. So I began a series of memory stories. The idea seemed blessedly simple. Each piece would focus on a significantly blurry space of time. From the meager scraps of events that I remembered and the more substantial hunks of feeling that I could own up to, I would make up details, episodes, even people, with such abandon as seemed necessary for the good of the story; but I would not alter the remembered feelings.

"This resolution not to alter feelings seems to me now singularly obtuse. The feelings most useful to fiction are the same ones the soul uses and is used by: they are not subject to invention or alteration, only to discovery and complication. At the time, however, the resolution seemed noble enough and was perhaps necessary to get the stories begun.

"When it came time, some three or four memory stories later, to begin 'Lady of Spain,' I jotted down a few incantatory phrases: *playing the accordion at the ward — the gray ladies — strange men — Mother's empathy, compassion — passion.* Then I actually wrote the title — the only time I can remember a title coming first. Thus equipped, I wrote the first sentence with heady confidence: 'Again I strap on the big accordion.'

"The real beginning would not come until much later, of course.

And the story would require numerous substantial revisions before yielding its true middle, its right ending. But I knew that something was under way, something that had to do with the shadowy image of a lady of Spain — with loveliness and music and with a whole lot else that only the craft of fiction could enable me to articulate.

"As for the ending, well, no story's ending has given me more trouble nor blessed me with such a sense of terrible release. When I had those last words, I wept over them. I really did. I felt cut to the quick. I can't explain it. I might have been standing in the path of stampeding angels. I felt illuminated. I wish I could explain it."

JOHN UPDIKE was born in Shillington, Pennsylvania, in 1932, and graduated from Harvard College in 1954. After two years on the staff of *The New Yorker,* he moved with his family to Massachusetts, where he has resided ever since. He is the author of twelve novels and seventeen other books, of which the most recent is a collection of short stories entitled *Trust Me.*

JOY WILLIAMS has written two novels, *State of Grace* and *The Changeling,* and a collection of stories, *Taking Care.* A new novel will be published by Random House early in 1988.
▪ "Harold Pinter was once explaining how he got the idea for one of his plays. He said something like: "I went into a room. I saw a man and woman talking. This gave me the idea for the play . . . " And he was speaking the truth, I'm sure. But why should a writer tell the truth when cornered as to how a piece of work came to be? The truth sounds so . . . literal. It's bad enough we have only words to work with. We must describe the work with words as well? It would be nicer to indicate our intentions so:

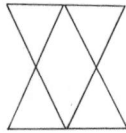

"But I will tell you how it would seem that 'The Blue Men' began. A friend of mine who lives on Nantucket had just returned from a vacation in Morocco. She said to me, 'We wanted so much to see the blue men, but we never did.' This remark enchanted me. I dwelled upon it for some time. That, to me, was the door to a room. I entered, and found my people there. Later, I found that what I wanted to write was a false resurrection story."

TOBIAS WOLFF received the 1985 PEN/Faulkner Award for fiction for his short novel, *The Barracks Thief.* He is also the author of two collections of stories, *In the Garden of the North American Martyrs* and *Back in the World.* He teaches at Syracuse University.

▪ "I honestly don't remember what made this story first move in me. The sight of three soldiers in a mud-spattered jeep on the coast highway? An oppressive sense of mortality, certainly, quickened by the recent deaths of friends. Beyond that I can't say. My best stories find their forms in spite of my intentions, not because of them. They take me by surprise, and leave no trail."

100 Other Distinguished Short Stories of the Year 1986

SELECTED BY SHANNON RAVENEL

ABBOTT, LEE K.
The Beauties of Drink: An Essay. *The Iowa Review,* Vol. 16, No. 2.

ADAMS, GAIL GALLOWAY
Inside Dope. *The North American Review,* September.

ANDRES, KATHARINE
The Right Word. *The Threepenny Review,* Spring.

ATWOOD, MARGARET
In Search of the Rattlesnake Plantain. *Harper's,* August.

BANKS, RUSSELL
Adultery. *Mother Jones,* April/May.
The Fish. *The Agni Review,* No. 23.
Hostage. *Esquire,* April.

BEATTIE, ANN
Home to Marie. *The New Yorker,* December 15.

BENNETT, JAMES GORDON
Dependents. *The Virginia Quarterly Review,* Winter.

BERGLAND, MARTHA
An Embarrassment of Ordinary Riches. *New England Review and Bread Loaf Quarterly,* Spring.

BOSWELL, ROBERT
Edward and Jill. *The Georgia Review,* Winter.

BROWN, MARY WARD
Let Him Live. *Shenandoah,* Vol. 26, No. 2.

BUSCH, FREDERICK
Gravity. *The Ohio Review,* No. 36.
Orbits. *The New Yorker,* January 20.

CANIN, ETHAN
Where We Are Now. *The Atlantic,* July.

CARLSON, RON
Phenomena. *Writer's Forum,* Fall.

CARVER, RAYMOND
Blackbird Pie. *The New Yorker,* July 7.

COGGESHALL, ROSANNE
Peter the Rock. *The Southern Review,* January.

COLWIN, LAURIE
I've Got What It Takes (but It Breaks My Heart to Give It Away). *GQ,* May.

CONNELLY, JOHN
Basques. *The Greensboro Review,* Winter.

COOVER, ROBERT
Aesop's Forest. *The Iowa Review,* Vol. 16, No. 1.

CORRINGTON, JOHN WILLIAM

LOEB, KAREN
Departures. *South Dakota Review,* Summer.

McGUANE, THOMAS
A Man in Louisiana. *Shenandoah,* Vol. 26, No. 2.
Partners. *Playboy,* December.
McILVOY, KEVIN
The Cuevas. *The Missouri Review,* Vol. 9, No. 1.
The Complete History of New Mexico. *Indiana Review,* Winter.
MARTONE, MICHAEL
An Accident. *Northwest Review,* Vol. 24, No. 3.
MATTHEWS, JACK
How Uncle Fox Really Got His Name. *Western Humanities Review,* Spring.
MATTISON, ALICE
Great Wits. *The New Yorker,* May 19.
MINOT, STEPHEN
A Death in Paris. *Black Warrior Review,* Fall.
MOORE, ELIZABETH
Savannahs. *Cimarron Review,* April.
MORTENSEN, PAULINE
Side Effects. *Cimarron Review,* October.
MOYER, KERMIT
Tumbling. *Hudson Review,* Winter.
MUFSON, JACOB
The Savior. *St. Andrews Review,* No. 31.
MUKHERJEE, BHARATI
A Wife's Story. *Mother Jones,* January.
MUNRO, ALICE
Fits. *Grand Street,* Winter.
White Dump. *The New Yorker,* July 28.
MURPHY, YANNICK
Delaware. *The Malahat Review,* June.

NORDAN, LEWIS
Sugar, the Eunuchs, and Big G.B. *The Southern Review,* Autumn.

OATES, JOYCE CAROL
Señorita. *Northwest Review,* Vol. 24, No. 1.

OHLE, DAVID
The Log of the Pipistrel. *The Missouri Review,* Vol. 9, No. 2.

PAINTER, PAMELA
The Real Story. *Harper's,* October.
PAYNE, PEGGY
The Pure in Heart. *The Crescent Review,* Spring.
PROULX, E. ANNIE
Heart Songs. *Esquire,* October.

RADU, KENNETH
Moment of Impact. *The New Quarterly,* Winter.
RAVA, SUSAN
Celeries. *The Crescent Review,* Fall.
RESS, SUZANNE
The Lost I.D.s of Manuella and Carmella Diores. *Ascent,* Vol. 11, No. 2.
REYNOLDS, SALLIE
Cusie. *Prairie Schooner,* Spring.
ROBISON, MARY
Trying. *The New Yorker,* September 8.
ROSENBLATT, SARI
Miss McCook. *The Iowa Review,* Vol. 16, No. 1.

SCHUMACHER, JULIE
Dividing Madelyn. *New Letters,* Summer.
SHACOCHIS, BOB
Where Pelham Fell. *Esquire,* January.
SMITH, LEE
Goodbye, Sweetheart. *Redbook,* February.
SPARK, DEBRA
The Incorrect Hour. *The North American Review,* June.
STARK, SHARON SHEEHE
May Angels Lead You Home. *The Atlantic,* December.
STROUT, ELIZABETH
In Love. *Ascent,* Vol. 12, No. 1.
SWICK, MARLY

Editorial Addresses of American and Canadian Magazines Publishing Short Stories

When available, the annual subscription rate, the average number of stories published per year, and the name of the editor follow the address.

Agni Review
P.O. Box 660
Amherst, MA 01004
$8, 10, Sharon Dunn

Alfred Hitchcock's Mystery Magazine
Davis Publications
380 Lexington Avenue
New York, NY 10017
$19.50, 130, Cathleen Jordan

Amazing
Dragon Publishing
P.O. Box 110
Lake Geneva, WI 53147
George Scithers

Amelia
329 East Street
Bakersfield, CA 93304
$6, 10, Frederick A. Raborg, Jr.

Analog Science Fiction/Science Fact
380 Lexington Avenue
New York, NY 10017
$19.50, 70, Stanley Schmidt

Antaeus
The Ecco Press
18 West 30th Street
New York, NY 10001
$20, 15, Daniel Halpern

Antietam Review
33 West Washington Street
Hagerstown, MD 21740
$3, 10, Ellyn Bache

Antioch Review
P.O. Box 148
Yellow Springs, OH 45387
$18, 20, Robert S. Fogarty

Apalachee Quarterly
P.O. Box 20106
Tallahassee, FL 32304
$12, 10, Allen Woodman, Barbara Hanby, Monica Faeth

Arizona Quarterly
University of Arizona
Tucson, AZ 85721
$5, 12, Albert F. Gegenheimer

Ascent
English Department
University of Illinois
Urbana, IL 61801
$3, 20, Daniel Curley

Atlantic
8 Arlington Street
Boston, MA 02116
$9.75, 25, C. Michael Curtis

Aura Literary/Arts Review
P.O. Box University Center
University of Alabama
Birmingham, AL 35294
$6, 10, rotating editorship

Bellowing Ark
P.O. Box 45637
Seattle, WA 98145
$12, 5, Robert R. Ward

Bennington Review
Bennington College
Bennington, VT 05201
$4, 10, Nicholas Delbanco

Black Ice
Black Ice Press
571 Howell Avenue
Cincinnati, OH 45220
20, Dale Shank

Black Warrior Review
P.O. Box 2936
University, AL 35486
$5, 12, Janet McAdams

Boston Review
991 Massachusetts Avenue
Cambridge, MA 02138
$9, 6, Mark Silk

Brown Journal of the Arts
Box 1852
Brown University
Providence, RI 02912
rotating editorship

California Quarterly
100 Sproul Hall

University of California
Davis, CA 95616
$10, 4, Nixa Schell

Calyx
P.O. Box B
Corvallis, OR 97339
$18, 2, Margarita Donnelly

Canadian Fiction
Box 946
Station F
Toronto, Ontario
M4Y 2N9 Canada
$30, 16, Geoffrey Hancock

Capilano Review
Capilano College
2055 Purcell Way
North Vancouver
British Columbia
Canada
$9, 5, Dorothy Jantzen

Carolina Quarterly
Greenlaw Hall 066A
University of North Carolina
Chapel Hill, NC 27514
$10, 20, rotating editorship

Chariton Review
Division of Language & Literature
Northeast Missouri State University
Kirksville, MO 63501
$4, 10, Jim Barnes

Chattahoochee Review
DeKalb Community College
2101 Womack Road
Dunwoody, GA 30338
$12.50, 25, Lamar York

Chelsea
P.O. Box 5880
Grand Central Station
New York, NY 10163
$9, 6, Sonia Raiziss

Chicago Review
5801 South Kenwood
University of Chicago

Chicago, IL 60637
$10, 20, Steve Heminger, Robert Sitko

Choteau Review
Box 10016
Kansas City, MO 64111
David Perkins

Christopher Street
249 West Broadway
New York, NY 10013
$24, 12, Charles Ortleb

Cimarron Review
208 Life Sciences East
Oklahoma State University
Stillwater, OK 74078
$10, 15, John K. Crane, Mary Rohberger

Clockwatch Review
Driftwood Publications
737 Penbrook Way
Hartland, WI 53029
$6, 5, James Plath

Colorado Review
360 Liberal Arts
Colorado State University
Fort Collins, CO 80523
$5, 10, Steven Schwartz

Columbia Magazine of Poetry and
Prose
404 Dodge Hall
Columbia University
New York, NY 10027
$4.50, rotating editorship

Commentary
165 East 56th Street
New York, NY 10022
$33, 5, Norman Podhoretz

Confrontation
English Department
C. W. Post College of Long Island
University
Greenvale, NY 11548
$8, 25, Martin Tucker

Conjunctions
33 West 9th Street
New York, NY 10011
$16, 5, Brandford Morrow

Cotton Boll/Atlanta Review
P.O. Box 76757
Sandy Springs
Atlanta, GA 30358-0703
$10, 12, Mary Hollingsworth

Crazyhorse
Department of English
University of Arkansas
Little Rock, AR 72204
$8, 10, David Jauss

Crescent Review
P.O. Box 15065
Winston-Salem, NC 27103
$7.50, 24, Bob Shar

Crosscurrents
2200 Glastonbury Road
Westlake Village, CA 91361
$15, 10, Linda Brown Michelson

Crucible
Atlantic Christian College
Wilson, NC 27893
Agnes H. McDonald

CutBank
Department of English
University of Montana
Missoula, MT 59801
$6.50, 10, Craig Holden

Denver Quarterly
University of Denver
Denver, CO 80208
$12, 10, David Milofsky

Descant
P.O. Box 314
Station P
Toronto, Ontario
M5S 2S5 Canada
$18, 20, Karen Mulhallen

Epoch
251 Goldwin Smith Hall
Cornell University
Ithaca, NY 14853
$8, 15, C. S. Giscombe

Esquire
2 Park Avenue
New York, NY 10016
$17.94, 15, Rust Hills

event
c/o Douglas College
P.O. Box 2503
New Westminster
British Columbia
V3L 5B2 Canada
$8, 10, Maurice Hodgson

Fantasy & Science Fiction
Box 56
Cornwall, CT 06753
$17.50, 100, Edward L. Ferman

Farmer's Market
Midwest Farmer's Market, Inc.
P.O. Box 1272
Galesburg, IL 61402
$6, 5, John E. Hughes

Fiction International
Department of English
San Diego State University
San Diego, CA 92182
$12, 25, Harold Jaffe, Larry McCaffrey

Fiction Network
P.O. Box 5651
San Francisco, CA 94101
Jay Schaefer

Fiddlehead
The Observatory
University of New Brunswick
Fredericton, New Brunswick
E3B 5A3 Canada
$14, 20, Michael Taylor

Five Fingers Review
100 Valencia Street
Suite 303

San Francisco, CA 94103
$8, 5, John Hish

Florida Review
Department of English
University of Central Florida
Orlando, FL 32816
$6, 16, Pat Rushina

Formations
P.O. Box 327
Wilmette, IL 60091
$15, 2, Jonathan and Frances Brent

Four Quarters
LaSalle College
20th and Olney Avenues
Philadelphia, PA 19141
$8, 10, John Christopher Kleis

From Mt. San Angelo
Virginia Center for the Creative Arts
Sweet Briar, VA 24595
8, William Smart

Frontiers
Women's Studies Program
University of Colorado
Boulder, CO 80309
$14, Katni George

Gargoyle
Paycock Press
P.O. Box 30906
Bethesda, MD 20814
$10, 25, Richard Peabody, Gretchen Johnsen

Georgia Review
University of Georgia
Athens, GA 30602
$9, 15, Stanley W. Lindberg, Stephen Corey

Good Housekeeping
959 Eighth Avenue
New York, NY 10019
$14.97, 24, Naome Lewis

GQ
350 Madison Avenue

New York, NY 10017
$18, 12, Trish Deitch Rohrer

Grain
Box 1154
Regina, Saskatchewan
S4P 3B4 Canada
$9, 15, Brenda Riches

Grand Street
50 Riverside Drive
New York, NY 10024
$20, 20, Ben Sonnenberg

Gray's Sporting Journal
205 Willow Street
South Hamilton, MA 01982
$23.50, 8, Edward E. Gray

Great River Review
211 West 7th
Winona, MN 55987
$7, 12, Orval Lunda

Greensboro Review
Department of English
University of North Carolina
Greensboro, NC 27412
$5, 16, Lee Zacharias

Harper's
666 Broadway
New York, NY 10012
$18, 15, Eric Etheridge

Hawaii Review
University of Hawaii
Department of English
1733 Donaghlo Road
Honolulu, HI 96822
$6, 12, Zdenet Kluzek

Helicon Nine
P.O. Box 22412
Kansas City, MO 64113
$15, 8, Gloria Vando Hickock

Hoboken Terminal
P.O. Box 841
Hoboken, NJ 07030
$6, 15, C. H. Trowbridge, Jack Nestor

Hudson Review
684 Park Avenue
New York, NY 10021
$16, 8, Paula Deitz, Frederick Morgan

Indiana Review
316 North Jordan Avenue
Bloomington, IN 47405
$10, 20, Pamela Wampler

Iowa Review
EPB 308
University of Iowa
Iowa City, IA 52242
$12, 10, David Hamilton

Isaac Asimov's Science Fiction
  Magazine
380 Lexington Avenue
New York, NY 10017
$19.50, 100, Gardner Dozois

Jewish Monthly
1640 Rhode Island Avenue NW
Washington, DC 20036
$8, 3, Marc Silver

Kansas Quarterly
Department of English
Denison Hall
Kansas State University
Manhattan, KS 66506
$12, 43, Harold Schneider, Ben Nyberg,
  John Rees

Karamu
English Department
Eastern Illinois University
Charleston, IL 61920
John Guzlowski

Kenyon Review
Kenyon College
Gambier, OH 43022
$15, 15, Philip D. Church, Galbraith M.
  Crump

Ladies' Home Journal
3 Park Avenue
New York, NY 10016
$20, 10, Constance Leisure

Latitude 30° 18'
1124B Regan Terrace
Austin, TX 78704
$5.50, 5, Joseph Slate

Lilith
The Jewish Women's Magazine
250 West 57th Street
New York, NY 10019
$12, 5, Julia Wolf Mazow

Literary Review
Fairleigh Dickinson University
Madison, NJ 07940
$12, 25, Walter Cummins

Little Magazine
Dragon Press
P.O. Box 78
Pleasantville, NY 10570
$16, 5

McCall's
230 Park Avenue
New York, NY 10169
$9.95, 20, Helen DelMonte

Mademoiselle
350 Madison Avenue
New York, NY 10017
$12, 14, Eileen Schnurr

Malahat Review
University of Victoria
P.O. Box 1700
Victoria, British Columbia
V8W 2Y2 Canada
$15, 25, Constance Rooke

Mark
2514 Student Union Building
University of Toledo
2801 West Bancroft Street
Toledo, OH 43606
$6, 10, Zona Gabe

Massachusetts Review
Memorial Hall
University of Massachusetts
Amherst, MA 01002

*$12, 15, Mary Heath, John Hicks, Fred
    Robinson*

Michigan Quarterly Review
3032 Rackham Building
University of Michigan
Ann Arbor, MI 48109
$13, 10, Laurence Goldstein

Mid-American Review
106 Hanna Hall
Department of English
Bowling Green State University
Bowling Green, OH 48109
$6, 15, Robert Early

Minnesota Review
Department of English
State University of New York
Stony Brook, NY 11794
$7, Fred Pfeil

Mississippi Review
Southern Station
Box 5144
Hattiesburg, MS 39406-5144
$10, 25, Frederick Barthelme

Missouri Review
Department of English, 231 A&S
University of Missouri
Columbia, MO 65211
$10, 25, Speer Morgan, Greg Michalson

Mother Jones
1663 Mission Street
San Francisco, CA 94103
$12, 5, Michael Moore

MSS
Department of English
State University of New York
Binghamton, NY 13901
$10, 30, Liz Rosenberg

Nantucket Review
P.O. Box 1234
Nantucket, MA 02254
$6, 15, Richard Burns, Richard Cumbie

Nebraska Review
Writers' Workshop
ASH 215
University of Nebraska
Omaha, NE 68182
$5, 10, Art Homer, Richard Duggin

Negative Capability
6116 Timberly Road North
Mobile, AL 36609
$12, 15, Sue Walker, Ron Walker

New England Review and Bread Loaf
   Quarterly
P.O. Box 170
Hanover, NH 03755
$12, 10, Sydney Lea, Jim Schley

New Letters
University of Missouri
5310 Harrison
Kansas City, MO 64110
$15, 10, David Ray

New Mexico Humanities Review
P.O. Box A
New Mexico Tech
Socorro, NM 87801
$8, 15, John Rothfork

New Orleans Review
Loyola University
New Orleans, LA 70118
$20, 15, John Biquenet

New Quarterly
English Language Proficiency
   Programme
University of Waterloo
Waterloo, Ontario
N2L 3G1 Canada
$10, 5, Peter Hinchcliffe

New Renaissance
9 Heath Road
Arlington, MA 02174
*$10.50, 10, Louise T. Reynolds, Harry
Jackel*

New Yorker
25 West 43rd Street

New York, NY 10036
$32, 100

North American Review
1222 West 27th Street
Cedar Falls, IA 50614
$11, 35, Robley Wilson, Jr.

North Dakota Quarterly
University of North Dakota
P.O. Box 8237
Grand Forks, ND 58202
$10, 4, Robert W. Lewis

Northwest Review
369 PLC
University of Oregon
Eugene, OR 97403
$11, 10, John Witte

Ohio Journal
Department of English
Ohio State University
164 West 17th Avenue
Columbus, OH 43210
$5, 4, Don Citino

Ohio Review
Ellis Hall
Ohio University
Athens, OH 45701
$12, 20, Wayne Dodd

Old Hickory Review
P.O. Box 1178
Jackson, TN 38301
$5, 5, Drew Brewer

Omni
1965 Broadway
New York, NY 10023-5965
$25, 20, Ellen Datlow

Ontario Review
9 Honey Brook Drive
Princeton, NJ 08540
$8, 8, Raymond J. Smith

Other Voices
820 Ridge Road

Highland Park, IL 60035
$15, 20, Delores Weinberg

Oxford
Bachelor Hall
Miami University
Oxford, OH 45056
$4, 7, Gail R. Neff

Paris Review
541 East 72nd Street
New York, NY 10021
$16, 15, George Plimpton

Passages North
William Boniface Fine Arts Center
7th Street and 1st Avenue South
Escanaba, MI 49829
$2, 12, Elinor Benedict

Pequod
536 Hill Street
San Francisco, CA 94114
$9, 5, Mark Rudman

Piedmont Literary Review
Piedmont Literary Society
P.O. Box 3656
Danville, VA 24543
$10, 10, David Craig

Plainswoman
P.O. Box 8027
Grand Forks, ND 58202
$10, 10, Emily Johnson

Playboy
919 North Michigan Avenue
Chicago, IL 60611
$22, 20, Alice K. Turner, Teresa Grosch

Playgirl
3420 Ocean Park Boulevard
Suite 3000
Santa Monica, CA 90405
$20, 15, Mary Ellen Strote

Ploughshares
P.O. Box 529
Cambridge, MA 02139
$14, 25, DeWitt Henry

Poetry East
Star Route 1
Earlysville, VA 22936
$10, 5, Richard Jones

Prairie Schooner
201 Andrews Hall
University of Nebraska
Lincoln, NE 68588
$11, 20, Hugh Lake

Present Tense
165 East 56th Street
New York, NY 10022
$14, 5, Leonard Krigel

Primavera
Ida Noyes Hall
University of Chicago
1212 East 59th Street
Chicago, IL 60637
$5, 10, Ann Gearen

Prism International
University of British Columbia
Vancouver, British Columbia
V6T 1W5 Canada
$10, 12, John Schoutsen

Puerto del Sol
P.O. Box 3E
New Mexico State University
Las Cruces, NM 88003
$5.75, 12, Kevin McIlvoy

Quarry Magazine
P.O. Box 1061
Kingston, Ontario
K7L 4Y5 Canada
$16, 10, Allan Brown

Quarry West
Porter College
University of California
Santa Cruz, CA 95060

Quarterly
Vintage Books
201 East 50th Street
New York, NY 10022
$6.95, 50, Gordon Lish

Quarterly West
317 Olpin Union
University of Utah
Salt Lake City, UT 84112
*$6.50, 10, Christopher Merrill, Ann
   Snodgrass*

RE:AL
Stephen F. Austin State University
Nacogdoches, TX 75962
$4, 5, Neal B. Houston

Redbook
959 Eighth Avenue
New York, NY 10019
$11.97, 35, Kathy Sagan

Richmond Quarterly
P.O. Box 12263
Richmond, VA 23241
$10, 10, Welford D. Taylor

River City Review
P.O. Box 34275
Louisville, KY 40232
$5, 10, Richard L. Neumayer

River Styx
Big River Association
7420 Cornell
St. Louis, MO 63130
$9, 10

A Room of One's Own
P.O. Box 46160
Station G
Vancouver, British Columbia
V6R 4G5 Canada
$10, 12, Robin Bellamy

Rubicon
McGill University
853 rue Sherbrooke Ouest
Montreal, Quebec
H3A 2T6 Canada
$8, 10, T. Peter O'Brien

St. Andrews Review
St. Andrews Presbyterian College
Laurinsburg, NC 28352
$12, 10, Susan Ketchin Edgerton

Salmagundi
Skidmore College
Saratoga Springs, NY 12866
$10, 2, Robert and Peggy Boyers

San Jose Studies
San Jose State University
San Jose, CA 95192
$12, 5, Fauneil J. Rinn

Saturday Night
70 Bond Street, Suite 500
Toronto, Ontario
M5B 2J3 Canada
Robert Fulford

Seattle Review
Padelford Hall, GN-30
University of Washington
Seattle, WA 98195
$6, 10, Charles Johnson

Seventeen
850 Third Avenue
New York, NY 10022
$13.95, 12, Bonni Price

Sewanee Review
University of the South
Sewanee, TN 37375-4009
$12, 10, George Core

Shenandoah
Box 722
Lexington, VA 24450
$8, 10, James Boatwright

Sinister Wisdom
P.O. Box 1023
Rockland, ME 04841
$14, Melanie Kaye/Kantrowitz

Sonora Review
Department of English
University of Arizona
Tucson, AZ 85721
$5, 10, Antonya Nelson, Scott Wigton

South Carolina Review
Department of English
Clemson University

Clemson, SC 29631
$5, Richard J. Calhoun, Robert W. Hill

South Dakota Review
University of South Dakota
P.O. Box 111 University Exchange
Vermillion, SD 57069
$10, 25, John R. Milton

Southern Magazine
P.O. Box 3418
Little Rock, AR 72203
$15, 12, James Morgan

Southern Review
43 Allen Hall
University Station
Baton Rouge, LA 70893
$9, 20, Lewis P. Simpson, James Olney

Southwest Review
Southern Methodist University
P.O. Box 4374
Dallas, TX 75275
$10, 15, Willard Spiegelman

Sou'wester
Department of English
Southern Illinois University
Edwardsville, IL 62026
$4, 10, Joanne Brew Callander

Stories
14 Beacon Street
Boston, MA 02108
$20, 30, Amy R. Kaufman

Story Quarterly
P.O. Box 1416
Northbrook, IL 60062
$12, 20, Anne Brashler

Telescope
15201 Wheeler Lane
Sparks, MD 21152
Julia Wendell, Jack Stephens

Tendril
P.O. Box 512
Green Harbor, MA 02041
$12, 12, George E. Murphy, Jr.

Texas Review
English Department
Sam Houston State University
Huntsville, TX 77341
$4.20, 15, Paul Ruffin

Threepenny Review
P.O. Box 9131
Berkeley, CA 94709
$8, 10, Wendy Lesser

Toronto South Asian Review
P.O. Box 6986
Station A
Toronto, Ontario
M5W 1X7 Canada
$15, 5, M. G. Vassanji

TriQuarterly
1735 Benson Avenue
Northwestern University
Evanston, IL 60201
$16, 30, Reginald Gibbons

U.S. Catholic
221 West Madison Street
Chicago, IL 60606
The Rev. Mark J. Brummel, CMF

University of Windsor Review
Department of English
University of Windsor
Windsor, Ontario
N9B 3P4 Canada
$10, 40, Eugene McNamara

Virginia Quarterly Review
One West Range
Charlottesville, VA 22903
$10, 12, Staige D. Blackford

Wascana Review
English Department
University of Regina
Regina, Saskatchewan
S4S 0A2 Canada
$13, 10, Joan Givner

Waves
79 Denham Drive

Richmond Hill, Ontario
L4C 6H9 Canada
$8, 20, Bernice Lever

Webster Review
Webster University
Webster Groves, MO 63119
$5, 5, Nancy Schapiro

West Branch
Department of English
Bucknell University
Lewisburg, PA 17837
$5, 10, Karl Patten, Robert Taylor, Jr.

Western Humanities Review
University of Utah
Salt Lake City, UT 84112
$15, 10, Jack Carlington

William and Mary Review
College of William and Mary
Williamsburg, VA 23186
$3, 5, rotating editorship

Wind/Literary Review
RFD #1
P.O. Box 809K
Pikeville, KY 51501
$6, 20, Quentin R. Howard

Writers Forum
University of Colorado
P.O. Box 7150
Colorado Springs, CO 80933-7150
$8.95, 15, Alexander Blackburn

Yale Review
250 Church Street
1902A Yale Station
New Haven, CT 06520
$14, 12, Mr. Kai Erikson

Yankee
Yankee, Inc.
Dublin, NH 03444
$15, 10, Edie Clark